THE 13TH CONTINUUM

JENNIFER BRODY

THE 13TH CONTINUUM

The Continuum Trilogy
BOOK 1

Turner Publishing Company
424 Church Street • Suite 2240 • Nashville, Tennessee 37219
445 Park Avenue • 9th Floor • New York, New York 10022

www.turnerpublishing.com

The 13th Continuum

Cover design: Maddie Cothren
Book design: Glen Edelstein

Library of Congress Cataloging-in-Publication Data

Names: Brody, Jennifer.
Title: The 13th Continuum / by Jennifer Brody.
Other titles: Thirteenth Continuum
Description: New York, New York : Turner Publishing Company, [2016] | Series: The Continuum trilogy ; Book 1 | Summary: "One thousand years after a cataclysmic event leaves humanity on the brink of extinction, the survivors take refuge in continuums designed to sustain the human race until repopulation of Earth becomes possible. Against this backdrop, a group of young friends in the underwater Thirteenth Continuum dream about life outside their totalitarian existence, an idea that has been outlawed for centuries. When a shocking discovery turns the dream into a reality, they must decide if they will risk their own extinction to experience something no one has for generations, the Surface"-- Provided by publisher.
Identifiers: LCCN 2015037764| ISBN 9781681622545 (pbk.) | ISBN 9781681622552
(hardback)
Subjects: | CYAC: Science fiction. | Totalitarianism--Fiction.
Classification: LCC PZ7.1.B758 Aak 2016 | DDC [Fic]--dc23
LC record available at http://lccn.loc.gov/2015037764

[9781681622545]

Printed in the United States of America
15 14 13 12 11 10 9 8 7 6 5 4 3 2 1

To all the dreamers who have wondered "what if . . ."
and had the guts to write about it.

CONTENTS

PART III: THE BEACONS 181

PART IV: AETERNUS ETERNUS 245

PART V: THE SURFACE 329

Maybe there is a beast . . . maybe it's only us.
—William Golding, *Lord of the Flies*

Man is a fire-stealing animal, and we can't help building machines and machine intelligences, even if, from time to time, we use them not only to outsmart ourselves but to bring us right up to the doorstep of Doom.
—Richard Dooling, *The Rise of the Machines*

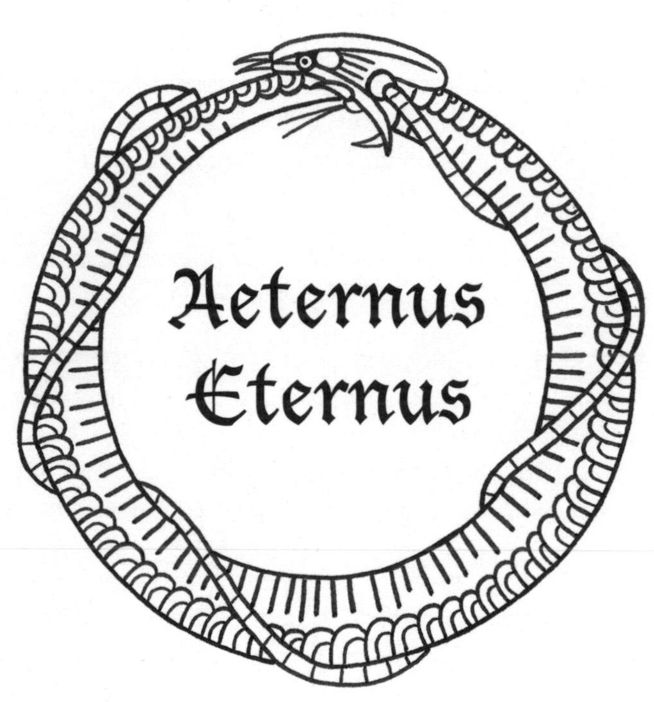
Aeternus
Eternus

Chapter 0
THE DOOM

It was well past midnight when Sari woke to the alarm blaring through the White House. Frightened, she rubbed the sleep from her eyes.

A strobe light pulsed in the darkness and illuminated the room. On and off, she could see her backpack slumped astride the foot of her bed, a mess of clothes and toys strewn across the floor waiting to get her into trouble with her mother, and her desk with the shiny, new tablet computer that was a gift from her father for her tenth birthday last week (or so the card said, though it was probably selected and purchased by his staffers).

But the angles and corners of the room felt all wrong, just like the strangers in suits who now followed her family everywhere they went. "Mr. President," they called her dad. Those men gave her the creeps. Her pulse quickened as she regretted how much her life had changed over the last year, ever since her father won the big election.

New city. New house. New bedroom. New school. New teachers. New friends.

Everything had changed.

Everything.

The alarm continued its shrill cry.

Sari pushed herself up and hugged her backpack to her chest. Ever since the move, she kept it filled with her most prized possessions just in case—her antique picture books, dog-eared and crumbling to pieces, the snow globe of the Eiffel Tower that her grandmother had given her, and the porcelain doll collection that she should have outgrown, but never had, though it ashamed her to admit it.

She padded across the room, the creaky floorboards registering her presence, and twisted the doorknob. The heavy door swung wide open. Soldiers with big guns, Secret Service agents, and staffers fled past her door. Some she recognized, but most were strangers. None of them noticed her. They were too afraid, she could tell.

They'd held emergency drills before, but they were orderly affairs with everyone following the safety procedures calmly. This time was different—something was definitely wrong. Her thoughts immediately leapt to her family.

Did something happen to them?

And, more urgently—where were they?

She had to find them.

Even though her heart was thumping, Sari stepped into the hall, dodging a befuddled man who staggered past. She could hear him muttering to himself. "The doom, the doom, the doom . . ." His lips wobbled and his eyes darted around, seeing everything and nothing all at once. "The doom, the doom, the doom, the doom . . ."

She flattened herself against the wall and let him pass out of sight. The man never noticed her. Being short and scrawny had its benefits. She always won when she played hide and seek with her sister, who was five years older and tall like their father.

She had reached the end of the hall when she heard pounding feet behind her. Though it was hard to see through the darkness, which was broken up by blinding flashes of light, a group of men in suits stormed into her bedroom. They might have been Secret Service agents, but she wasn't sure, nor did she think it wise to stick around and find out what they wanted. Besides, adrenaline was thumping through her heart, rushing through her veins, and screaming in her brain. It yelled one thing over and over:

Run!

The instinct to flee was primal, terribly strong, and impossible to resist. Sari took off running down the hall. The strobe lights lit her way. She dodged a bronze bust and an ornately carved table with a ceramic vase on it. Their shadows stretched out as if to grab her, but the dark tendrils passed over her harmlessly.

She heard shouting and pounding feet behind her—the men were closing in. She dashed around a corner, sprinted down a long hallway, and skidded to a halt at a dead end. That was when she heard the footsteps right behind her. She was trapped. Her mouth tasted like metal, which only happened when she was really and truly afraid.

Step, drag, step.

It wasn't the men—it was somebody else. In a blind panic, Sari tried the doors on either side of the hall, but they were locked and wouldn't budge.

Step, drag, step.

The footsteps were louder now.

Step, drag, step.

In the flashing of the lights, Nana stepped into the hall. At the sight of the old woman, Sari broke into a smile. "Nana," she said, rushing into the woman's waiting arms, careful not to knock her over. Sari buried her face in her grandmother's silken robe and inhaled the familiar scents of soap and rosewater.

For as long as she could remember, Nana had watched her and Elianna during the day while their parents worked long hours on her father's campaigns, making sure that they finished their homework, and then filling their heads with stories of the olden days, before robots ran errands for their owners and flying cars filled the skies, thick as flies sometimes.

In the sweltering heat of the Tulsa summers, they'd pick and eat mulberries together, the fruit staining their lips and teeth dark purple, and in the brisk chill of winter they'd huddle up by the flickering gas fire and stitch needlepoint pillows with soft velvet backings. Following the big election, Nana had moved into a modest bedroom in the Executive Residence, even though she'd never lived outside of Oklahoma.

But when Sari looked up, she saw an unfamiliar expression on her grandmother's face—her mouth was folded down into a frown. "Child, come on now," Nana said. "We've got to hurry."

"Yes, Nana," Sari said. She knew better than to argue with her or ask any questions. The tone of her voice told her as much.

Grasping her cane with one hand and Sari's hand with the other, Nana led the way through the White House's intricate warren of rooms connected by hallways. *Step, drag, step.* Despite her pronounced limp, she moved swiftly. *Step, drag, step.* A few minutes later, they slipped through an emergency exit. Sari sloshed into the mud, slipping in the deep tire tracks that marred the lawn. Nana yanked her up.

"Careful, child," she said. "God's about to pitch a fit."

The alarm was even louder out here, and the flashing was brighter. It wasn't just from the emergency lights. Bolts of lightning pulsed in the stormy sky. Thunder—lightning's darker paramour—crackled so loudly it shook the ground beneath their feet. This night was brighter than most days, and Sari could see clearly. People were fleeing from the grounds, making for the exits in vehicles and on foot. She glimpsed kitchen staffers, housemaids, and soldiers. They all looked panicked. Behind the tall gate, on Pennsylvania Avenue, the streets were clogged with military vehicles and people carrying bags and possessions. Likewise, the skies were jammed with transports.

Sari spotted a little boy, who couldn't have been older than three, dragging a filthy teddy bear down the street. He struggled to keep pace with the mob. His face and hands were smeared with dirt, and his upper lip was bloody. *He must have fallen*, Sari thought. Their eyes met for a split second—her on one side of the gate, him on the other.

Something terrible had happened. She could see it in his eyes. They were wide and glassy, full of fear. But she had no idea what it was. She stood there, frozen in place, and watched as the mob swept him away, like a gigantic wave snatching a seashell from the shore, until Nana urged her forward again.

They reached the South Lawn, where Marine One was waiting with its engines already revving up. Her father, mother, and Elianna were stooped under the helicopter's spinning blades. Gusts of wind kicked up by the rotors tore at their clothes and hair. A group of Secret Service agents were guarding them and yelling into their communicators.

The President's eyes fell on Sari and widened. Ignoring the agent who tried to restrain him, he ran over and scooped her up.

"Oh, Sari, thank God." He checked her over for injuries. "You scared us half to death! Where were you? They checked your room, but you weren't there. We've been looking for you everywhere."

Sari cast her eyes down in shame. "Sorry, Dad. The alarm scared me, so I ran away and got lost. Nana found me and brought me here."

Her dad nodded, a grim look on his face. His hair was whiter now. Ever since he had become the President, the white hairs had begun to outnumber the rest.

One of the agents approached them and handed her father a secure communicator. "Mr. President," he said. "It's time."

Her dad nodded and set Sari down. Nana took up her hand again, and they followed the two men toward Marine One, whose engines were now roaring. The rotors blew back their hair and kicked up bits of gravel. Sari tasted grit on her tongue, and her eyes stung from the debris.

Her dad scanned his thumbprint on the communicator's screen. "Aeternus eternus," he said into the mouthpiece. He had to yell to be heard over the helicopter.

The communicator beeped its recognition and automatically connected the call. Less than a minute later, there was somebody else on the other end of the line. Sari glimpsed his face on the screen—he looked like a kindly grandfather who was still dressed in his red sleeping gown after being woken up from an unintentional nap.

"Mr. President, I hoped we'd never have to have this conversation," the old man said in lieu of a formal greeting. His voice was deep and sonorous, full of gravitas. Sari could just hear him over the noise of the rotors.

"So did I, Professor," her dad said. "The time has come. You must activate the Continuums and seal the chambers."

"It will be done," the man said without hesitation.

"And Professor?" her dad said. He paused, the way that he did in his speeches to add weight to his words. "Thank you for everything you've done for us."

"Don't thank me yet," the man said. "There's still a long road ahead, and the outcome is far from certain."

"But you've given us a chance," her dad said. He looked down at Sari, and then over at Elianna and her mother.

"A chance is all it is—the rest is up to you," the man said.

With that, the line went dead.

"Hurry, Elijah," her mother urged as her father gathered Sari up and lifted her into Marine One. As she climbed into the cabin and joined her mom and sister, she knew her grandmother was right behind her and would be coming with them. They'd never gone anywhere without her. But when Sari looked back, she saw her below them, still on the ground. She made no move to join them. Sari would only later remember all that followed in flashes of memories, as if they too were illuminated by the strobe lights.

"Nana!" she cried out as the door slammed shut. She pounded on it with her fists, but a pair of burly arms restrained her. They belonged to a Secret Service agent. "Nana!" she cried again, but her grandmother only lifted a twisted hand to wave good-bye.

Sari tilted her tear-stained face to her father.

"Why isn't she coming?"

"She wasn't chosen," her father said as Marine One lifted off the ground. He rested his hand on her shoulder, but his face was stoic. "You must let her go now."

Sari knew then that she'd lost her father. He was fully the President now and didn't belong to her anymore. She turned to her sister, who could always explain things that she didn't understand, but Elianna was sobbing in their mother's arms.

"But I choose her!" Sari cried, writhing in her seat. "I choose her! Why doesn't anybody ask me what I want? I would have chosen her!"

The last thing that Sari remembered was Nana growing smaller and smaller as Marine One ascended into the stormy skies.

o o o

Though the flight was bumpy and treacherous, Sari barely noticed, nor would she have cared if they'd crashed. She was too upset about her grandmother to feel anything else.

About twenty minutes later, they landed at the United States Naval Academy in Annapolis, Maryland. As Sari climbed from the helicopter, a violent explosion rocked the ground, but whether it was from the thunderstorm still raging in the dark sky or something far more insidious, she did not know and was too scared to ask.

Ten-foot electrified fences guarded by soldiers with German shepherds surrounded the Naval Academy. Hundreds of people were queued up outside the fences in a desperate attempt to get through to the docks. Sari heard their screams and pleas for help. It reminded her of her father's rallies, only this was far more frenzied and desperate. One man spotted her dad and shouted at him: "President Wade!"

Sari didn't know whether her father didn't hear the man's cries or just chose to ignore them.

Armed soldiers drove her family in a shuttle to the docks, where a massive submarine awaited them. A giant 13 marked its hull next to a strange circular symbol. As they got closer, Sari realized that the circle was actually a golden serpent swallowing its own tail. Inside the snake, two words were inlaid in an elaborate script.

Aeternus Eternus

She'd heard her father speak them into the communicator before they boarded Marine One. But when she turned to ask him what they meant, he was busy greeting other people who were lining up to board the submarine.

"Senator Sebold," he said to a man in a gray suit.

The senator's piercing green eyes found her father and held his gaze. A grave look passed over his face. "Mr. President, glad to have you with us, even under these circumstances."

Her dad greeted another senator whom Sari had seen at the White House, a famous musician who had performed at the inauguration, and a high-ranking naval officer. She could tell that he was important from his uniform with all its badges and medals. They must have been *chosen*, she guessed, correctly. Though why exactly they'd been chosen—or, more to the point, who exactly had done the choosing—remained a mystery to her. All she knew was that her grandmother should have been among them.

At this thought, her tears threatened to make an encore appearance. She bit down hard on her lip, hoping the pain would be enough to keep the waterworks at bay. The briny, metallic tang of blood flooded her mouth.

Sari stepped onto the gangplank, right as another explosion shook the earth. Screams followed from the crowd outside the fence. One man tried to climb it and was electrocuted. He was dead before his body hit the ground. The gangplank buckled and swayed. Sari had to cling to her dad to keep from falling into the harbor. Frigid water sloshed onto the dock and soaked her feet.

In the chaos that followed, Sari and her family were rushed into the submarine. The interior was sparse and outfitted with benches and restraints, meant to transport a large number of people. Every seat was soon filled with frightened men, women, and children. Sari sat between her father and sister.

Elianna helped her buckle her harness, tightening the bulky straps to fit her thin frame.

Once it was secure, Sari looked up to see a man in a long crimson robe. To her eyes, he looked like a priest, but not from any religion she'd ever encountered. Elianna paled when she saw him. The man slipped his hand inside his robes and produced what looked like a golden bracelet. It shimmered in the dim light of the interior deck. The same symbol that marked the hull—the serpent entwined around the two strange words—was etched into its luminous surface.

He knelt and presented the bracelet to her father.

"Mr. President, the Beacon."

"Thank you, Professor," her dad said.

He accepted the bracelet, but instead of tucking it away or latching it around his own wrist, he turned to the older of his daughters.

"Elianna, your wrist, please."

Though he said it kindly, even fondly, it wasn't a request. Elianna returned his gaze, and an understanding passed between them—from father to daughter. Sari didn't know what it was, and this scared her. She tasted metal again.

"Yes . . . Papa," Elianna said. Her voice wavered only slightly, but Sari noticed it.

Elianna slid her sleeve back, exposing the tender flesh of her right wrist. With her other hand, she plucked the bracelet from her father's outstretched palm. She turned it over in her hands, its surface casting off fragments of golden light.

"It's so light, like it barely weighs anything at all."

Suddenly, the Beacon's solid façade split open. Sari was awed by the sudden transformation—the liquid shifting of the metal—and how it took on a life of its own in her sister's grasp. Elianna hesitated, her eyes glued to the reformed armlet.

"Go ahead," her father said. "This is your duty."

With his urging, and under the professor's careful watch, Elianna latched the Beacon around her wrist. The symbol glowed with a blinding flash of green light as the device sealed itself around her flesh. Her face went slack, and her pupils dilated all at once. A soft whimper escaped from her lips in a rush of breath. Her lungs had emptied themselves. Then, just as swiftly as the Beacon had come alive, it went dark again.

Elianna blinked once, then twice. She examined the bracelet and flexed her fist, her muscles rippling underneath her caramel skin. On closer inspection, Sari saw that the Beacon had welded itself to her sister's flesh, almost like it had become a part of her.

The professor leaned over and inspected her wrist. He murmured approvingly. "It appears it's properly integrated," he said to her father. "A very strong bond, just like we'd hoped." He shifted his gaze to Elianna. "How do you feel, my dear? Any dizziness? Disorientation? Weakness? Nausea?"

She bit her lip. "I guess, a little," she said. "My brain feels fuzzy and kind of . . . jumbled."

"That should pass as you grow accustomed to carrying the Beacon," the professor said. "Just drink plenty of fluids, and this will be difficult I'm sure, but try to get some rest tonight." He patted her wrist and slid her shirtsleeve back down, concealing the bracelet from view. Now Elianna looked no different than she had a moment before. Satisfied that the Beacon was in place, he rose from his knees and bid them farewell.

"Aeternus eternus," he said with a bow.

"Aeternus eternus," her father echoed. A grim expression stole across his face, deepening his already deep worry lines. "May God have mercy on our souls."

The professor didn't reply to that. Instead, he bobbed his head again and exited the sub with a swishing of his robes.

An alarm sounded and a red light flashed, followed by the announcement: "All hands below deck."

Naval officers streamed inside and manned their stations. Two of them sealed the thick door shut. Sari watched it close until it severed her view of the outside world. The final sucking of air as the door latched tight felt decisive and permanent. Without any shred of doubt, Sari knew that she'd never lay eyes on that world again.

Then, with a great revving of its engines, the submarine dove into the ocean, descending deeper and deeper, until the surface was miles above it and no light could penetrate.

o o o

In another part of the country, Professor Divinus and his sworn brothers and sisters made their way across Harvard Yard, their crimson robes rustling around their ankles. The same symbol that marked the submarine was emblazoned on their lapels.

Divinus had just spoken to the President, and the concern was etched into his face. "The time has come," the President had said. Though Divinus had predicted it would happen, he'd always hoped that he was wrong, a strange thing for a scientist to wish.

As they passed Memorial Hall, the ancient building erected to honor soldiers slain in the Civil War, Divinus found himself remembering when he'd first come to Harvard, some sixty years ago. *Sixty-four, to be exact*, he reminded himself. He'd been a skinny, eighteen-year-old kid with a head full of burning ambition. Though he had aged significantly in the ensuing decades, his freckled skin shriveling up and his hair turning from carrot orange to white, he was still skinny underneath it all.

Divinus and his companions traversed the stairs that led up to Widener Library, a building that had been largely abandoned by both the students and faculty, and the neglect showed in the decaying of its exterior—the subtle corroding of its many steps, the oxidization of the columns, and the layer of soot that covered it from top to bottom.

"Easy there, Theo," Professor Singh said.

Though not as spry as he'd been in his undergrad days, Divinus kept up with Professor Singh, the youngest of his sworn brothers at forty-two years of age. Singh was the chair of Harvard's Astrobiology Department and the author of several bestselling books on the topic. His eleven other companions were also distinguished professors from a variety of fields, each pledged to serve with him until their deaths.

At the top of the stairs, Divinus paused by the columns and looked back at the world behind him. Panicked freshmen were fleeing from the dormitories and streaming into the Yard. *The news must have broken,* Divinus thought. Many were talking into communicators, doubtless to family and loved ones. Most were crying, but a few brave souls sat together in a circle serenely holding hands, resigned to their fates.

The chaotic scene felt reminiscent of the black and white photographs from two centuries ago, when a group of students protesting the Vietnam War had taken over University Hall. Only something felt different about this gathering. After a moment, Divinus settled on the missing element—it was hope. The students in the photographs had it. In fact, one could argue that it had fueled their radical actions.

But these students had none.

Despite the many years of his life dedicated to the Continuum Project, Divinus couldn't believe that the Doom had finally come. He had always hoped against hope that the probability of their destruction would remain only that—a probability. But as with so many things in his life, he had been right. He forced himself to look away. There was nothing he could do for them now.

Divinus and his companions—thirteen in all—proceeded into Widener Library and hastened through its marble halls. The derelict building had once been a repository that housed millions of books, back when people still read such things, before the worldwide conversion to digital. Divinus sniffed the air and sneezed. They could remove the musty books from the library, but they couldn't remove their smell.

He approached a gilded doorway marked by their seal.

"Aeternus eternus," Divinus said. His sworn brothers and sisters repeated the phrase in unison, their voices echoing through the corridor.

The computer registered their identities and beeped its approval. Only then did the door dilate, granting them access to the elevator. They filed inside, the thick doors contracted, and they began to descend at blinding speed. Divinus felt his ears pop as they adjusted to the pressure. They were journeying miles beneath the surface.

He rubbed his nose and sneezed again, wondering how scholars had ever relied on moldy, old manuscripts for their research. Suddenly, an explosion rocked the elevator shaft. Divinus fell into Professor Singh, who caught him. They exchanged a solemn glance. No words were uttered aloud, but they understood each other perfectly.

The end was coming soon now.

A short time later, their descent halted and the door dilated. As Divinus stepped through it, panels mounted on the ceiling flashed on and illuminated the cavernous room. It was as immense as a football field, and this was only the first chamber. Rows upon rows of the golden machines stretched out in all directions, thousands of them. Clear panels on the front permitted a glimpse of their precious cargo.

"Hello, Professor Divinus," said a male voice so lifelike that it was hard to believe it belonged to a computer. "I received the newsfeed from the surface. Is it time?"

"Noah, seal the chamber," Divinus said.

"Yes, Professor," Noah said.

Even though Divinus tried to keep his face devoid of emotion, he still flinched when the thick door contracted behind him, entombing them inside the First Continuum. The air instantly felt heavier—and staler, too. Was this how the pharaoh's servants felt when they were buried alive inside the pyramids with their ruler?

He shook his head to clear it. He would have plenty of time to ponder that great mystery later. Now he had many things to do.

Divinus crossed the chamber, his eyes falling on the cryocapsules. Inside each one, suspended in cryogenic stasis, were delicate embryos. This room held mammals. Through the clear panels, he glimpsed their contents. *Panthera tigris. Elephas maximus. Ursus maritimus. Mephitidae.* Incubator after incubator filled with beings. Thousands upon thousands of them.

This was his life's work, automated to survive his passing.

Divinus entered the control room. Professor Singh claimed the seat to his right while the rest of his sworn brothers and sisters took their places around the room. The holographic monitor in front of Divinus lit up with the words:

THE NATIONAL OPERATION TO ARCHIVE HUMANITY

He manipulated the screen, pulling up information on the other Continuums. Twelve green lights appeared before him. His eyes grazed over the data for each of them—oxygen levels, water and food supplies, power reserves generated by the reactors and stored in batteries, and the progress of the elevators, submersibles, and transports.

Everything looked to be in order. He swiped the first green light. "The Second Continuum, this is Professor Divinus," he said, contacting the first of the space colonies. "Have the transports arrived yet? Over."

There was a pause, only a few seconds long, but to Divinus it felt like an eternity. He held his breath and waited. All of his careful preparations hung in the balance.

"Roger that, the first transport is docking," said a voice that Divinus recognized as belonging to General Milton Wright. "All systems are go. Over."

His sworn brothers and sisters broke into elated cheers, but Divinus kept his composure. Still eleven more to go, he reminded himself. He moved swiftly to contact each of them. To his great relief, all the evacuation vessels got off more or less on schedule. Only one encountered any major difficulty—a transport bound for the Third Continuum suffered an engine problem that was quickly repaired.

Regretfully, a few of the Chosen missed their ships, but that was to be expected. Alternates, who had been waiting at the ports and praying that their numbers would come up, filled their spots. For them to live, somebody else had to die. Divinus wondered if they thought of that morbid trade-off when their number was called, as he did in his private musings, when his thoughts went unbidden to the dark place.

Once Divinus had ascertained that the last of the submersibles had dived into the trenches, the elevators had carried their final load of passengers into the bowels of the earth, and the transports had left the atmosphere far behind, he allowed himself to feel a modicum of relief.

"The first stage is complete," he announced.

And that was when it happened.

A thunderous explosion shook the vault and threw them around. Warning symbols flashed and an alarm shrieked. As Divinus braced himself, he knew that the Doom had reached its pinnacle. He shut his weary eyes and pictured the chain reaction occurring miles above them on the exposed surface of the Earth—the release of energy, the incineration, and the millennium of obliteration that would inevitably follow.

Another blast roiled through the chamber, more violent than the last. The alarm blared again. Each of the twelve green lights blinked out in rapid succession. Their communication lines had been severed. Divinus called out to Noah for help, though he knew that nothing could be done now that the Doom was underway.

And so, just as Divinus had predicted, with a great flash of light followed by a deafening rumble, the world of men was unmade at last.

PART I
POST DOOM

Superstition always directs action in the absence of knowledge.

—Isaac Asimov, *Foundation and Earth*

The sea is everything. It covers seven tenths of the terrestrial globe. Its breath is pure and healthy. It is an immense desert, where man is never lonely, for he feels life stirring on all sides. The sea is only the embodiment of a supernatural and wonderful existence. It is nothing but love and emotion; it is the Living Infinite.

—Jules Verne, *Twenty Thousand Leagues Under the Sea*

Excerpt from
THE JOURNAL OF PRESIDENT ELIJAH WADE
(First President of the Thirteenth Continuum, Milwaukee Deep, Puerto Rico Trench)

[1 P.D.] . . . Still no communication from the Surface, though against all odds, we are thriving down here in the blackest depths of the ocean. As a first order of business, my fellow colonists held an election. There was no campaigning this time. No speeches. I didn't even toss my hat into the ring. But my fellow colonists—the Founders of the Thirteenth Continuum—elected me as their first President. It is an honor that both thrills and humbles me. I feel the weight of their survival squarely on my narrow shoulders . . .

[4 P.D.] . . . Though countless attempts have been made to contact the other Continuums—radio messages, electronic communications, even an unmanned probe—all have ended in abject failure. Our messages were met with silence, and the probe lost contact with us the instant that it left the trench. It was most likely destroyed by whatever hell rages beyond our safe harbor under the sea. For all intents and purposes, we are on our own . . .

[7 P.D.] . . . It saddens me to report that one of our colonists, Clyde Donovan, went stir crazy (cabin fever is a common ailment down here). He stole a sub and made for the Surface. The last transmission that we received from him was the sound of screaming, followed by static, and then silence. The noises that he made—more animal than human, tormented, and amplified by the receiver—have haunted my dreams for weeks. Whether anything still survives up there is a mystery that only God knows the answer to . . .

[15 P.D.] . . . Every day I see what mankind is capable of: our resilience, our innovative spirit, our capacity for adaptation under exigent circumstances. Our citizens work tirelessly to produce the food, water, and power that keep us alive. But every day, I am also reminded of the Doom that we unleashed upon the world. The two sides of our psyche: creation and destruction. Which will win out? I can only hope the former . . .

[23 P.D.] . . . A viral epidemic has spread through the colony. It has already halved our numbers. I lost my wife of thirty-eight years, Veda, to the scourge. Thank God my daughters still survive, even if they are having difficulty coping with the loss of their mother. Hell, we all are. The Pox-like ailment begins with a fever and rash and ends with massive internal hemorrhaging. Our doctors have never encountered its like. *A mutation*, they say. I've instituted emergency quarantines, but I do not know if they are enough. Meanwhile, a new religious fervor is also sweeping through the colony, perhaps due to the virus, or the extreme isolation of the deep, or both. The followers have donned red cloaks and call themselves The Church of the Oracle of the Sea . . .

[36 P.D.] . . . Sometimes I still dream of the world as it was. In my dreams, I am always a child back on my family's farm in Tulsa. The images are scorched into my mind. The tall grass, so verdant that it burns my eyes. The landscape crawling with living, breathing things—groves of trees, flocks of birds, mammals of every ilk and temperament, swarms of insects. The feel of the spring breeze kissing my face. The stars at night, bright pinpricks as endless as the universe. Even the withering heat of the Oklahoma summer. Down here, there is no weather, and it is always dark and cold. *Always*. But by the time I wake, the dreams are gone, and with them, any memory of the Surface . . .

[44 P.D.] . . . Will we last a thousand years? Is there anything left on the Surface? Or dare I ask, is there still a Surface? Or has it been consumed by the Doom? Are we the only ones left—the last outpost of human civilization? Only the long years ahead will tell. I am old and weak now, and must bequeath the world to my only surviving daughter—and her children and her children's children. May they survive the long years in the dark of the sea, to one day return to the Surface and repopulate its lands, planting and tending to them until they are as green and lush as they are in the depths of my dreams.

—THE NATIONAL OPERATION TO ARCHIVE HUMANITY

Excerpt from
THE RECORDS OF THE GOVERNMENT OF THE THIRTEENTH CONTINUUM

PREAMBLE TO THE CONSTITUTION OF THE THIRTEENTH CONTINUUM
Signed by President Elijah Wade on May 1, 1 P.D.

WE THE PEOPLE of the Thirteenth Continuum, in Order to form a more perfect Union, establish Justice, insure domestic Tranquility, provide for the common defense, promote the general Welfare, and secure the Blessings of Liberty to ourselves and our Posterity, do ordain and establish this Constitution for the Thirteenth Continuum.

AMENDMENT IX
Passed by Congress on July 21, 52 P.D.
Ratified on August 7, 52 P.D.

Article 1 of the Constitution of the Thirteenth Continuum shall be amended as follows:

(1) The Congress of the Thirteenth Continuum shall be dissolved.
(2) All legislative Powers herein granted shall be vested in a Synod, comprised of seven [7] members, each appointed by the President for life terms.
(3) No further Elections shall be held, effective immediately.
(4) This is to ensure the Protection and Safety of the Colony.

AMENDMENT XII
Passed by the Synod on June 10, 53 P.D.

Article 2 of the Constitution of the Thirteenth Continuum shall be amended as follows:

(1) The Office of the President of the Thirteenth Continuum shall be dissolved.

(2) All executive Powers herein granted shall be vested in the Synod.
(3) No further Elections shall be held, effective immediately.
(4) If Vacancies arise on the Synod, by Resignation or otherwise, then the other Members of the Synod shall appoint a Successor at their sole discretion, and in accordance with their Internal Procedures.

AMENDMENT XV

Passed by the Synod on September 13, 55 P.D.

Article 3 of the Constitution of the Thirteenth Continuum shall be amended as follows:

(1) The judicial Power of the Thirteenth Continuum herein granted shall be vested with the Synod, effective immediately.
(2) The judicial Power shall extend to all Cases, in Law and Equity, arising under this Constitution and the Laws of the Thirteenth Continuum.
(3) The Trial of all Crimes shall be adjudicated by the Synod, with a Majority rule (herein defined as at least four [4] votes) determining Guilt.
(4) Sentencing shall also be determined by Majority rule of the Synod.

AMENDMENT XIX

Passed by the Synod on December 30, 55 P.D.

Article 5 of the Constitution of the Thirteenth Continuum shall be amended as follows:

(1) Sections contained herein pertaining to the Separation of Church and State shall be stricken from the Record. Specifically, Article 5, Section 8, stating, "the Government shall make no law respecting an establishment of religion or prohibiting the free exercise thereof" is hereby stricken from the Record; any laws based thereon are hereby Void and Ineffective.
(2) The Church of the Oracle of the Sea shall be hereby recognized as the official sanctioned Religion of the Government of the Thirteenth Continuum.

(3) Furthermore, the Head Priest of The Church of the Oracle of the Sea shall be granted a permanent seat on the Synod, effective immediately.

AMENDMENT XX
Passed by the Synod on January 14, 56 P.D.

Article 5 of the Constitution of the Thirteenth Continuum shall be amended as follows:

(1) Any Citizen convicted of worshipping a False Idol, or desecrating the Oracle, shall be Punished by being *put out to sea*.
(2) Citizens are required to attend weekly Services at The Church of the Oracle of the Sea. All Citizens shall be assigned a Day (Monday through Saturday) based on their compartment number when they must attend Services.
(3) Any Citizen convicted of more than three [3] unexcused Absences, or more than five [5] instances of Tardiness, shall be Punished by being *put out to sea*.

AMENDMENT XXII
Passed by the Synod on April 13, 56 P.D.

The Constitution of the Thirteenth Continuum shall be amended as follows:

(1) Article 10 shall be added to the Constitution.
(2) It shall read as follows: Books, Documents, Images, and Records (both printed and electronic) from Before Doom are hereby ordered Destroyed.
(3) Furthermore, any reference, in either verbal or written Communication, to Before Doom, or use of the Blasphemies is hereby Prohibited.
(4) Any Citizen convicted of possessing the aforementioned Technology and/or Materials, or using the Blasphemies shall be Punished by being *put out to sea*.

—THE NATIONAL OPERATION TO ARCHIVE HUMANITY

Chapter 1
NO DISSENTERS

Deep in the blackest depths of the ocean, the automatic lights came on in the Thirteenth Continuum, as they had at the same early hour like clockwork, day in and day out, for the last thousand years.

There was no natural light down in the trench, for the sun could not penetrate the miles of saltwater and rock that shielded this remote human outpost. If not for the Animus Machine generating electricity and oxygen, the Aquafarm and the automatic lights, the heating systems and the desalinators, all begat by the Founders, they would have perished long ago. Instead, against all odds and in total isolation, the Thirteenth Continuum had thrived, though it had not grown due to strict population controls.

Nevertheless, much had been forgotten, lost to the long years. For the past has a way of becoming first memory, then history, and eventually legend, before finally fading from the collective remembrance altogether, as if it had never existed at all. This lengthy process of forgetting can be hastened along by acts of willful destruction.

By order of the Synod, all records and properties from Before Doom were destroyed in the Great Purging. The same fate had befallen the submersibles that brought them there. Even speaking the very words—*the Surface*—had been deemed an offense punishable by being put out to sea, a death sentence in the deep water. The Head Priest of The Church of the Oracle of the Sea had even given his holy blessing to the Synod's decree. And nobody dared to disobey the Church; they knew what fate awaited sinners.

In this way, a millennium had come and gone in the Thirteenth Continuum, and life continued pretty much as it always had, with one exception. Somewhere in the depths of the colony, in a locked chamber where few were permitted to enter, a secret deliberation was taking place.

"How long did he say?"

"Eight months. At the most."

"It could be less?"

"Yes."

"There will be deaths?"

"If he is to be believed, we shall all perish."

This was met with silence. And then: "Could he be wrong about this?"

"Well, he's never been wrong before. There's no reason to suspect that this time is any different."

"But can he be trusted? That's what I want to know."

"There was that incident with his daughter, but she was punished."

"Not harshly enough, in my opinion."

"Perhaps, but we need him. He's not replaceable. At least . . . not yet."

Another silence engulfed the chamber while they considered how to proceed. It was a few seconds before the one who was their leader spoke.

"I have consulted the Oracle," he pronounced. "It pains me to say it, for our people have already suffered so much, but there is only one course of action—I must have more sacrifices."

This was met with approving murmurs.

"That would lessen the burden on the system."

"And appease the Holy Sea."

"All in favor say *aye*."

Nobody hesitated—their unanimous voices echoed through the chamber, stopped only by the thick barrier of the locked doors. It had been settled then.

There were no dissenters.

Chapter 2
THE ENGINEER'S DAUGHTER

The dream ended abruptly when the automatic lights flashed on. This was followed a few seconds later by the jarring and unmistakable sound of her father's yelling.

"Myra, wake up!" he bellowed from the kitchen.

Myra groaned once, then a second time, flipped over, and buried her head under the scratchy blanket with the big hole in it. The hole was already there when she claimed the blanket from the Com Store on her last shopping trip. It also smelled funny, like it clung to the memory of its past claimants even now, long after their bodies had been given to the Holy Sea. The light leaked through the fraying fibers, cajoling her tired brain into wakefulness. This made her groan for a third time.

She'd meant to patch it up—really, she had, as the Oracle was her witness. But somehow, she'd never quite gotten around to it. *There are just too many things that need fixing around here*, she decided, *and not enough time to mend them all.*

Despite her many complaints (according to her father, complaining, loudly if necessary, about any given object or situation was synonymous with being sixteen years old), Myra had grown fond of that blanket, gaping hole and all. It was a raggedy and partially useless thing. Hence, it reminded her an awful lot of herself.

Not willing to surrender to waking yet, she squeezed her eyes shut and tried to recall her dream, which had already dissolved into smoke under the harsh glare of the lights.

Was it the mermaid one again?

She knew that she should have outgrown such childish dreams by now, and she had tried to harden her heart against them, for it seemed like that was what you did when you grew up. But every night, her mind rebelled against her and conjured up vivid fantasies that contrasted starkly with the drabness of her world. In the clutches of her sleep, she could be anything.

Some nights, she dreamed that she was a mermaid who could swim through the saltwater, immune to the crushing pressure and the lack of oxygen, like in the fairytales of old that her mother used to tell her before bed. The stories always began the same way.

"Far out in the ocean," her mother would recite, as she lay curled up next to her daughter on the narrow bunk, weaving adventures like delicate threads out of thin air, "where the water is as blue as the prettiest cornflower and as clear as crystal, it is very, very, very deep."

"How blue is a cornflower?" Myra would ask.

Her mother would shake her head with a sad smile.

"I don't know, honey. Just picture the bluest blue you can possibly imagine." And that's what Myra would do, although she always suspected it paled in comparison to the real thing.

But in her favorite dream, she wasn't anything except Myra Jackson—a scrawny girl with a pale face dotted by freckles and crowned with a heap of russet hair.

In this dream, it wasn't her that was different.

It was everything else.

She would wake to the automatic lights the same as always, but instead of her father yelling for her to wake up, it was her mother, though Myra could scarcely remember what her voice sounded like anymore. Its exact tenor had been swallowed up by the years that had passed, one of the many things that had been stolen from her prematurely. Her mother had died while birthing her little brother.

Myra knew that it wasn't his fault. It was nobody's fault. At least, that's what her father always told her. But no matter how many times she repeated that mantra, sometimes the sight of her brother still brought back the memory of his arrival into this world, when he'd emerged from their mother's womb red-faced, squalling, and baptized in a river of blood, and of how much they'd both lost right then.

But the truth of the dream didn't matter at all. In her imaginings, her mother's voice was the sweetest sound that she'd ever heard—light and sonorous and full of love. *Myyyr-rrraaaaaa!* Her mother had chosen Myra's name, and it only sounded right when it rolled off her lips, but that hadn't happened for going on eight years now—

"Myra Jackson, wake up this instant!" her father yelled. There was an edge to his voice now. And he had used her full name, which was never a good sign. "You're going to be late . . . again!"

Resistance was futile.

Myra heaved off the blanket and struggled from her bunk. She glanced across the tiny room, even though she already knew what to expect. The other bunk was empty and the blanket, which also sported a few sizable holes, was tucked under the mattress flawlessly.

Tinker always got up as soon as the lights came on. Of course, Tinker wasn't her brother's real name. His given name was Jonah, the same as their father. But long before he could speak, when he was still in swaddling clothes, he would take apart and reassemble anything that he could get his grubby little hands on—furniture, light fixtures, appliances, tools. He was always tinkering, and so the nickname stuck.

But despite his many oddities, or perhaps because of them, Myra loved him more than anything in this world. They'd both suffered from losing their mother, and that suffering had bound them together.

Myra fished a rough-spun dress and hempen sandals out of her trunk, slipped them over her head and onto her feet, respectively, and raked one hand through her hair. It got stuck in a tangle, and she ended up wrenching out a clump of curls when she yanked it free. She considered brushing her hair out, but nobody in the Engineering Room cared what her hair looked like, and besides, it would probably be soot-covered, grease-smeared, or worse by the end of the day.

After splashing some cold water on her face, Myra padded into the living space. Their assigned compartment was identical to all of the others, even down to the Synod-issued furniture, which had been patched up more times than she could count. Her father always had to repair something that had broken, but resources were scarce and everything was precious.

There was the main living area—an austere room with a low ceiling, pipes jutting out of the concrete walls, and an ever-present chill in the air. A washroom with a composting toilet and a water-recycling shower, which never got quite warm enough for Myra's taste. Two tiny bedrooms—her father's and the one that she shared with Tinker. And a cramped kitchen with a rusty two-burner stove, a shallow basin, an icebox, and tarnished countertops that never seemed to come clean, no matter how many times she scrubbed them. They were ancient like everything else in the compartment.

Her father and brother were already well into breaking their fast at the kitchen table. Blueprints covered every square inch of space not taken up by breakfast, but this was nothing new. Tinker was tapping away on his computer. This also was nothing new. They didn't notice her enter the room. *Also nothing new*, she thought.

Myra sat on a wobbly chair at the kitchen table. She helped herself to a bowl of creamy rice porridge, ladling it from a crusty pot on the table into a chipped, earthen bowl. She topped it with a sprinkling of nori, a type of dried seaweed, to please her father, and a generous dollop of rice syrup to please herself. She had a serious sweet tooth. She started eating, relishing the sugary taste.

"You passed," her father said. He didn't look up from his blueprints, nor did he express any feeling about the matter. He also didn't elaborate. He just stated the facts.

"I know," Myra said through a mouthful of porridge. "Royston told me yesterday."

Her father had come home late last night, so they hadn't had a chance to discuss the results of her Apprentice Exam. As the Head Engineer, he worked around the clock, and when he did eventually stumble home, his work always seemed to follow him there, too.

Last week, Myra took the test with a group of five other pledges. Royston Chambers, the Engineering Pledge Master, administered it in a dank, smelly corner of the Engineering Room. The test took over six hours and involved both written and practical problems. She'd spent the better part of the last two years preparing for it, and now their scores, which would determine their futures, were finally in.

Yesterday, Royston took each pledge aside to inform them of their results. Though she had felt confident after taking the test—perhaps overly so—as more days had passed, that confidence had eroded into insecurity, and then worry, and finally downright panic. It was a relief to learn that she'd passed. The same wasn't true for all the pledges. Those who failed became Hockers, cast out of their chosen trade and forced to fend for themselves.

"You start as an apprentice next week," her father said.

"Royston told me that, too," she replied. It came out a bit snarky, but it got his attention, which she supposed had been the point. Her father looked up from his blueprints. It took a moment for his dazed expression to wear off.

"Myra, listen to me. You're the youngest person that's ever taken the test."

"Tell me something I don't know," she muttered, tossing her hair back and looking away. She hated being reminded of her age—and worse yet, the reason that she wasn't still in school.

"Fine, you got a perfect score. You're the first to do that, too."

Myra stopped chewing and nearly choked on her porridge. "Holy Sea, really? Swear it on the Oracle?"

Even Tinker was paying attention now. He looked up from his computer and punched his thick glasses up the bridge of his nose.

"On the Oracle and the Holy Sea," her father said. "Even I missed a few questions, though that was ages ago."

While his voice still contained no emotional inflection, a hint of pride played across his features. It was brief—like a light bulb that flickers on only to burn out a split second later, but Myra detected it. It wasn't much in the way of paternal affection, but she'd take it. She was tempted to add that she hadn't studied, that for her the test had been easy, but she didn't want to brag. Besides, her father probably already knew that, too. Nothing went on in the Engineering Room without him knowing about it.

"But remember," her father cautioned, lowering his voice. "You can't tell anybody your score, not even your friends. This has to stay inside our family."

"Papa, I know," Myra said with an exaggerated sigh. "I can only say if I passed or failed," she added to satisfy him, though everybody knew about the Synod's decree.

It worked—her father went back to his blueprints and Tinker went back to his computer. She took another bite of porridge and frowned at the bland taste. She dumped in more syrup. *You start as an apprentice next week*. Those were her father's words. They ran through her head again, thrilling and terrifying her at the same time.

It didn't quite seem real to her yet.

Most kids didn't pledge to a trade until after they turned sixteen and graduated from the Academy, but since Myra was expelled two years ago (she preferred not to think about the Trial, as it had become known), she was forced to pledge to her father's trade early. She loved Engineering—the puzzles of the moving pieces; the grime, the rust, and the grease that found their way onto her clothes and under her fingernails; the feel of a wrench in her hand; and the satisfaction of completing a repair to a vital system.

She knew that what she did every day kept her little world humming along without a hitch, unlike when she attended the Academy of the Oracle of the Sea, where she'd never understood what the lessons she memorized had to do with her actual life. Her classes had always seemed so pointless. She loved the certainty of being an Engineer.

And she had a knack for it, too. It could have been in her genes all along. As far back as she could trace that side of her family—the Jackson side—they had all been pledged to Engineering. Probably even dating back to the Founders, though most of that history had been destroyed in the Great Purging. But that wasn't an issue, because nobody much cared about history anymore. The subject wasn't even taught at the Academy.

And now, Myra Jackson—the daughter of Jonah and Tessa Jackson—was going to be the youngest Engineering apprentice ever. She liked the sound of that.

Chapter 3

THE FIRST WARNING

The lights in the compartment flashed off and on, and a tone sounded one time.

This was the First Warning for Factum, or the working class, to report to school or their chosen trade, whichever applied. Myra spooned up the last of her porridge and stood up from the table while her father rolled up his blueprints. The colony functioned on a strict schedule. On their assigned day, they also had to attend services at the Church. Any Factum caught scrimping on their duties, or skipping them altogether, risked getting demoted to Hocker status. Nobody wanted to end up a Hocker, not if they could help it. Myra nudged her brother to make sure she had his attention.

"Tink, time for school. I know you don't want to go, but we're Factum and rules are rules."

Tinker looked up from his computer, and his pupils focused as if he were noticing her for the first time that morning. His computer was a rarity in their world. He'd built it himself from scavenged parts. Some came from the Spare Parts Room in Sector 10 or the Com Store, but most had been ferreted home by their father, plucked out of old machines that couldn't be repaired or discovered in long forgotten parts of the colony where only the Engineers dared to venture anymore.

Tinker hopped up, stowed the computer in his rucksack, and slung it over his shoulder. Through it all, he didn't utter a single word, but his lack of response was normal. He didn't start talking until he was over four years old, and now, at twice that age, he had the ability to speak and a large vocabulary—at least according to his impressive test scores—but, more often than not, he still chose to keep silent. It also didn't help that he was small for his age and often got bullied by bigger kids at school.

"Tinker, have a good day at the Academy," their father said, draining the last dregs of his tea and stashing the blueprints in his satchel. "Myra, I'll see you after you drop your brother off. I'm assigning your team to a water leak in Sector 7."

She envisioned a map of the colony and zeroed in on the area that housed the Aquafarm. "Oh, water leaks, my favorite."

"Just be thankful it's not a sewage leak," he replied. Though his voice remained serious, a smirk pulled at his lips. "We've got one of those, too."

"Thank the Oracle, or I might start to regret my pledge choice."

"In that case, I might start to regret assigning your team to the water leak," he said without missing a beat. "It's not too late to switch the assignments. I'm sure Erwin wouldn't mind giving up sewage—"

"Say no more!" she cut him off and flashed the biggest, most cheerful grin she could muster. "Who doesn't enjoy a little hypothermia first thing in the morning?"

Then, before he really did decide to switch the assignments, she seized Tinker by the arm and shuttled him toward the door. She swiped the tattoo on her wrist under the scanner. It beeped its approval, and the thick door dilated.

The corridor was filled with Factum headed to school or work. Everyone was dressed in the same rough-spun clothes—the women in crude dresses, and the men in coveralls and loose-fitting tunics. Most wore sandals, but a few lucky Factum had boots. Some clutched satchels or pulled rickety carts, while others went empty-handed.

Myra stepped into the corridor with Tinker in tow. As far as she could see down either side of the passageway were identical doors that led to other compartments. Their only distinguishing features were the numbers that marked them—descending to the left, ascending to the right. Odd numbers on one side, even on the other.

Suddenly, a Patroller stepped out from a doorway. He was dressed in black from head to toe. A steel pipe was strapped to his waist by a chunky bit of rope. It was imprecise yet deadly, and therefore the Patrollers' weapon of choice.

Myra thought for a second before settling on his name—Jasper Waters. He'd been a few years ahead of her at the Academy and was only an apprentice. She wondered if he'd been watching her compartment, waiting for her to emerge. A chill worked its way up her spine, and she stepped in front of Tinker reflexively.

"Hurry, let's get out of here," she whispered to her brother. She tugged him in the opposite direction. The crowd soon absorbed them, and Jasper vanished from view. But his appearance had rattled Myra. Even as she ducked and weaved through the corridor, she kept thinking about the Patroller.

A few minutes later, they exited Sector 2, which housed the living compartments. The colony was divided into ten sectors connected by corridors that were tightly sealed and heavily fortified to protect them from the deadly pressure of the seawater surrounding them. If viewed from the outside, the colony would have resembled a giant block with nine blocks spawning off it like the spokes on a wheel.

Even though the Synod had instituted controls that kept the population at around two thousand, the corridors were jam-packed with people. Myra navigated through the narrow passages from memory, but if she were to get lost, she could swipe her wrist at any terminal along the way and the central computer would project a holographic map, complete with a tiny figure representing her current location. She could also tell the computer her destination—*The Academy of the Oracle of the Sea,* in this instance—and it would project the best route.

How the central computing system functioned was mostly a mystery now. It had been created by the Founders—she knew that much. But how it was programmed, why it could recognize their speech, or how it projected such realistic holographs seemed more like magic now, like something out of one of her mother's fairytales.

Sure, they had Programmers, but their knowledge was mostly limited to troubleshooting problems that arose. They could plug in pieces of code here and there. When chips blew out, sometimes they could locate a replacement in the Spare Parts Room, but, more often than not, they'd have to route around that part of the system. Lately, more and more chips were blowing out, and more and more parts were being routed around. She'd heard her father complaining about it last week.

"Hey, did you see that?" Tinker said in a raspy voice. It sounded raw and ragged from disuse. He tugged at her sleeve, pulling her toward the window.

She turned to look just as a monstrous creature swam past. It had a wide mouth filled with rows of jagged teeth and spindly antennae that protruded from a bulbous head. The end of the longest antenna was positioned right in front of its mouth and glowed with eerie, bluish light. *Bioluminescence*, her father called it.

She was so surprised that Tinker had actually spoken that she almost forgot to respond.

"That's good luck," she said and mussed his fine, blond hair. "Anglers usually avoid the lights."

"Good luck," Tinker repeated and punched his glasses up. "For both of us?"

"Yup, I saw it too."

Tinker smiled his lopsided smile, but then it faded from his lips, replaced by another expression altogether.

"I was thinking . . . what else is out there?"

His eyes were fixed on the small circular window, peering not at the fish hovering inside the halo cast by the exterior lights, but at the murky darkness that lay beyond it. That darkness—where their lights could no longer penetrate—formed the very edge of their world.

Oblivious Factum streamed around them, focused only on the day ahead and the tasks at hand. *Tuck your head down and do your work* was a common saying.

"Oh, all sorts of creatures," Myra said. "Stingers and jellies."

"And . . . krakens?" Tinker said.

She fixed him with a stern expression. "You've been listening to Maude's stories again, haven't you? You know better than that."

His guilty expression said it all. Maude was the Hocker who lived across the corridor in Compartment 519 and traded homemade candy at the Souk for extra provisions. As punishment for getting kicked out of school or their trades, Hockers lost half their Victus or Synod-issued rations. And they were a superstitious lot by nature.

Myra knelt down and looked Tinker squarely in the eyes. "Don't listen to Maude. There's no such thing as krakens," she said, picturing the giant, tentacled monsters that often appeared in the Hockers' tales. "Besides, we never go out there. The colony protects us, remember? We're safe, as long as we stay in here."

Tinker didn't reply—he just took in what she said soundlessly—but he didn't look afraid anymore either. She breathed a sigh of relief. The last thing that she needed was to deal with his nightmares tonight. He was prone to them. They both turned back to the window as the angler's razor-sharp teeth snapped shut with terrifying speed, as if grasping for something just out of reach.

Myra flinched back from the window. And then, as unexpectedly as it had appeared, the creature darted out of the reach of the lights, swallowed up by the gloom.

They continued down the corridor. Soon it widened again and the windows vanished. The human traffic grew thicker.

Myra glanced down at the green arrows illuminated on the floor. A sign flashed beneath her feet that read SECTOR 5. As she rounded the bend, two arms latched around her torso and squeezed together, ensnaring her between them.

She felt warm breath tickling her throat.

"Myra Jackson, hold it right there."

Chapter 4
TEACH YOU A LESSON

Myra's first instinct was fear driven—*the 'Trollers had her!* But she forced herself to relax and take stock of the situation. Her heart rate slowed and the rational part of her brain sparked to attention. She breathed in through her nostrils, and that's what did it. She'd recognize his scent anywhere—spice and sweat with a hint of perfumed soap underneath, the kind that only the Plenus could get.

At his smell, her heart pitter-pattered in her chest. *Traitor,* she thought. She was referring to her heart, but the term could have just as easily applied to him. Before she could enjoy his embrace too much, she twisted away and stomped on his foot. It had its intended effect.

"Holy Sea, what'd you do that for?" Kaleb yelped. He released her to tend to his wounded extremity. She could tell that he wasn't hurt that badly.

"You can't just go around grabbing people in the corridor like that," she said. "Somebody has to teach you a lesson."

He massaged his foot gingerly. "Point taken . . . but did you have to use so much force?"

"It wasn't that much. Force equals mass times acceleration. I used just enough to make you release me, not enough to break a toe."

He tried to look aghast, but it was terribly adorable. "Break a toe? What kind of monster are you?"

"The nice kind," she shot back. "Otherwise I would have actually broken it—not just considered it. Don't be such a wimp. Pretend you're Factum for one second."

Kaleb put a little pressure on his foot, testing it out. Just as she had guessed, it bore his weight easily. He didn't even flinch. The only thing damaged was his ego.

"Good as new!" he proclaimed.

The smile was back on his face now, the one that he'd probably been wearing behind her back while he held her captive in his arms. It lit up his face, enhancing each of his highborn features, from his glossy black hair, to his sharp cheekbones, to his deep, emerald eyes.

Even now, after everything they'd been through, she still wondered why he chose to share it with her. Kaleb was Plenus with a father on the Synod. He could have had any girl in the colony, but for some inexplicable reason he had picked her. It was maddening and infuriating and perplexing and—worst of all—it defied all rationality.

But it hadn't ended well.

Sure, it had started out great. For two glorious years they courted until The Trial put a stop to that—and every other good thing in her life. After she got expelled from school, Kaleb abandoned her. All of her friends from school did. That was really the only word for it.

They *abandoned* her.

Kaleb stopped talking to her. Stopped kissing her. Stopped coming by her compartment. Stopped everything. Just stopped.

The heartbreak that followed was worse than everything else that happened during that dark time. It kept her up at night, sobbing into her pillow, and haunted her like a ghost during the day, turning up when she least expected it and scaring her half to death. It got so bad that for a while she didn't even recognize herself anymore. Who was this creature with dark circles under her eyes who cried at the drop of a hat?

But time had a funny way of changing things. Slowly, but surely, over the last few months, Kaleb started talking to her again. All of her friends from school did. Eventually, she let them back into her life, just as they let her back into theirs.

But not all the way.

The Trial had changed her. It had made her more cautious with her affections. And she'd sworn a sacred oath to herself that she was done with *courting*, done with *kissing*, done with *Kaleb Sebold*. Being lonely was better than nursing a broken heart.

At least, this was what she told herself. And to her brain, it all sounded perfectly reasonable—necessary even. But her heart wasn't convinced, that much was clear. Like she said, it was a traitor.

"So, did you miss me?" Kaleb asked as Myra and Tinker fell in with him. He shot her a sideways glance. "Haven't seen you around the corridors lately."

Myra thought about it—*had she missed him?*

Usually, she saw her friends when she walked Tinker to school in the mornings, or after work in the corridors on the way home, but for the last few weeks, she'd been holed up in the Engineering Room studying for her test.

"Nope, I didn't," she said with a straight face.

"A little?" Kaleb prodded.

"Not even. Don't flatter yourself."

"A teeny-tiny bit?" His grin widened, daring her to resist it.

"No," she said sternly, but this time she smiled in spite of herself.

"There, I knew you missed me," he declared. His eyes lingered on her face, and she felt blood warming her cheeks. A second passed, then another, until—

"Missed us," bellowed a jovial voice.

They turned to see Rickard, who had finally caught up to his best friend. He smiled his goofy grin when he reached them. "You missed us, don't you mean?"

"Like a bad case of the Pox," Myra said.

"That much, huh?" Rickard said and laughed, his big frame shaking. He was broad-shouldered and sturdy like his father, who was the Head Patroller. This had made her wary of him at first, but his tough exterior was just a façade, nothing more. Underneath it all, he was one of the kindest, most generous people that she'd ever met.

"Myra, there you are!" Paige called out in a breathless voice. She forced her way through the crowd, juggling a big stack of books. Her eyes darted around the group. They'd all started as First Years together. "So . . . did you tell them yet?" she said with barely concealed excitement.

Myra dug her foot into the floor. "It's nothing."

"Myra, it's not nothing," Paige said. "Myra passed her Apprentice Exam. My cousin Erwin told me last night. I'll bet she's been studying like crazy. That's probably why we haven't seen her around."

"Like I said, it's nothing," Myra said.

"Please, don't be so modest," Paige said, but her reaction wasn't unusual. There were few things that she considered as important as studying and tests. "You're the youngest person that's ever passed the test."

"Impressive, Engine Rat," Rickard said and pounded Myra on the back harder than was necessary, making her wince.

Kaleb let out a long whistle. "An apprentice already? We haven't even pledged yet."

Myra looked down, trying not to show how much this bothered her. "That's only because I got a head start," she said in what she hoped was a neutral voice. "And I got lucky, too. I could have easily become a Hocker."

An awkward silence fell over the group. They'd never discussed The Trial. She caught Tinker watching her with a concerned expression. Finally, Rickard broke the tension.

"By the Oracle, I'd love to get kicked out of school! No

Headmaster Crawley, no Religious Studies lesson taking up the whole afternoon, and no Baron Donovan."

"Yeah, I certainly don't miss that stuff," Myra said.

Paige caught her eye with a knowing smile. "Sweetfish?" she asked. They'd been best friends ever since their teacher paired them together for a math lesson during their First Year. Thanks to Paige's focus and Myra's math skills, they'd earned top marks and quickly become inseparable.

Myra arched her eyebrow.

"Do you even need to ask?"

o o o

"Fresh fish rolls!" bellowed a Hocker with yellowing teeth and stained coveralls. His voice carried through the Souk. "Get your fish rolls! Salty and briny, made from yesterday's Victus!"

Myra, Tinker, and her friends—Kaleb, Rickard, and Paige—proceeded into Sector 5 and headed for the large marketplace set right in the middle. They had a little bit of time before they had to swipe in at the Engineering Room and the Academy, respectively. Factum poured into the market from the corridors that spawned off Sector 5, the most central sector. Some pushed old carts or wheelbarrows laden with rusted hunks of metal, broken computer parts, or other scavenged goods for bartering with the Hockers. Others carried provisions from their Victus that they could spare, such as rice flour, sugar, or kelp bars, which didn't taste very good, but were full of nutrients. This made them popular with the Hockers, who had lost half their Victus. For them, malnutrition was a chronic malady.

"Who wants stinky fish rolls when they can have my crispy skewers?" another Hocker bellowed at the top of her lungs. "Spicy, fresh off the grill! Get 'em while they're hot!"

"Who you calling stinky?" the first Hocker spat. "I seen where she gets her fish, I have!" He squeezed his nose shut. "Fresh fish rolls, made from yesterday's Victus!"

Their verbal warfare escalated with each shout. The Souk

was garish and frenzied, but also exhilarating and tempting at the same time. Even the low ceilings and ever-present chill in the air couldn't stifle its liveliness. Myra saw handwoven baskets, tie-dyed scarves in every pattern and color imaginable, fermented fish rolls wrapped in rice and crispy seaweed (which she detested, though most considered them a delicacy), crudely stitched dolls made from swatches of old fabric, curried fish that smelled pungent and spicy and made her mouth water uncontrollably, and prickly sandals woven from hempen thread.

A scratchy voice cut through the crowd. "If it isn't Myra Jackson, my best customer!"

Myra turned to see Maude waving at them from behind her booth on the far side of the Souk, which was piled to the ceiling with the homemade candy that she traded for extra provisions. Myra snatched up Tinker's hand, and they made a beeline for her booth.

"You want the usual, sweetheart?" Maude said with a toothless grin. She wore a motley skirt, decorated with fraying swatches of fabric and mismatched buttons. Unlike most Hockers, she was a little on the plump side from sampling too much of her own product, which also accounted for her missing teeth.

"Of course," Myra said. "How long have you known me?"

Maude held her hand at waist level. "Since you were wee high and getting into all sorts of trouble. From what your father tells me, not much has changed."

Myra blushed. "Well, I'm a bit taller."

"But still a troublemaker?"

"Aye," Myra said, casting her eyes down. There was no point in denying it—everybody knew about The Trial.

"Good girl," Maude said. "I'd expect nothing less."

Her gaze shifted to Tinker, whose hand was stuck deep in a pile of hard candy. "And hello there, Tinker! Where are your manners? I know you're not much for talking, but how about a wave?"

Guiltily, Tinker yanked his hand free and waved. A shy

smile crept onto his lips and a little color into his cheeks. This made Maude chuckle.

"Now, who else do we have today?" Her eyes flashed over their faces. "Kaleb, Rickard, and Paige. I'd say it's the usual bunch. Let's see, it's licorice twists for Kaleb, ginger snaps for Rickard, and lemon pastries for Paige. That about right?"

Maude made it her business to know the name of every kid in the colony and what type of candy they preferred.

"That's right, ma'am," Rickard said.

"Well, what are you waiting for?" Maude said. "I baked the peanut butter brittle fresh this morning. Oh, and there's a new flavor of hard candy—caramel apple."

They didn't need to be told twice. Myra plucked up two handfuls of the plumpest sweetfish in a variety of colors and presented them to Maude, who nodded at the impressive pile.

"That all for today, sweetheart?"

While Maude wrapped up the candy in burlap cloth, something caught Myra's attention. They were standing on the outermost edge of the Souk and had a full view of Sector 5. Nervous energy rushed through the market like a current of electricity. Further down the sector, beyond the Infirmary, a large crowd was gathered in front of the Church. Something was definitely going on. She had a bad feeling about it.

"Maude . . . what's the commotion?" she whispered.

Maude looked up and followed her gaze.

"Got a 'Troller drunk on firewater last night," Maude said in a hushed voice, referring to the homemade liquor that she brewed on the side. Alcohol was forbidden to Factum and Hockers, but since the Patrollers indulged in firewater just as much as everybody else, they tended to turn a blind eye to both its manufacture and consumption.

"What'd he say?" Myra said in a low voice. She glanced over at her friends and brother, but they were busy picking out candy.

"He only hinted to it, mind you. And he was a bit tipsy, but it sounds like the Red Cloaks have got themselves a new sacrifice," she said, using the Hockers' slang term for the priests. "That's the fifth one this month. Looks like the Holy Sea will run red today."

Though Maude trafficked in information just as much as candy and firewater, clearly she took no pleasure in delivering this news.

"The Hockers are growing restless," she went on. "Most of the sacrifices come from within our ranks. If Padre Flavius isn't careful, he could end up with a revolution on his hands."

"A revolution?" Myra said, shocked. "But the Hockers wouldn't stand a chance, not against the 'Trollers and their pipes."

"Aye, the 'Trollers have their pipes, but we outnumber them two to one. And maybe we could convince some Factum to join us. Hockers aren't the only ones who are unhappy with the Synod."

"Still, it would be dangerous. A lot of people would die."

A dark expression clouded Maude's face. "There are things worse than dying."

"Like . . . what?" Myra asked.

"Living without freedom, for one thing," Maude said as she finished tying up the bundles of sweetfish with red string.

Her words chilled Myra. Hockers were only allowed to be in three places in the entire colony—Sector 2, which housed their living compartments; Sector 5, which housed the Souk and the Church; and the corridors that connected those two places. If they were caught anywhere else, then they could be arrested and sent before the Synod.

Maude handed over the candy. "Don't listen to me," she said with a dismissive wave. "I'm just a gossipy old widow with too much time on my hands. Now, don't eat them all in one sitting."

Myra tried to offer payment for her sweetfish and the suckers Tinker was picking out. "Here, take these," she said, fishing some kelp bars out of her pocket, but Maude waved her off.

"I won't hear of it, sweetheart. The help your father gives me around my compartment is payment enough. I mean it, now not another word."

Myra waited while her friends settled up with Maude. No matter what type of payment they offered, everybody left her stall with something sweet. Come to think of it, Myra had never seen her turn any kid away empty-handed, regardless of their status.

"Good-bye," Myra said as she backed away.

"It's not good-bye," Maude said. "It's see you later."

"See you later," Myra revised her statement.

That satisfied Maude, and she waved them off. "Now, all of you, get out of my sight. The Final Warning will be flashing before you know it."

Chapter 5

THE SENTENCING

As Myra departed the Souk with her pockets brimming with candy, the lights dimmed throughout the entire colony, and the tone sounded twice this time. This was the Second Warning.

Right away, the crowd of Factum at the Souk began to disperse. Soon the Hockers would start breaking down their stalls and preparing for the close of the market.

"Hurry up. We're late," Paige said, always the official task-master of their group. "Rickard, that means you."

Rickard was loitering by a booth that sold spicy crab rolls. He stuffed the rest of a ginger cookie in his mouth. "Just trying . . . to maximize my free time," he mumbled between chews.

"You won't have any free time if you get marked tardy again," Paige said. "Mr. Richardson has it out for you."

"Lynch, you heard her," Kaleb said. "Your dad will kill you if you get another one."

That settled it—they hurried away from the Souk.

As they passed the Infirmary, Myra spotted an orange flag hoisted over the door and a long line snaking out the front.

Though the doctors worked tirelessly, there were never enough appointments to go around. Plenus always got seen first, followed by Factum, and then Hockers if there were any spots left. Often they never got seen at all.

Paige's mother, the Head Doctor, was busy triaging a patient in the line. The elderly man looked like he was having trouble breathing.

"Another health warning?" Myra asked.

Paige followed her gaze to the flag. "Oh, right, I heard my mom talking about it this morning. There was another allergen release from the Aquafarm. The Synod issued a warning, but it's nothing serious, just some excess pollen from the new batch of crops or something."

"Guess that explains the long line," Myra said.

Paige nodded. "And the orange color."

Orange signified some kind of air contamination, blue was for water contamination, and yellow meant the flu. The flag that they all feared the most was red. That meant that there was another Pox outbreak. The last one occurred almost thirty years ago and killed over a hundred people, including Maude's husband and children.

They neared the Church. Since they'd left the Souk, the crowd gathered in front of it had grown larger. A priest was speaking from the top of the steps, which wound up to the entrance in a tight spiral. The centerpiece of the Church was the Oracle itself—a conch shell gilded in precious metals. When held to one's ear, the Holy Sea could be heard rushing and roaring through it and delivering sacred messages.

Myra knew she should keep going—the Final Warning would be flashing shortly. But curiosity got the better of her. She signaled her friends, and they pushed through the crowd to get a better view.

"People of the One True Colony under the Holy Sea," Padre Flavius spoke to the crowd in his deep baritone.

Now that Myra was closer, she could tell that this was no ordinary sermon. A group of Patrollers lurked behind the priests in their black uniforms. She spotted Jasper, the apprentice from the corridor, and Head Patroller Lynch, Rickard's father.

"The Oracle teaches us that the Holy Sea provides everything we need," Padre Flavius said. He had a black beard, waxed to a fine point, beady eyes set a little too close together, and thin lips that he liked to purse whenever he disapproved of something, which seemed to happen quite often. The other priests flanked the Head Priest in their matching crimson robes. "The water we drink, the air we breathe, the food we eat."

The crowd voiced their support.

"Amen!"

"But through his sins, mankind brought the Great Doom upon himself. A mighty scourge rose up and devoured the Earth, turning it into ash and fire. But the Holy Sea saved the Chosen People. She delivered them into her sacred waters. She cleansed them of sin and gave them a Safe Harbor."

Padre Flavius hoisted up the Oracle in front of the crowd. It gleamed and shimmered under the automatic lights. And it had its intended effect. The crowd rumbled again: "Amen!"

One woman threw herself at Flavius's feet. "Padre, save me!" she wailed, flopping around on the ground.

Padre Flavius reached into his cloak and produced a vial of Holy Seawater. He sprinkled some on her forehead, and she writhed in ecstasy. The crowd roared its approval.

Once they had settled down, Padre Flavius passed the Oracle to another priest for safekeeping and then turned to Rickard's father.

"Head Patroller Lynch, please bring out the prisoner so we may bestow our punishment upon the heathen."

Paige's face drained of color. "It's a . . . sentencing," she whispered.

The Synod conducted trials in secret, but once their verdicts were rendered, they left the dirty business of dispensing sentences to Padre Flavius. He quite enjoyed it, too. He'd already given more sacrifices to the Holy Sea than his last five predecessors combined. Rather than rebelling against him, the crowd—a rowdy mix of Factum and Hockers—seemed to relish the spectacle. They shouted praises and cheered him on.

Myra snuck a glance at Kaleb. Did he know about the sentencing? It would have been a secret, but his father sat on the Synod. It was possible that he'd let something slip at home.

"Yes, Padre," Rickard's father said.

He signaled to his men, and they ducked into the building and disappeared around the spiral. Their shadows could be seen circling deeper and deeper into the structure, which was modeled after the Oracle itself, even down to its pinkish, translucent walls.

While they waited, the crowd outside was going wild with anticipation. People started speculating about the identity of the heathen. One man—an enterprising Hocker from the look of him—was taking bets, marking them down in a ledger.

"Man or woman?" he called out.

Factum and Hockers shouted out their guesses.

"Adult or child?"

Better odds were given if you could guess the heathen's class. Most speculated that he must be a Hocker. Even better odds if you got his or her name right. People started shouting out names, some of which Myra recognized. It sickened her to listen to them.

A few minutes later, the Patrollers emerged from the building, dragging a prisoner behind them. Ropes bound his wrists and ankles. They had torn bloody tracks into his flesh. Splotchy bruises and open wounds crisscrossed his back. They looked like they had been inflicted by the Patrollers' pipes.

The prisoner fought a losing battle, digging his heels into the ground and gnashing his teeth. Jasper gagged him with a filthy piece of cloth, and then they threw him down at Padre Flavius's feet.

The man rolled onto his back with a groan.

Myra gasped when she saw his face.

It was Carter Knox.

Though his features were bloody and badly misshapen, there was no mistaking him. He was also pledged to Engineering, though he was a few years older than her and already a Master Engineer. They'd worked together for the last two years, and he was one of her father's favorite workers.

"Before the Synod, this man has confessed to uttering an *Unholy Blaspheme*," Padre Flavius said, reading from a scroll. "And plotting to return to the *Place That Shall Not Be Named.*"

The mob screamed profanities at Carter.

"Drown the heathen!"

"Traitor, the Holy Sea save him!"

There was only one thing that he could have said to provoke such a reaction. *The Surface*, Myra thought, careful not even to mouth the words. Angry tears pooled in her eyes and flowed down her cheeks.

She lunged toward Carter, but two arms snaked around her torso and restrained her. This time she didn't twist away from Kaleb, or try to free herself. "Please, we have to help him!" she cried, though she knew it was suicide to even consider such a thing. "They're going to kill him!"

"Myra, there's nothing we can do," Kaleb hissed in her ear. "Padre Flavius is looking for any excuse to come after you. Don't be stupid! You can't save him."

She looked at him in surprise—this was the first time he'd even come close to acknowledging what had happened to her. Mostly, they'd just avoided the topic. *He knows more than he's let on*, she realized.

"You can't win," Kaleb whispered. "Not against them."

Overcome by the helpless feeling that swept through her, Myra sagged in Kaleb's arms. He kept them wrapped around her, and it morphed into an embrace. Still, she didn't try to stop him or shrug him off. This was a slippery slope—one that she'd already slid down before—but she couldn't help herself. Not in the face of so much brutality.

"He was just telling a joke," an old man yelled from the crowd. Myra wondered if it was Carter's father. "That's all it was! He was just having a bit of fun—"

Before he could finish, Jasper leapt into the crowd and started beating him with a pipe. Myra saw blood splatter and a piece of a tooth fly into the air. Once the old man had been subdued, Jasper dragged his limp body away, most likely to the Penitentiary in Sector 3. Kaleb was right—you couldn't win. Not against the Synod and the Red Cloaks and the Patrollers. They held all of the power, and they knew it.

"Carter Knox, I hereby sentence you to be put out to sea," Padre Flavius said. "May the Holy Sea cleanse you of your sins, lest you bring the Doom upon us all."

Carter let out a moan when he heard his punishment. A rumble surged through the crowd. One woman yelled, "Serves the sinner right!"

"He don't deserve the Safe Harbor!"

A man swirled his finger over his heart, a superstitious gesture. "He'll bring the Doom upon us—cast the heathen into the Holy Sea!"

With a flick of his wrist, Padre Flavius commanded the Patrollers to take him away. They wrenched Carter, kicking and screaming, through the Souk. The bloodthirsty crowd trailed behind them, yelling profanities and calling for his demise. Myra watched in disgust as they left. They were headed for the Docks in Sector 10. Back when they'd had submersibles, that's where they'd been housed, by the portals that opened to the sea. Her father had told her about them in secret.

Now it was where the executions were held.

Myra pictured Carter's naked body being forced into a portal and locked inside. Padre Flavius, or maybe Rickard's father, would press a button, and then the chamber would open to the sea, allowing the super-pressurized saltwater to rush in. It would instantly crush him. Carter wouldn't last one second after the water hit his fragile human body.

He was already a dead man.

Myra shrugged off Kaleb's embrace. "Hey, let's get out of here," she said. She had to swallow hard to keep the bile from backing up into her esophagus. It didn't work, not entirely. She tasted bitterness.

Grabbing Tinker's hand, she yanked him toward the Academy. She used more force than she intended, and poor Tinker had to scramble to keep up with her. Kaleb and Paige followed after them silently, but Rickard hung back, his eyes glued to the angry horde's procession through the Souk. Their cries could still be heard:

"Put him out to sea!"

"Kill the heathen!"

"He'll bring the Doom on us!"

Clearly, Rickard wanted to watch the execution. Though it would make him late for school, he wouldn't be marked tardy today. Mr. Richardson wouldn't want to be seen as interfering with official Church business, or else he risked suffering the same fate as Carter Knox and countless others who Padre Flavius had put out to sea.

"Rickard, you coming?" Myra called back. She hated to think that one of her friends would enjoy watching another one of her friends suffer.

"Be right there," Rickard said after a lengthy pause. He wrenched his gaze away from the mob. As he caught up to them, relief surged through Myra. She was glad that he wasn't going to watch. It would have driven a wedge between them, and she didn't want that. She'd already lost her friends once, and she didn't want to lose any of them again.

"Wouldn't want to be tardy, now would I?" Rickard said.

This provoked a scowl from Paige. "Very funny."

"You heard him, let's go," Myra said. Not waiting for a response, she broke into a sprint, wanting to put as much distance between her and the Church as possible.

Chapter 6

THE TRIAL

"If I run faster, then I won't have to think about it."

Myra chanted this to herself as sweat dripped down her forehead. She was breathless and soaked by the time she arrived outside the Academy, a modest building constructed from cinderblocks sealed with concrete. It was nothing compared to the opulence of the Church or the Synod's chambers, which occupied all of Sector 6.

Skidding to a halt, she brushed the sweat from her eyes. They were stinging, but whether it was from the tears or the perspiration—or maybe both—she wasn't sure. She doubled over to catch her breath. It took a moment for the dizziness to pass. *It must be the allergen release*, she thought, remembering the orange flag above the Infirmary.

A second later, Tinker, Kaleb, Paige, and Rickard arrived by her side. They'd all made it before the Final Warning. Everybody was winded, but poor Tinker more so than the rest.

Myra was about to say good-bye to him when she spotted three large figures lurking by the school's entrance. *Baron Donovan. Gregor Crane. Horace Grint.* Their names flashed through her head. They were the reasons that she walked Tinker to school every morning.

"Baron and his crew," Myra said under her breath.

Frustration coursed through her—she hated feeling so helpless. She wanted to walk her brother to his classroom, but she had to leave him outside. The Synod had banned her from coming within one hundred feet of the school.

Kaleb draped his arm protectively over Tinker's shoulders. "Don't worry. We'll make sure he gets to class."

"Thanks. I mean it," Myra said.

She knelt down by her brother and straightened his rucksack's straps. She cast a wary glance toward Baron and his crew. "Tink, you know the drill, right? Maude will walk you home after school, and I'll see you when I get off work."

After he had come home with two black eyes in one week, courtesy of Baron and his crew, she'd enlisted Maude's help to keep him safe.

Tinker nodded and waved good-bye.

"Later, Engine Rat," Rickard said.

"Don't be a stranger now that you're an apprentice," Paige added, bobbling her armload of textbooks. Kaleb just aimed one of his dazzling smiles at her. Myra felt her heart hiccup in her chest—the traitor.

Then Kaleb steered Tinker toward the school. Her brother was headed for his Third Year classroom, where Mrs. Pritchard would be waiting for him. She was a prim woman who lacked any sense of humor whatsoever, or so Myra thought. She'd been her teacher, too.

Myra watched him walk away, his rucksack bouncing on his shoulders, until he vanished inside the school with her friends, swallowed up by the gray cinderblocks.

o o o

Myra was halfway across the Souk when the entire sector plunged into darkness again, and the tone rang out three times.

This was the Final Warning—she was officially late. She needed a way get to work quickly. Though most of the

Patrollers were probably at the execution, she didn't want to risk being caught out in the corridors. Her eyes swept up and down the Souk. The Hockers, even the few stragglers, had already packed up and left for the day.

Myra stole across the empty market to the far side. To her right was the corridor that led to Sector 4, which housed the Engineering Room—but she didn't go that way.

Instead, she knelt next to a grate set unobtrusively into the wall. She slipped her hands through the narrow slats, felt around, and unfastened the latch. She glanced back to make sure she wasn't being watched, and then slithered through the tight opening and into the pipe. The grate snapped shut behind her, locking into place with a satisfying click. This pipe only carried air, so it was safe. She fished out her flashlight and aimed the beam into the murky darkness.

In this way, she began her journey to Sector 4, taking her secret ways. Hidden beneath the walls, the ceiling, and the floor were all sorts of pipes and ducts. Some were in constant use, like the sewage and water lines, but many had been shut down or abandoned long ago. She first discovered them as a kid, when she snuck a look at her father's blueprints. Laid out in pale blue lines etched onto dark blue paper was an entire world that existed beneath the world that she knew.

A furry, black rat scampered ahead of her, but Myra didn't startle or flinch in any way. Instead, she smiled fondly. "Hey there, little guy," she cooed to the rat.

Nobody knew exactly how the rats had wound up in the colony. Some thought they'd stowed away on the submersibles and hitched a ride into the colony, while others thought people had deliberately smuggled them down here. Regardless, they'd quickly invaded their new digs and settled into the pipes and ducts.

The rat cocked its head at her, trying to determine if she was friend or foe. Maintenance workers were always trying to exterminate them, but they never succeeded in wiping them all out. If there was one thing you could say about the rats—they were survivors. That's what Myra liked most about them.

They had that in common. She'd made it her secret mission to aid and abet their tiny rebellion against Maintenance.

"You're starved, aren't you?" she said and dug in her pocket. She tossed some sweetfish to the rat, who snatched the candy in its jaws and then scurried off, disappearing down another pipe.

Myra continued through the labyrinth of pipes and ducts, at times crawling on all fours when the passage narrowed. *Poor Carter*, she thought. The image of him being put out to sea flashed through her head again.

His naked body, prickled with gooseflesh, as he stood in the massive portal. The thick door trapping him inside. The way his eyes would go flat when he realized that there was no escape. The deluge of seawater rushing in to claim him in an implosion of blood and tissue. And, worst of all, the cheers of the crowd when it was done.

While she hadn't known Carter overly well, she'd gotten used to seeing his smiling face at work every day. His crooked teeth and goofy grin were welcome distractions from her grueling pledge duties. *It could have just as easily been me that was put out to sea*. The thought raced through her head before she could stop it.

Despite her attempts to forget The Trial, it tended to pop up at times like these. Instead of trying—usually in vain—to push it from her mind, she allowed the memory to surface in its full glory. Her teacher, Mrs. Simon, assigned her class to write a story. Right away, Myra knew what she wanted to write about—her favorite fairytale.

When she got up to read it to the class, everything started out just fine. The class looked bored, Baron cracked jokes to his crew, and Mrs. Simon nodded along approvingly. The story began with the mermaid princess living under the sea.

"Far out in the ocean, where the water is as blue as the prettiest cornflower," she read to the class, "and as clear as crystal, it is very, very, very deep."

But when Myra got to the middle—specifically, the part where the mermaid princess drinks the witch's magic potion, sprouts legs, and leaves her father's sea kingdom so she can live on dry land—Mrs. Simon's mouth dropped open in horror.

"Oh my, now Myra," she said. "Everything we need is under the sea. It's blasphemy to suggest otherwise." She snatched the story from Myra's hands and scrawled a big red "F" at the top. "Now, sit back down. Your story time is over."

"But Mrs. Simon—" Myra said.

"Young lady, are you talking back?" Her face turned a disturbing shade of crimson. "Students aren't allowed to ask teachers questions. You know that."

"But—"

"But nothing. Now sit. Back. Down."

Right then, something in Myra snapped.

She wasn't sure if it was all the years of listening in silence, or studying textbooks with black lines crossing out words, sentences, pages, even whole chapters sometimes, which made learning a daily exercise in code decryption. Every story, scientific formula—even math equations—always had gaping holes. Or maybe it was Mrs. Simon's suggestion that there was something deeply offensive about her mother's story.

Regardless of the reason, Myra felt her mouth opening—almost of its own accord—and the words spilling out. She was helpless to stop it from happening.

"How do you know that everything we need is under the sea?"

Her question rang out loud and clear and true, ricocheting through the classroom. And once she'd asked it—once the words had left her mouth—she couldn't take them back.

Mrs. Simon's face turned fully purple now, and she screamed for help.

Headmaster Crawley came running.

The Patrollers were called.

The Synod was notified.

Head Patroller Lynch came to the Academy to arrest Myra. He bound her wrists with rope in front of the entire class, while Mrs. Simon and Headmaster Crawley watched. He confiscated her story as evidence. Though it was a work of fiction, everybody was taking it seriously. Then, he carted her off to the Penitentiary.

Located in Sector 3, the Pen—the Hockers' slang term—was a smelly, dank place. The Head Patroller locked her up with the other prisoners, though due to her young age, he granted her a private cell. Most prisoners weren't so lucky. The Pen was overcrowded. Many were awaiting trials, though how long that would take was anybody's guess. The Synod's processes for administering justice were secret.

The automatic lights burned in their sockets during the day, but as a special form of torture, the Patrollers had covered them with thick casings so the darkness never ceased. Soon Myra lost track of the hours of the day, and after a while, she lost track of the days of the week, too.

At first, she dreamed of escape. Using her hands—her eyes were useless in the dark—she felt out the dimensions of her cell. It was a steel cage. Through the bars that crisscrossed the ceiling, she could make out a grate covering a vent. Air hissed out, chilling her hands. It was tantalizingly close, yet unreachable all the same.

Myra wasn't allowed to converse with the other prisoners. No visitors were permitted, but she overheard a Patroller named Bates laughing about how her father had shown up, begging to see her. He'd sent him away with "a good shove." Eventually, Myra came to realize that silence was the worst. It was worse than the darkness and the cold and the filth. It was the one thing that could drive you really and truly crazy.

And for a time, she did go a little crazy.

She couldn't say how long they kept her locked up. Long enough to break her, she supposed. But eventually they did come for her.

A flashlight shone into her cell, blinding her. She scampered to the darkest corner and tried to shield her eyes from the searing light. As her vision cleared, she could make out the Head Patroller's silhouette framed in the entrance to her cell. Two of his men flanked him, including Patroller Bates, who kept the flashlight aimed at her face.

"Hey, Kiddo," Lynch said, not unkindly. He tossed her a towel, a bar of soap, and a clean set of clothes. "Let's get you cleaned up for the Synod, okay?"

She hugged the clothes to her filthy body. "What's wrong with how I look now?" she croaked out. Her voice was weak and raspy from disuse. A smile crept onto her lips. She wanted them to know that they hadn't broken her, at least not entirely.

Her trial before the Synod was conducted behind the locked doors of their chamber in Sector 6. The final verdict—and it wasn't unanimous—stated that she hadn't broken the law. At least, not technically speaking. Her story and question didn't contain the banned words, nor did they reference anything Before Doom. Therefore, the Synod was unable to levy their favorite punishment of putting her out to sea.

When Chancellor Sebold read that part of the verdict, Padre Flavius glared at her from his cushioned bench. Nevertheless, Myra nearly fainted with relief. Her father—who had come to testify on her behalf—also went white with relief.

Even though she avoided a death sentence, the Synod branded her a heathen and banned her from the Academy, lest she corrupt other youths. Expulsion usually resulted in Hocker status, but her father convinced the Synod to let her pledge early to Engineering. They always had a shortage of pledges, and he argued that keeping her hidden down in Sector 4 was the best way to prevent her from corrupting others.

But she'd been lucky—very, very lucky.

And now she had to be extra careful. She'd seen the look on Padre Flavius's face when Kaleb's father read the verdict that spared her life. She knew that he felt like he'd been cheated out of a sacrifice—and he'd be willing to do anything to change that.

Just then, a blast of air blew the hair back from her face, snapping her back to the present. Myra waited for it to subside, and then took the pipe to the right, which led in the direction of Sector 4. She had to hurry if she didn't want to be late to work.

Or rather, any later than she already was.

Chapter 7

THE ANIMUS MACHINE

Myra peered through a rusty grate at the empty corridor below.

She slipped through it and landed in a crouch to cushion her fall. She swiped her wrist under the scanner. It beeped its approval, and the thick door dilated and admitted her to Sector 4. As she stepped into the Engineering Room, she was greeted by a blast of hot air and the smell of grease, her favorite scent in the world. If she listened closely, she could hear the scraping of wrenches being applied to pipes, the low thrum of generators churning out electricity, and the soft hiss of the Animus Machine puffing out oxygen.

A boy pushing a cart loaded down with parts almost plowed into Myra. She had to jump back to avoid being flattened. "Watch it, Pledge!" she yelped.

"Sorry, Engine Rat," he said. "Didn't see you standing there." His face was covered with more freckles than bare skin. While he looked familiar, she didn't know his name. He'd probably been a year or two ahead of her at school.

Hearing the commotion, Royston stepped out of his office. His coveralls and face were stained black with grease and soot and the Oracle knew what else.

"Delivery from the Spare Parts Room!" the boy announced.

"Well, I can *see* that," Royston said. He snatched a rusty hunk of metal from the cart and inspected it. A frown creased his face. "Who authorized the delivery?"

"Decker," the boy said. "Stan Decker. From Dissemination."

"Wasn't expecting anything until the end of the week."

The boy's cheeks flamed red, the same color as his hair. "It's a special delivery for the Head Engineer. I was supposed to say that up front, but I guess I forgot."

"Right, I can sign for it then," Royston said.

Myra knew that she should find Darius, her assigned apprentice. He would be furious with her for turning up late again. But she still had a million pesky questions rattling around in her brain. Even the brisk jaunt through the pipes hadn't quieted them down. So she made a beeline for her father's office in the back of the sector.

On the way there, she passed by the Animus Machine. Not for the first time, she marveled at its impressive size, stunning design, and brilliant golden hue. It was slurping and hissing and puffing away, laboring to transform saltwater—their most bountiful and endless resource—into the oxygen they breathed, the hydrogen they used for power, and the heat that prevented them from freezing to death under the icy water.

A symbol was engraved on its surface—a creature swallowing its own tail, entwined around two words. "Aeternus eternus," she whispered.

She had no idea what they meant. She'd asked her father about them once, but he didn't know either. This wasn't surprising. So much of their knowledge had been destroyed in the Great Purging or forgotten over the years. And it wasn't just the words that they didn't understand anymore. Nobody alive—not even her father—knew how the Animus Machine worked. Unlike other machines, it didn't have any gears, joints, screws, or any moving parts, for that matter. None visible to the naked eye at least.

It's less like a machine, she thought, *and more like a living organism.*

She reached her father's office, finding the door cracked slightly. He was working on some blueprints at his desk. Myra rapped her knuckles on the doorframe.

He looked up with a startled expression. "Myra, there you are!"

He wasn't happy with her, she could tell, but relief was the stronger emotion. He reshuffled papers on his desk, concealing the blueprints from her view. Curious, she pushed the door open and stepped into his office. The room was cramped and dingy, with just enough room for a desk and a rusty filing cabinet shoved in the back corner.

"You're late . . . again," he said. "What were you thinking? I was just about to send Royston out to look for you. You're just lucky the 'Trollers didn't catch you."

Myra cast her eyes down. "Guess they were too busy putting Carter out to sea."

His face collapsed, making him look ten years older. He shut the door and scanned his wrist to lock it. He didn't return to his desk but started pacing.

"Royston told me. You saw the Sentencing?"

She nodded. "There was a crowd gathered at the Church. We saw it on the way to school . . . it was pretty hard to miss. And, well, they were enjoying the spectacle."

"Tinker too?"

"We all saw it—Paige, Rickard, and Kaleb were with us." A fresh wave of sadness swept through her, but she forced herself to finish. "The 'Trollers beat an old man bloody in the crowd. I'm not sure, but maybe it was Carter's father."

"Tell me you didn't go to the Docks."

"Of course not! But we were definitely in the minority."

Her father ran one hand through his thinning hair. The dark circles under his eyes looked darker. She wondered how much he'd been sleeping lately. He had been working around the clock. Abruptly, he reached over and pulled her into an awkward embrace.

"Myra, promise you'll be careful," he said and squeezed her tighter. "I already lost your mother. I couldn't bear to lose you, too. By the Oracle, swear it."

"Uh . . . right . . . I swear," she said, taken aback by his sudden outburst.

He almost never expressed emotions this way. Hugs were a rare thing in her household. Her mother had always been the one to dispense such gestures, giving them out daily and without hesitation.

After nearly suffocating her, he finally let go. "No more loitering after the Final Warning, not anymore. I expect you here on time, that clear? The 'Trollers are itching to catch you doing something wrong."

She let out a weary sigh. "Tell me something I don't know."

He frowned. "This isn't a joke, Myra. You saw what they did to Carter. And, well, next time they won't hesitate. You know what the seawater will do to you, right?"

The image of Carter being put out to sea rushed through her head for the third time that day. "It'll crush me instantly," she said. "I won't last a second."

That seemed to satisfy him. "Now, go find Darius and get to work. I've assigned your team to repair the water leak in Sector 7. Oh, and you might want to grab a pair of rubber boots from the supply closet. From what I hear, it's a gusher."

Myra grimaced—the last thing she needed was to get soaked with icy water. This was already shaping up to be a lousy day. *I wonder what else can go wrong*, she thought glumly. But she didn't dare complain. He was already angry with her for being late. So instead, she trudged off in search of Darius and a pair of boots, praying that they'd be enough to shield her from the gusher that awaited them in Sector 7.

o o o

Some seven hours later, with her clothes soaking wet and her hair even more tangled than it had been that morning, Myra packed up Darius's tool rig and prepared to leave Sector 7, where they had been working to repair a water leak all day. Lately, it seemed like there were more leaks, both from cracks in the exterior walls and burst pipes.

When they had first arrived in Sector 7, which housed the Aquafarm, Myra had tasted the water gushing from the wall. It was salty, not a good sign. That meant that seawater was leaking in from outside. It had taken them most of the day to stanch the leak, and by that time, she'd been soaked with water. Even Darius got drenched, though he usually preferred to shout orders while she struggled to do the work by herself.

Myra returned to Sector 4 and flashed her wrist under the scanner. Of course, Darius hadn't offered to accompany her back to the Engineering Room. By now he was probably home, eating hot fish stew and warming himself under a blanket.

"This is my last day as a pledge," she whispered to herself. It had been her mantra all day.

The Engineering Room was deserted. Everybody had already left for the day. Even her father's office door was closed, with no light leaking under it. Myra crossed the sector, lugging the heavy tool rig. With every step that she took, it banged against her shin, where it was sure to leave a bruise. Her fingers were purplish and pruned from the water, and her teeth chattered. She wasn't sure if she'd ever get warm again.

She reached the supply closet and shoved the tool rig inside, giving it a kick for good measure. Water sloshed out of the side of her boot, slopping onto the floor. With some effort, she stripped off the rubber boots and peered at her sodden feet.

"Bloody icy water," she muttered. "Bloody boots. Bloody tool rig."

She heard a familiar chuckle coming from behind her. She turned to see Royston. His soot-covered lips slid back to reveal his white teeth. He had a thick roll of blueprints tucked under one arm and a bag slung over his shoulder.

"Need a little help?"

"Is it that obvious?" She allowed her exterior to soften a bit. Royston was one of the few people that she trusted implicitly. "Holy Sea, it's been a tough day."

A dark expression passed over his face. "Aye, that it has."

While they didn't dare mention Carter by name, it was clear that they were both thinking about him. All day while Myra was working in Sector 7, her thoughts kept drifting back to the Sentencing. Over and over again, she kept picturing him getting shoved into a portal and crushed by seawater. It had almost driven her crazy.

"But cheer up, this was your last day as a pledge," Royston said, deftly changing the subject. "Excited to start as an apprentice?"

"I won't miss Darius, if that's what you mean."

He nodded. "He's a tough one, no doubt about it, but this is a trade for tough people. Sooner or later, you'll thank me for the assignment."

"Later being more likely."

This provoked another chuckle from Royston.

"Oh, that reminds me! Your father had a meeting down in Sector 10, so he won't make it home for dinner. He asked me to let you know."

"Yeah, and what else is new?"

Royston fixed her with a concerned expression. "Myra, you know . . . Jonah loves you and Tinker, too. He just has a hard time showing it, that's all. Ever since Tessa . . ." He trailed off, the pain evident on his face. Royston wasn't just her father's second in command—he was also his best friend.

"Yup, I know," Myra said with a sigh.

He nodded and turned to go. "Catch you later, apprentice."

As Royston headed for the exit, Myra's gaze lingered on the blueprints tucked under his arm. Her thoughts snapped back to that morning—and to the plans that her father had hidden when she'd knocked on his door.

She knew that she should head home. Tinker would be waiting, with dinner simmering away on the stove. Even the automatic lights had dimmed slightly, signifying that day would soon transform into night. But curiosity got the better of her. She wanted to find out what he was hiding. Plus, she loved reading blueprints—tracing her fingers over the blue lines, learning how the pieces fit together to create something larger than the sum of their parts. She simply couldn't resist the chance to study some new ones.

Myra stole across the sector to her father's office. She tried the door, but it was locked and wouldn't budge. Her eyes darted to the scanner where she could swipe her wrist, but it would only deny her access. Even worse, it would summon the Patrollers. Only her father could unlock this door.

But she didn't need doors to get around.

Using the pipes that jutted from the wall, she climbed to the ceiling, slipped into a vent, and slithered through it. She came to a halt when she reached the grate above her father's desk. She leapt through it, expertly landing in a crouch. The automatic lights dimmed even more. It was later than she had realized—evening was upon her.

She crept over to the desk, using her flashlight to light the way. Papers and blueprints were strewn across it. Organization had never been her father's strong point. She shuffled through them, careful to preserve the appearance of disarray. He would notice if he returned to find a tidy desk. Her eyes fluttered over diagrams of machines and other important papers, but they weren't what she was looking for.

She rifled through his desk drawers. No luck there. Next, she tried the filing cabinet shoved in the corner. Still nothing caught her eye. She peered under the desk. She searched through a crate of wrenches, hammers, crowbars, and screwdrivers. She even rummaged through the case that held a drill but found nothing aside from a replacement battery and some different sized bits. No luck there either.

She chucked the drill back under the desk, where it landed on the floor. But instead of the usual dull thud, it made a hollow sound.

She froze when she heard it, registering the abnormality. She rapped her knuckles on the concrete, feeling out where the space was concealed. She hit upon it at last. She peered closer. She could just make out razor-thin cracks that formed an opening. Using a crowbar, she pried off the panel and thrust it aside, revealing a secret compartment.

The space was about two feet by two feet square and looked like it had been drilled out of solid concrete. Her eyes fell on a thick set of blueprints tucked inside. Her pulse quickened, as she plucked them out and unfurled them in front of her. What she saw made her heart feel like it might jump out of her chest—these weren't diagrams of machines. They weren't even maps of the sectors. Her eyes zeroed in on a single word printed at the top in her father's neat handwriting: SUBMARINE.

Not only was that a blasphemous word, but possessing blueprints of it was strictly forbidden. Either could result in being put out to sea. Her heart pounding in her ears, she shuffled through the pages, other words popping out at her now: HUMAN-OCCUPIED. DEEP-OCEAN. STEEL CASING.

She struggled to make sense of what was staring her in the face. She thought back to the dark years, the time immediately following her mother's death. Her father had come a little unhinged with a squalling infant and a rowdy eight-year-old who couldn't grasp why her mother wasn't ever coming home again. She often woke in the middle of the night to find him pacing in an endless loop or weeping in his bunk.

The darkness finally lifted around the time that she turned ten, but by then, she started to come a little unhinged herself. She acted out in school, fighting with Baron and becoming a permanent fixture in detention.

And then the Trial happened.

But even those dark years couldn't fully explain this. She held in her hands what could easily be her father's death sentence. Fear stabbed through her heart like a fiery dagger. A hundred questions charged through her brain, but before she had a chance to puzzle through them, she heard the sector door beep and then dilate with a slurp.

Her eyes darted to the blueprints held in her sweaty palms. Somebody was coming—she had to hide.

Chapter 8
THE HEATHENS

The sound of footfalls reached Myra's ears.

She glanced at the blueprints clutched in her clammy palms. As quickly as she could, she shoved them back into the secret compartment and replaced the panel. Then, she climbed into the vent and clicked off her flashlight. Darkness flooded back into the tight space. She pressed her ear to the grate and listened to the footsteps—it sounded like more than one person. This made her heart pound even faster. The footsteps halted right outside the office. The scanner beeped its approval, and the door swung inward.

Three dark shadows extended across the room. They shuffled inside and then shut the door behind them. The lock clicked back into place with a beep.

"You're sure it's safe to meet?" said a gravelly voice.

"It's never been safe. You know the risks."

That was her father.

"You don't think he talked, do you?" said a higher-pitched voice.

Her father again: "Then we wouldn't be standing here, would we?"

He flipped a switch, causing harsh light to envelop the office. Myra peered through the grate at the two men with her father. She recognized the first one—Stan Decker, the Dissemination worker who oversaw the Spare Parts Room. Like the items over which he presided, he looked broken down. His back hunched over at the shoulder blades, his cheeks were pockmarked, and he had more than a few missing teeth.

Her father started pacing. "We're just lucky he withstood their torture, but we need to hurry. The Synod is growing suspicious . . . we're running out of time."

He turned to the other man, whom Myra didn't recognize. He had wiry spectacles wedged over a bulbous nose. His mustache was waxed and twisted to fine points.

"Bishop, tell us what you found," her father said. That jogged Myra's memory—the man was Philip Bishop. His twin daughters were in Tinker's class.

"Well, it wasn't easy," Bishop said in his nasal voice. "I dug into Records as far as I dared. The Synod keeps careful watch over us. They tried to erase everything, and they did a bloody good job, but I managed to salvage some drives and rebuild them—"

"In layman's terms?" Decker interrupted.

"Right. I've pieced together a timeline."

From her hiding place, Myra had to strain to see through the grate. Decker and her father exchanged a solemn glance. "So, were our guesses correct?" Decker asked.

"It's been a thousand years," Bishop confirmed.

"Since the Founders?"

"Yes—based on my calculations."

"Could you be wrong?"

"Well, it's possible," Bishop said. "There are lots of holes in the data."

"But what if he's right?" her father said. "Doesn't it make sense with all the leaks and the machines breaking? This place wasn't built to last forever. We were meant to leave." He paused to let that sink in. "There's a chance the Surface is livable again."

Myra nearly gasped when she heard him speak the banned words. The Surface was destroyed in the Doom. It was blasphemous to suggest otherwise.

Decker shot him a reproachful look. "A chance is all it is—you can't know that."

Bishop bobbed his head. "He's right. We could all perish if we go up there—"

"We'll perish for sure if we stay down here," her father cut in.

Bishop looked like he'd just been slapped in the face. His eyes darted from Decker to her father. He punched his spectacles up the bridge of his nose. "Jonah . . . what do you mean? We'll perish for sure?"

Silence engulfed the room. Myra found herself holding her breath. Decker exchanged a freighted look with her father. "You haven't told him yet?"

"I wasn't sure if I could trust him completely."

"Well, he's proven himself now," Decker said. "He deserves to know the truth, especially after what happened to Carter. We're all in this together."

A dark look passed over her father's face, but he didn't speak yet. Clearly, whatever he had to tell Bishop—whatever the truth might be—he was having a hard time voicing it.

Decker placed a supportive hand on his shoulder and squeezed it. "Go ahead, you can tell him—it's happening regardless."

Her father sucked in a sharp breath. "The Animus Machine is breaking down."

Bishop's face drained of color. "But . . . are you sure?"

"More than sure—the levels are already dropping. It explains the increase in visits to the Infirmary. People are complaining of headaches, nausea, dizziness, vomiting, fatigue, shortness of breath. It's not caused by an allergen release—it's hypoxia. So far the symptoms are mild, but as the levels decrease, it's only going to worsen."

"I don't understand," Bishop said. He wrung his hands together as if trying to ward off what was coming. "What's hypoxia?"

It was Decker who answered: "It means we're all going to suffocate to death."

Bishop turned to her father. "But can't you fix it? You're the Head Engineer!"

"Believe me, I've tried," her father said, pacing even faster. "For the better part of the last year I've been trying. By the Oracle, I don't even understand how the bloody thing works. Only the Founders knew, and they're dead."

"No, no, no . . . I won't believe it," Bishop stammered.

Myra found herself thinking the same thing, but her father was almost never wrong, especially when it came to the machines. And, well . . . there was more. She'd been experiencing some of those very same symptoms lately. Of course, she'd blamed it on the allergen release, but now she realized it was due to something far more insidious:

They were running out of oxygen.

"Tell him how long we've got left," Decker said.

"Eight months at the most, before the levels drop too low." Though her father didn't say it directly, it was clear from his expression that it could be less.

"But somebody has to alert the Synod!" Bishop said.

Her father's shoulders sagged as if the invisible burden that he'd been carrying around had just come into physical being. "I went to them as soon as I realized what was happening. They heard me out and then deliberated behind closed doors. When they returned, Padre Flavius delivered their answer. He said that due to our sins, we had brought another Doom upon ourselves. And he offered their solution—more sacrifices. He claimed that it would lessen the burden on the system and appease the Holy Sea."

Bishop threw his hands up. "But that's madness!"

"My thoughts exactly," Decker muttered.

"Padre Flavius said whatever happens is the Oracle's will,"

her father went on. "I didn't dare mention the Surface. I would have been arrested on the spot."

"Who else knows about this?" Bishop asked.

"Nobody, not even the other Engineers," her father said. "I'm the only one who monitors the Animus Machine. Before the Synod let me go, they swore me to secrecy. And for a second, I thought Padre Flavius was going to have me arrested to keep me quiet, but he needs me to keep this place running. At least, for as long as I can."

"And the orange flag over the Infirmary?" Bishop said.

"Just a story the Synod concocted to explain away the symptoms. They don't want anyone to know the truth. They're afraid that unrest would sweep through the colony. They're worried it could incite a revolution."

"About bloody time!" Decker swore. "A revolution is just what we need."

Jonah shook his head. "No, it's too dangerous! The 'Trollers have everyone under their thumbs. The Plenus would be against us. We'd have the Hockers, but most of the Factum would side with the Plenus. We'd be severely outnumbered. Even if by some miracle we did win—if we overthrew the Synod—it still might be too late. We don't have much time left."

Her father stopped pacing and turned his gaze on them. "We only have one choice if we want to survive."

"The Surface," Bishop said and swirled his hand over his chest.

"Exactly!" her father said and knelt under his desk. He pried open the hidden panel, pulled out the blueprints, and unrolled them on his desk, covering it entirely.

"Look, I've already drawn up the plans."

"And once we're up there, then what?" Bishop said. "What if it's desolate and uninhabitable? Or worse—there's no land, just endless ocean? Tell me, what then?"

Her father got that stubborn look that he always got when he'd already made up his mind. "I'm going to the Surface. It's our only chance. Now, who's with me?"

Their silence was answer enough.

"Jonah, I'm on your side," Decker said eventually. "You know that. But if we're not careful, we could find ourselves taking a swim in the Holy Sea, just like Carter."

This prompted Bishop to drag his hand across his chest again.

"And there's still the matter of the Beacon," Decker said.

Myra's ears pricked up. She leaned closer to the grate and peered down at them, struggling to hear better. Her father looked up from his blueprints.

"Right, I was just getting to that. Bishop, tell him the rest of it."

Bishop nodded. "At Jonah's request, I searched through Records for any mention of the Beacon. It seemed hopeless until I stumbled upon some old pictures of Elianna Wade. They weren't destroyed or quarantined because they're not from Before Doom."

Decker exchanged a hopeful look with her father. "The eldest daughter of Elijah Wade, the first President and one of the Founders? That sounds promising."

"Yup, that's her," Bishop said.

He rummaged through his pocket and extracted a picture. "This was taken in the early years of the colony." He pointed to the first girl in the image. "That's Elianna and that's her younger sister, Sari. Now, I can't be sure, but it looks like Elianna is wearing a bracelet that matches the description of the Beacon."

Myra strained to see the picture through the grate. The older girl looked about the same age as Myra and also had curly, dark hair. But that was where the similarities ended. She was tall, curvaceous, and wore a serious expression on her face, as if some great burden had been placed on her shoulders. The younger girl in the picture—Sari Wade, according to Bishop—also had curly, dark hair, but otherwise looked nothing like her sister. She was petite and thin, with a goofy grin affixed to her childish face.

Myra's breath caught in her throat—Sari could have been her twin. She was the spitting image of Myra at that age, and her mother before her. The resemblance was unmistakable. Her father seemed to pick up on the resemblance to his late wife. A haunted look flashed over his face, the same one that he'd worn after her death.

Bishop gestured to Elianna's wrist. "I magnified the image, and there's no separation between the bracelet and her skin. Also, look at the marking on the outside. That's a snake swallowing its tail entwined around the words *Aeternus Eternus*."

"The Founders' seal," Jonah said.

Decker leaned over for a closer look. "Well, I guess it could be the Beacon," he said. "It does match the description, but it's hard to tell. How can we be sure?"

"But she's always wearing it," Bishop said.

He extracted more pictures of the Wade family. As he flipped through them, the sisters seemed to age before Myra's eyes. Elianna filled out and Sari grew taller—though not as tall as her sister—and transformed into a young woman, too. And then tiny wrinkles and a few gray hairs appeared on their heads, as middle age set in.

Some pictures showed them dressed up and attending events with their parents (Myra guessed their identities from their resemblance). In one photograph, the President spoke to a crowd, while his wife and daughters watched from the front row. Another depicted the Wade family visiting the Infirmary, though it looked brand new in the picture. The next one showed Elianna cutting a red ribbon that stretched across its entrance. In every picture, she had the golden bracelet affixed to her right wrist.

Bishop flipped through image after image, but then they abruptly ceased.

"Elianna is never without the bracelet," Bishop said. "I rebuilt some drives, remember? Well, there were lots of gaps in the data, but one of them contained excerpts from President Wade's journal entries. According to one of the passages, once the Beacon bonds with a Carrier—that was his word choice—it can't be removed."

"Unless they die," Decker guessed.

Bishop had one last picture in his pocket. He pulled it out now. "This was taken at Elianna's funeral. According to my timeline, she died in the second great Pox epidemic that decimated the population. She was seventy-one years old."

The image was indeed of a funeral. Elianna's lifeless body was laid out on an altar. A veil covered her prone form, obscuring the damage that the Pox had wrought on her skin. Sari was dressed in black and knelt beside her sister. Her head was bowed in prayer, the sorrow apparent on her face. She was holding Elianna's right hand.

Decker leaned in to study the picture. "She's not wearing the bracelet—it's gone."

"Exactly," Bishop said. "Someone must have removed it from her wrist."

"Did somebody else claim it?" Decker asked.

"Well, I don't know," Bishop said. "After this last picture of Elianna alive," he tapped it with his finger, "the Beacon vanishes from the archives."

Decker furrowed his brow. "Maybe it's not the Beacon after all. Maybe it's just some fancy jewelry that she liked to wear when she got dressed up."

"It's possible . . ." Bishop said.

"Or maybe it is the Beacon!" Jonah cut in and started pacing again. "What if, after she died, her father—or maybe her sister, removed it from her wrist?"

"Then why didn't they start wearing it themselves?" Decker said.

"Well, I don't know," Jonah said, running one hand through his hair. "It's just a theory. But right around the time she died—isn't that when the Synod took over and started destroying everything from Before Doom in the Great Purging?"

"That's right," Bishop confirmed. "It's on my timeline."

Decker frowned. "All that proves is that the Synod probably destroyed the Beacon along with everything else. That doesn't exactly help us."

Jonah thought for a moment. "Maybe they did destroy

it . . . or maybe Sari hid it! She was alive during the Great Purging, wasn't she? Older . . . but alive?"

Bishop nodded. "That's correct."

"Think about it. Sari would have known the importance of the Beacon. Based on the President's journal entries, we've finally been able to verify its purpose. The Beacon is supposed to guide us back to the Surface so that we can rendezvous with the other colonies—if any have survived the period of exile—and restart life up there."

Myra's heart nearly leapt out of her chest. She'd always been taught that the Holy Sea had saved the Chosen People in the Safe Harbor. That the rest of mankind—all of the heathens—had perished in the Doom. It was like spending your whole life as an only child, only to wake up and discover that you had siblings. And that they lived in another world, one that you'd also never known existed. It was almost too much to process.

She struggled to stay calm—she didn't want to blow her cover—but it was a losing battle. Her heart raced anyway, and her breathing sped up. She started to feel lightheaded, which brought with it a feeling of dread. They were running out of air.

"Even if Sari hid the Beacon," Decker said. "This was a thousand years ago we're talking about. She could have hidden it anywhere. Where would we start?"

"Another dead end," Bishop said. "So . . . now what?"

A few seconds of silence passed while they considered this.

"I say we stick to our plan," Jonah said at last. "And we continue to search for the Beacon. Without it, we have little chance of reaching the Surface."

That settled it. They flipped off the light and filed out of the office. The scanner beeped as the lock clicked back into place. Myra didn't move until they had crossed the Engineering Room and exited the sector. Only then did she begin her journey home, taking her secret ways. She had to hurry if she was going to beat her father home and avoid his pointed questions. She was already in enough trouble for being late to work.

While she climbed through the pipes on wobbly legs, she

thought about everything that she had just overheard. The words raced through her head, speeding faster and blurring together. She struggled to make sense of it all, failing miserably.

There was only one thing she knew for sure:

If her father failed, then they were all doomed.

PART II
THE RETURN FROM EXILE

No man can be an exile if he remembers that all the world is one city.

—C.S. Lewis, *Till We Have Faces*

Human beings may be miserable specimens, in the main, but we can learn, and, through learning, become decent people.

—Orson Scott Card, *Ender's Game*

THE SECOND CONTINUUM

. . . The first of the three interstellar colonies of the Continuum Project, built into a space vessel originally designed to study extraterrestrial life-forms . . .

. . . Under the leadership of Supreme General Milton Wright—the first leader of the Second Continuum and formerly a general in the United States Army in the time Before Doom—they adopted the primary values of *Efficiency*, *Productivity*, and *Discipline*. All colonists were trained to be soldiers and attended the Agoge, a military school . . .

. . . Their days consisted of regimented blocks of twenty-four hours with each minute accounted for in the strict schedule. Compulsory activities included Morning Calisthenics, Battle Strategy, Emergency Drills, and Flight Training. Their marriages were arranged at birth and regarded as necessary only for reproduction and population maintenance, rather than romantic affairs of the heart. Eventually, even emotions themselves came to be despised as inefficient and signs of character weakness . . .

. . . In this military society, the highest honor for any soldier was to perish in battle. Even so, they held no funerals, viewing such rites as sentimental and inefficient. Instead, the bodies of the deceased were unceremoniously dumped into the incinerator that helped to power the ship, so that even in the throes of mortality, a soldier could commit one final act of productivity . . .

—THE NATIONAL OPERATION TO ARCHIVE HUMANITY

Chapter 9

NO MERCY IN THE FACE OF WEAKNESS

Captain Aero Wright

The golden blade arced through the air, barely missed his neck, and clanged into the armor protecting his shoulder. It went numb from the impact and the electric shock. *Any closer and I'd be a few inches shorter*, Aero thought as he spun out of the way. His opponent grinned and raised his sword to strike again.

"No mercy in the face of weakness," the boy said. Though he was on the cusp of manhood (they both were), his opponent was still more boy than man. He had quoted from their teachings at the Agoge. His opponent wouldn't wait for him to recover.

Aero ducked behind a towering redwood, careful not to trip over its roots. Above him, the tree thrust its shrouding of leaves toward the blazing-hot sun. Sweat had accumulated under his helmet and dripped down his face, stinging his eyes. But he didn't allow himself to get distracted—it could mean the difference between life and death.

At his unspoken command, the Falchion in his left hand morphed from a broadsword into a shield. *Sometimes the best offense is a good defense.* This was another one of their teachings. Aero raised his shield just in time for his opponent's Falchion—still in the form of a curved blade—to slam into it. His arm throbbed, but the shield withstood the impact. His opponent's blade ricocheted off in a shower of sparks.

Aero had made the right decision.

They were both soldiers in the Interstellar Army of the Second Continuum, fighting with morphing weapons called Falchions. Each Falchion bonded with a soldier and would only respond to his or her commands. They could shift into spears, shields, knives, and blades of varying sizes and weights. The only type of weapon they could not become were those with moving parts, like guns or bows.

But this versatility could just as easily pose an obstacle. Choosing a weapon form added another level of decision-making to a battle, and indecision could cause the weapon to melt down. Aero had seen it happen on more than one occasion. The soldier would be carted away by Medical for psychiatric observation, and then the Forgers would have to remake the defunct weapon in a painstaking process that could take months.

Losing one's Falchion was the greatest humiliation that a soldier could suffer, so Aero went to great lengths to control his thoughts just as carefully as he controlled his muscles. His opponent swung again, and Aero parried again. This went on for a few more seconds—the *clanging* and the *sparking* followed by retreating, and then the *clanging* and the *sparking* again. They circled each other in the dappled sunlight of the forest. The ground was pliant and covered in dried leaves that crackled underneath their boots.

"Captain Wright to the bridge," came the summons. Aero heard it through the communicator wired into his helmet. They needed him in the control room.

He had to finish this.

To the soldiers watching on the monitors, the fight thus far would have appeared one-sided, with Aero on the losing side. But appearances were deceiving.

His opponent swiped at him again. Their Falchions clashed together, the boy's in the shape of a curved blade, and Aero's in the form of a shield. Golden sparks cascaded from the point where they touched. The Falchions carried an electric charge. Aero smelled fire—it tasted acrid on his tongue. The leaves on the ground started to singe and smoke from the sparks. Only the dampness of the soil kept them from combusting.

A few more seconds of this, Aero thought as he deflected another blow. It wasn't a conscious calculation exactly—rather his instincts, which had been honed meticulously over the last eleven years by the Drillmasters at the Agoge, told him what to do. His opponent was winded now. His chest heaved and hiccupped as he struggled for breath. His hands were probably aching from the weight of his Falchion. There was a quivering in his muscles and unsteadiness to his stance. He was off balance and struggling.

Now, and only now, was it time to attack. In a process that took mere seconds and almost no conscious thought at all—no more than it took to raise his arm or lift his foot—Aero commanded his Falchion to morph back into a broadsword. The golden metal liquidly shifted and rearranged itself into a long, sturdy blade. It was heavier than the sword clutched by his opponent, but it had a longer reach and could inflict more damage.

And Aero wasn't tired.

He wasn't even breathing hard. He had conserved his strength, and now he was ready to deploy it. He sprung an attack on his opponent, swiftly and efficiently. The boy never stood a chance. Aero's muscles unfurled themselves and released the elastic energy stored within them. His sword—heavy as it was—cut through the air like it weighed nothing at all. He slashed and spun and stabbed in a blur of golden sparks.

Now the boy was retreating, but he hadn't given up yet. He didn't morph his Falchion into a shield. *Fool*, Aero thought. Even a general knew when the battle was lost and it was time to surrender. In one smooth motion, Aero knocked the boy down and kicked the Falchion out of his hand. The boy hit the ground hard. His helmet flew off from the impact. It clattered and spun on the leaf-covered dirt.

Aero stood over the boy with his Falchion raised over his head in a two-handed grip. *Only a boy*, he thought again. *What a pity he didn't fight better.*

Fear flashed across the boy's face. "Mercy," he begged. "*Mercy.*" Aero didn't flinch. "No mercy in the face of weakness," he said as he swung his Falchion and took the boy's head off in one clean slice.

o o o

Everything went black as the simulation ended.

The lights flashed on, flickering and then stabilizing. Aero shrugged off his helmet, morphed his Falchion into its default form—a lightweight, curved blade—and sheathed it in the scabbard belted to his waist. He was alone in the simulation chamber; his opponent was in another chamber. Sweat stood out on his brow. He was breathing hard and adrenaline still pumped through his veins, but he wasn't debilitated in the way that his opponent undoubtedly was. He could fight again right away if necessary.

When Aero had programmed the simulation and selected the venue, he had fully engaged the safety controls to prevent any physical harm from befalling them. However, that wouldn't save them from the psychological damage that resulted from experiencing death. There was no safety control that could protect a soldier from that.

He caught sight of his reflection in the steel door. His brown hair was a mess—drenched in sweat and matted from the helmet. He kept it short like every soldier, even the women. His brown eyes weren't anything special, but his vision was sharp, a characteristic he valued more than attractiveness. He also valued his height. He stood over six feet tall. That gave him an advantage when he fought. A patch of pink tissue stood out from his brow, just above his left eyebrow. Like a good soldier, he wore his scar like a badge of honor.

Aero punched the button by the chamber door. With a hiss, it dilated. Wren was waiting outside with a grin. She was dressed in a lightweight silver uniform with the Ouroboros seal emblazoned in crimson on the shoulder. Aero would have noticed that Wren was quite beautiful—with her spiky, blonde hair and hazel eyes—if he'd cared about such things. He strode from the chamber without giving her a second look.

"Captain, ten minutes to finish him?" Wren said as she jogged after him. There was a playful lilt to her voice. She relieved him of his helmet and tucked it under her arm. "You finished me in five, and I'm twice the soldier. What took so long?"

"Lieutenant, it's not about winning," Aero said. Then, in explanation: "And I could have finished him faster, but I was testing him, looking for weaknesses."

"You're always so serious," she said with a shake of her head. She brushed a few rebellious strands of hair from her brow. "Where's the fun in that?"

"It's not about fun either," he said with a frown. He hated how serious he sounded, but it was just his natural state. *His default form*, he supposed.

"Oh, please, it's a little bit about fun," she said with that grin again. She punched a button in the wall. A hidden door hissed and opened, revealing a storage room. "The adrenaline, the frenzy of battle, and the triumph of vanquishing your opponent!"

This bordered on insolence, but their relationship exceeded the traditional leader and subordinate roles, so Aero overlooked it. They were friends, if you could call it that. The idea was a foreign concept in their world.

"What's the point in always winning if you can't enjoy it?" Wren said, her hazel eyes flashing and defying him. They appeared more green than brown today, he noticed against his will. He shook his head in exasperation. Why was she always pushing his buttons this way? Why couldn't she just follow orders like the other soldiers?

"Careful," he said. "I could report you."

"Oh yeah? For what?" she asked with an arch of her eyebrow. She set his helmet on a shelf, next to the other helmets. Additional simulation equipment filled the room.

"*Intentional expression of emotions*," Aero quoted the violation. "The Majors could find you psychologically unsound and remove you from command."

"Well, it's not intentional," Wren said, and perhaps this was true. She had never learned to hold her tongue, even at the Agoge, when it had threatened her with expulsion. Only her prowess as a soldier had saved her from that fate. "And I'm not expressing anything, except maybe my opinion. You're reading into my words."

This also could have been true, although Aero would never admit to feeling anything for her. They'd both been betrothed to others since their births.

Wren was like this—hotheaded, volatile, and emotional. And deep down—if Aero thought about it, which he tried not to do if he could help it—he would have realized that he admired her for these traits, envied her even. She was comfortable with her emotions in a way that he'd never been. Many had questioned his decision when he'd chosen her as his first lieutenant. Soldiers were supposed to be detached. But she had another quality that he valued above the rest—she was unfailingly loyal. She had never let him down.

"Look, the point is to know my soldiers," Aero said. "And the best way to know them is to fight them. *A soldier reveals his or her truest self when facing death.*"

This was yet another teaching, one that he believed with all of his heart. He found himself remembering his Krypteia, the final test to graduate from the Agoge and become a soldier in the Interstellar Army of the Second Continuum. The arena for the Krypteia changed every year depending on the ship's location. However—unlike the battle in which he'd just fought—the Krypteia was no simulation.

Aero had been dropped in an escape pod onto a tiny planet orbiting Pulsar B1257+12. It had a toxic atmosphere, more ice than earth, and few places to seek cover from the carbon dioxide snowstorms that raged constantly on its surface. His only weapon was his Falchion. Other experienced soldiers had been planted in the arena. His objective was to survive twenty-four hours and then make it to a predetermined rendezvous point. If he failed, then they would abandon him there to perish.

And I did almost fail, he thought with a shudder. The soldiers had attacked him mercilessly. They were better armed, carrying blasters in addition to their Falchions. And they outnumbered him, too. Aero fought them off, but just barely. The planet also served as an opponent—hurtling ice and snow and wind at him. His spacesuit deflected some of it, but soon his teeth were chattering and his hands had gone numb.

Death had haunted his every step and had almost taken him a time or two. Once, a soldier surprised him from behind and fired his blaster. Aero raised his Falchion—in the shape of a shield—just in time to intercept most of the blast, but the shot grazed him. It left a scar above his left eyebrow.

Another time, overcome by the freezing wind and sleet, he had sat down to rest. Just for a second. But that second turned into minutes. Soon he was covered up to his shoulders by carbon dioxide snow. His eyelids started to droop, and he considered giving into the tiredness and the cold, but something in him rallied. It had almost been too late—another few minutes, and he might never have roused again. Somehow, he cut himself free using his Falchion and its electric charge to sever the ice that bound him.

He had arrived at the rendezvous point on time, frozen and stumbling and a shell of himself, but he had survived. The scars that marked him—the slash above his left eyebrow, and the three toes and tip of his right pinky finger that had to be amputated due to frostbite—would never leave him. And those were only the visible ones.

But he had faced his own death and fought his way back to life. That was the final lesson that the Agoge taught him. He knew that he could survive anything now.

"Well, I still think you could have finished him faster,"

Wren said. She pushed the button that closed the door to the storage room. "Even if you were testing him."

Her voice and the soft hiss of the door jerked Aero out of his memory. For a brief moment, he'd been back on that icy rock of a planet orbiting Pulsar B1257+12, shrouded in that blanket of carbon dioxide snow that had almost been his undoing.

He shook his head to clear it, just as there was another hissing sound. The door to another chamber dilated. They both turned to look. A lanky boy named Zakkay stepped unsteadily from the chamber. He was a private in the unit that Aero commanded. They were both sixteen, like all the soldiers in their unit, and had attended the Agoge together.

After graduation, soldiers were assigned to different units based on their ranking. Some specialized in combat, like Aero's unit, while others served as engineers and supervised the ship's systems and transports. Still others staffed the clinics—Medical, Procreation and Population Maintenance, and Euthanasia. Soldiers with lower rankings operated the Mess Hall, overseeing the production and distribution of provisions.

Zakkay wore a dazed expression, one that Aero recognized well. It was the same look that all his opponents wore after they'd faced him in simulated battle—he was still disoriented from having just died a moment before. Zakkay wavered on his feet. His pupils remained fixed and dilated, and his hands shook slightly.

"Private, should we call Medical?" Aero said.

He didn't respond—didn't even tilt his head up.

"*Zakkay*?" Aero tried again. Still receiving no response, he turned to Wren. "Lieutenant, call Medical. Inform them it's a psychological injury—"

"I'm fine," Zakkay interrupted. "Just disappointed in myself."

"Everybody loses to Captain Wright in Falchion-to-Falchion combat," Wren said with a hint of a smile. "You know that. I think you fought well."

"Not well enough. I wanted to distinguish myself in combat."

Anger flashed over his face, and he threw down his Falchion, the golden metal clanging on the floor. It was in the form of a curved blade. Aero exchanged a pointed look with Wren, and he could tell they'd reached the same conclusion:

Zakkay was not ready for command.

It wasn't that he had lost the simulated battle—every soldier lost to Aero. Not only was he undefeated in Falchion-to-Falchion combat, but he'd also earned top marks at the Agoge and graduated with a ranking of first in his class. That was why he was a captain and the leader of a combat unit. Rather, it was Zakkay's reaction to losing. Every commander lost a battle at some point, but they had to stay focused to win the war.

A few other soldiers from his unit stepped into the corridor. Per Aero's orders, they had been watching the simulation on the monitors. They saluted when they saw him, and then a few of them broke into grins and clapped. Aero noted their identities—Tristan, Hoshiko, Starling, Etoile, and Xing. They were all privates.

While it was tempting to bask in the glow of their applause, now wasn't the right time. Aero put on his serious face. "All of you, back to work," he ordered. "This was meant to be a training exercise. I want you to write up a full analysis of the battle and the strategies for tomorrow. Then we'll go through the video feed and discuss it."

His eyes shifted to Zakkay. "You too, Zakkay." His gaze pivoted to the boy's Falchion, which rested haphazardly on the ground. "Clearly, you still have many lessons left to learn. For one, take proper care of your Falchion at all times, even if you've just lost a simulation. If you're not careful, I'll report you to the Majors for being an emotional hazard."

"Yes, sir," Zakkay said, though there was an undercurrent to his voice. He was still angry. The battle had riled up his emotions, which was dangerous.

Aero made a mental note to keep a closer eye on him before he handed off command to Wren and headed for the bridge.

o o o

While Aero navigated through the ship's many corridors and levels, he thought about why he'd been summoned to the bridge. *We must be close now*, he decided. *They must have made visual contact.*

He wondered what his reaction would be when he saw Earth projected on the monitors at long last. He had seen pictures, of course—detailed, high-resolution images of a planet cloaked in vivid greens and lustrous blues, peeking out from underneath a smattering of brilliantly white clouds. In all of his travels, through distant galaxies and their many solar systems, Earth was the most striking planet that he'd ever encountered. Other planets had rings and many moons and even two suns sometimes. They boasted colors that defied the imagination, but none of them had spoken to him the same way.

None had called to him.

But those images were from Before Doom.

He had also seen a few images taken from space right after the Doom struck. They showed no greens or blues or whites anymore—just the angry reds and smoky blacks of fire and ash. His people may have mastered interstellar travel at speeds approaching that of light, but they had no science that could undo the damage that had been wrought. *Only time could heal the planet*, Aero had learned at the Agoge.

And now that time had finally elapsed.

It had been a thousand years since his people had fled from Earth and the Doom that had befallen it. A thousand years of incineration and contamination and toxicity that had rendered its surface uninhabitable. A thousand years of exile—of going from planet to planet, from solar system to solar system, searching for a new Earth—one that they had never found. And now, per their orders, they were finally returning home.

This word bore no emotional connotation for Aero—he meant it in a purely functional way. At least, this was what he told himself.

It was where his ancestors had been birthed and lived.

No more, no less. Just the origin point of his people's great nomadic history, where the components of their vessel had been dreamed up and manufactured (the ship itself had been assembled piece by piece in outer space, or so he'd learned in The History of the Continuum Project).

And now it was the place to which he must return.

A mixture of emotions roiled up in him just then. He felt the gamut of them run through him—dread, joy, anxiety, and, last of all, hope. He tried to suppress them and the confusion that they ushered in, for he hated the way that feelings clouded his critical thinking and obscured his judgment. And mostly, he feared them, for he knew that they made him unpredictable, dangerous even. He didn't want to be an emotional hazard.

A good soldier is an unaffected one.

This was another teaching—perhaps the most important one. He mentally cursed himself for not having fully mastered it yet. He was no better than Zakkay, whom he'd lectured not five minutes ago for this same shortcoming.

But at this moment, as he walked to the bridge, it was a losing battle. He couldn't muscle his way through it—couldn't parry it into exhaustion and surrender. He had to give in. He had to surrender this time. And so he did—he let go of himself.

Home, he thought again. He felt the emotions in their full potency, though they frightened him. *We're finally going home.*

Chapter 10
THE SECRET ROOM

Myra Jackson

I have to find the Beacon.

As soon as the automatic lights flashed on and Myra's eyes fluttered open, her brain coughed up this directive and spat it out for her consideration. When the lights wrenched her from sleep, she usually felt groggy and disoriented. But this morning was different. A rare sense of clarity washed through her, filling her with certainty.

She couldn't fix the Animus Machine and prevent them from running out of oxygen, but she could search for the Beacon. She'd heard everything that her father knew and she'd seen the pictures of the Wade family. From studying blueprints of the colony, she knew the layout better than anybody, even the Master Engineers. And using her secret ways, she could access places that nobody else could—long forgotten places.

She considered going to her father and offering to help. She could hear him rattling around the kitchen, putting the kettle on for tea. But she quickly dismissed the idea. He'd be furious with her for breaking into his office and forbid her from getting involved. He would claim it was too risky, especially with the Patrollers and the Synod already suspicious. Her protests—that it didn't matter if they were all going to die anyway—would fall on deaf ears. His natural instinct was always to protect her.

But she didn't want to disobey her father or have him watching her every move, so she decided not to say anything. *What he doesn't know can't hurt him*, she thought. And if she did succeed where nobody else had—if she did find the Beacon—then she could always go to him and explain everything, and then he wouldn't even be angry.

Myra climbed from her bunk. Her father didn't even have to yell for her to wake up. It was Sunday—the Day of Rest—because on the seventh day the Holy Sea bestowed the Oracle on the Chosen People, but she didn't plan on resting. She was in the middle of buckling on her sandals when she caught Tinker scrutinizing her from his bunk.

"Hey, don't give me that look," she said with a twinge of irritation.

Her sudden urge to wake up must have drawn his attention. Sometimes she wished that her brother wasn't quite so observant. Or, better yet, that she had a room of her own. A little bit of privacy would have been a welcome thing.

o o o

"Busy day planned?" her father said. He didn't look up from the blueprints scattered on the kitchen table. Clearly, he wasn't planning on resting either.

"Yup. I'm gonna meet . . . Kaleb, Paige, and Rickard . . . at the Souk," Myra said in between shoveling porridge into her mouth. "I want to pick up a few things . . . before I start as an apprentice tomorrow. Some new sandals and maybe some coveralls."

Though it was Sunday, the Souk would be in full swing. Hockers never took a day off, not if they wanted to avoid malnutrition and starvation, and Sunday was their busiest day. Instead of shutting down after the Final Warning, the market stayed open to service Factum who had free time to devote to shopping.

"Sounds like a good plan," her father said. He shifted his gaze from the blueprints to his son's ratty sandals and threadbare tunic. "Tinker, want to join your sister?"

"Does he have to?" Myra said.

The last thing she needed was her brother following her like a second shadow. She didn't actually have plans to meet up with her friends and instead hoped to avoid them. Her father shot her a disapproving look. She could tell that he was about to launch into one of his famous lectures about *putting family first*.

"I don't want to go to the Souk," Tinker said, softly but firmly.

They both looked at him in surprise.

"Fine, have it your way," their father said. He knew better than to press Tinker. He gathered up the blueprints and rose from the table. "I've got to get to work."

That settled it—breakfast was over. Myra dumped her bowl in the basin and joined her father by the door. He swiped his wrist, and they both stepped outside. The corridor was mostly deserted. A few Factum strolled by, but they didn't appear to be in any rush. They lacked the frenzied energy that they'd possessed only yesterday. Her father turned down the corridor that led to Sector 4.

"Have fun at the Souk," he called over his shoulder.

"Planning to work late tonight?" she asked, alarmed by the needy quality in her voice. "Right, no worries if you are," she backpedaled. "I was just wondering."

He turned back with a weary sigh. "Don't I always? I'll try to make it home for supper."

It was an empty promise. She couldn't remember the last time he'd sat down to supper with them. Though she often pushed him away by complaining and acting difficult, it was only a defense mechanism. If she pushed him away first, then he couldn't desert her. The truth was that she craved more time with him—but lately all she got was less. And that wasn't likely to change, not with what she'd learned recently.

All these thoughts whirred through her brain, but all she said was, "Great. See you then."

As Myra hurried down the corridor and rounded the bend, two dark shadows emerged from a compartment. "Follow the heathen," Patroller Bates hissed. "I've got the father." The dark figures diverged, each heading down a different corridor.

o o o

Myra knew that Jasper was following her again. Since the Trial, she'd learned to keep an eye out for 'Trollers—their black silhouettes slinking between doorways, the heavy footfalls of their chunky boots, the clanging of their pipes as they walked. She'd caught him tailing her yesterday when she walked Tinker to school.

And she didn't like it one bit.

Finding the Beacon was going to be hard enough without a Patroller breathing down her neck. Keeping track of him out of the corner of her eye, she led him on a roundabout route through the Souk. It was packed with browsing Factum. She darted around booths, skirted between rowdy Hockers, and dodged carts. A haggling match broke out between a Factum and two Hockers. She headed straight for it.

Moving fluidly through the crowd, she ducked around a booth and exited the Souk. She glanced back. Jasper was caught up in the commotion, just like she'd hoped. Sure that she'd lost him, Myra ducked down an empty passage. Only then did she pry open the grate and vanish from the corridor as if she'd never been there at all.

She peered through the grate as Jasper entered the corridor. He staggered around, his pipe unsheathed. "Bloody heathen, where'd she go? The Holy Sea take her," he muttered before he gave up and disappeared back into Sector 5.

Serves him right for tailing me, she thought and grinned.

But the smile evaporated a second later. She was lucky that the Souk was so busy today. It wouldn't be as easy to lose him next time. She'd have to be more careful. With that thought, she began her journey through the pipes, taking her secret ways.

About ten minutes later, Myra arrived at her destination. In front of her, the pipe bottomed out. She leapt down and set her flashlight on the floor, illuminating the room. It was on the large side and smelled of rust, mildew, and aerated chlorine. Pipes protruded from the walls at haphazard angles, casting intricate shadows. This was where she always went when she wanted to be alone or needed to solve a difficult problem—or both.

She retrieved the satchel of sweetfish from her pocket. A few rats crept out and twitched their noses at the air. Unlike when Maintenance invaded the pipes with their lethal poisons and traps, the rats weren't afraid of her. She'd been coming here since she was a kid. "Here you go," Myra cooed and tossed them some candy. A squabble broke out, but they quickly settled it with the biggest ones claiming the most sweetfish.

Myra laughed at their antics, but then she dragged her attention away and focused on the reason why she'd come to the secret room. And then she thought.

And thought.

And thought some more.

But nothing.

Not even a hint of something.

Her mind was as empty as a blank chalkboard.

Frustrated, she downed a handful of sweetfish. While her jaw worked to grind up the candy, she considered the obstacles confronting her search. For starters, Sari Wade had lived over nine hundred years ago. If the Beacon wasn't lost or destroyed—likely possibilities—then she could have hidden it anywhere. It wasn't very big, about the size of a large bracelet. The colony was made up of ten sectors connected by corridors, not to mention the labyrinth of pipes and ducts and their countless nooks and crannies.

Though Myra knew the layout better than anybody, it would still take her years to search everywhere. And she didn't have years—only eight months.

At the most.

Her stomach lurched at this unpleasant reminder, though it could have been from eating too many sweetfish. Not for the first time, she wished that she'd been taught history. Her knowledge of the past was like a patchwork quilt, crudely sewn from scraps of religious doctrine, tantalizing tidbits that her father or Maude let slip, and the stories that circulated through the Souk. The worst part was that she had no way to separate the rumors from the truth. And lately, she'd come to learn the truth could be just as outlandish—if not more so—than the gossip that the Hockers dreamed up at the Souk.

Myra thought about where to find the Beacon for another hour, without making any progress. Already, her search was a disaster. A rat crept out of a pipe and cocked his head.

"Hey there, little guy," she said to the rat. "Where's the Beacon? It's gold . . . and shiny . . . and about this big. I'll give you this sweetfish if you lead me to it."

She held up the candy to tempt the rat, but he just twitched his nose. This worked in her mother's fairytales, where animals often possessed magical qualities, but not in real life. She tossed the piece of candy to the rat anyway.

Suddenly, loud banging noises erupted from a pipe.

They reverberated into the room. The rat snapped its head in the direction of the noise. His nostrils twitched at the air. Not waiting to discover the source of the racket, he snatched up the candy and darted down another pipe.

Maybe it's just the clanking of a pipe, Myra thought. But then more noises echoed into the room, and this time they were accompanied by cursing. It sounded like more than one person. Fear surged through her. On a few occasions, she'd encountered Maintenance workers laboring on the pipes, but today was Sunday, so they had the day off.

That was a bad sign.

Her thoughts snapped back to Jasper. She was sure that she'd lost him at the Souk—or so she'd thought. Her heart rate sped up. She scooped up the flashlight and clicked it off.

Darkness flooded the room once more. She ducked behind a pipe.

As the noises grew louder and louder—heading straight for her and the secret room—she held her breath and waited for the intruders to reveal their identities.

She didn't have to wait long.

Chapter 11
STERN'S QUEST

Captain Aero Wright

"Captain Wright to the bridge."

Aero marched through the corridors, obeying the order that had reached him during the simulated battle. A window on the starboard side drew his attention. The enormous solar sails propelled them toward Earth. From his vantage point—on the second of the ship's three levels in the main hull—he could just make out his destination.

The bridge jutted out of the bow like a spindly appendage. An elevator shaft connected it to the body of the ship. Though it couldn't be glimpsed by the naked eye yet, Aero could tell from their reliance on the solar sails and reduced speed that they were nearing Earth. *Another few days and it will be hovering right outside this window.*

For a second, he lost himself in the beauty of the scene—the impossibly brilliant stars set against the vacuum of outer space. The darkness of space was so extreme that it couldn't even be called black, though that was the closest approximation. It was more like the complete absence of color—of everything, in fact.

This was the backdrop against which he'd lived his life, lodged inside this spacecraft, only occasionally journeying down to the surface of planets and moons, which invariably proved hostile and toxic, each in its own special way. As he had come to learn, the universe was a solitary and barren place. For all he knew, they were the only ones who had survived the millennium of exile—a terrible and haunting thought.

During the Doom, the space colonies lost contact with the Earth-bound colonies, an unforeseen consequence of the devastation. The other two space colonies, the Third and Fourth Continuums, both expired in untimely fashions. The Third Continuum—an enclosed city on the surface of Mars—lasted exactly 157 years. An air leak finished them off, though they'd been barreling down a self-destructive path long before that event. By the time the Second Continuum reached them on a rescue mission, most of the colonists had already suffocated to death. They'd managed to save only eighty-six of them.

The Fourth Continuum had fared better for a time. They lasted almost three hundred years, but that good fortune did not hold. In the year 296 P.D., while the Fourth Continuum was orbiting the dark side of Uranus, it vanished. Why the ship had traveled to that location—or what had befallen it—nobody knew to this day. Under the command of Supreme General Bryant Stern, the Second Continuum traveled to their last known coordinates.

When they reached Uranus, they found no trace of the ship or its crew. Stern sent out communications and deployed units to inspect the planet's moons. A surface mission was out of the question. If the Fourth Continuum had crashed onto Uranus, then it would have sunk through the upper layers of hydrogen and helium and then into the liquid icy center of the planet. There would have been nothing left of the ship or its crew to find.

For months, the Second Continuum waited around for any sign of them, orbiting Uranus and beset by indecision. Eventually, Stern was forced to conclude that unless any of the Earth colonies survived, they could be the only ones left—the last outpost of human civilization. With the Doom still ravaging the surface of the Earth, rendering it uninhabitable for another seven hundred years, Stern arrived at a decision. The Second Continuum would travel outward through space and set its sights on a new mission—to find another planet to call home. This would eventually become known as Stern's Quest.

And so, for the better part of the last seven hundred years, under the rule of twenty-seven subsequent Supreme Generals, the Second Continuum had traveled from planet to planet—from solar system to solar system—in search of a new home, one that they had never found. Stern's Quest had ended in abject failure. And now, per Supreme General Arthur Brillstein's new orders, they were finally returning to Earth.

Aero dragged his eyes from the window and continued to the bridge. On his way, he passed by many familiar areas—the Barracks, the Mess Hall, the Clinics, and the passageway that led to the Docking Bay, which housed their transports. The ship's populace always hovered right around three thousand, since reproduction was strictly regulated by the Clinic for Procreation and Population Maintenance.

He rounded a bend and came upon possibly their most important institution—the Agoge. The military school's arched doors were thrust open. Made from the same material as the Falchions, they were engraved with the Ouroboros seal entwined around the words Aeternus Eternus.

A unit of children—not much older than five—ran through their daily calisthenics routine on the terrace. They sported fresh buzz cuts, and their uniforms bore no insignia, apart from the seal. The Forgers hadn't even bestowed their Falchions on them yet.

"One . . . two . . . three . . . four . . . five!" the Drillmaster called out in a staccato rhythm. He carried a golden staff with him. If he caught any students slacking off, he whacked them, leaving a painful welt. Aero had felt its sting on many occasions.

"One . . . two . . . three . . . four . . . five!"

The students cycled through their exercises—push-ups,

jumping jacks, lunges, repeat. Aero had been put through these very same drills when he'd first arrived at the Agoge. Before that, like all children under five, he'd lived in the Natal Barracks with his mother. There was really only one word for that time in his life—utopia.

He and his mother had existed in their own special world without drillmasters, commanders, orders, or training. Their thrice-daily meals provided the only structure to their days. Over the years, he saw other mothers move out of the Natal Barracks when their children came of age, never to return. Those kids—who'd been his playmates and his confidants—then vanished from his life.

But he still felt unprepared when his fifth birthday finally arrived. His mother woke him first thing in the morning. He wasn't allowed to take anything. They didn't even eat breakfast. Instead, she marched him up to the Agoge and handed him over to the Drillmasters. She didn't even say good-bye. Through his tear-blurred vision, he watched her walk away and knew that she was walking out of his life for good.

At first, he felt furious at his mother, and then at the cruel system that had torn them apart. And lastly, he felt terribly, terribly sad, until he learned to numb himself and feel nothing at all. But he supposed that had been the point. The Drillmasters wanted to break him of his attachments. They put him through endless exercises to teach him to suppress his emotions. They wanted him to never feel anything ever again.

A good soldier is an unaffected one, or so they taught.

He turned his anger inward and devoted himself to his studies and training, and it began to pay off. Last year, he had graduated first in his class, and now he was in charge of his own combat unit, the highest assignment for a new soldier.

"Soldiers, fall in!" the Drillmaster barked. They'd reached the end of their routine. They fell into a U-shaped formation and marched in place. "Forward march!"

They paraded in formation back toward the Agoge to resume their lessons, but still Aero lingered behind and watched them from the corridor, lost in a dreaded swirl of memories, until an announcement came blaring over the loudspeakers: "Captain Wright to the bridge."

It was Major Doyle's voice.

He didn't sound pleased to issue a second summons.

Aero cursed himself for loitering outside the Agoge, swept up in the recollection of a past that he could never reclaim. It was a completely inefficient use of his time, especially when duty required that he be elsewhere.

He hit a few buttons on a computer panel set invisibly into the corridor's smooth wall. "This is Captain Wright. I'll be there in five. Over."

He didn't wait for the response from Major Doyle. Instead, he about-faced and marched as quickly as he could to the elevator that would carry him to the bridge.

Chapter 12
INVASION OF PRIVACY

Myra Jackson

Voices echoed into the secret room, reaching Myra in her hiding place behind a pipe. Feeling the rapid thumping of her heart, she crouched lower and listened.

"By the Oracle, I dunno how she fits in here!"

Adrenaline rushed through Myra's veins, but then she relaxed slightly. "I know that voice," she muttered. That was followed by more banging noises and then:

"Help, I'm stuck."

"Holy Sea, you eat too many cookies!" grumbled another boy.

"Shut up and help me push!" said a girl.

Actually, Myra recognized all three of their voices. Annoyance surged through her. She located the pipe from which the noises were emanating and peered inside to see Rickard's face. It was dirty, sweaty, and flushed. She immediately pinpointed the source of his discomfort—his broad shoulders were wedged inside the narrow pipe. She shifted her eyes to the two faces behind him—Kaleb and Paige. They clutched flashlights and were pushing on Rickard from behind, but he looked like he hadn't budged an inch.

Myra glared at them.

"Hey, keep it down—unless you want the 'Trollers to show up."

"Look, it's Myra!" Rickard said.

"About bloody time," Kaleb said. "I thought we'd never find her."

"Or get out of here alive," Paige added in a sulky voice.

Rickard ignored their complaints. "Holy Sea, am I glad to see you."

"Well, I wish I could say the same thing," Myra said, allowing the irritation to seep into her voice. "I came here to be alone. Now spit it out—how'd you find me?"

"By the Oracle . . . get me out . . . of here . . . " Rickard said, flailing his arms and trying to free himself from the pipe. "And . . . I'll tell you whatever . . . you want to know."

Myra arched her eyebrow. "Anything?"

"You name it. Just get me out."

Myra climbed into the pipe and seized his hands. They were so big that they engulfed hers entirely. "On the count of three . . . " she called to Kaleb and Paige.

"One . . . two . . . *three*."

Myra pulled on his arms while they pushed him from behind. A few seconds and a lot of cursing later, Rickard finally came unstuck. Both he and Myra went flying back into the room. She tucked herself into a tight ball and rolled to lessen the impact, but Rickard didn't fare quite as well. He landed in a puddle with a mighty splash. But it didn't appear to bother him at all. He was too relieved to be free of the pipe.

Myra retrieved her flashlight while Kaleb and Paige joined them in the room. Myra surveyed her friends—they were dirty, soaking wet, and scraped up from their journey through the pipes. Kaleb shot Myra a sheepish glance. It made him look even more alluring somehow. She tried to ignore the pitter-pattering of her heart.

"Now, really, how'd you find me?" Myra demanded.

Her friends exchanged uneasy looks but didn't answer.

"Look, I know you had help getting in," Myra said. "Which means you'll need help getting out. So if you don't tell me, then I'll leave you here with the rats."

Paige shuddered in revulsion. "Rats?"

"Yup, big ones. Hairy. Sharp teeth. Oh . . . and famished."

Paige finally cracked. "He brought us here."

She pointed to the pipe. Myra heard rustling sounds, and then Tinker poked his head out. She was shocked to see him. Unlike her friends, he didn't appear sullied from the journey. Myra checked him over for injuries and then leveled her gaze on him. "Tink, what were you thinking, crawling through the pipes like that? It's really dangerous. What if you'd gotten lost or hurt? What then?"

He just shrugged his shoulders.

"Seriously, how'd you find me?" she said.

He pointed to the pipe.

"You followed me?"

He nodded once in confirmation.

"Then why didn't you lose my trail?"

He furrowed his brow. "I've been following you," he said softly.

She looked at him in surprise. "For how long?"

"Always."

She couldn't believe it. "I never . . . knew," she stammered.

Tinker smiled crookedly, unzipped his rucksack, and retrieved his computer. The tap-tap-tap of his fingers on the keyboard echoed through the room. She knelt beside him, glimpsing the complex code on the monitor. It looked like a bizarre language.

"Tink, why'd you bring my friends here?" she asked.

"I was worried. You've been acting . . . abnormal."

He fell silent, his pupils dilated, and his face went slack, as if the act of communicating had sapped his strength. Paige's voice drew Myra's attention.

"He showed up at my compartment looking for you. You said we had plans to meet up at the Souk, but I checked with Kaleb and Rickard and well . . . "

Myra grimaced at her lie. "Right. I had to come up with some excuse to get out of my compartment. My dad's been acting weird lately, really worrying about me."

"That makes sense," Paige said. "Anyway, it's not like you to lie. So we decided to find you. Tinker insisted that you'd be here since it's where you always go when something is bothering you. So, really, tell us, what's going on?"

Myra dug her toe into the floor. "I'm just nervous to start as an apprentice."

"You didn't seem nervous yesterday," Paige said.

"Well, I am now."

Kaleb shook his head. "No way. I don't buy it; you love Engineering. You couldn't wait to be an apprentice." Myra opened her mouth to deny it, but he stopped her. "Seriously, don't bother trying to lie again. You're terrible at it. Like the worst. Ever."

He had her cornered, but something held her back. Something big. Something she usually tried to ignore. She crouched down and wrapped her arms around her chest.

"Even if it's something, I can't tell you."

Paige looked offended. "And why not?"

Myra kept her eyes glued to the floor. "Because . . . I just can't."

"Try harder," Paige insisted.

"Just bloody tell us already," Rickard added.

Kaleb fixed his gaze on her. "By the Oracle, we're not leaving you alone until you do."

That's what finally did it. Myra glared at him, her eyes flashing. "That's funny since you didn't seem to have a problem leaving me alone after I got expelled."

Her words ricocheted around the room. Kaleb looked like she'd just slapped him in the face. "Myra, really, it's not what you think," he said in a pained voice.

"Oh, yeah? Since I recall having lots of alone time back then, like tons of it. Months and months, in fact." She turned her gaze on Paige and Rickard. "You abandoned me, all of you, right when I needed you the most. You were supposed to be my friends, so why should I trust you now?"

Silence engulfed the room, as her words hung in the air. She'd finally given voice to it—the question that she'd never been brave enough to ask. Tinker's hand snaked up and clasped her palm. He squeezed. She felt gratitude flooding through her. Her friends had abandoned her, but not Tinker. She squeezed back and turned away from them.

"Cowards, just like I thought," she said in disgust. "I'm out of here."

"No, Myra, wait," Kaleb said. "Really, I can explain everything."

He tried to grab her shoulder, but she twisted away. "That won't work this time," she said. Even her heart—usually a traitor—didn't react to his touch. She shuttled Tinker, more roughly than she intended, toward the pipe that led back to Sector 2. Kaleb glanced helplessly at Paige and Rickard.

"It's time, isn't it?" Paige said.

Rickard nodded. "We've kept it from her for too long."

Myra pivoted back toward her friends. "Kept what from me?"

Kaleb's face twisted up with agony, but still he said nothing.

"Three seconds, then I'm gone," she said. "Three . . . two . . . *one*."

"Myra, I didn't have a choice! I had to . . . abandon you."

She couldn't believe her ears. A cruel smile pulled at her lips. "Well, that's a strange explanation. You had to. Nice, very nice. Well, I have to go now."

"After the 'Trollers arrested you, I made a deal with my father. I was afraid they'd keep you locked up forever . . . or worse." He swallowed hard. "I panicked, I didn't know what to do. My parents, they never approved of our courting; they wanted me to marry into a Plenus family, not Factum. They said it would bring shame on us."

Myra stared at him in surprise. Of course, she'd known it was unusual for Kaleb to court somebody like her, but since it had never seemed to bother him, she hadn't given it much thought. "Seriously, I had no idea . . . why didn't you ever tell me?"

He looked at her the way he used to back when they courted. "Myra, I didn't want you to feel less than."

Her heart started pounding, but she forced herself to stay calm. "So, then what happened?"

"Well, my father refused to help, of course. He said I'd gotten what I deserved for courting below my position. Those were his exact words. So, I threatened to do something crazy to get myself arrested, so I could join you in the Pen—or even the Holy Sea, if it came to that. Finally, my mother couldn't take it anymore. She convinced my father to lobby the Synod to spare your life." He hesitated, but then forced himself to finish. "But on one condition."

"The condition . . . what was it?"

"I had to stop courting you." He wrenched his hand through his hair, the fear, anguish, and longing evident on his face. "Believe me, that's the last thing I wanted to do, but I didn't have a choice. My father made me swear not to tell you about it, so I decided to disappear from your life. I thought it would be the best thing. For both of us."

"Paige, Rickard, what about you?" Myra said.

"Our parents ordered us to stay away from you," Paige said. "They were scared we'd get into trouble just for being your friend. And that we'd be next."

"I guess that makes sense," Myra said, thinking through everything. "But then why'd you start talking to me again? What was it . . . about a year later?"

"One agonizing year," Kaleb said with a grim smile. "One morning, I saw you walking Tinker to school, and I just couldn't help myself anymore."

"I remember that," Myra said, thinking back. "You waved to me from across the corridor. I was so surprised I didn't even wave back. Then I saw you the next day, only you actually talked to me. I think you asked me how pledging was going."

Kaleb flashed a sheepish smile. "Yeah, it wasn't very smooth."

Myra's face softened, but then she snapped back to reality. "But what if your father finds out?"

A furious expression stole over Kaleb's face. "A few

months ago, an informant ratted me out. He told my father that he'd seen me consorting with a known heathen."

Myra swallowed hard. "So what did he do?"

"My father confronted me, and we had a huge fight."

"What'd you tell him?"

"That we're just friends, nothing more. I promised to stop courting you, not to stop talking to you. My father backed down but reminded me not to break my promise, that it could be really bad for both of us. So since then, I've had to be really careful."

Myra felt blood flushing her cheeks."Right, we're just friends."

"Exactly," Kaleb agreed, but the way his eyes lingered on her face made her wonder if that was the whole truth. "Actually, it's a relief to tell you."

A giddy feeling swept through Myra, and she found her self nodding. It was a relief. That dark time right after her expulsion replayed in her mind, the images whirring in rapid succession, but she saw everything through a different lens this time. The events shifted and rearranged themselves in order to accommodate this new information. She caught up to the present moment and reached a conclusion:

This changes everything.

"I'm . . . so sorry," she said. "So very, very sorry. I always thought it was your choice to stop being my friends. I can't believe I've been holding a grudge when you were just protecting me. You have no idea how hard it was to lose my friends."

"Sure we do," Paige said. "It was hard on us, too."

"Him most of all," Rickard said, jerking his thumb at his best friend. A little color crept into Kaleb's cheeks. An awkward second passed, then another.

"All right, let's hug it out," Rickard said. He stretched his big arms, engulfing all of them into one giant embrace. "Myra, apology accepted!" he declared with a grin.

Once he released them, Myra turned to leave, but Kaleb stopped her. "Nice try, Jackson, very smooth," he said. "But you still haven't told us what's going on."

The smile faded from her face. "You have no idea what you're asking."

"Seriously, I don't care. I'm sick of lies and half-truths." Kaleb studied her face for a moment, and then came to a realization. "You know something, don't you?"

"Maybe, but that doesn't mean you have to know."

Paige took the bait. "Does it have to do with the Synod?"

"Sort of . . . yes . . . in a way."

Paige fired off a rapid string of guesses. "The 'Trollers? The Hockers? The Church? The Academy? The Com Store? The Victus? The allergen warning?"

Myra's face gave it away—she flinched on that last part.

Paige backtracked quickly. "What about the allergen warning?"

"It's . . . a lie," Myra said.

"What do you mean?" Rickard said. He glanced at his friends. "We've seen the long lines, haven't we? And the orange flag? How else do you explain that?"

Myra nodded. "Right, people are having trouble breathing, but it's not because of a bloody allergen release or whatever rubbish the Synod claims."

"Trouble breathing," Paige repeated. "That's right. My mother's been talking about the symptoms. Shortness of breath, dizziness, oxygen deprivation . . . "

Horror swept over her face as it dawned on her. "Something's wrong with the Animus Machine, isn't it?"

The words hung in the air and then dispersed as if sucked away. Aside from the faint dripping of water and the soft hiss of the air vents, the room was deadly silent.

"It's not too late—you don't have to know," Myra said, but her voice sounded weak even to her ears. Paige took two steps toward her and seized her by the shoulders.

"Myra, tell us everything," Paige said. "Just start from the beginning. Please, we have a right know the truth, don't we? No matter how horrible it is."

Myra took in her face and knew that she was right—they did have a right to know, for it affected each of them equally, regardless of their parents' status. Shielding them from the truth wouldn't keep them from suffocating to death.

"Are you sure?" Myra asked. "It's not too late. You can still back out."

Her eyes tracked over their faces, coming to rest on Tinker. After a few more seconds passed and she sensed no hesitation, not even a tremor, she knew that they'd made their choices. *We're in this together now*, she thought. She started pacing around the room; she knew that if she stopped, she wouldn't be able to go through with it.

"The Animus Machine is breaking down."

Even though she kept her eyes fixed on the floor, she still heard their gasps. "And my father can't fix it. In eight months, maybe less, we're going to run out of oxygen."

Myra kept pacing and talking, and the story poured forth like water from a burst pipe. She told them everything, sparing no details, not even when Paige started to sob quietly and Tinker flinched away in fear. Not even when Kaleb and Rickard went pale with shock, which gradually dissolved into downright horror. Through the tears and the palpable sense of dread and regret, Myra told them every single thing.

And when she was finished, she took a deep breath to stay her own tears and studied their faces. As much as they looked like they didn't want to believe her, she could tell that they did. She saw myriad emotions cascading over their faces, but doubt wasn't one of them. Then she levied her question on them, the one that had been plaguing her.

"So how do we find the Beacon?" Her voice reverberated through the shadowy room. "According to my father, it's our only hope if we want to survive."

Chapter 13
POSSIBILITIES

Captain Aero Wright

The elevator door dilated with a soft hiss.

Aero stepped through it and onto the bridge, catching sight of Earth for the first time. Though still too far away to see with the naked eye, the sensors had captured its likeness and magnified it on all five of the monitors. His first reaction to the planet was—*not very impressive*. Earth possessed none of the verdant greens or sapphire blues—shrouded in their blanket of white clouds—of the planet Before Doom, nor did it resemble the angry, volcanic orb that it had become right after the Doom.

Instead, a dreary, grayish world filled the screens. Swirls of storms plagued its atmosphere, obscuring any view of the surface. But even that, Aero imagined, would be equally colorless—and most likely lifeless, too. He could tell from the harried movements of the Majors that they were trying to run scans on the surface but were encountering difficulty. The storms were probably interfering with their instruments.

Supreme General Brillstein stood at the front of the bridge with his eyes fixed on Earth. Aero waited before announcing himself, savoring this time spent in the presence of his father. It was a rare treat. After he had waited for as long as he could without drawing unwanted attention, he saluted. "Sir, you summoned me to the bridge?" he said.

Brillstein did not turn to face his son. "At ease, Captain," he said. "Stand by for orders." There was no emotional inflection in his voice, nor any acknowledgment that Aero was his son.

"Yes, sir," Aero said with another salute. Then, he moved his left foot to shoulder width—exactly twelve inches apart—and clasped his hands in the small of his back. He could move a little bit, except for his right foot, which had to stay rooted in place. But he had to remain silent until given further instructions. In short, he had to wait.

There were few things that Aero hated more than waiting.

It was boring, maddening and, worst of all, inefficient. He occupied himself by observing the Supreme General. He was tall—nearly as tall as Aero—with a lean frame and gray-flecked hair. He wore the same uniform as his soldiers, except for the ornate insignia that marked him as their most senior commander. The only other thing that made him appear any different was the golden armlet latched around his right wrist.

The Beacon, Aero thought. The device pulsed with greenish light, which seemed to grow brighter the closer they got to Earth. He wondered if the steady throbbing of the light mimicked his father's heartbeat. Regardless of how the connection functioned, the Beacon was a peculiar device. The First Ones made it using the same ancient science as the Falchions. Brillstein had inherited it from the last Supreme General after he passed away. They were of no relation. The only reason that the Majors had chosen him was because of his young age—he had just turned sixteen—and his high ranking.

And now, as they drew closer and closer to Earth, the Beacon seemed to be commanding them just as much as the man who carried it.

"Major Vinick, any life-forms reported yet?" Brillstein said.

"No sir, not yet," Vinick said. "We're having trouble

getting a clean read on the surface with these storms. They're interfering with our instruments."

Vinick had dark eyes and darker hair. Along with his hooked nose, these features gave him a slightly threatening appearance. He was Brillstein's second-in-command, and they'd graduated from the Agoge together. Vinick had a better combat record, but he didn't score as well on the written exams, which carry equal weight at the school. Thus, Vinick graduated second in their class. Had his grades been only slightly higher, he would be wearing the Beacon and would be their Supreme General—not Aero's father.

"Keep trying, Major," ordered Brillstein. "If there are any life-forms down there, even just the possibility of life-forms, I want to know right away."

"Yes, sir; these damned storms have got to let up sometime."

"Sometime might be too late. We'll be close enough to send the first squadron on a reconnaissance mission in four days. I don't want to send them in blind."

Vinick narrowed his eyes, and a dark expression clouded his face. "Sir, about the reconnaissance mission?" he said.

Brillstein frowned. Though the Majors functioned as his advisors, he didn't like to have his decisions questioned. "Proceed," he said, though his tone indicated with caution.

Vinick gestured to the control panel. "Well, I've been thinking, should we even be looking for life-forms? I say we scan for resources, rare minerals, technology."

"Major, your suggestion has been duly noted," Brillstein said.

"Noted—but not acted upon," Vinick replied. His voice remained flat, but his eyes locked onto the monitors hungrily. "Why don't we plunder this dead planet for anything valuable, then continue on our search for a new home?"

"Stern's Quest is finished," Brillstein said as the Beacon blazed with green light. "Our true mission—given to us by the First Ones—is to recolonize Earth."

"Of course, sir! I'll keep scanning for life-forms."

"That's better, Major." Brillstein turned to Aero. "Captain Wright, your unit will be the first boots on the ground. I want you leading the reconnaissance mission to Earth. Your orders are to search and scan for any and all life-forms. Is that understood?"

"Yes, sir," Aero replied. His heart skipped a beat and rejoiced. His father had chosen his unit for this historic mission—and by extension—him.

"Inform your soldiers and begin preparations," Brillstein said. "This mission will be challenging. It's possible that you'll be the first people to set foot on Earth in more than a thousand years. And if not, then you'll have to be prepared. We don't know what has happened to the other colonies—and whether they will be friend or foe."

Aero wasn't sure if it was his imagination, but Brillstein's pupils dilated slightly, and it seemed like his mind was somewhere else—searching, probing for something. Aero shifted his gaze to the Beacon, which was pulsing faster and glowing brighter.

"Yes, sir," Aero said. "We'll be ready."

"I suggest you run a few training simulations. And get your weapons checked by the Forgers. Make sure they're freshly charged. Even if you don't encounter other people, there's still the possibility of mutations."

Aero had learned about this in the Science of the Doom. Some biologists theorized that certain tenacious species might survive by burrowing deep underground or living underwater. However, the radiation might have caused them to mutate. And in the absence of natural predators, they could have grown larger and more hostile.

"Yes, sir," Aero said. "I was already planning on it."

Just then, something flickered in Brillstein's eyes. *Was it pride?* Aero wondered. But just as quickly as it had appeared, it was gone.

"Of course," Brillstein said, breaking their eye contact and turning back to the monitors. "Your unit will deploy in four days, that clear? Soldier dismissed."

"Yes, sir," Aero said with one last salute.

Before he exited the bridge, his eyes flicked back to the

monitors. On second thought, maybe his reaction to Earth had been too harsh. Who knew what stirred beneath the swirl of storms on this unknown world on whose surface he would soon touch down? Now the emotions were back stronger than ever, afflicting him like the tempests on Earth.

A rebellion was stirring in his heart and his head and his loins and the tips of his nine intact fingers and seven toes. And for the first time, Aero thought he understood the reason for his emotions—Earth represented possibility. It held the possibility that he might live a life other than the one that had been ordained for him since the moment of his birth.

No, scratch that.

Since the moment of his conception.

This uninhabited terrain, no matter how much of a toxic wasteland, was a free and wide-open space. It had not yet been colonized, restricted, divided up, and regulated. There were no rules down there against love and family and emotions. And though these things frightened him—and he wasn't sure that he wanted to experience them—he knew that he wanted to have a say in his life, no matter what path he ultimately chose.

Possibility, he thought again, relishing the feel of that word rolling around in his head like a loose screw, shaking up everything he'd been raised to believe.

Chapter 14

CONTRABAND

Myra Jackson

Myra's voice reverberated through the secret room. Her question about how to find the Beacon hung in the stagnant air. Not even the rats that had crept out of the darkness to listen to her story could provide an answer. She studied her friends' faces, assessing their condition. Thankfully, some of their shock seemed to have subsided. A little color had crept back into Rickard's cheeks, Paige had stopped crying, and Tinker was back to tapping on his computer. Of them all, Kaleb seemed to have taken the news the best.

"Holy Sea, I can't believe there are other colonies," he said at last.

Myra looked down. "Well, we don't know if they survived the exile."

"Still, they did exist," Kaleb said. "That goes against everything we've been taught by the Red Cloaks, the Chancellors, the teachers. They're a bunch of liars."

Paige hunched over and wrapped her arms around her chest. She'd always believed in the value of her studies and devoted herself to being the top student at the Academy.

Learning that they'd been taught falsehoods affected her the most.

But Rickard had no such qualms. "By the Oracle, I knew the teachers were two-faced prigs! And that studying was a complete and total waste of time."

Myra arched her eyebrow. "Is that why you got so many tardies?"

"Yup, I knew school was bloody useless."

"Revisionist history," Kaleb said. "You're worse than the Synod."

Paige jabbed her finger in Rickard's face. She looked angry, not an inappropriate emotion given the circumstances. "Rickard Lynch, if you're so much smarter than the rest of us, then tell me this—where did Sari Wade hide the Beacon?"

Rickard thought for a moment. "Well, let me see. If I had to hide something . . . and everybody was looking for it . . . then I wouldn't want to be caught carrying it around the corridors . . . so I'd hide it in my compartment." He finished with a triumphant grin.

"Genius work, Lynch," Paige said. "You just stated the obvious."

"Obvious, maybe—but that doesn't mean I'm wrong."

"Don't you think 'Trollers would have searched her compartment already? Look, I'll admit the history is sketchy, but the Synod wanted to destroy everything from Before Doom in the Great Purging. The Beacon would have been a prime target, right?"

"Well, it was just a suggestion," Rickard said glumly.

Myra started pacing around the room. Something was nagging at her. Needling at her brain. It had to do with what Rickard had just said. *Hidden the Beacon . . . in her compartment . . . inside of her compartment . . . inside of it . . . during the Great Purging.*

"Actually, Rickard might be onto something!" she said. "We do repairs on the compartments when wiring goes haywire or pipes burst, stuff like that. And the Engineers are always finding things hidden in the walls."

"Contraband," Kaleb said. "I've heard about that."

Myra nodded. "Usually, it's stuff like firewater or the perfumes and caviar that only the Plenus are supposed to get, but sometimes we find things that people hid during the Great Purging. Of course, we have to turn anything we find into the 'Trollers."

"Right, my father is always complaining about it," Kaleb said. "The Plenus stuff goes to the Synod, so they can arrest the Factum or Hockers for dealing in black market goods, and harmless items go to Dissemination for the Com Store's shelves."

"And the stuff from Before Doom?" Myra asked.

"That's easy—it gets destroyed," Kaleb said.

Her eyes locked onto his face, and she felt a chill working its way up her spine. She could tell they were both thinking the same thing—they'd always made a great team.

"Paige, thoughts?" Myra said. "Could the Beacon be hidden in her compartment, like inside the walls or in a secret panel, like contraband?"

"I guess it's possible," Paige said after a moment.

Rickard grinned. "I knew it."

"Not so fast, Lynch," Paige said. "I'm not finished. It's possible—but I'm still skeptical. It would be really risky to hide it there . . . but I've got another idea."

"What is it?" Myra asked.

"Maybe she left a clue," Paige said.

Myra shot her a puzzled look. "A clue?"

"Right. Well, think about it," Paige said. "Sari wanted to hide the Beacon from the Synod, but she also would have wanted the right people to find it later on, otherwise that would have defeated the entire purpose of saving it. So maybe she left a clue behind."

"That's brilliant," Myra said. "A clue, of course!"

Paige looked pleased. "Well, it's what I would do."

Myra zeroed in on the map of Sector 2 in her mind and focused on it. "Let's see, there are nine hundred compartments, so how do we know where she lived?"

"We could track down her descendants," Kaleb said.

Myra shook her head. "The assignments are randomized, so they wouldn't live in the same one anymore. Also, I doubt they'd know—we're talking a thousand years ago."

"Maybe there's an old directory in Records?" Paige said.

"My mother was pledged there, remember?" Myra said. "It's heavily restricted. Nobody who isn't pledged there can get inside."

Kaleb nodded. "You're right about Sector 9, it has all the normal security and extra protections, too. I don't think even you could break in there."

"The grates?" Myra said.

"Yup, they're welded shut. Padre Flavius upgraded the security."

Myra thought for a moment. "Well, any other ideas?"

When nobody answered, she started pacing again, trying to come up with an idea . . . even just the hint of an idea . . . but nothing leapt to mind . . . *blank* . . . *empty* . . . *useless*.

She felt a tug on her sleeve. She looked down impatiently and grimaced. "Tink, not now," she said. "Can't you see I'm trying to think?"

He tugged more impatiently and started to gesture.

"You're just going to have to say it. Out loud. Not with your hands."

"Fine," he rasped. "I know how to find her compartment."

Myra knelt down to face him.

"Tell me *how*," she said with bated breath.

Tinker broke into his lopsided smile. "Just ask the computer."

"Your computer?" Myra glanced at the unwieldy hunk of metal clutched in his tiny palms. "But . . . how would your computer know where Sari Wade lived?"

He shook his head vigorously. "Not my computer."

"Then which computer?"

"The big computer—the one that the Founders programmed. It knows everything, since it was here before the Chosen People arrived."

"But I thought the Programmers encrypted the archives?"

"They encrypted the archives, that's true," Tinker said, "but the Programmers couldn't put controls on everything. They need the computer to run important things, stuff they don't even understand anymore. That's why they couldn't just erase the files. Everything would shut down—the automatic lights, the Animus Machine, the Aquafarm, the doors, the scanners. Without the computer, everything would stop working."

"By the Oracle, you're right!" Myra said. "The computer does run everything. That's why the Engineers can go home at night—the systems are automated."

Paige furrowed her brow. "But how do we use the computer to find her compartment? If they locked up the archives, then we can't access those."

"Not directly," Tinker agreed.

"So then . . . how?" Myra asked.

"Just scan your wrist at any terminal," Tinker said. "Then ask the computer to direct you to *Sari Wade's Compartment.* It'll project a map like it does for every location in the colony. I'll bet it'll even give you directions if you request them."

"Just ask the computer," Myra repeated. A proud smile crept onto her face. "Tinker, that's genius! I would never have thought of that, not in a million years."

Tinker blushed. "Well, it's kind of obvious."

"Maybe to you," she said and mussed his hair. She jumped to her feet. "Come on, let's find a terminal."

As Myra led them from the secret room through the labyrinth of pipes and ducts (she selected a route that could accommodate Rickard's larger size), she realized that it felt like a heavy weight had been lifted from her shoulders. She still felt a little pressure, but the burden seemed lighter somehow. It felt less, well, burdensome.

After a bit of thought, she settled on the reason: *I'm not alone in this anymore.*

She glanced behind her. Her companions crawled in tandem through the pipe, their faces lit by the glow of their flashlights. Despite her earlier protests, she was grateful they'd invaded her privacy. Yet that wasn't the only reason. After feeling stuck all morning, it felt like they were finally getting somewhere.

Like they might stand some kind of a chance.

Chapter 15

NO ONE IS SAFE

The Synod

"Why did you summon us?" asked their leader.

The others regarded him in silence. Eventually one of them spoke, her voice echoing through the locked chamber. "An informant came forward. He claims that one of the Factum pledged with him was snooping around Records for the Beacon."

At that word, several of them hissed. A few swirled their hands over their chests. The leader's eyes narrowed to slits.

"Did he find anything? Maybe something we overlooked?"

"He took a few pictures from the archives, but they'd been cleared. But I'll have the Patrollers snatch him out of his compartment, just in case."

The leader grabbed a cracker laden with caviar from the golden platter. He nibbled on it, relishing the delicacy reserved for those of his stature.

"What's the Factum's name?"

"Bishop. His wife was a troublemaker, too."

"Oh, yes, I remember her." His lips twisted back in pleasure at the memory. "After the birth of her twin daughters, she defied our orders for sterilization. Of course, we convicted her and sentenced her accordingly. We can't have Factum overpopulating the colony, now can we? She didn't go to the Holy Sea willingly. It was quite a challenge."

He glanced down where a jagged, crescent-shaped scar marked his wrist. She'd bitten him when he forced her into the portal, but that didn't alter her fate.

"It's been eight years since we've had a case like this one," he went on. His voice surged with irritation. "I thought we'd handled it."

"What was the name of the last Factum?"

"Tessa Jackson," supplied somebody else. "We caught her searching through Records for any reference to the Beacon. One of her coworkers snitched on her. And . . . well . . . we all remember what happened after that." His eyes darted to their leader.

"Are the two Factum connected?" he asked. "Bishop and Jackson?"

Silence engulfed the chamber. The leader shifted on his cushioned throne. He took a long gulp of rice wine from his goblet and popped another cracker in his mouth. He ground it up with his teeth and swallowed. "Well, are they?" he asked.

"We don't know," she said quickly. "At least not yet. But once we commence our interrogation, Bishop will talk, I'm sure of it. More than that Knox boy."

Their leader frowned and snatched up another cracker. "What makes you so certain?"

"Because this Factum has more to lose," she said. She leaned forward, the light catching her sharp cheekbones. "*Two* more things, to be specific."

"Ah, I like how you think, Chancellor. Proceed then," he said with a flick of his wrist. "But keep me informed. I want to know everything this heathen divulges, especially if he has new information. The profane object slipped through our grasp once, and I don't intend to let that happen again. I'm going to find it—and destroy it."

He clenched his fist, crushing the cracker with a sickening crunch.

"We'll begin the interrogation shortly," she agreed.

"If you have to arrest his daughters to get him to talk, then do it. Relations of heathens must also be considered heathens and cast into the Holy Sea. Nobody is safe, not in this dark time. Sinners now threaten us from all sides. If we are not vigilant—if we do not root them out from our midst—then this new Doom will consume us."

"By the Oracle, it will be done!"

"Amen!"

"The Holy Sea save us!"

Only one member appeared troubled by this turn of events, but he didn't speak his mind, for he also had more to lose. One thought flashed through his head:

Now no one is safe.

Chapter 16
THE CLINIC

Captain Aero Wright

"Captain Wright," the nurse read off an electronic chart.

Her steely gray eyes combed the sterile waiting area. A red cross marked the sleeve of her uniform, signifying that she served in a Medical Unit. None of the soldiers stood up from the hard metal benches. She peered down at the chart again.

"Captain Wright?" she called more uncertainly.

This time, Aero stood up and saluted.

It wasn't that he didn't hear her the first time, though that's how he would have explained it if anyone challenged him. No, he had heard her perfectly. Her no-nonsense voice had cut right through him. If it had been up to him, the second she had called his name he would have bolted through the door, never to return to this godforsaken place.

He hated the Clinic for Procreation and Population Maintenance; hated the way the nurses and doctors made him feel like nothing more than a hunk of flesh they wanted to manipulate to their advantage; hated how they poked and prodded him and took his vitals, never once looking him in the eye;

hated that soon he'd have to return here for his first conjugal visit, following the Connubial Service before the Magistrate.

He hadn't received his summons yet, but he knew that it was only a matter of time now that he'd graduated and turned sixteen. A few of the soldiers in his unit had already received their official letters from the Clinic.

"Pre-deployment health screening," the nurse read off his chart. "Is that correct, Captain?"

"Yes, that's correct," he said.

She led him back through the sterile corridors. They did not speak or make small talk. He glanced at the closed doors that lined the walls on each side. He'd been born in one of these rooms, though of course he had no memory of it, or any pictures to tell him what he had looked like as an infant, or even as a young child. Such things had no place in their world. He could only conjure up the image of his newborn self, basing it on a combination of guesswork and things that his mother had told him when he was still a child at the Natal Barracks. It was a fuzzy rendering at best.

The nurse led him to a small examination room and ordered him to change into a plastic gown. The nurse did not leave the room or avert her eyes. Under her watch, Aero removed his uniform piece by piece and pulled on the flimsy plastic. The gown gaped open in the back, but modesty was an emotion, and thus he wasn't supposed to feel it.

He sat on the examination table. It felt cold against his backside. Goosebumps erupted on his flesh. The room smelled vaguely like rubbing alcohol and vinegar, and something sweet that he couldn't quite place. In a practiced manner, the nurse took his vitals. She probed him with cold metal instruments that lit up and typed notes in the electronic chart that had been his since birth. She did not look at his face. She did not ask if anything hurt. Put simply, she did not care. But Aero didn't squirm when she touched him or shy away from her needles and instruments. Instead, he did his best to make it easy for her to perform her duty, as he had been trained.

"Dr. Hendricks will be with you shortly," she announced

when she was finished. Then she took his chart and marched out of the room, leaving him alone.

Aero tried to occupy himself and stop the fidgeting of his hands by focusing on his upcoming deployment. The grayish swirl of storms still plagued Earth's atmosphere, making a descent to the surface a suicide mission. Yesterday, he'd received orders from the Supreme General postponing his deployment until after the storm lifted. How long that would take was anybody's guess. Some of the Majors thought days, others weeks, and still others thought that the storm could last months. For now, he had to wait. They all had to wait.

He ran through the list of everything that he had to do to ready his unit for their deployment, even down to the minutest details. And then he ran through it again. Nothing could be overlooked, nothing left to chance. He wished the damned storm would lift so he could cease all this waiting around and spring into action. Only when he was moving—fighting—leading—did he feel at home in his own skin.

Aero wasn't sure how long the doctor kept him waiting. At the Clinic, time seemed to bend and stretch, both growing, but also sometimes contracting, until he had no sense of its passage at all.

Was it minutes? Half an hour? Longer?

He had no clue. Regardless, the door to the room flung open, bringing with it a rush of chilled air and a stern man with graying hair, spectacles, and a red cross on his uniform's sleeve. Aero tried to stand and salute, but the doctor demurred.

"At ease, Captain," he said, his eyes fixed on Aero's chart. Like the nurse, he also did not meet his patient's gaze. "Your vitals look good," he mumbled, half to himself. "Actually, better than good . . . flawless. Captain, you're in tiptop shape. Is this Falchion response time accurate? Very impressive."

"Thank you, sir," Aero replied in a crisp voice, though he wasn't sure if he could take any credit. Sure, he trained hard, but the Clinic had molded his genetics.

The doctor didn't reply. He sat down at the desk and typed rapidly in Aero's chart. The typing seemed to go on forever. At last, the doctor finished and swiveled back around to face his patient. "Captain, you're medically cleared for deployment."

Aero felt a rush of relief. Though he knew that he was in *tiptop shape*, he had feared the health screening would uncover some hidden flaw in his body, some deficit that had lain dormant and only now reared its ugly head, some hitch in his genetic makeup that would prevent him from deploying, or worse, land him in a noncombat unit.

"Thank you, sir," Aero replied.

The doctor nodded and scrolled through Aero's chart. "I see here that you've just come of connubial age." His eyes scanned the screen. "But you haven't received your summons yet. If you'd like to make a donation before you deploy, I could put in a request to the Magistrate to expedite your Connubial Service. Captain, it would be a substantial loss for the colony if you died before you procreated."

Dr. Hendricks looked at him expectantly.

Aero didn't answer right away. He knew that he was supposed to want to perform his duty—to make a donation, as the doctor put it—but something held him back. The only reason the doctor cared if he died was purely pragmatic. He was a top-ranked soldier with genes that he wanted to propagate through the species. That was all he was to him.

"Who is she?" Aero said at last.

The doctor frowned in disapproval. "You know I can't tell you the name of your betrothed," he said frostily. "It's against regulations. And for your own good, I might add. To prevent you and your betrothed from forming emotional attachments, which can be highly dangerous—"

Knock! Knock!

The sharp rapping on the door startled them both. The doctor opened it to reveal the nurse. She whispered something urgently in his ear, and alarm swept over his face. He muttered something to Aero about an emergency delivery and then darted from the room with the nurse on his heels. The door swept shut behind them.

Aero's eyes darted to the surveillance camera in the corner of the room. Then they shifted to the doctor's desk. And to the medical chart that he'd accidentally left there.

Aero knew that he should stay right where he was—that such things were kept secret for a reason—that knowing the name of his betrothed wouldn't change his fate. But he found himself moving anyway. Angling his body to block the view of the camera under the guise of slipping back into his uniform, he scrolled through his chart, speed-reading the pages the way that he'd learned at the Agoge, effortlessly memorizing every detail. Finally, he found the right page. It was printed under his name in bold.

"Betrothed to **Danika Rothman.**"

Underneath her name was Supreme General Brillstein's signature signing off on the pairing.

Danika Rothman, Aero thought. *Who are you?* Her name didn't ring a bell. No face popped into his head. No memory of her surfaced. She was just a stranger, he supposed. Just another soldier doomed to the same loveless fate as him.

This wasn't an accident.

His eyes blazed over the chart, drinking in every last detail about her, sparse though they were. She had trained in a different unit at the Agoge. That was no surprise. Betrothed never trained together, and they also never served together once they graduated, not even after being wedded. That was why they were paired at birth—so the Clinic could ensure that they were kept apart. She had earned high marks at the Agoge and also served in a combat unit. Her stats were impressive, almost as impressive as his. If they had been in the same unit at the Agoge, she would have been second in their class.

According to the chart, the Clinic had paired them together because they were born just days apart and their genetics check was clean. If the pairing ultimately proved faulty for some reason—due to illness, death, inability to produce offspring, or some other affliction—then the Clinic could annul it. This happened, though rarely. Over the course of a thousand years, they had almost perfected the science of reproduction.

The Connubial Ceremony itself would be a purely administrative process, where they would meet for the first time and sign paperwork for the Magistrate. Shortly thereafter, the Clinic would schedule them for their first conjugal visit, a routine sixty-minute affair slotted into their already-packed schedules.

Aero would check in with the receptionist, as he had for all of his appointments. A nurse would take his blood pressure and vitals, just as she had today, before she led him back to a sterile room in another wing of the Clinic. This room would contain a bed and nothing else. Danika would probably be waiting for him there like a dutiful soldier.

Maybe she'd be perched on the edge of the bed. She might already be undressed (this was what Aero hoped for—he didn't want to go through the awkward process of removing her uniform). It was possible that she'd be nervous the first time. He'd been warned that she might bleed a little and that this was *perfectly normal*. He'd also been told that it might be physically pleasurable and that this was also *perfectly normal*.

The one thing that Aero always wondered about was the lights.

Did they stay on during the procedure?

On the one hand, that would make it easier to navigate the complexities of their bodies. But on the other hand, the shroud of darkness might smooth over the interaction and make it easier to feel what he was supposed to feel—which was nothing at all.

So far, Aero hadn't gotten up the nerve to ask anybody about the lights. He'd sat through instructional classes at the Agoge, which explained in precise, mechanical detail how the act itself—the act of procreation—was performed. A few techniques had even been suggested to hasten the procedure. But they had never mentioned the lights.

And even if he got Danika pregnant following one of their visits, he would not be permitted to contact his offspring or play any role in their lives outside the bounds of official duty. He scrolled through the chart some more, memorizing every detail, even the garbled medical language, but he learned little else about his betrothed.

A rebellion was stirring within him. It was growing stronger with each passing second. He realized, suddenly, that he had no intention of following through on the Supreme General's orders and wedding Danika Rothman. This should have worried him—terrified him, even—but it didn't.

Not even close.

It made him feel more alive than he'd ever felt in his entire life.

He pulled on his uniform, slipped from the room, and returned to his unit's Barracks. He nodded to Wren and his other soldiers. Answered her logistical questions about the training schedule and assured her that he'd been medically cleared for deployment. He mechanically performed his duties and spoke those words, going through the motions of life, but all the while, thoughts of his betrothed danced through his head.

Chapter 17
JUST ASK THE COMPUTER

Myra Jackson

The corridor in Sector 2 was deserted.

Myra signaled to her friends before she slithered through the grate. Kaleb, Rickard, Paige, and Tinker followed behind her and gathered in the corridor. The grate snapped shut, clicking back into place. It was Sunday evening, so most Factum were probably home in their compartments cooking supper and getting ready for the busy workweek ahead. Since the Souk was closed, most Hockers were home, too.

But they still needed to hurry or else their parents might start to worry and come looking for them. The last thing that Myra needed was Chancellor Sebold catching her with his son, doing something suspicious-looking with the computer.

"Come on, it's over here," Myra whispered.

She approached the computer terminal and swiped her wrist under the scanner. A green light shot out, scanned her tattoo. The computer beeped its recognition.

"Myra *Jack*-son," said a male voice. Though Myra had heard it many times before, the voice was so lifelike—so warm and genuine—that sometimes she still found it hard to believe that it belonged to a computer. "How can I help you today?"

"Computer, can you direct me to Sari Wade's compartment?"

Myra held her breath in anticipation. Kaleb, Tinker, Paige, and Rickard waited behind her. The computer took only a few seconds before it supplied an answer.

"Sari *Wade* lives in Compartment *7-1-5*. Projecting a map . . . now."

A green light shot out of the scanner and resolved into a three-dimensional, holographic map of the colony. It zoomed in and focused on Compartment 715.

"Would you like directions, Myra *Jack*-son?" the computer asked.

Myra checked to make sure that the corridor was still empty. "Sure, that would be great," she said—just for fun this time. She already knew the way.

"Projecting route to Compartment *7-1-5*."

A thin beam of green light morphed into a tiny female figure. Then, a green arrow extended away from the figure, wending its way through the holographic corridors, halting in front of a compartment that looked identical to all the others, except for the number that marked it. That was where Sari Wade—the daughter of the Founders—had lived and breathed, loved her husband, raised her children, taken her morning and evening meals, slept and risen to the automatic lights that still shone in their fixtures.

She felt Kaleb's breath on her neck and his lips tickling her earlobe. "Incredible, isn't it?" he whispered, giving voice to her innermost thoughts.

"Incredible doesn't even begin to describe it," Myra said.

They had played with the mapping feature when they were kids and the world around them was brand new and enthralling and full of mysteries, before they'd grown older and impervious to its charms. She couldn't believe that they'd ever taken this miraculous tool for granted, that it had faded into the background of their lives, this technology that the Founders had given them but that they could no longer replicate.

"Start *guidance?*" asked the computer.

"No, thanks," Myra said. If she'd responded in the affirmative, then green arrows would have lit up on the floor, directing them to Compartment 715.

"Do you require any more assistance?" asked the computer.

"Nope, that's all—thank you."

"*Good-bye.*"

The terminal went dark, falling back into sleep mode. Myra wondered how much time would pass before somebody woke it up again. *Probably a lot*, she decided. Almost nobody used the computer this way anymore; it was too easy to know your way around.

"Compartment 715," Myra whispered to her friends. "Nice work, Tink." He grinned crookedly. "So . . . how do we get inside? I'm guessing it's occupied."

"What if we broke in when nobody's home?" Rickard said.

Myra shook her head. "Too dangerous—what if the 'Trollers catch us?"

"How about ringing the bell and asking to take a look around?" Kaleb said.

"Well, that wouldn't give us much time," Myra said. "I want to open up the walls, look for secret panels, that sort of thing. I'll need a few hours at least, plus it'll make a bloody racket. There's no way they'd let us do that, not while they're home."

They fell silent, as they racked their brains.

"Wait, I've got an idea!" Myra said. "Who wants to be my pledge?"

They all looked confused, but then a smile crept onto Paige's face. "I think Kaleb would enjoy that privilege very much. He's always wanted to pledge to Engineering."

Kaleb scowled. "And why would I want to be her pledge?"

"Well, tomorrow I start as an apprentice," Myra said. "And I won't have an assigned pledge yet, but nobody outside Engineering knows that."

"But why not Rickard or Paige?" Kaleb asked.

"Because your father is on the Synod," Myra said grimly.

"The Oracle forbid . . . if the 'Trollers caught us . . . they'd probably go easier on you, right?"

"My thoughts exactly," Paige said.

"But won't somebody recognize me?" Kaleb asked.

Myra broke into a grin. "Not with the disguise I've got in mind. Also, nobody will suspect that a Plenus kid would pretend to be a Factum pledge."

Rickard grinned at the prospect. "Kaleb doing manual labor. Wow, I can't even picture it."

"Hey, I labor all the time . . . on lots of things," Kaleb said weakly.

"Very persuasive, Sebold," Myra said with a laugh. "Tomorrow, we can ring the bell and say there's a gas leak or something like that. That way, they won't question us if we make a lot of noise and tear open the walls. And maybe the floor, too."

"The floor?" Kaleb said. "Isn't that a bit much?"

Myra shrugged. "It's the only way to know for sure if the Beacon's hidden there." She broke into a devilish grin.

"Besides, I enjoy demolishing things—it's very liberating."

From the look on Kaleb's face, it was clear that he wasn't convinced.

"Oh, come on, it'll be fun," she said and nudged him.

His cheeks colored at her touch. "Fine, I'll be your Engine Rat," he said. "But don't think that gives you permission to haze me. I know what goes on in the Engineering Room."

"Just a little hazing?"

"Absolutely not."

"A teeny-tiny bit?"

"Don't even think about it," he said, but he was smiling now. "I could still change my mind, you know. Engineering has got to be at the bottom of my pledge list."

"Fine, no hazing—but you have to carry my tool rig."

"Your what?"

Before he could question her further, Myra changed the subject. "Let's meet at my compartment after you get out of school. Tinker can let you in. I'll get there as—"

The sound of pounding feet reached their ears. It sounded like more than one person.

"Who'd march down the corridor on a Sunday night?" Paige asked.

"I dunno . . . " Rickard said. "Sounds like—"

"The 'Trollers," Myra finished. "Quick, over here . . . "

She signaled to her friends, and they ducked into the nearest doorway and pressed themselves against the wall. Her breathing sped up and her heart thudded in her throat.

A second later, the Patrollers stepped into the corridor. Their pipes were untethered and clenched in their fists. Myra spotted Rickard's father and Jasper. He was smiling, never a good sign. Kaleb raised his finger to his lips, indicating that they should stay quiet. The Patrollers marched up to Compartment 357 and triggered the lock. It beeped and dilated, and then they barged inside. Myra heard a familiar voice cry out.

"By the Oracle, get out of my—"

But it was cut off as the Patrollers began beating him with their pipes. She heard a nauseating thud as a body hit the ground, but still the pipes clanged. Two children were sobbing. Compartment doors starting beeping and dilating up and down the corridor as Factum and Hockers stepped outside to see the commotion. Some quickly ducked back into their compartments and locked their doors, but others loitered around. They whispered nervously among themselves, their eyes glued to Compartment 357.

Soon a crowd had formed in the corridor. Myra stepped out of the alcove where she'd been hiding, and slipped between the bodies. The sounds of struggle continued.

Head Patroller Lynch's voice echoed into the corridor. ". . . by order of the Synod, you're under arrest . . . "

A second later, the Patrollers emerged from the compartment, dragging a body behind them. Myra's eyes fell on his battered face and widened—it was Bishop. He'd been in the secret meeting with her father. His daughters—twins, about Tinker's age, with red hair and matching dresses—ran after their father. But Jasper jerked them back by their collars and threw them down on the ground. He raised his pipe to strike them.

Before she could stop herself, Myra lurched into the corridor. She felt Rickard reach for her to pull her back, but he was too late. She slipped through his fingers and threw herself between the girls and Jasper's pipe, shielding them with her body.

"Mercy!" she cried out. "They're only young children!"

Jasper's lips wrenched into a vicious grin. His teeth were crooked and discolored, and his black hair stuck to his sweaty brow. Blood spatters flecked his cheeks.

"Heathen, you want a taste of this?"

Myra didn't even flinch—she stared him down. "Not like I haven't tried it before!"

The Factum and Hockers appeared torn. Unhappy rumbles tore through the crowd, and Jasper hesitated. Myra heard whispers. "Children now . . . what's next?"

"That girl . . . she's a heathen. The Oracle save us."

"Should've put her out to sea . . . "

Head Patroller Lynch halted his progress. His eyes swept up the corridor as he took in the situation—Jasper about to strike Myra, her protecting the twins, his son behind them, the uneasy crowd—and saw that it was spiraling out of control.

"Patroller Waters, stand down!" he ordered.

Jasper looked furious but lowered his pipe.

"Go on now, get out of here," Myra whispered to the twins.

They scampered back into their compartment, but their frightened eyes lingered on their father's prone body until the door contracted and cut off their view. The Head Patroller's eyes flicked over to Myra and then came to rest on his son. They narrowed.

"Rickard, go home . . . now."

He sounded furious.

"But father—"

"Now," he repeated. "We'll discuss this later."

"Yes, sir," Rickard said, casting his eyes down.

"Now, everybody back to your compartments," he ordered. "Unless you'd like to join our friend here." He gestured to Bishop, who was writhing on the ground.

The crowd began to disperse, doors contracting up and down the corridor. Myra reached down and clasped Tinker's hand, dragging him away from the Patrollers. Her friends trailed behind her. Myra could feel Jasper's eyes boring into her back. If he'd hated her guts before, then she'd just made it a hundred times worse.

Somehow she made it back to her compartment on unsteady legs. She felt paralyzed by fear. If the Patrollers had arrested Bishop, then her father was also in danger. Before she triggered the door and vanished inside, Kaleb caught her eye.

"Still want to do this?" he whispered, his voice thick with concern.

She set her lips and nodded once. "Meet me back here after school."

She glanced in Rickard's direction. He and Paige had continued down the hall toward their compartments. Rickard looked dejected. Kaleb followed her gaze.

"Don't worry. He can take care of himself."

"But it's my fault."

"It's Padre Flavius's fault. You did the right thing. The rest of us . . . " Shame crested his face. "We're . . . cowards. You're the brave one. Always have been."

"I'm not brave, just reckless."

"Well, I know what I saw," he said, backing away. He lifted his hand in farewell and then turned around.

As Myra stepped into her compartment and met her father's worried eyes, one thought flashed through her head—they needed to find the Beacon.

And fast.

Chapter 18
THE ORDER OF THE FOUNDRY

Captain Aero Wright

Aero came to a halt before a golden door that looked like it had been hewn from one solid sheet of metal, but when he hit the button next to it, the door rippled and morphed liquidly, dilating into the walls. He stepped through it and into the Foundry.

Before his upcoming deployment, he had many tasks to accomplish, charging his Falchion foremost among them. He'd received his orders only yesterday, and already he had run a flight simulation with his unit, placed orders with the Mess Hall for provisions and the Engineers for two transports to carry them to Earth. He always put his soldiers and their needs first, but now he had to service his weapon.

Scattered throughout the large room located in the bowels of the ship, the Forgers—known collectively as the Order of the Foundry—worked to produce new Falchions and reforge old ones. Their crimson robes swished as they labored with controlled, precise movements. It took a tremendous amount of time and effort to fashion a new Falchion, so whenever a soldier died, the Forgers remade the weapon and bestowed it on a student at the Agoge.

Aero remembered his Bonding Day well—how the forger had come to the school, bearing his Falchion. How he had taken the sacred oath, seized the hilt, and felt the weapon sink itself into him, melding with his flesh and his mind in a way that felt simultaneously invasive and exhilarating. Since that day, Aero had never let his Falchion out of his sight. But the Forgers did not just give—they also took.

Once a year, they came to the Agoge to select students to join their Order. They watched the students train and examined their test scores, but nobody knew what qualities they sought or why they chose certain students. Sometimes they picked kids with impressive test scores and poor combat records, but other times it was just the opposite. Even Aero—who had tried to decipher their ways for years—was left mystified.

One year they selected a boy named Xander from his class, though once he became a Forger, he left that name behind, along with any hope of becoming a soldier. The Forgers didn't use individual names, as their entire purpose was dedicated to their ancient science. They referred to each other only as brother or sister.

Suddenly, a warm voice cut through the foundry. "Well, if it isn't Captain Wright."

Aero recognized it right away. He turned to see the Forger who had bestowed his Falchion on him. He'd been old back then, but he was even older now, possibly the oldest of the bunch, though he did have some competition. He looked up from a strange apparatus. Like most things that had to do with the Foundry, its function eluded Aero. It was the size of a backpack and the same golden hue as the Falchions.

The Forger set it aside, crossed the room with a swishing of his robe, and came to a stop in front of Aero. He smiled, and his eyes flashed with youthful energy. "Captain, what brings you to the Foundry?"

Aero greeted him with a salute. "Supreme General Brillstein selected my unit to be the first boots on the ground, and we deploy as soon as the storms lift."

He tried to keep his voice devoid of emotion, but pride

could be heard coloring it, and underneath that, a little bit of self-consciousness. The Forger noticed it, but it didn't seem to bother him. A twinge of a smile pulled at his lips.

"The Supreme General is a wise man," he said. He did not elaborate, though Aero wished that he had. Now, he would probably spend the better part of the day, and maybe most of the night, dissecting his cryptic statement.

"So, let me see it," the Forger said.

Aero pulled his Falchion—in its default form—from the scabbard belted to his waist. The golden weapon shimmered and flashed as if delighted to be unsheathed. He offered it to the Forger, the only other person that he'd permit to touch his blade. The old man murmured as he examined it. "Very nice. Top notch craftsmanship . . . one of the best blades we've ever produced, no doubt about it."

With more strength and speed than seemed possible from somebody his age, he whipped the sword through the air. He shifted his gaze from the deadly weapon to Aero.

"How has it been responding to your commands?"

"Like it's directly wired into my brain," Aero replied.

"No delays? No glitches or hesitations?"

"Negative," Aero said. "Just this week, I triumphed over three more opponents in simulated battle, two of my soldiers and a captain from another combat unit. I'm still undefeated in Falchion-to-Falchion combat."

The Forger frowned. "*War is deception*," he quoted from their teachings. "You won't remain undefeated forever, mark my words."

Aero felt a chill, but before he could question him further, the Forger handed the Falchion back, hilt first. "Now, I want to see you morph it. First try . . . trident."

Aero felt his fingers encircling the hilt and thought—*Trident*. The golden metal morphed instantly, narrowing and elongating and then sprouting three sharp points.

"War hammer . . ." the Forger said.

Aero shifted the trident into a hefty, blunt hammer. It was an inelegant weapon, but it could inflict severe damage on an opponent. At the Agoge, the Drillmasters had schooled him endlessly on weapon forms.

"Labrys . . ." the Forger said.

Again, the Falchion responded to Aero's unspoken command, liquidly shifting and remaking itself into the double-headed ax. He whipped it through the air.

"Excellent response time," the Forger said. "You have talent, there's no doubt. It responds to your commands faster than most. Pity I didn't choose you from the Agoge when I had the chance. You know, I considered it. It kept me up for several nights."

Aero jerked his head up. "You wanted to . . . choose me?" He scanned the room, his gaze landing on the Forger formerly known as Xander. Instead of the uniform that he'd worn at the Agoge, he was dressed in a crimson robe. His head was shaved clean, exposing his pale scalp.

That could have been me, Aero thought.

The old Forger nodded. "Even back at the Agoge, your talent was unmistakable. Your instincts for battle were strong, but other students were equally capable. It was your connection with your Falchion that set you apart from the rest."

This caught Aero by surprise, but then understanding washed over him. Though he'd never spent much time thinking about it, the Forger was right—his Falchion did respond to his commands faster than others. "Then why didn't you select me?"

The Forger thought for a moment before responding. "I knew that you were meant for other things and your path lay elsewhere. Let's just say, it would have been selfish to claim you for our Order and prevent you from fulfilling your destiny."

"What do you mean—what destiny?"

The Forger frowned. "I shouldn't have spoken of it. Suffice it to say, I couldn't choose you. It would have gone against our teachings. You were meant to be a soldier."

The Forgers had many teachings, some of which overlapped with the Agoge, but many that did not. Usually, nobody outside their Order was privy to them. It was rare for the Forgers to speak of them to outsiders.

"Thanks . . . I think," Aero said. While the Forgers and the nature of their work had always fascinated him, he couldn't fathom not being a soldier.

"Be careful what you thank me for," the Forger said. "I fear that a long, dark path lies ahead for you. Trouble is brewing."

"Trouble," Aero repeated. "What kind of trouble?"

He wondered if the rumors had filtered down to the Foundry. Last night, he'd caught his soldiers gossiping in the barracks. A rumor was swirling around the ship that the Supreme General had chosen his unit out of nepotism—because Aero was his son.

"Now, don't listen to me," the Forger said with a dismissive wave of his hand. "These are just the worries of an old man who has seen too many years and spent most of them down here with the Falchions." He reached for Aero's weapon. "The station is free, so let's get it charged."

Before the Forger turned away, he admired the Falchion. "It's a thing of beauty, is it not?"

Both of their reflections were visible in the golden blade.

"The most beautiful thing in all of the world," Aero said.

The old man reached his gnarled hand up. "Just remember that your greatest weapon is up here," he said as he tapped him on the forehead. Then, he reached down and tapped him on the chest. "And in here. Don't ever forget that."

"Yes, sir," Aero said, even though he didn't agree. The Falchion was undoubtedly his greatest weapon. And maybe his head, for it issued the commands.

But what did his heart have to do with any of this?

The Forger swished over to a charging station and set the Falchion over a golden platform, where it levitated on thin air. He manipulated a few levers. A force field entombed the weapon, and a greenish vapor—almost like mist—filtered into the chamber.

While Aero waited for his weapon to charge, he mulled the old man's words over in his head. He knew that he should feel honored that they'd almost chosen him to join their Order, but it only added to his confusion. He'd always believed that his destiny to become a soldier was a certain thing, with no other paths that he might have taken.

A fixed, unchanging, completely undeniable thing.

Now he realized—as his Falchion liquidly shifted and pooled in the transparent enclosure—that his destiny was a lot more like his weapon:

A constantly changing, constantly shifting, malleable thing.

And, for the first time, he realized that he didn't know what his future held. He'd never dreamed that his unit would be the first people to set foot on Earth since their ancestors had fled from it over a millennium ago, but his father had chosen them. *The Supreme General is a wise man*, the Forger had said. But he had also cautioned that trouble was brewing—and that a long, dark path lay ahead.

Aero knew that this should have frightened him—this sudden uncertainty in the midst of a life that had always felt so predetermined. But it didn't, not even a little bit. Rather, it made him feel happy—the happiest that he'd felt in a long time, maybe since he was five years old. *Happiness*, he mused. It was a strange sensation.

A few minutes later, the Forger returned with his Falchion. Aero gripped the hilt and felt the fresh charge surging through the blade. It traveled up his arm, through his central nervous system, and zapped his neural synapses. He tested the weapon out, whipping it through the air. It cut and shifted effortlessly under his direction.

Now he was ready for what came next.

Whatever that may be.

Chapter 19
IT'S BETTER IF YOU STINK

Myra Jackson

News of Bishop's arrest had spread through the colony like a new batch of firewater. It cast a shadow over Myra's first day as an apprentice.

Though the Engineering Room clanked and hummed along and the Engineers went about their duties, Myra could sense the unease in their clipped voices, in the absence of laughter and razzing, and in the way that Royston kept dropping his tools, cursing his clumsy hands, when usually his grip was ironclad. Her father stayed in his office with the door closed and locked. He never isolated himself that way, not during the day, when his workers might need his help or just a kind word of encouragement.

Last night, after Myra returned home and informed him of Bishop's arrest, he headed straight for the door, leaving her with an admonishment to stay put. "But Papa, you can't go," she protested. "The Head Patroller ordered everybody to stay home—"

He silenced her with a distracted wave.

"Myra, I've got enough on my mind without you giving me trouble, too. Please, just watch your brother, and I'll be home before the lights go out, I promise."

His words stung, but they did their job. She didn't try to stop him again. Instead, she watched him leave with fear gnawing at her insides. She did her best to comfort Tinker, who was also worried. In the dim glow of evening, she stayed awake in her bunk, waiting for the extinguishing of the lights or the slurping of the compartment door, whichever happened first. Her father beat the lights and made it home before curfew.

But just barely.

o o o

"Here, put these on," Myra said.

She thrust the coveralls and rubber boots at Kaleb. She'd just arrived home from work to find him lounging on her sofa. As usual, he was dressed in freshly laundered clothes that smelled like perfume—the kind that only the Plenus got in their Victus—which simply would not do, not if he wanted to pass for an Engineering pledge.

Kaleb sniffed the coveralls and grimaced. "These reek to the Holy Sea!" He held them out at arm's length. "Don't you have a less . . . revolting pair?"

Tinker let out a laugh from the kitchen, where he was busy cooking dinner. He stirred a pot of gingery fish stew with a wooden spoon. It smelled delicious.

"Well, it's better if you stink," Myra said. "Engineers are a dirty bunch, you know that. You can't exactly waltz in there smelling like perfume, now can you?"

"You may have a point—but I don't have to like it."

He made a show of pulling off his tunic, revealing his chiseled torso. Making matters worse, he slipped off his trousers and stood there—in the middle of her living space—in only his undergarments. Their eyes met, and he flashed a devilish grin.

"I can keep my clean undies, can't I?"

Myra felt blood rushing to her cheeks. "Uh . . . right.

Nobody can see those anyway, so I guess it's fine . . ." She dragged her eyes off Kaleb and distracted herself by running through their plan.

"Tinker, they're Factum? You're positive?"

"Yup, Velma and Walter Thompson," he reported. "She's Dissemination and he's Janitorial. They have two daughters, Celia and Hilda. They're First Year and Third Year. I asked around school, and eventually somebody knew who lived there."

"That's perfect—they don't know us."

Once Kaleb was fully clothed again, Myra smeared his exposed skin—his face, neck, and hands—with axle grease. She handed him a cap, which he pulled low over his brow. His disguise in place, he stood up and bent his knees, testing out the coveralls.

"So . . . do I look as hideous as you hoped?" he asked.

Myra surveyed her handiwork. "Tinker, what do you think?"

He looked over from the kitchen. "Wow, I don't even recognize him! He does look hideous."

Satisfied, Kaleb started for the compartment door, but Myra stopped him. She aimed her finger at her newly issued tool rig. It was a perk of her apprentice status. The metal box was stuffed to the brim with heavy-duty tools.

"Not so fast, pledge—you have to carry that."

His gaze fell on the tool rig, and he frowned.

Not waiting for him to object, she hurried to the door, triggered the scanner, and stepped into the corridor. It was packed with Factum trudging home from work. Myra entered the fray and started down the passageway. Her family lived in the 200 section; they were headed for Compartment 715.

Kaleb lumbered behind her, muttering curses every time the tool rig bumped his shin. She glanced back and couldn't help but grin.

"What're you smiling at?" he grumbled.

"Oh, I think I like you this way."

"What . . . way?"

She arched her eyebrow. "A little bit . . . scruffy."

He looked surprised then pleased by her comment. She turned back around and they continued on. As they rounded the next bend, people pushed up against her in a logjam. "Hey, can you tell what's going on up there?" she whispered to Kaleb.

He was taller and could see over the crowd, but before he could answer, a loud voice reverberated down the corridor. "Factum, Hockers, this is a checkpoint!" Jasper barked. "New security measures, by order of the Synod! For your protection and safety!"

Myra tried to slow her progress, but the crowd kept sweeping her forward. Even though they weren't in possession of anything illegal, aside from the work order that she'd forged to get them into the compartment, Kaleb's disguise could provoke unwanted attention. "A checkpoint?" she hissed to him. "Since when do they have checkpoints?"

"Since they arrested Bishop?" he whispered back.

"Padre Flavius must be cracking down."

Kaleb caught her eye. "Think he knows about, well, you know . . ."

"No idea, but we have to assume the worst. It would certainly explain the checkpoint. Maybe he's looking for it."

Kaleb nodded. "Then let's get out of here."

They turned to leave, but another Patroller stepped in front of them and blocked their progress. It was Patroller Bates. A menacing smile stretched across his pudgy face.

"Heathen, just where do you think you're going?"

"Uh, nowhere, sir . . ."

He placed his hand on his pipe. "Get into line now—or else."

Patroller Bates forced Myra and Kaleb into the line for the checkpoint. Myra didn't dare resist. When she'd been locked up in the Pen, he'd been one of her cruelest captors. Ahead of them, Factum and Hockers stripped off their jackets and sandals to be patted down, opened their rucksacks, and allowed the Patrollers to search their carts.

Jasper paced up and down the line. "Factum and Hockers, this is a checkpoint! Open your bags and carts! Prepare to be searched! For your protection and safety!"

Myra glanced nervously at Kaleb. He was still in his disguise—the hat and dirty coveralls—and his face was smeared with black grease. But it wouldn't hold up under close scrutiny. Somebody was bound to recognize him.

Jasper spotted Myra in the crowd. "Heathen, line up! Arms above your head!"

He ambled over to her, enjoying himself. "Ever been . . . patted down?" he whispered, his wet breath kissing her earlobe. It stunk of spoiled fish and firewater.

She cast her eyes down, willing herself not to tell him off. Her mind flashed back to when they'd taken her to the Pen. She'd endured pat downs . . . and worse.

"Yup . . . I mean, of course, sir."

"Spread your legs, nice and wide," he ordered. He ran his hands over her body. She felt his fingers lingering on her breasts and then a painful pinch. She gasped, but bit down on her tongue to keep from resisting.

"Nice . . . for a heathen," Jasper slurred.

Revulsion rose up in her and tears sprung to her eyes, but she stayed put. She wanted to keep his attention on her—and not Kaleb. She risked a glance at him and saw the furious expression on his face. *Don't try anything stupid*, she mouthed to him. He obeyed, but he didn't look happy about it.

Jasper's hands traced over her hips and jabbed at her crotch. She heard something crinkle in her pocket. Fear seized her heart, and she tried to twist away, but Jasper had her pinned. He yanked it from her pocket, his eyes sweeping over the crumpled page.

"Well, well, what do we have here?"

"Uh, just a work order, sir," Myra said. "There's a gas leak."

"Compartment 7-1-5," he read. "Thompson residence."

"That's right, we're headed there now."

Jasper looked up, his eyes falling on Kaleb. "And who do we have here?"

"Just my pledge, sir," Myra said.

"Name, Engine Rat?" Jasper barked at Kaleb.

"Uh . . . it's . . . Quentin . . . uh . . . "

Jasper gripped his pipe. "Rat got your tongue, boy?"

"No, sir! It's Quentin . . . Reed."

Jasper narrowed his eyes. He patted Kaleb down and, finding nothing, started rifling through the tool rig. As he straightened up, something caught his attention. Jasper took a step toward Kaleb and sniffed him. He leaned in closer, sniffed again.

"Pledge, is that . . . perfume?"

"Uh, no, sir," Kaleb said. "Must be . . . a mistake."

Jasper scowled. "Only Plenus get perfume! Trading in the black market is a crime, boy. How'd you like to smell the Pen? It stinks like piss down there."

"Don't think I'd like it one bit, sir."

"And what's that muck on your face?"

"Grease, sir. Must be from work."

"Wipe it off, Engine Rat."

Jasper's hand twitched over his pipe, making Myra's heart lurch in her chest. It wouldn't take much for him to arrest them. Clumsily—and as slowly as possible—Kaleb started wiping his face with his sleeve. Jasper started to look annoyed.

"Faster, boy! Not like I have all bloody day."

Suddenly, a scuffle broke out ahead of them.

"Hey, that's mine!" a Hocker yelled.

Myra turned to see Patroller Bates pocketing something shiny. It looked like a flask of firewater.

"Bloody thief, gimme that back!" the Hocker slurred drunkenly. He took a slow motion swing at Bates, but the Patroller easily ducked it. He pulled out his pipe and went to work on the man. Myra started to feel sick to her stomach. The crowd surged up behind her and Kaleb for a better view of the action. When Bates stepped back, the Hocker was immobile and drenched with blood. His body looked . . . broken.

Bates dabbed his face with a handkerchief, wiping away the blood like it was nothing more troublesome than sweat. "Patroller Waters, cart him to the Pen!"

"Yes, sir!" Jasper said. He thrust the work order at Myra and waved them through the checkpoint. "Move along, Factum," he ordered. "Move along."

They didn't need to be told twice. Myra and Kaleb hurried away down the corridor. They didn't dare breathe a word until they were well out of sight of the checkpoint. The area ahead was mostly deserted due to the bottleneck behind them.

"Holy Sea, that was close," Myra whispered. Her heart was still pounding dully in her chest, but that wasn't the worst of it. She felt violated by Jasper's touch.

"Too close," Kaleb said.

"Jasper saw the work order and the compartment number. What if he decides to check it out? He'll realize it's forged and that nobody reported a gas leak."

"And that there's no Quentin Reed."

"Also, it won't take him long to trace the number back to Sari Wade. What if he informs the Synod? Padre Flavius will figure out that we're after the Beacon."

"Then we have to hurry," Kaleb said.

"And hope that Jasper is as dumb as he looks?"

"Well, we might be in luck there."

This provoked a smile from Myra—a small one. They may not have their freedom, she thought, or even enough to eat in many cases, but at least they still had a sense of humor, and not even Padre Flavius could rob them of that.

A few minutes later, they arrived at Compartment 715 and rang the bell. An electronic chime emanated from behind the door. She heard the shuffling of feet and muffled voices. She looked back, half expecting Jasper and a group of Patrollers to come charging after them. A second later, the door dilated to reveal a middle-aged woman.

"Can I help you?" the woman said. Her clothes looked nicer than most Factum and her sandals less worn. The perks of a Dissemination job.

Behind her in the living space, Myra glimpsed two girls playing with a handmade doll, the kind the Hockers traded at the Souk. A man dressed in filthy coveralls was slumped back on the sofa, her husband most likely. Some kind of spicy fish stew was bubbling away in the kitchen, filling the compact space with its pungent aroma.

"Ma'am, is this Compartment *7-1-5*?" Myra said in her best official voice. She pretended to consult the work order. "Thompson residence?"

"Yes, that's right. I'm Velma Thompson."

Myra handed her the paperwork. "Mrs. Thompson, we're from Engineering. We've traced a gas leak back to your compartment, and we're here to repair it."

"A gas leak?" Velma repeated, absently scanning the work order. She stepped out of the way to let them inside. "Right, yes, of course. Come right in."

"Velma, who is it?" her husband yelled from the sofa. Myra could detect the faint odor of bleach and cleaning chemicals wafting off him.

"Walter, they're from Engineering. They say there's a gas leak."

He trudged over and snatched the work order from his wife. "A gas leak, huh?" he said, scrutinizing the paperwork.

"That's right," Myra said. "We'd like to start in the bedrooms, if possible."

Velma steepled her fingertips under her chin. Unlike her husband's rough, calloused hands, hers looked soft and unblemished. "Is it serious?"

"Well, it could ignite and blow up the whole sector," Myra said with a straight face. "Does that count as serious?" Out of the corner of her eye, she caught Kaleb stifling a grin. She kicked his shin to make him cut it out. He winced and stopped smiling.

"Oh my, thank the Oracle you're here!" Velma said.

Her husband nodded his permission, and she led them to the back of the compartment. "This is our bedroom," Velma said. "You can start in here."

Myra shut and locked the door. The bedroom looked the same as every other bedroom in the colony, even down to the Synod-issued furniture. Two small bunks and two trunks took up the entirety of the space. Despite the sparse furnishings,

Myra felt a thrill just knowing that Sari Wade had lived within these four walls.

Kaleb set the tool rig down with a thud. Myra rifled through it, pulling out a drill, a crowbar, and a hammer. She fitted in a drill bit. "Just how much demolition are we talking about here?" Kaleb asked, warily eyeing the tools piling up at their feet.

Myra fired up the drill. It made a high-pitched whirring noise. Kaleb flinched away, inviting an eye roll from her. "As much as it takes. You can start by searching the furniture, checking the trunks for false bottoms, hidden panels, anything like that. And search the bunks. Don't forget the mattresses. I'm going to work on the walls first."

With that, she fired up the drill and started dismantling the wall panels.

o o o

Two and a half hours later, both Myra and Kaleb were drenched with sweat.

Kaleb had searched the bunks and the trunks and examined every object in the room, including Velma's figurines. Myra had searched behind the wall and ceiling panels and checked the floor for hidden compartments. But they hadn't found anything interesting, aside from a flask of firewater hidden under Walter's mattress.

"Well, that's it," Myra said as she screwed in the last wall panel. She wiped the sweat from her brow and sank to her knees. She was beyond exhausted.

"Should we try the other bedroom?" Kaleb started.

But then the automatic lights dimmed, signifying that day would soon transform into night. Myra scowled at the light fixtures. "The Holy Sea take these lights! If we could control them, maybe we could work later. And we can't come back tomorrow."

"Not with the checkpoint," Kaleb agreed. "It's too risky."

He followed her gaze to the ceiling, squinting at the lights. "Wait a second, I've got an idea!"

"Hurry up, spit it out."

"We have searched everywhere—except the automatic lights."

Myra leapt to her feet. "By the Oracle, you're right! They're one of the oldest things in this compartment. I can't believe I didn't think of them."

Kaleb smirked at her. "Well, they are your nemesis."

Using the drill, Myra went to work on the lights. She unscrewed the casing. The first two screws came out easily enough, but the third one had rusted into place. But she was used to working on ancient machines. With a little more effort, she pried it out and lifted off the covering. It resisted stubbornly, but with one last tug, it came away.

She set it aside and turned her attention to the fixture itself. At first glance, nothing looked out of the ordinary. The long, thin tubes glowed dimly. She felt around behind them, when suddenly her fingers brushed the outline of a panel.

Her breath caught in her throat. "Wait, I think there's something back here!"

"Well, what is it?" Kaleb whispered.

"Not sure yet, let me see."

She probed the panel, and, at her touch, it swung inward and divulged a secret compartment. She felt around inside, her fingers brushing up against a hard edge.

It shifted under her touch.

"Holy Sea . . . I found something!"

"Is it the Beacon?" Kaleb asked.

She fished the object out and examined it, her face falling.

"No, I don't think so," she said, her voice thick with disappointment. "Looks like a book of some sort."

Dust obscured the cover. She brushed it off, slowly uncovering a drawing. It depicted a mermaid with flowing red hair swimming through the ocean. She read the text printed just above it: "*The Little Mermaid* by Hans Christian Anderson."

Her eyes widened. She knew this story—knew it very well.

She opened the stiff cover. The spine crackled as if it hadn't been manipulated in a long time. She thumbed through the pages. Detailed illustrations accompanied the text, still vivid despite their age. She read the first paragraph.

"Far out in the ocean, where the water is as blue as the prettiest cornflower, and clear as crystal, it is very, very deep; so deep, indeed, that no cable could fathom it: many church steeples, piled one upon another, would not reach from the ground beneath to the surface of the water above. There dwell the Sea King and his subjects . . ."

She traced her finger over a drawing of a flower, following the delicate curve of its bright blue petals. *So that's a cornflower*, she thought with a shiver.

"Myra, you know this book, don't you?" Kaleb said. "It sounds like that story you told our class, the one that got you expelled."

"Yeah, I think it's the same one," Myra said.

"But . . . how is that possible?"

She felt that familiar tug of longing, accompanied by an undercurrent of grief. "My mother used to tell it to me. It was my favorite bedtime story."

"Your mother? Then how'd she know it?"

"Well, I didn't mention this before because . . . I guess it didn't seem important at the time . . . but I think she might be descended from the Wade family. Maybe that explains why she knew this story? Maybe the story got passed down through her family?"

Kaleb's gaze shifted to the book. "Do you think it belonged to Sari?"

"I don't know, but it's certainly old enough," she said. She started flipping through the book. "These pages feel like they could fall apart in my hands."

When she reached the very last page, her breath caught in her throat. "Wait, there's an inscription!"

Kaleb craned his neck to see the page. "What does it say?"

"For you who seek enlightenment, you have taken the first step," Myra read in a hushed voice. "I've hidden the Beacon in a safe place to protect it from the Synod. They're hell-bent on destroying everything my father worked so hard to build—that we all worked to build. My time is running short now—they will be here any minute.

Hidden in a city of old,
Untouched by the Doom,
It is always damp and cold.
There lies the buried treasure
That will light the way home,
So that the world that ended
May be remade once more.

"Good luck—you're going to need it," Myra finished reading. "Yours truly, Sari Wade." Below her name, she had scrawled the date in her looping cursive:

"May 7, 65 P.D."

"Sixty-five Post Doom," Kaleb said. "It did belong to her!"

They both stared at the inscription. Myra couldn't believe that her father's hunch had proven correct. Kaleb scanned the riddle, his brow furrowed in thought.

"What do you suppose that means?"

Myra frowned at the cryptic message. "No bloody clue."

Suddenly, the automatic lights dimmed even more, casting the room into shadow. This was followed by a sharp knock. "Almost finished?" Velma called through the door.

Myra started, nearly dropping the book. "Uh, yes, we just finished patching it up!"

"Oh, thank the Oracle," Velma said. "I'm so glad you found it."

Me too, Myra thought, though she was referring to Sari Wade's book.

Kaleb peered over her shoulder. "What do we do about the checkpoint?" he whispered. "That book is contraband—it's highly forbidden. They'd toss us straight into the Pen. They probably wouldn't even bother with a trial this time."

"Before they put us out to sea," Myra said feeling her chest constrict. She thought for a second. "We hide the book in the secret room. We're just lucky the 'Trollers got us coming—and not going. Or else we'd be in real trouble."

Her eyes skimmed the inscription. The idea of the book falling into the wrong hands terrified her. If Padre Flavius found the Beacon first, he'd destroy it—and any chance they had of returning to the Surface.

Good luck—you're going to need it.

Those were Sari Wade's words, and now Myra realized just how true they were. They needed all the luck they could get if they were going to find the Beacon in time.

PART III
THE BEACONS

May it be a light to you in dark places, when all other lights go out.

—J.R.R. Tolkien, *The Fellowship of the Ring*

Ignoring isn't the same as ignorance, you have to work at it.

—Margaret Atwood, *The Handmaid's Tale*

Chapter 20

RELATIONS OF HEATHENS

The Synod

"Arrest the daughters."

"Both of them?"

The leader's face contorted into a scowl. "I think I made myself perfectly clear." His voice wavered, barely containing the fury.

"But are you sure that's prudent?" said another. "Many Factum and Hockers won't like it. And with the new checkpoints and random searches, they're growing restless. We've had a few . . . situations. And, well, they seem fond of their children."

"It's for their own safety and protection. You know that."

"Of course, sir," the man backtracked.

"We shouldn't have waited two days. That was a grievous error. If you can't handle the business of this Synod, then perhaps we should discuss replacements."

"No, no, that won't be necessary."

The leader's eyes lingered on his face. "I've consulted the Oracle," the leader said eventually. "They're abominations—the spawn of heathens. May the Holy Sea claim that whole cursed family. Arrest them, throw them in the Pen, torture them a little, and then see how their father feels about talking."

"By the Oracle, it will be done."

"Aye," the other five voices echoed.

There was a sharp rap on the locked door. Silence engulfed the chamber. The leader opened it to reveal a man dressed in black. "Well, what have you found?"

The Head Patroller handed over a thick stack of pictures. "We ransacked Bishop's compartment. As we suspected, he'd hidden them. We had to pry off the wall panels, but there they were, along with a stash of firewater."

The leader's lips twisted with pleasure as he fanned the images out in his palm. His eyes shifted from the girl's face to her wrist, where a golden armlet was fastened.

"The Beacon," he said under his breath. The other members swirled their hands over their chests. His eyes darted from the images to the man in black.

"Head Patroller, I've got a job for you."

Chapter 21
ENEMIES CLOSER

Myra Jackson

Myra spent her second day as an apprentice working on a ruptured water main in Sector 8, which housed the Docks that opened to the sea.

When she arrived in the sector, she took in its pitiful state. Nobody worked here anymore, not since the submersibles were destroyed in the Great Purging. The floors were covered with a thick layer of dust. It seemed like even Janitorial neglected it now. A large area had been sectioned off with thick tarps. The signs posted above it read:

DANGER:
Structurally Unsound

NO TRESPASSING:
By Order of Engineering

Many years ago, the Master Engineers had deemed the area in danger of collapse. Though it was slated for restoration, it always seemed to fall to the bottom of the long list, as the sector was no longer considered vital to the functioning of the colony. Instead, Engineering just performed triage whenever leaks sprang up and threatened to flood it.

Before she got to work, Myra peered into one of the portals, meant to house a large submarine. It was dotted with circular windows. In the halo cast by the exterior lights, the landscape looked rocky, desolate, and bereft of life. But that was only an illusion. Most life-forms were skilled at staying out of the reach of the lights. The reality was that the water teemed and shuddered with the vibrations of the living—the gelatinous and the transparent and the bioluminescent—all tossed together in the primordial sea.

All of this valuable space that once sheltered a mighty fleet of submersibles, Myra thought, *now has only one terrible purpose*. She wondered how many people had lost their lives here—how many heathens Padre Flavius had forced into these portals, exposing their fragile bodies to the incredible and terrible power of the sea. *Too many to count*, she decided.

This made her feel sad.

Her thoughts drifted to her father. He'd been holed up in his office all morning with the door shut. The only visitor he'd received was Decker. She thought of his plans for the submersible. She'd never spent much time thinking about what lay beyond the thick walls of their colony. Not only was it futile to speculate about, since they had no way to leave, but it was also dangerous, especially with Padre Flavius running things.

But the what ifs ran through her head now. And for the first time she thought:

What if I could make my father take me?

Of course, it was unlikely that she could convince him—he would claim it was too risky. But what if she found the Beacon first? Not only would that prove she was worthy of being included on such a voyage, but it would also give her a bargaining chip. Once the Beacon bonded with a Carrier, it could only be removed after that person died.

So what if she bonded with the Beacon?

In this way, as Myra gazed into the portal that opened to the sea, a plan began to sprout and take root and blossom in her mind. Now she was more determined than ever to find the Beacon, if only to prevent her father from leaving her behind.

○ ○ ○

When Myra returned to the Engineering Room, Royston cornered her by the supply closet. His shadow fell over her, blocking out the automatic lights. "How'd it go in Sector 8?" he said.

She looked up from packing her tool rig. Her clothes were soaking wet, and she was running late. "Another gusher," she said. "We all got drenched."

He nodded, but then his face turned serious. "Well, you had a visitor today."

Her heart thumped in her chest. "Uh, really?" she managed. "Who was it?"

"Patroller Waters stopped by to see you."

Royston's eyes were glued to her face. She tried to keep it blank, even though her heart was thudding in her throat.

"Right, what did he want?"

"Something about a work order for a gas leak."

Fear prickled at her scalp and sent shivers gushing through her body. "That's strange; since when do 'Trollers care about gas leaks?"

"Funny, I asked him the same thing."

"Did he say anything else?"

Royston nodded. "He was looking for a pledge named Quentin Reed. Odd, since there's nobody by that name down here. He claimed the boy worked for you, said he stopped you at a checkpoint." Royston scratched his head. "Know anything about that?"

Myra swallowed hard. "Uh, nope," she said quickly. A little too quickly. She busied herself with stashing her rig in the closet. "So . . . what'd you tell him?"

"That I've got more bloody gas leaks than I know what to do with," he said. "I explained about the old pipes, and how they like to explode on occasion. Offered to give him a demonstration if he'd like to stick around. Alas, he wasn't interested."

Myra tensed. "That all?"

A twinkle lit up Royston's eyes. "Oh, and that of course I knew Quentin, said he was fixing a sewer rupture in Sector 10, under your supervision. Awful when that happens, just awful. I made sure to mention the stink and how it gets everywhere. He left pretty quickly after that."

She couldn't believe it—he'd lied to a Patroller to protect her.

"Look, I don't like to pry, you know that," Royston said. "Your business is your business, and these are strange times. But anything you want to tell me?"

She looked down. "Nope . . . nothing really."

"Well, I'm here, if you change your mind."

He turned to go. The Engineering Room was nearly empty.

"Oh, and Myra," he called back over his shoulder. "The 'Troller may have left—but he'll be back, mark my words. He's one determined bastard."

o o o

Light flooded into the pipe, chasing out the darkness.

Over the soft hiss of air and the steady drip, drip, drip of water, Myra heard voices. She headed straight for them until the pipe ended, and then she leapt from its mouth and landed on the ground in a crouch. Her eyes grazed over the people already gathered in the secret room—Rickard, Kaleb, Paige, and Tinker.

"You're late," Paige said in lieu of hello.

"More checkpoints," Myra said, still out of breath from her jaunt through the corridors. "I had to take a roundabout route. Also, I got held up at work."

"Another water leak?" Paige guessed.

"Yup, but that's not what made me late—Jasper stopped by."

Kaleb paled. "What did he want?"

"He was asking questions about a gas leak and a pledge named Quentin Reed. Royston covered for me, but he'll be back. And with friends, I'll wager."

"He knows," Kaleb said.

"He suspects," Paige cut in. "It's different."

"Either way—it's not good," Myra said.

Paige set her lips. "Then we have to hurry."

Myra retrieved Sari Wade's book from its hiding place inside a pipe while Tinker pulled a blanket out of his rucksack and spread it out on the floor. They camped in a circle around the flashlights and emptied their pockets. Sweetfish, cookies, apples, dried seaweed, and rice crackers piled up. Rickard produced a flask of firewater and took a pull, grimacing as it blazed down his throat. They didn't call it firewater for nothing. He passed the flask around.

"Where'd you get this?" Kaleb said and threw back a shot.

Rickard grinned. "Siphoned it off my father's stash. The 'Trollers are supposed to confiscate the stuff and destroy it, but really, they just keep it for themselves."

"That's illegal," Paige said.

"Or as I like to call it—fun. Wouldn't kill you to have a little."

Paige shot Rickard a disapproving look, but she didn't refuse the flask. She took a dainty sip and passed it to Myra. As the fiery liquid hit her stomach, Myra felt the tight knot that had formed relent slightly. *Liquid courage*, she thought, choking down another shot. She handed the flask back to Rickard and flipped to the inscription in the book.

At the sight of the loopy cursive, her vision blurred and her head throbbed with dullish pain, but she forced herself to read the riddle again for the hundredth time, just in case they'd overlooked something. Her voice reverberated through the room:

HIDDEN IN A CITY OF OLD,
UNTOUCHED BY THE DOOM,
IT IS ALWAYS DAMP AND COLD.
THERE LIES THE BURIED TREASURE
THAT WILL LIGHT THE WAY HOME,
SO THAT THE WORLD THAT ENDED
MAY BE REMADE ONCE MORE.

Paige pulled out a notebook and poised her pen over the blank page. "Well, let's start at the beginning, shall we? *Hidden in a city of old—*"

"Who made her the leader?" Rickard said.

"You want do it, Lynch?" Paige shot back.

"Enough," Myra cut in. "We're wasting time."

Tinker tapped away on his computer. "Definition of city," he said, his eyes glued to the screen. He'd downloaded the dictionary from the big computer. "A sizable human dwelling with commerce and culture," he read. "A vital, important, large-sized town."

They considered this question as the flask wound its way around the circle again, though Myra made sure it bypassed Tinker.

Kaleb took a swig and grimaced. "I'll bet she means our colony. It's a city, right?"

"Maybe," Tinker said. "But it's not old, or at least, it wasn't when she wrote that. I think she's referring to a city on the Surface."

"But how'd she hide the Beacon up there?" Kaleb said.

Paige nodded. "It would be impossible. And if she does mean a city on the Surface, then how could it be untouched by the Doom? It just doesn't make any sense."

A cryptic smile pulled at Tinker's lips. "That's why it's a riddle." He tapped and then read: "Definition of riddle, a statement that is challenging or perplexing to understand; a conundrum; an enigma."

"Well, if she meant to be perplexing, then she certainly succeeded," Myra said with a frustrated sigh. She got no argument there. They continued debating the meaning of the riddle for another two hours with little progress until the flashlights started to dim. The batteries were running low. Myra stifled a yawn and shut the book.

"Meet back here tomorrow?" she said.

Paige exchanged a glance with Rickard and Kaleb. "Uh, right, we can't tomorrow."

"Why not . . . " Myra started but then remembered. *The Initium Ceremony*. She'd been so focused on the Beacon that it had completely slipped her mind. If not for her expulsion, then it would have been her graduation, too. "It's official—I'm a bad friend."

"Not true, Jackson," Paige said. "Just preoccupied, like we all are."

"Understatement of the century," Myra said. She busied herself with putting the book away. "Time flies—it's tomorrow afternoon, isn't it?"

"Noon," Paige said. "At the Church."

Though she stated the location, it was unnecessary. The ceremony was always held in the Church since it was the only gathering place large enough to accommodate the graduating students, their families, the heads of the trades, and the Plenus.

"Well, have you made your decisions?" Myra said.

Paige bit her lower lip. "I'm ninety percent sure."

"The Infirmary?" Myra said.

Paige nodded. "I should just commit already, stop agonizing."

"Yup, agonizing is for suckers," Rickard said and took a swig from the flask. His cheeks had acquired a rosy glow. "I already decided—I'm pledging to the Patrollers."

Myra arched her eyebrow. "A 'Troller, huh?"

He put on a menacing face. "That firewater I smell on your breath? I'll toss you in the Pen if you don't hand it over!"

They clapped at his convincing performance. He took a bow and downed another shot, but then turned serious. "Though, I was thinking—"

"Never a good idea, Lynch," Paige said.

"Hey, I think all the time."

"Not very hard."

Rickard scowled, but then finished. "I was thinking . . . I could keep an eye out for us. Like spy on them, since I'll be on the inside, working right under their noses."

Myra nodded once. "Friends close—enemies closer."

"Exactly," Rickard said.

"That's a great idea."

Everybody's attention turned to Kaleb, who'd been quiet ever since the topic of the ceremony came up. *Unusually quiet,* now that Myra thought about it. She caught his eye.

"So . . . are you?" she asked him.

He met her gaze and held it.

"Am I what?"

"Gonna pledge to the Synod?"

Pain flashed across Kaleb's face. The expression looked strange on him, unnatural even. While the trades accepted all pledges, regardless of their parents' status, only the children of Plenus could pledge to the Synod. It was another second before he spoke.

"I always thought that I'd follow in my father's footsteps."

"Thought," Myra said. "Past tense."

Kaleb didn't deny it.

"You're having doubts?" Paige said.

"Well, that's one way to put it."

"What's on your mind, man?" Rickard said, passing the flask to Kaleb, who accepted it gratefully and took a big swallow. "What they did to Myra?"

Kaleb wiped his lips. "That and everything else. Now, I'm thinking maybe Dissemination, or even Farming might be safer choices. I'd like growing things, I think. And being Factum isn't so bad, really, if you think about it."

"Nothing is safe," Myra said. "Not anymore."

Kaleb's eyes locked onto her. They were bloodshot and shadowed by dark circles. Myra could see the angst and the dread buried in them. He really had been struggling with this decision, she realized. It must have been keeping him up at night.

"Sorry, that was harsh," she said.

"Don't ever apologize for speaking the truth," he said. "I guess I just hate the idea of pledging my life to them when they're prepared to sit on their hands and watch us all suffocate to death."

"They're not just sitting on their hands," Myra said. "They're sacrificing more people to lessen the burden on the system and prevent another Doom. My father said as much. And, well, there's really only one word for that . . ." she trailed off.

"Murder," Kaleb said under his breath. "Trust me, I can't even look at my father anymore without thinking about it, and it's driving me crazy. He knows something is wrong, but I've been avoiding him, leaving early, coming home late."

Myra rested her hand on his shoulder and squeezed. "I hate to say this, especially since I know what it feels like to not have a choice, but you have to pledge to the Synod. Your father's already suspicious. If you choose another trade and become Factum, won't he be angry and start asking questions . . . and maybe even open an investigation?"

"You're right, it would infuriate him."

"Well, we can't take that chance, right? We all have to do everything we can if we're going to survive beyond the next few months."

Kaleb exhaled and clenched his fists together. His knuckles turned white. He looked like he was going to refuse, but then the episode seemed to subside.

"Fine, I'll do it," he said through gritted teeth. "I'll pledge to the Synod."

He said those last two words with so much rancor that it made Myra shudder. Graduating students were supposed to take pride in where they pledged, not dread it. Myra hoped that he could at least pretend to be excited tomorrow. She didn't want his father—or any of the Plenus, for that matter—to suspect that something was amiss.

They were already in enough danger.

Chapter 22

THE RED PLANET

Captain Aero Wright

"This isn't Earth—this is Mars."

Clad in a lightweight spacesuit, Aero stood in a swirl of red dust. Everything about this world looked enflamed and murky. Even the sky above him glowed with fierce light, as if a red-tinted filter had been placed over the sun. As he spoke, he paced up and down the row of his soldiers. His left hand rested lightly on the hilt of his Falchion.

"Or rather, this is a simulation of Mars," he said. That meant that they weren't really standing on the Red Planet—each soldier was actually locked inside a simulation chamber on the ship—but it felt real all the same.

"The Majors haven't been able to get a clean read on Earth's surface due to the storms. I'm hoping they'll lift soon; I don't want to go in blind. But a good soldier is prepared, no matter what the circumstances." Aero gestured to the rocky, desolate terrain surrounding them. "Mars is the closest approximation of Earth Post Doom."

An uneasy rumble tore through his soldiers.

"According to our calculations, Earth should have a more

intact atmosphere with breathable oxygen," Aero continued. "But the terrain should appear similar. I adjusted the gravitational force and atmosphere of Mars so we could run test drills today."

He watched as Zakkay's eyes shifted to the vista and narrowed. He was studying the remains of the Third Continuum, as they had existed the last time their ship had been in the vicinity of the Red Planet. Aero had come across this rendering in the computer's archives. In the hazy distance, a clear dome stretched up toward the sky, entombing a city of towering skyscrapers. They appeared to be in a state of decay. Encircling the buildings, Aero glimpsed the slums where the underclass had lived.

"In the first drill, we'll encounter survivors from another colony, and they'll prove hostile. Therefore, this will be a battle sequence." He gestured for his soldiers to split into two groups. "Lieutenant Jordan will lead the insurgents; I'll command the other side."

Wren grinned and sidled over to lead her section of fifteen soldiers. When Aero divided them up, he made sure that Zakkay was on his team. *Keep your allies close and your enemies closer*. This was another of their teachings.

"Oh, and I've set the simulation controls to wound."

This got his soldiers' attention. Nervous murmurs ran through the unit. Usually, when they ran simulations, the safety controls were fully engaged, preventing a soldier from sustaining even a scratch in the real world. Aero hadn't set them to kill, so there was still a level of protection. Nobody would die today. But he wanted his soldiers to be on their toes.

Aero ran his thumb over the stump where his pinky finger used to be. Consequences, even painful ones, were how you learned.

"We'll be fighting only with Falchions today—not blasters," Aero said. "Even if we encounter hostile survivors on our deployment, the Supreme General has ordered that they be taken alive for questioning, is that understood?"

"Yes, sir!" came the reply from his soldiers.

In a smooth motion, Aero unsheathed his Falchion and gestured in the direction of the Third Continuum. "Soldiers, forward march!" he ordered his group.

They formed up into ranks and paraded after him over the rocky terrain, their boots kicking up puffs of red dust. Their role was to explore the surface and search for survivors. Wren and her soldiers' role was that of the insurgents.

Soon they would launch their attack.

o o o

Aero led his soldiers over the surface of Mars.

They neared the outskirts of the Third Continuum. Aero squinted against the sun at what remained of the once magnificent colony. Hundreds of years ago, there had been paved roads crisscrossing the surface for robotic vehicles that mined precious minerals and delivered them to the enclosed city. But the red sand had consumed them long ago. Aero marveled at how a civilization—which took hundreds and hundreds of years to rise up from the lifeless dust and grow and evolve—could be wiped out in one fell swoop.

Right when his unit passed a jagged rock formation, which blocked out the sun and cast the area into shadow, Wren sprung her attack. Her soldiers leapt from behind the rocks, their Falchions unsheathed and giving off a golden glow even in the scarlet light.

But Aero was ready for the attack. He raised his Falchion and morphed it into a broadsword, just in time to meet Tristan's Falchion, in the shape of a katana, otherwise known as a Japanese samurai sword. *Clang!* A shower of golden sparks erupted from the point where they connected. Aero ducked and spun away. Tristan—a spry boy with a fierce fighting style—advanced on him again, and Aero parried again.

Around him, his soldiers were locked in furious battle. The shuffling of boots and clanging of Falchions was deafening. Dust kicked up by the soldiers clogged the air, making it hard to breathe and even harder to see.

Out of the corner of his eye, Aero saw Zakkay fighting

Starling. He fought with a battle-ax while she swung a spiked mace. She was winning; Zakkay was retreating. She backed him up against the rock formation. Desperately, Zakkay tried to morph his Falchion into a shield, but he hesitated; he loathed going on the defensive. It was only for a second, but that was enough—his Falchion melted down into a puddle of gold.

The liquid metal pooled at his feet.

Zakkay let out a piteous wail and sank to his knees. The bond had been severed. Now the Forgers would have to remake the weapon. *The pain of losing one's Falchion must be excruciating,* Aero thought, though he didn't know from experience. He'd never suffered indecision in the heat of battle; his Falchion had never melted down.

In the face of Zakkay's surrender, Starling halted her attack. The computer took note of his despondent state, and Zakkay began to flicker and fade before their eyes. The simulator was pulling him out.

"Zakkay, we'll see you after we finish the battle," Aero yelled, as he parried another of Tristan's blows. He'd programmed the timer for one hour, but the simulation would end sooner if one side triumphed before that time had elapsed.

And then Zakkay was gone, as if he'd never been there at all.

Tristan advanced on Aero with his Falchion, and now Starling, free of her opponent, turned her attention on him, too. Tristan thrust his katana while Starling swung her spiked mace. Aero bobbed away from the mace's sharp spikes, but he didn't get his sword up fast enough to deflect Tristan's blow.

The katana clipped Aero's left shoulder. He felt a sharp sting and then heat as blood gushed from the wound. He clenched his fist and felt pain shoot up it. *This is going to make it much harder to fight*, he realized. As Tristan swung again, Aero switched his Falchion to his right hand. Though his damaged finger would inhibit him, it wouldn't slow him as much as a wounded shoulder. And he fought just as well with his right hand.

Aero met Tristan's katana and knocked it away, and then ducked as Starling's mace slammed into the rock formation above his head. Shards flew into the air. Aero's heart hammered in his ribcage, but he forced himself to calm down and take stock of the situation. Around him, the battle bucked and reared like a wild beast—it had taken on a life of its own. Wren was locked in fierce combat with Xing, a short, burly soldier.

"Soldiers, to the higher ground!" Aero yelled as he deflected another blow from Tristan and dodged another swing of Starling's mace.

In a fluid motion, Aero morphed his Falchion into a shield, slung it over his back, and then scrambled up the rock formation. His soldiers amassed around him. Xing slipped away from Wren and claimed the spot to his right, while Etoile, a grim-faced girl, took his left flank. Soon they all stood atop of the uneven rocks.

"Soldiers, retreat!" Wren called out, pulling her soldiers back. He could tell from her expression—a mixture of fury and frustration—that she'd realized her error. She'd made a critical mistake when she forfeited the higher ground. Though Aero's side was outnumbered since they'd lost Zakkay, they had the strategic advantage now.

"Attack!" Aero yelled as he leapt at Wren.

He shifted his Falchion in midair back into a broadsword and connected with Wren's Falchion, still in the shape of a curved sword called a talwer. His soldiers followed his lead, raining down on the other side in a shower of golden sparks.

Wren grinned fiercely and swung at Aero, forcing him back against the rock formation. She was an impressive soldier, and Aero was wounded.

"You won't finish me in five minutes this time!" she said and pressed him back further. The coarse rocks scraped against his wounded shoulder.

"Don't bet on it!" he grunted.

He kicked out his right leg, jabbing her in the knee, and down she went. When she landed, her Falchion skittered away.

She scrambled after it on all fours. Her fingers closed around the hilt. She turned back to meet Aero's blow, right as the ground began to shake and undulate beneath them. Her face contorted in alarm.

"What the hell—" she began, but she never got a chance to finish.

Suddenly, a chasm split the earth, running right under the battlefield. One second they were standing on solid ground and the next they were in free fall. Aero had time for only one thought—he didn't program any environmental interference into the simulation.

And then he was falling.

Without hesitation—almost without even thinking—he morphed his Falchion into a pickaxe and swung at the wall of the chasm with all his strength. The sharp end connected with the rock face—and sunk in just enough to halt his descent. His right arm jerked back, but he managed to hang on. And then he was dangling over thin air.

Starling and Tristan both plummeted past him, their screams following them down. Abruptly, they went silent as the chasm swallowed them whole.

Aero clung to his Falchion's hilt with one hand—the right one with the missing finger. His left hand was slick with blood and his shoulder was damaged. How long could he hold on like this? To his immediate right, he saw that Wren had copied his maneuver and also hung by her Falchion from the cliffside. Relief washed through him that she had reacted quickly.

The other soldiers must have been standing far enough away from where the earth had split open and were probably unharmed. But two of them—Tristan and Starling—had tumbled into the abyss below. Aero had heard their screams and witnessed their descents as if in slow motion, and he was only now processing it.

"Computer, disengage the simulation!" Aero yelled.

Nothing happened.

"Computer, end the simulation at once!"

Again, nothing.

He was still dangling in midair on the rendered surface of Mars.

Is this a computer malfunction?

That was his first thought, but it was followed immediately by something far more sinister—*did somebody tamper with the simulation?* That would explain the earthquake. It would also explain why the computer wasn't responding to his verbal commands. It was possible to program the simulator so that only somebody from the outside could end the sequence. If that had happened, then it meant that they were trapped here.

And if so, did they also meddle with the safety controls?

Aero had set them to wound, which meant that Tristan and Starling would be shaken when they emerged from their simulators. Shaken, but alive. However, if somebody had switched them to kill, then the soldiers were assuredly dead. This thought chilled him to the bone. And with the computer not responding to his commands, he had no way to know if Tristan and Starling had survived. He had to assume the worst: *We could all perish now.*

"What the hell is going on?" Wren yelled. "Is this some kind of trick? To surprise us?" *She thinks I programmed it*, Aero realized. "Well . . . it really worked!"

"No, no, I didn't program any environmental interference."

"Damn it, then how?"

"Somebody must have tampered with the simulation!"

Wren's face went white with fear. "Then what else did they tamper with?"

He set his lips. "I don't know."

"Tristan and Starling?"

"We have to assume the worst."

She took this in grimly. "How long until . . . it's over?" she grunted, gripping her Falchion with both hands. They were both fatigued from the battle.

"At least half an hour, but the computer isn't responding to my commands. Only somebody from the outside can pull us out now." Aero looked up at the sky. "Zakkay, if you're watching on the monitors, disengage the simulation! You have to pull us out!"

Nothing happened.

They were still stuck in the simulation.

Aero wasn't surprised—there was no way to know what kind of state Zakkay was in right now. He could be comatose, for all they knew. He turned back to Wren.

"Starry hell, I don't know about you, but I can't hold on for half an hour. Plus, they could have switched off the timer, too. We have to climb—it's our only chance."

They began to scale the cliff, slowly and unsteadily, using their Falchions as pickaxes. Aero searched out footholds and handholds, and then pulled his Falchion out of the rock and sank it into a spot above his head. In this way, he used the versatile weapon to pull himself higher. Wren mimicked his method. Below them stretched only empty space. One wrong move could mean their deaths, so he did his best not to look down.

The fresh blood on his right hand almost sent him plunging to his doom, but Aero managed to hold on to his Falchion somehow. Wren—who was lighter than Aero and uninjured—fared better. She reached the top of the cliff ahead of him, and Hoshiko and Xing pulled her to safety. Aero kept climbing, even though his shoulder throbbed.

A few minutes later, though it felt like an eternity, he stretched his hand up and felt it gripped by Hoshiko. It was the best feeling in the world. Aero transferred his weight over to that hand and yanked his Falchion from the rock. It resisted at first but then came free. Hoshiko started to hoist him out of the chasm, but then his right hand, which was still slick with blood, slipped from Hoshiko's grip.

One minute he was suspended in midair, and the next he was falling.

"No!" Wren cried in anguish.

She reached out for Aero, but her hand grasped only air. The effort almost sent her tumbling after him, but Xing wrenched her back at the last second. Hoshiko looked stunned, with his lips formed into a perfect circle. His hand, the one that had gripped his commander, was stained crimson with blood.

The world above Aero began to recede.

It grew smaller and smaller.

He fell, as if in slow motion, deeper and deeper into the chasm. The wind ripped at his spacesuit, fluttering the thin fabric, and tore at his flesh. He watched Wren's face as he descended—tear-stained and contorted with abject horror. She was always so emotional, he thought, but at least she had been saved. This knowledge comforted him.

A state of peacefulness washed over him as he accepted his own death.

And then everything went black.

Chapter 23

THE INITIUM CEREMONY

Myra Jackson

Myra watched the Initium Ceremony from the pews.

She'd come to help her father and Royston with the new pledges. Padre Flavius opened the ceremony with a prayer, and then Headmaster Crawley called each student up to the pulpit to announce their pledge choice. Paige pledged to the Infirmary while Rickard pledged to the Patrollers, and, true to his word, Kaleb pledged to the Synod.

Myra breathed a sigh of relief when Kaleb announced his decision and joined the Plenus in the elevated benches behind the altar. His mother blithely kissed his cheek, while his father squeezed his eldest son's shoulder. They both looked proud and—most importantly—unsuspecting that Kaleb had ever harbored any doubts.

But it wasn't all good news.

Baron also pledged to the Patrollers, as did Horace and Gregor, who made up the rest of his crew. This wasn't unusual—the Patrollers always proved a popular choice, especially with the boys. Luckily, Rickard could keep an eye on them. Most of their waking hours would be spent training together for the Apprentice Exam.

As Myra watched the ceremony unfold, she felt a pang of regret. She wondered what it would feel like to stand behind the pulpit and announce her trade. She'd made her decision, or, more accurately, it had been made for her behind the locked doors of the Synod's chamber. It was either that or Hocker status. But there was no use dwelling on it or trying to change it. The past was as inflexible as the Synod's rules.

By the end of the ceremony, Engineering had collected two pledges—Roland Minsk, whose father was a Master Engineer, and a feisty girl named Charlotte Park, whom Myra had always liked. As she took in their hopeful faces with their wide eyes and eager smiles, she wondered if they'd made the right decision. She certainly hoped so.

"Welcome to Engineering!" her father greeted them. "The next two years will be the most challenging—but also the most rewarding—of your lives."

Though he tried to sound cheerful, Myra could see that the dark circles under his eyes had darkened and the lines around them had deepened. Too much work and too little sleep were taking their toll on him.

"Let's go, pledges," he said. "Follow me, we're heading to the Engineering Room for your Pledge Orientation. Hope you like getting your hands dirty."

Roland and Charlotte laughed nervously, but Myra knew that he wasn't joking. At her orientation, Royston had given her a broken hydraulic valve and told her that she couldn't go home until she fixed it. It had taken four hours—and countless attempts—but with her fingers aching and her head throbbing, she'd finally succeeded. In Engineering, it was sink or swim, and the new pledges would start working right away.

o o o

The compartment door dilated with a slurp.

"There's a welcome sight for sore eyes," Maude said in her

scratchy voice. She stood in the doorway of her compartment, balancing frothy mugs in her arms.

"Sorry I'm late," Myra said, kissing Maude hastily on the cheek. "Pledge got his finger stuck in a pipe, and I had to rush him to the Infirmary."

Maude chuckled. "I seem to recall that was you not so long ago," she said, making Myra blush. "Now get in here, before these ginger beers go flat."

Myra stepped into the compartment, where she was immediately greeted by the sound of jovial voices. Kaleb, Paige, and Rickard sat around the kitchen table. She took in the living space, which resembled a miniature Souk. Old shoes, iron pots, boxes of preserved foodstuffs, and other junk littered the room while the kitchen was overflowing with candy. And this didn't even include the robust trade that Maude did in firewater.

She'd transformed the spare bedroom into a distillery. Through the cracked door, Myra glimpsed the coppery vats and zigzagging pipes used to produce the potent brew. Most evenings, Maude's compartment would be packed with Factum and Hockers stopping by for a drink, but tonight it had been reserved for a special occasion.

Myra joined her friends at the table. Frothy mugs soon appeared in front of them, courtesy of Maude. Myra sipped it thirstily, savoring the spicy taste.

When she looked up, she caught Kaleb smirking at her.

"What's so funny?" she said.

He reached over and wiped away the foam mustache that had accumulated on her upper lip. She colored at his touch—it was an intimate gesture. Rickard and Paige exchanged a knowing look, making it even worse. Before Myra could think of something witty to say that would diffuse the situation, Maude's voice cut through the tension.

"Make way!" she called out. "Or else!"

They hoisted their mugs off the table in the nick of time as Maude heaved a massive buttercake onto the table, the legs creaking under its weight. Paige handed out plates while

Maude dispensed slices, each gluttonously large. Then she joined them at the table and raised her mug. It was also filled with ginger beer, though based on her flushed cheeks, Myra suspected that it was spiked with firewater.

"To the new pledges!" she declared and toasted them. "May you work hard and prosper! In other words . . . not end up a Hocker like me."

They cheered and clinked their mugs together.

Myra dug into the cake. It was fluffy and buttery, spiked with fresh vanilla and iced with sugary frosting—in short, positively scrumptious. She polished off her piece and asked for another. While she waited for Maude to slice it, her eyes roved around the table, taking in her friends' faces. *One last night, before we all dissolve into separate factions*, she thought. Most pledges only associated with pledges from their trades.

Paige caught the look on Myra's face. "By the Oracle, I'm going to miss seeing you guys at school."

"Even me?" Rickard said.

"Right—even you, Lynch."

Rickard grinned. "Ah, I'll miss you, too."

"Well, you could always make friends with Baron," Myra said, spooning up her second piece of cake. "You both pledged to the 'Trollers."

He shuddered. "I'd rather be sacrificed to the Holy Sea."

They all laughed, except for Kaleb. He pushed his plate away as if his appetite had fled from him. "Nothing is going to change," he said in a bitter voice.

The happy banter evaporated.

"What do you mean?" Paige asked.

"We're all pledged to different trades now, but we have to stay friends, no matter what." His eyes darted to Myra. "No way I'm letting them split us up again."

"You think it's intentional?" Paige said.

Kaleb nodded. "Think about it! Why can't you switch trades if the first one isn't right? Why does flunking out automatically make you a Hocker? Why can only the children of Plenus pledge to the Synod? Well, I've been thinking a lot lately, maybe more than I have my whole life, and they want to divide us up—we're weaker that way."

Silence fell over the table.

"My boy, you're smarter than I thought!" Maude said. She leaned in closer and whispered. "Of course that's what the Synod wants! If we're too busy worrying about our status and resenting each other, then we'll never realize who the real enemy is."

"Wait, you knew about this?" Myra said.

"Of course, sweetheart," Maude said. "Most Factum and Plenus think Hockers are dim-witted and slow, but nothing could be further from the truth. Well, you'd have to check with Records, but I'll wager we were top students at the Academy. I know that I was. Trust me, we wouldn't survive a month as Hockers if we weren't shrewd."

"You had high marks?" Paige said in surprise.

Maude grinned proudly, exposing her missing teeth. "Yup, I was the top student in my class."

"Then how'd you end up a Hocker?" Paige said.

"Oh, I pledged to Records and flew through the pledge process. Anyway, after I took the Apprentice Exam, I was sure I'd aced it—but when my Pledge Master pulled me aside, he told me that I'd flunked. Well, before that, I'd never failed a test in my life." She sipped her beer. "The only thing I could think was . . . maybe I did too well."

"They kicked you out on purpose?" Rickard said.

Maude shrugged. "Now, I don't have proof—and it can't leave this room—but that's exactly what I'm saying. And I'm not the only Hocker that feels that way."

It wasn't news that most Hockers believed that they'd been wronged by the pledge process. They could be heard grumbling about it at the Souk, but Factum and Plenus tended to regard their complaints as excuses for their failure and nothing more.

"But that can't be. I don't believe it," Paige said in shock. "They want the smartest people working in the trades! That's why they test us."

"According to who—Padre Flavius?" Myra said. "Think about it; I'll bet they were afraid to have Maude pledged to Records since they handle sensitive information." The wheels turned rapidly in her head. "Maybe the two-year pledge process isn't to train us for our Apprentice Exams . . . maybe it's to identify potential troublemakers."

"Troublemakers, huh?" Maude said. "That's what you think of me?

Myra blushed and looked down. "Sorry, I didn't mean it."

"Of course I'm a troublemaker!" Maude said, slurping from her mug. "We both are, sweetheart. But I think the Red Cloaks would prefer the term heathen."

The conversation dried up at the table. This cast a shadow over what had been a happy celebration. Pledging had taken on a whole new meaning.

"Well, it makes sense," Myra said eventually. "If somebody is a Hocker, they're easier to control. Why else are they only allowed in three areas? And they lose half their Victus, which forces them to focus on survival, rather than starting a rebellion."

Maude patted her on the shoulder. "Sweetheart, that's exactly what I think, and I've had a lot more time to puzzle through it. I know the Hockers better than any of you. Trust me, we're a savvy bunch, smarter than most Factum. Otherwise, we'd starve."

"Because Factum are just supposed to tuck their heads down and perform their duties and not ask questions . . ." Myra trailed off. Something was nagging at her.

Maude caught her eye. "What is it, sweetheart?"

"Well, then, why wasn't I kicked out after I took the Apprentice Exam?"

Maude gave her a knowing smile. "Your score was high?"

Myra nodded quickly—this was dangerous territory. You weren't supposed to tell anybody your score. It was strictly prohibited and could result in Hocker status. "It wasn't just high—it was perfect."

They all took this in for a moment.

"I'm not surprised," Maude said eventually.

Paige shook her head. "Of course it was! I should have known."

"Well, it makes sense if you think about it," Kaleb said. "That's why you have to keep your score a secret. And why the penalties are so high if you reveal it. If we don't know anybody else's score then we can't figure out that the whole system is rigged."

Myra furrowed her brow. "That still doesn't explain why I'm not a Hocker right now."

"There's only one explanation," Maude said. "Your father must be protecting you. He reports the scores to the Synod, doesn't he? I'll bet he tampered with your test, made it look like you barely squeaked by. That way they won't worry about you."

Myra thought back to the day that she learned her score. "He did make a point of telling me to keep it a secret. He was afraid I'd tell somebody my score."

"Because it'd get you into trouble," Maude said. Then more urgently: "Myra, who'd you tell about your score? This is important! Think . . . "

"Nobody! I mean, Royston knows, but he wouldn't tell. He's worked for my father his whole life. Tinker knows, but he doesn't talk much. And now, you know."

Maude took a swig of beer. Her cheeks had acquired a rosy glow, but her eyes remained sharp. Thoughts whirled through Myra's head, but one chased out the others and demanded her attention. She knew that she had to ask for Maude's help.

"Maude . . . well, I can't tell you what exactly," Myra said. "But something big is happening." She glanced at her friends to make sure they didn't object. "We're looking for an object . . . it's really old . . . about the size of a bracelet."

"How old are we talking here?" Maude asked.

"Really, really old. So old it could get us into trouble."

Maude narrowed her eyes, taking on a cunning appearance. "Well, certainly not in Records. Anything that old was destroyed in the Great Purging."

"Well, it was worth a try," Myra said. "Thanks anyway."

"Not so fast, sweetheart! There's one place I'd check. Anybody can access it and, well, old things tend to slip through the cracks. Let's just say the Factum pledged there aren't exactly the brightest lot. They always kick out all the smart ones."

"But where's that?" asked Myra. "Anybody can access it?"

Maude grinned and supplied the answer. "The Com Store! Of course, the useful stuff gets claimed, like clothing, blankets, and shoes, but there's a ton of junk that's been overlooked. I'd be willing to bet that a lot of it is really old. So old that Dissemination doesn't know what it is anymore."

"I can't believe I didn't think of it," Myra said, picturing the dusty storeroom that took up the entirety of Sector 1. It was stuffed to the brim with possessions that had been confiscated from people after they died. Factum were granted two tickets a year and could claim only three items. Hockers had to trade for tickets while Plenus could visit the store anytime and claim as many items as they desired.

Factum always envied Plenus for that privilege. And they looked forward to their two shopping trips all year long. There was nothing like digging through the old boxes, even if you could only claim three objects, and practical ones at that. Maude was right—an object like the Beacon, which on the surface didn't appear to serve any real purpose, might have been overlooked. It couldn't keep you warm at night, that was for sure.

"Anybody got a ticket stashed away?" Myra asked hopefully. "What about you, Kaleb? Your parents are Plenus. You've got to have at least one, right?"

Even though Kaleb was now pledged to the Synod, he was still technically Factum until he passed the Apprentice Exam. Kaleb cast his eyes down. "Well . . . I kind of like . . . shopping."

Myra arched her eyebrow at his pressed tunic and newly-claimed shoes. "Right, I should have known." Her eyes roved around the table. "Anybody else got one?"

Paige shook her head. "I needed new shoes, a blanket, and . . . undergarments." Rickard sniggered, drawing an elbow from Paige. "Well, what about you, Lynch?"

"Nah," Rickard said. "Factum use them up right away; you know that. There's never enough to go around. The store is always packed when tickets get issued."

"Yeah, of course," Myra said. "My family already used up ours too, and new ones won't be issued for three more months. That's a long time to wait."

Paige spoke up. "We could try to sneak in."

"By the Oracle, that's risky," Kaleb said. "The penalties for theft are steep."

Silence fell over the table. Myra ran through their options in her head, each one more dismal than the last. At this rate, they were never going to find the Beacon.

"You Factum sure are a greedy bunch!" Maude said with a chuckle. "You don't understand the need to save up for the hard times ahead. Let me see. I must have a few tickets squirreled away somewhere. I just have to look for them."

She stood up from the table, but Myra stopped her. "Maude, we couldn't possibly! You need them."

Maude set her hands on her wide hips. "Do I look hungry to you? Or like I'm lacking anything?"

Myra glanced at her kitchen. Rations packed the pantry shelves, not to mention the boxes of provisions piled high in the living space. Even though Maude was a Hocker, she never seemed to go hungry. She was a bit on the plump side, which was unusual for anyone in the colony, let alone a Hocker.

"No, no, of course not," Myra was forced to admit.

"Know why? Because I'm the best Hocker there is," Maude said with a hint of pride coloring her voice. "Between the candy and firewater, I'd say I'm doing bloody well. The truth is that I'm way better off a Hocker than I ever was a Factum."

"Maude, are you sure?" Myra said. "You could trade for a lot with them."

"Positive, sweetheart! Now not another word."

Maude trudged over to a trunk, flipped it open, and started rifling through it. Objects clanked together, and dust motes floated up and clouded the air. She fished out several objects and chucked them aside—flashlights, spare batteries, the lid to a cast iron pot, a raggedy doll. "By the Oracle . . . got to be in here . . . somewhere," she muttered.

Finally, she straightened up with a big grin. "Told ya I had some stashed away!"

Maude fanned out the golden tickets. Myra couldn't believe her eyes—five tickets. She'd never seen so many in the possession of a single person. She'd always pitied Maude for her status and feared becoming like her, but now she realized that Maude really did have it better than most Factum—and maybe some Plenus, too.

Myra looked at her friends and smiled.

"Who wants to go shopping tomorrow?"

Chapter 24
MIDNIGHT INTRUDERS

The Synod

She was in the grip of a terrible dream when a noise roused her.

She bolted upright in her bunk. Slowly, stubbornly, her eyes adjusted to the dim room. Her sister was sound asleep in the other bunk. She crawled from her bed, dragging her blanket with her, and shook her sister. "Ginger . . . did you hear that?"

"Stella . . . just . . . go back to sleep," her sister mumbled and flipped over.

Sleep meant more nightmares, and she'd already had enough of those for one night. She let her sister sleep and padded into the living space, the scratchy blanket shrouding her shoulders. The door to the other bedroom was shut. She shuddered when she saw it. The compartment felt strangely hostile. Only a few days ago, it had felt like home. Now it was something else altogether. She didn't feel safe here, not anymore.

She was headed for the sofa, hoping that it would offer

some respite from her nightmare-ridden sleep, when suddenly the compartment door beeped.

It dilated with a loud slurp.

Four shadows spilled into the living space.

She opened her mouth and screamed.

Chapter 25

COLLATERAL DAMAGE

Captain Aero Wright

Aero was shocked by the bright lights and the sudden rush of consciousness.

He was dead. This couldn't be happening. He'd let go—he'd felt himself die. He panicked and scrambled to his feet, knocking Wren down in the process.

But she didn't seem upset, not even a little bit.

"Starry hell, you're alive!" she gasped. "I thought we'd lost you."

Aero blinked at her in confusion. The disorientation was overwhelming. His head was spinning, his eyes burned from the light, and he felt nauseated. He doubled over and retched once, then a second time, and spat on the floor. He stayed hunched over and tried to take stock of himself. His shoulder throbbed, and blood seeped from the wound. He felt Wren's cool hands applying a bandage to his arm.

"Hold still, you're making it worse," she said. "Medical should be here soon. They're on their way."

It took Aero another minute to realize where he was—on the floor of his simulation chamber. A few soldiers from his unit had gathered in the doorway. They wore frightened expressions. He saw Hoshiko, Xing, Etoile, and, lastly, Zakkay. He looked shaken, more so than the rest. There was a sickly greenish pallor to his skin.

"What happened?" Aero said. He searched his memory, finding it full of holes. "The last thing I remember is . . . the earthquake . . . and falling . . . and then nothing."

Wren studied his face. "Zakkay heard your order over the monitors and disengaged the simulation. Well, it looks like a computer malfunction triggered the environmental interference and caused the timer to switch off."

"Anything else?" Aero said.

"The safety controls were reset." When she said that last part, her voice wavered. Aero also noticed a shift in the room, as if all of the oxygen had been sucked out of it.

More memories came rushing back now, and two soldiers plummeting past as he clung to the cliffside was one of them. He felt the nausea return with a vengeance but forced it back down. He didn't want to appear weak in front of his soldiers, not when they were already frightened. Or at least any weaker than he already did.

"Tristan and Starling?" he asked.

Wren set her lips, and that was when he knew. His hunch had proven correct—the safety controls had been changed to kill. Pain flashed across her face.

"They're dead . . . every last bone in their bodies was shattered."

What she didn't say directly was that the same thing could have happened to him had Zakkay acted only one second later. If he'd been only slightly more despondent over the loss of his Falchion—some soldiers even went catatonic—or even a tiny bit slower to disengage the simulator and pull them out, then Aero would be a shattered corpse lying on the floor of his simulation chamber, too. He did not believe in god or fate.

Luck—and nothing more—had saved his life.

"I want to see them," he said. "Starling and Tristan."

Wren shook her head. "You can't."

"Damn it, Wren! That wasn't a request—it was an order."

"Sir, I know an order when I hear it," she said, biting down on every word. "You can't see them because the Euthanasia Clinic already took them away. They'll do an autopsy, and then the bodies will be sent to the incinerator. You'll get the report."

"How long have I been out?"

"Less than fifteen minutes."

"Why did Euthanasia respond faster than Medical?"

She shrugged. "Zakkay called them at the same time."

This detail bothered Aero—he felt it nagging at him. He shifted his gaze to his soldiers, who stood in the threshold of the chamber. Some were bruised and bloodied, but none were dirty or covered in red dust, for that had existed only in their minds.

"Soldiers, out!" Aero said. He was acting unstable but didn't care. He needed to talk to Wren alone. "Everybody out now, except for the First Lieutenant."

"Yes, sir!" the soldiers said with crisp salutes. They started out of the chamber, but Xing hesitated. "Only, sir, what do you want us to do when Medical arrives?"

"Send them away. Tell them I'm fine."

His eyes darted to Aero's shoulder. "But sir, you're bleeding."

"That's another order, Private."

Xing didn't protest further—he knew better than to defy a direct order. He retreated from the chamber, the door contracting behind him with a soft hiss. He was probably relieved to be away from his volatile commander, Aero thought ruefully.

"Well, that was rash," Wren said. Her arms were folded across her chest, and she looked seriously ticked off. "And you are bleeding, quite profusely, I might add."

He looked down at his shoulder. The bandage that she'd applied was now stained crimson with blood, but this didn't make him feel queasy. A good soldier didn't flinch at the sight of blood. Nor did it concern him greatly. He knew from his extensive medical training that the wound wasn't anything serious. More of a superficial laceration really—maybe even a little bit of soft tissue and nerve damage—but he would survive.

Wren approached him with her hands raised in mock surrender. "Permission to approach the Captain and apply pressure to his wound?"

"Permission granted," he said reluctantly.

She knelt beside him and pressed down on the wound with firm, even pressure. He winced as the pain flared up again and tried to hide it, but she noticed.

Their eyes met, and she held his gaze. "Well, that's a nasty wound."

"Damn Tristan and his katana! He was a good soldier, wasn't he?"

Her eyes flashed with pain. "The best," she said. "Starling, too."

He glanced at the injury and grimaced. "He got me fair and square; I'll probably have a scar. It's been a long time since anybody's scratched me."

"Sure you don't want Medical?"

"No, just keep applying pressure. The bleeding has got to stop eventually."

What he didn't want to say—at least not until he had more proof—was that he didn't trust them right now. He didn't trust anyone, in fact. What had happened moments ago—what had cost two of his soldiers their lives—was no malfunction.

Wren pulled a fresh bandage from the first aid kit and applied it to his wound. While Aero waited for the bleeding to subside, and hopefully some of the pain too, he observed her face—her short blond hair, drenched with sweat, and steely blue eyes. But there was something startling and unfamiliar about her countenance now. *Tenderness*, he decided.

There was a softness to her features—around the edges of her eyes and corners of her lips—as if she'd dropped the tough mask she always wore. Despite all the years that he'd known her and fought next to her, he'd never once glimpsed this side of her. They were close now, mere inches apart. Perhaps closer than they'd ever been before.

His pulse quickened, and he felt the heat of blood trying to gush from his wound. He could also feel Wren's cool fingers on his shoulder, holding the torrent at bay. Something stirred deep inside him—something powerful and unsettling. He didn't want to face it, so he tried to disengage his emotions and focus on his capacity for reason.

Mercifully, the feelings began to fade, replaced by stark clarity. "That was no malfunction," he said in a low voice.

Her eyes snapped to his face, alert and probing. "But why would somebody tamper with the simulation?"

"To kill us," he said simply. "Or, at least, to render our unit incapacitated."

"Incapacitated from what?"

"From leading the reconnaissance mission."

"Well, they certainly succeeded! Two of our soldiers are dead, and they almost killed us—both of the commanders. Not to mention the psychological damage. If that were true, then it'd be treason! Who would do something like that?"

"Somebody who doesn't want us to be the first boots on the ground."

She set her lips—she knew he was right.

"Zakkay? He got out before the controls were reset. Otherwise, he'd have been trapped in the simulation like the rest of us. And, well, he's rash and emotional. We both witnessed how he treated his Falchion the other day, and he has a motive."

"Because I defeated him?"

"Humiliated him, more like it."

Aero looked down in frustration—that had not been his intent, and she knew it. "Zakkay was my first thought, too. He's emotional and maybe even vengeful, but he's also reactionary. He doesn't have it in him to plot this way. Even if he was involved in the malfunction, he didn't act alone. This wasn't his plan—it's too complex."

"Then that points to somebody outside our unit."

"My thoughts exactly. We were locked in the chambers, engaged in the simulation. Anybody could have snuck into the control room and tampered with the computer. Another commander could have been jealous that their unit wasn't chosen. Maybe they were hoping that if they injured us, we'd have to step aside."

"It's possible. There's been some discontent in the barracks." She thought for a moment. "Zakkay said the control room was empty when he got there. We should search it anyway, just in case, though I'm guessing that whoever did this was careful not to leave any clues. And, well, I have a bad feeling this goes beyond a few rogue soldiers."

A moment of silence passed before either of them dared to say his name.

"Vinick?" Wren whispered.

"The thought crossed my mind."

"But it's just a hunch?"

"Well, I saw Vinick's reaction when the Supreme General issued my orders. He looked furious. I've also heard rumors that he's been stirring up the Majors by telling them that the Supreme General played favorites when he picked my unit."

"He's a lying sack of shit! Pardon my language, sir."

Aero grinned. "Couldn't have said it better myself! And he may be a lying sack of shit, but that doesn't mean he's a traitor. There's a difference."

"I know," she said with a frustrated sigh. "But Vinick is dangerous, mark my words. He has it out for you—hell, I think he's always had it out for you, ever since he realized you were Brillstein's son. He hates both of you, I'm sure of it."

"In that case, we have to be careful. We don't know how high up this goes. Let's post sentries at the barracks around the clock, and no more simulations."

"Obviously," she said, arching her eyebrow. "You couldn't get me back into that chamber if you tried. How much do you want to tell the soldiers?"

Like a good commander, she was always thinking about the welfare of her soldiers, no matter what the situation. "Not much," Aero decided. "Just that it was a computer malfunction, and we're investigating. That should satisfy them for now."

"And the reason for the sentries?"

"Training for the mission."

She nodded. "They should buy that. Are you going to file a complaint with the Majors?"

He shook his head. "Not until we know more. An official investigation would take too long; our unit is scheduled to deploy as soon as those storms lift. Even with the . . . loss."

His voice caught in his throat, but he forced himself to finish. "Our soldiers are still more than ready, and I don't want whoever tampered with the computer to know we're suspicious." He thought for a minute. "Also, don't you find it strange that Euthanasia responded faster than Medical?"

"Maybe . . . usually it's the other way around."

"Well, it's been bothering me," Aero said. "Of course, it could just be a coincidence. Maybe Medical got held up. But it's almost like Euthanasia couldn't wait to dispose of their bodies, like they were waiting for a call . . . expecting it even."

She gave him an uneasy look. "What you're suggesting would be a conspiracy—and a big one."

He frowned. "Look, I don't like it any more than you do. But right now, I don't trust anyone. Well . . . except maybe . . . you."

A thin smile played at her lips, erasing the frown that had been there only a moment before. Their eyes met, and a heated second passed, then another. The air in the room felt thicker, heavier. Aero didn't know if it was the disorientation from having died in the simulation . . . or something else altogether. He felt himself holding his breath.

But then Wren looked away and cleared her throat.

"Well, what do you know? It looks like the bleeding has stopped. Now, hold still while I bandage you up. I don't want you tearing open the wound again."

While Aero submitted to her ministrations, watching as she expertly fashioned a sling for his arm, he thought about everything that had just happened. He had lost two of his soldiers. He was now wounded. Somebody was trying to kill him—maybe even his whole unit. And tomorrow at 0900 hours, they were scheduled to deploy to Earth.

He would have to be careful now.
More careful than he'd ever been in his entire life.

Chapter 26
THE COMMUNIS STORE

Myra Jackson

"Ah, new shoppers!"

The Dissemination woman squinted at them through her thick glasses. They made her eyes look impossibly large. Myra proceeded into Sector 1, accompanied by Tinker, Kaleb, Rickard, and Paige, and approached her desk. It was littered with crumpled papers, and the air was clogged with dust motes. Further back, Myra glimpsed the rows upon rows of shelving, stacked to the ceiling and overflowing with confiscated objects.

The woman chuckled, but it morphed into a raspy cough. "And Factum, if I'm not mistaken."

"Yes, ma'am," Myra said. "Been a slow day?"

"More like a slow three months." She grinned as if pleased by the uptick in visitors. "Now, my dear, you do have tickets?"

They forked over the golden slips a bit reluctantly, and she tucked them into a rusty metal box and twisted the lock. Then, she pointed to the sign-in ledger.

"Full names and compartment numbers, and don't forget the date. Not your first trip, is it? You know the rules." She pointed to a placard mounted on her desk:

Attention Factum and Hockers:
Only three items may be claimed per trip to the *Communis Store*.
No exceptions. No excuses.
By Order of the Synod.

What the sign didn't state explicitly was that Plenus could claim an unlimited number of items. Oblivious to the inequity, the woman beamed at them. "After you make your selections, bring them up here so I can check you out. Now . . . any questions?"

After they'd signed in, she waved them off. "Happy shopping! May you claim good items today!"

As they turned away from her desk, the woman's gaze lingered on Myra, and the smile evaporated from her face. Myra noticed it. The woman gave her a bad feeling, but she tried to shake it off. Dissemination was known for its strange ways.

Too much time spent with objects and not people, she thought.

Myra caught up to her friends, and they ventured deeper into the aisles. She sniffed the air and sneezed. It smelled like a mixture of mold, dust, and decay, the stench that old things gave off. The shelves towered overhead, and the objects heaped on them looked unstable, like they could set off an avalanche at any moment.

"So . . . what's the plan?" Paige whispered. Her pale blue scrubs were spattered with blood, and she looked fatigued from her first day of work.

"Why do we always need a bloody plan?" Rickard said.

He was dressed in black from head to toe, the Patrollers' uniform. Every time Myra glimpsed his dark silhouette out of the corner of her eye, it sent a chill up her spine. She hadn't gotten used to seeing him that way. He snatched a shiny object from a shelf, his face contorting when he realized it was a chamber pot. He quickly dropped it.

"To keep from wandering off track, that's why," Paige said.

Kaleb's eyes roved over the shelves. Now that he was pledged to the Synod, he wore a velvety tunic in a rich shade of crimson. "The Wade section, we start there."

Myra nodded. "Right. Follow me, it's this way . . ."

She led them deeper into the store. The further they went, the more the shelves obscured the automatic lights, casting the area into shadow. Dust bunnies tumbled away from their feet. It looked like Janitorial hadn't swept this part in months. The inventory was organized alphabetically by the surname of the prior claimant. Myra scanned the rusty placards. *Sing. Siphon. Studebaker. Sweeting. Takata. Thatcher. Torrado. Tsu.*

Many of the objects looked old, though how old was hard to say. But Maude was right—a lot of the objects had probably been confiscated by Dissemination after the claimant died, placed on a shelf, and then completely forgotten. When she reached the end of the aisle, Myra heard a noise. It was faint—almost inaudible—but she heard it all the same. Her pulse quickened. Sometimes Patrollers were stationed inside the store.

"Did you hear that?" she whispered.

"Nope," Kaleb said while Tinker just shook his head.

"Probably just a rat," Rickard said. "This sector's full of them."

Paige didn't look thrilled to hear that.

They rounded the bend and stepped into the next aisle, where the "W" names commenced, when Myra spotted something on the floor—footprints.

"Hey, see those tracks? They look . . . fresh."

Paige frowned. "But the last entry in the ledger was weeks ago."

"Then they weren't made by a shopper."

Tinker produced a flashlight from his rucksack and aimed it at the floor. "The prints are different sizes," he reported in his soft voice. "Looks like three or maybe four people. And they were on the large side. Adult males most likely."

Myra set her lips—she didn't like the sound of that.

"And I think they made several trips," Tinker said. "They overlap a lot."

"Dissemination workers?" Kaleb said.

"Maybe," Paige said. "But nobody's died recently, at least not in the Infirmary, or I'd know about it. And there hasn't been a Sentencing . . . well . . . since Carter."

Myra winced at his name. "Right, so then nothing's been confiscated recently." She glanced at the shelves and their jumbled collection of objects. "And it doesn't exactly look like they do much maintenance around here. These shelves are a mess."

"Bunch of lazy prigs," Rickard said. He ran his finger along a shelf, the dust building up on it. He sniffed it and sneezed violently.

Myra led them down the aisle, her heart thudding in her throat. They reached the end and arrived at their destination—the four sections of shelving labeled *Wade*. She skidded to a halt and looked up, a horrible feeling sweeping through her.

"Oh . . . no," she stammered. "It can't be . . . "

The shelves were empty. Not a single object remained. They'd been cleared. Fresh footprints marred the floor and handprints the shelves. Dust motes swirled in the dim light as if they'd been stirred up recently.

She read the sign, then read it again:

QUARANTINED:
By Order of the Synod

"Quarantined," Paige said in a stunned voice. The word had a terrible finality to it. A second passed, and then: "But how'd they find out about the Wade family?"

Myra's mind reeled, grasping for an explanation. "The pictures of Elianna Wade," she said at last. "They arrested Bishop, remember? The 'Trollers must have found out where he'd hidden them."

"Or he told them," Rickard said.

"Under duress, if that's the case," Paige said.

Kaleb ran one hand through his hair. "Bloody stupid," he muttered. "I saw the 'Trollers dragging some crates into the

Synod's chambers this morning, but I thought they were just deliveries from the Victus. I should have paid closer attention."

Silence engulfed the group, and nobody spoke for a moment. Finally, Myra stood up, the blood rushing from her head and making her feel dizzy. It seemed completely hopeless, but something stirred in her—something deep. It refused to let her give up. She started pacing in front of the empty shelves, a determined look on her face.

"Well, should we search another section?"

"Right, we're assuming the Beacon was hidden in the Wade section," Kaleb said, "but we don't know for sure, so no point wasting the whole shopping trip."

Paige scanned the shelves. She was thinking hard from the looks of it. "Did Sari Wade ever change her last name? If she got married, or something like that?"

"Nope, not that I know," Myra said. "At least, my father never mentioned it." She ran through everything she knew about the Wade family. An idea struggled to surface, spurred on by what Paige had just said. Suddenly, something clicked into place.

"But I think my mother did."

Paige frowned at her in concern. "No offense, it's really terrible what happened to her, just awful . . . but what's your mother got to do with Sari Wade?"

Myra swallowed hard. "I think her last name was Wade."

"You mean before she married your father?" Paige said.

Tinker's eyes widened at the mention of his mother. They almost never talked about her. His lips moved, trying to form sounds: "Tessa . . . Wade . . . "

Kaleb's face lit up. "That's right, almost forgot about that! You knew the story from the book, didn't you? Your mother used to tell it to you before bed. You thought maybe it got passed down through her family, and she was related to Sari Wade."

"Well, it's just a guess," Myra said uncertainly. "But there's more. Remember the pictures of Sari? Well, she looked just like my mother. My father noticed it, too."

"We've got heirlooms that have been in my family for generations," Paige said. "Just some silly ceramic vases, but they've been reclaimed over the years. Think maybe your mother had something like that—an object that originally belonged to Sari Wade?"

Their eyes fell on Myra, and she felt her heart wrench painfully. She'd always avoided reclaiming any of her mother's things after she died. She hesitated and glanced at Tinker, but he met her gaze and held it. Then, he slowly nodded.

His meaning was crystal clear—*we have to try it.*

"Fine, let's do it," Myra said. "Before I change my mind."

o o o

As the automatic lights dimmed even more, signifying that nightfall was fast approaching, they arrived at the Jackson section.

Myra didn't want to be here—she wanted to turn around and run as fast as she could in the opposite direction, leave without checking out even a single item, sacrilege for Factum always in dire need of supplies, but she didn't do any of those things. Sucking in a deep breath, she forced herself to examine the first shelf. Her eyes combed over the dusty, tarnished objects. Something caught her eye, tucked all the way in the back. She retrieved it with shaking hands and held it up to the light—it was a needlepoint pillow.

Her eyes roved over it, taking in every knot and hue, every stitch of thread that she'd long ago committed to memory. The interwoven threads pulled together and resolved into a scene—the Sea King and his mermaid daughter swimming through an ocean of pale blue thread. Everything in her froze for a moment. And then, just like that, she was back in her family's compartment, a little girl of no more than five.

Her mother sat on the sofa after a long shift in Records, but she didn't go to bed yet. Instead, she was hard at work, stitching a pattern into a pillow that she'd claimed from the Com Store. It turned out to be a gift for Myra's sixth birthday. For the next two years, she'd slept with the pillow, until that horrible day when her mother never came home from the Infirmary. And then Dissemination came for her possessions.

Even after the next batch of tickets was issued, she still couldn't bring herself to face her mother's section. Over the years, she'd never reclaimed a single object; nobody in her family had. She'd done her best to block the memory out, but now it came roaring back like a burst pipe gushing water. She pressed the pillow to her face and inhaled its musty scent. When she exhaled, it felt like more than carbon dioxide left her body.

Blinking back tears, she knelt down and held out the pillow. "Tink, our mother made this . . ." Her voice dried up in her throat, but it didn't matter.

Understanding washed over his face. He hugged the pillow to his chest and grinned his lopsided smile. At that moment, as she took in her brother's face, she wondered why she'd waited so long to reclaim her mother's things. All at once, the pain and the fear rushed out of her. They were replaced by another feeling altogether—she felt her mother's love course through her, warming her from the inside out.

Through her tears, she squinted at the automatic lights, which were growing dimmer by the second. Then, she turned back to her friends and actually smiled.

"Come on, let's get started. We don't have much time."

As they searched through the Jackson shelves, Myra relished every object that had belonged to her mother. The sandals that she'd worn until holes ate through the soles (and nobody must have reclaimed them for that reason), and the red velvet ribbon that she'd used to bind her curly, black hair before trudging off to work. Myra reached the back of the shelf and pulled down the last object. A thick layer of dust obscured its surface.

A peculiar statue, she decided, *with a ball set on top of a sturdy base*. She held it up to the light to examine it, realizing that it was heavier than it had appeared at first.

Kaleb looked up from rifling through another shelf and wiped a sweaty strand of hair from his brow, leaving a smudge of dust in its place.

"Find something?" he asked.

"Not sure," she said as she studied it. She searched her memory. "Some kind of statue maybe. It does look familiar . . . maybe it belonged to my mother?"

Using the hem of her dress, she wiped some of the dirt away. When she finished with a small section, she clicked the flashlight on and aimed it at the round part. Her eyes widened when she saw what was inside. Now Paige was paying attention, too.

"Myra . . . what is it?"

"You see this round part? Well, it's made of clear glass . . . and it's filled with liquid." Myra looked closer, feeling a thrill. "And there's . . . something inside."

Her friends crowded around and peered over her shoulder. Inside the globe, submerged in the liquid, was a tiny model. There were buildings surrounded by pathways with miniature people walking along them. One structure rose taller than the rest, made out of crisscrossed metal bulwark that steepled upward to a sharp point. Everything was covered with what looked like ice—or at least that's what Myra thought it was.

She polished it off some more, revealing a bronze placard affixed to the base with a single word engraved in an ornate font:

Paris

"What's *Paaa-rrr-is*?" Rickard said.

"No idea," Myra said. "I've never seen that word before."

She flipped it over and examined the bottom. White debris broke off inside the model and swirled around in the water. The bottom was just as filthy as the rest of it, so she started cleaning it, slowly uncovering a message that had been scratched into the base:

Only the least among you may possess the treasure.
—S. Wade

"It did belong to Sari Wade!" she said. "Look at the handwriting. It's the same loopy cursive as the inscription in the book, isn't it? This object must have been passed down through the Wade family, reclaimed by each generation."

"Until it reached your mother," Paige said.

"Think it's from Before Doom?" Rickard whispered, his eyes darting around.

Myra ran her fingers over the statue, feeling the intricacy of the design. "Well, the craftsmanship does look ancient. I've never seen anything quite like it."

"Why didn't Dissemination quarantine it?" Kaleb said.

"Well, we don't even know what it is—so maybe they didn't either? Like Maude said, they probably don't know what half the junk down here is anymore. Plus, look at how filthy it is. You'd have to scrub it off just to see inside the glass."

Suddenly the lights dimmed again, casting the store into shadow. That was followed by the Dissemination worker's voice echoing down the aisles.

"Shoppers, last call for checkout—or all trips deemed null and void!"

Myra turned to her friends. "Hurry up, grab some stuff to check out."

It would arouse suspicions if they left with only one object. While her friends starting rifling through the shelves, Myra smeared dust back onto the statue, obscuring the view of the model inside and the message. Then, she grabbed two more objects—the needlepoint pillow and the ribbon. They hurried back up to the front of the store.

The woman grinned when she saw them. "Ah, there you are, my dears!"

They lined up to check out, with Myra going first. The woman produced a thick ledger and picked up the first of Myra's objects, squinting at it through her glasses.

"Nice choice, my dear," she said and scrawled down: *Needlepoint pillow of underwater scene with four mermaids (one male, three female)*. That was followed by: *Red velvet ribbon (1 in. wide by 10 in. long)*.

"Well, well, what do we have here?" She picked up the last object and examined it, turning it over in her hands. "Heavy thing, isn't it? And quite filthy, too. I'll reckon it's been down here a long time without being claimed." She looked at Myra expectantly. "Now, my dear, please state its name and purpose—or I'll have to quarantine it."

Myra felt her pulse quicken. That meant that Records would be called down to determine if it violated the Synod's decree prohibiting items from Before Doom.

"Uh, right, it's a . . . paperweight," she said.

The old woman pursed her lips in disapproval, and Myra's heart lurched in her chest, but then the woman set the object aside with the pillow and ribbon.

"Paperweight works for me."

She scrawled in the ledger: Paperweight with round ball atop sturdy base. Very heavy. Claimed by Myra Jackson, Compartment 516. And, lastly, she added the date.

"Just sign here, and you're checked out."

Relief coursed through Myra as she scribbled down her signature. The Dissemination woman packed her items into a crate and handed it to her. She repeated the same process with the others. Then, crates in their arms, Myra and her companions headed for the sector door. They were almost there when it beeped and dilated.

Four dark silhouettes were framed in the doorway.

They stormed through it.

Myra's eyes grazed over the Patrollers' faces—Jasper, Bates, and their new pledges, Baron and Horace. She glanced at Rickard, but he appeared just as shocked to see them.

Baron's eyes fell on Myra, and he grinned viciously. Jasper clutched a scroll in his hands with the Synod's official seal on it. He unfurled it and read: "By order of the Synod, all claimed items must be automatically quarantined. Effective immediately." He looked up and unsheathed his pipe. "Now hand 'em over!"

Chapter 27
THE LEAST AMONG YOU

Myra Jackson

The Patrollers advanced with their pipes raised.

Myra staggered to a halt, her heart thudding in her throat, and glanced at her friends, but they looked equally stunned. Her eyes darted to the crate cradled in her arms, where the statue rested against the pillow. She couldn't let it fall into the Synod's hands.

Paige caught her eye. "Automatic quarantine?" she whispered. "Since when?"

"Since Flavius is looking for you know what," Myra whispered back.

"Then why even let us into the store?" Rickard asked.

Myra's stomach twisted sickeningly. "Because he was hoping we'd lead him right to it." She glanced at the Dissemination worker cowering behind her desk. "She must have fetched the 'Trollers while we were looking. Bet they told her to alert them if there were new shoppers."

Myra fell silent as the Patrollers neared. Jasper pointed to her with his pipe and turned to Baron. "Pledge, relieve this heathen of her items," he ordered.

"Yes, sir!" Baron said.

He marched up to Myra and reached for her crate, but she didn't let go. "Hey, gimme that, or you'll pay!" he sneered. He raised his pipe to strike her, and Myra was prepared to fight back when Kaleb stepped in between them and shoved Baron.

And that was when it happened—a scuffle broke out. Myra saw Rickard throw a punch and land it on Horace's jaw, while Kaleb took a hit from Baron's pipe. His mouth was a bloody mess. Even Tinker got caught up in the melee.

"Tinker, no!" Myra yelled and tried to pull him to safety, but he scrambled after his rucksack. He must have dropped it in the chaos.

He crawled through the legs and pipes, wriggling across the floor. Myra started after him, but Jasper seized her. Paige leapt at him and tried to pull him off Myra, and they all collapsed to the floor. Finally, Bates broke it up. He hurled Kaleb to the ground, and then dropped Rickard with one well-placed punch to his jaw.

Myra saw her opening—she wrenched Tinker away from the Patrollers and kept her arms wrapped around him.

"Arrest them!" Bates said. "And toss 'em in the Pen!"

Myra felt her face contort in horror—more than anyone else, she knew what it was like to be carted off to the Pen and locked up in the unending darkness.

Jasper pulled out pieces of rope and passed them out to Horace and Baron. Baron jerked Myra's arms behind her back, while Horace restrained Tinker. They bound their wrists, cutting off the circulation. Jasper reached for Kaleb, but he struggled to his feet and rose to his full height, staring down the Patrollers with barely contained fury.

"Get your filthy hands off me!" He wiped the blood from his lips and spat. His eyes roved over the Patrollers' faces. "Do you Factum know who my father is?"

Jasper hesitated, his eyes darting to Bates.

"That's right," Kaleb went on. "Know what it's like to be a Hocker? Scrounging for your next meal? Arrest me—or any of my friends—and that's your future!"

An angry expression stole across Bates's face, but then he relented.

"Release them!" he ordered.

Baron looked uncertain. "But sir, they resisted—"

"Silence, Pledge!" Bates barked. "That was an order!"

Baron untied Myra's hands, but he didn't look happy about it. She rushed over to Tinker and checked him over for injuries. He had a cut on his forehead from the brawl and marks on his wrists but appeared otherwise unharmed. Kaleb straightened out his velvet tunic and started to gather up the crates, but Bates stepped in front of him.

"Not so fast!" he said. "Orders are orders. Tattle to your daddy if you want, but he's the one that bloody gave them. If your items pass inspection, they'll be returned."

Kaleb looked like he wanted to protest, but he recognized a futile situation when he saw one. He raised his hands in surrender and slowly backed away. Myra watched helplessly as the Patrollers gathered up their items, packed them into crates, and marched out of the store. They vanished through the sector door, and it contracted behind them.

o o o

"Curse the Oracle," Myra muttered as they walked down the corridor.

The image of the Patrollers leaving the store with their crates replayed over and over in her head. Kaleb laid a hand on her shoulder as if to comfort her, but she brushed it away. Furious tears swarmed her eyes and spilled down her cheeks. She imagined the look on Padre Flavius's face when he saw the message on the base of the statue.

Paige glanced at her in concern. "Myra, don't worry; we'll figure something out."

"Don't you get it? It's over! They took it. It's bloody over."

"Maybe it'll pass quarantine . . ." Rickard said, but even he sounded doubtful.

"Padre Flavius may be a bloodthirsty lunatic, but he's not stupid," Myra said, blinking back tears. "He'll find the message from Sari. He already knows about the Wade family. What if it leads him to the Beacon? If he finds it, he'll destroy it."

They fell into a poisonous silence. Myra could feel it eating away at her insides. She glanced at Tinker, but he didn't seem upset. Her eyes shifted to his rucksack.

Probably because his bloody computer is safe, she thought in annoyance. But then Tinker caught her eye. A lopsided smile stole across his face.

"Tink, what is it?"

He didn't answer—he just reached up and adjusted the straps of his rucksack. And that was when she knew. Her eyes darted back to the bulky bag.

"Holy Sea, you've got it, don't you?" she said.

He nodded once.

"You've had it this whole time?"

He nodded again.

"But . . . how?"

He glanced around to make sure they were alone. The lights would extinguish at any minute, so the corridor was deserted. "During the fight, when the 'Trollers got distracted, I slipped it into my bag. I'm little, so grownups don't tend to notice me."

Paige and Rickard broke into giddy laughter while Kaleb just looked impressed. Myra swept her brother up into a tight embrace.

"Oh, Tink, you saved us!"

She patted his full rucksack and felt a thrill. She couldn't wait to get home and head straight to her room, where she planned to stay up all night, studying the statue and the clue that Sari had left for them.

Only the least among you may possess the treasure.

Myra certainly hoped she qualified.

o o o

"Quick, he's gone to bed, turn the flashlight on."

Tinker whispered to Myra from his bunk, where he'd been

feigning sleep. Their father had just arrived home from work, right before the automatic lights shut off, and poked his head into their room before heading to his bedroom.

"Not yet," Myra whispered. "Let's make sure he's asleep."

They waited in the total darkness of their room. Myra counted under her breath: "One-one-thousand, two-one-thousand, three-one-thousand . . ."

Once she got to thirty, she thought they could risk using the flashlight. She clicked it on and then retrieved the statue from Tinker's rucksack. She flipped it over in her hands, taking note of any interesting features. The people wore thick layers of clothing and hats, and what looked like ice clung to the paths and buildings.

"What do you think that stuff is?" she asked. "Ice?"

Tinker clacked on his keyboard. "No, I think it's called . . . snow," he said. "Definition of snow," he read off the screen. "Ice crystals that fall from the sky in white flakes."

He tapped some more and then grinned.

"Tink, what is it? Spit it out."

"Myra, I found it," he said and tapped some more. "The object is called a snow globe." His eyes flashed over the screen. "Typically made of glass, a transparent orb filled with water enclosing a model, usually of a landscape or city. The snow globe is shaken up and then righted so that the snowflakes fall slowly through the water."

Myra followed the directions, shaking it up and then setting it on her trunk. They watched as the flakes drifted down, swirling around the tiny buildings and people, bundled up in their strange garments. "It's so beautiful," she whispered.

She pointed to the placard on the base:

Paris

"What does this word mean?"

He searched the dictionary. "Paris," he pronounced correctly. "The capital and largest city in France." He looked up. "It's a city from Before Doom."

"Wait, I think that explains the riddle."

She ran through the lines in her head to make sure:

Hidden in a city of old,
Untouched by the Doom,
It is always damp and cold.
There lies the buried treasure
That will light the way home,
So that the world that ended
May be remade once more.

The words that had stumped her for days now seemed to make perfect sense. It was an amazing transformation. She looked over at her brother excitedly.

"Based on the definition, Paris is a city of old," she said. "But since this is a model and not the actual city, it's untouched by the Doom." She gestured to the snow globe. "It's also filled with both water and ice . . . I mean . . . snow. So it's both damp and cold."

"And the scene never changes," Tinker said. "It's a model."

"Exactly, so it's always that way."

They both grinned, pleased to be on the right track finally. Myra flipped the snow globe over to examine the message carved into the base.

Only the least among you may possess the treasure.
—S. Wade

"What does this mean?" she asked. Tinker just shook his head and clacked on his computer. "Does least mean weakest?" she went on. "Or maybe smallest?"

"Not necessarily, it's too obvious." He typed a few more things. "Definition of least—smallest in significance; the smallest amount or degree."

"So, then who has the smallest significance? Hockers?"

Tinker shook his head. "They didn't exist back then, I don't think. The caste system wasn't put into place until after the Synod seized power."

"You're right, so what then?"

"The least among you . . ." he repeated with a furrowed brow. He looked up from his computer. "Wait a second, I think maybe I know what she meant!"

"What is it?" she said.

"The least among you—as in the youngest. She means kids, like us."

She thought for a second and caught onto his idea. "Right, that explains why the President didn't wear the Beacon, but his daughter did. I always wondered about that, since it seemed strange. It also explains why he didn't claim the Beacon for himself after she died. The same thing goes for her sister, because by that time—"

"Sari was already an adult," Tinker said.

"But why only kids?" Myra asked. "Why can't adults claim it?"

Tinker scrunched up his forehead like he always did when presented with a difficult problem. "The Beacon can only be removed after the Carrier dies, right?"

"Yup, according to the President's journal."

He gestured to his computer. "Maybe it's some kind of really advanced technology, like a computer that communicates directly with your brain, and it can only bond with somebody whose body hasn't finished growing yet. That would explain why you have to actually wear it."

Myra just stared at him. "Tinker, you're a genius!"

He blushed at her praise. "I just like solving puzzles."

"It's more than that—and you know it," she said and mussed his hair. Her gaze shifted back to the snow globe. "According to the riddle, it's buried in a city of old. Pass me a screwdriver from my rig, so I can open up the base."

Tinker dug through her tool rig and emerged with the tool. Myra went to work on the screws. They were rusty, and one was quickly stripped, but she was used to working on ancient machines. With a little more effort, she got them out and forced it open.

"Look, there's something in here."

Tinker watched over her shoulder as Myra fished out a black velvet bag. Her hands shook while she unfastened the ties and reached inside. Her fingers collided with something hard. She pulled it out, momentarily blinded by a flash of golden light.

And there it was—cradled in the palm of her hand.

The Beacon.

It looked the same as it did in Elianna's photographs. Unlike the snow globe, the Beacon didn't appear tarnished or rusted in any way. It looked brand new, like it had been fashioned only yesterday, which was astounding given its actual age. She ran her fingers over the golden surface. The metal gleamed vibrantly, casting off the dim glow of the flashlight. The same symbol that marked the Animus Machine was engraved onto its surface—a snake swallowing its own tail, entwined around two words.

"Aeternus eternus," she whispered.

Tinker's hands flew over the keyboard. "Origin: Latin," he read. "Whatever that is," he added with a frown. "Definition of Aeternus eternus," he went on. "Eternal, everlasting, without end—"

But before he could finish, something unexpected happened.

Myra's palm began to tingle and itch, and then to burn. Her first reaction was to cast the Beacon aside and cry out, but she found that she was frozen in place, as if an electric current were running through her body. She tried to move, but her muscles refused to respond to her commands. She was paralyzed, and this terrified her.

A greenish light began to emanate from the Beacon's golden surface—misty and dense. Suddenly, the Beacon split apart, the golden metal liquidly shifting.

"What's happening?" Tinker asked in a shaky voice.

But Myra couldn't respond. She was no longer in control of her body. Even her eyes were frozen, locked on the Beacon, so that she couldn't even tilt her gaze to see the frightened expression that was plastered on Tinker's face.

Something came over her and possessed her fully. In its

grip, she was helpless—merely a puppet of some larger force. Her limbs began to move of their own accord. First, her left hand grasped the Beacon, and then in one fluid motion, latched it around her right wrist.

"Myra, stop!" Tinker said. "We don't know if it's safe yet!"

He reached out to stop her, but he was too late.

With a blinding flash of green light, the cuff sealed itself around her flesh, the metal shifting and rearranging itself to fit the narrow dimensions of her wrist. The Beacon was locked in place—now only death could separate it from her flesh.

As the metal burrowed its sensors into her skin, Myra felt a searing pain worse than anything she'd ever experienced before, like a thousand fiery needles stabbing into her skin all at once. She tried to scream, but her jaw wouldn't open. She wanted to pry the Beacon from her wrist, but her arms were also immobilized.

The physical pain became something else altogether, as data traveled from the Beacon through her sensitive human nervous system to her brain. A thousand images forced their way into her thoughts, and this was excruciatingly painful. Her temples felt like they might explode. Strange places and people and events crammed their way into her mind, the likes of which she had never known, nor could she have ever imagined.

These thoughts were not her own, Myra realized—they belonged to somebody else. They became a part of her. She began to shake and convulse, foam frothing from her lips. Tinker shook her hard, trying to interrupt the seizure, but it didn't work. The strange memories overwhelmed and invaded her completely. And then, with a soft whimper and a great convulsion, Myra lost consciousness altogether as the world as she knew it faded away before her eyes.

It would never seem like the same world again.

PART IV
AETERNUS ETERNUS

Don't try to comprehend with your mind. Your minds are very limited. Use your intuition.

—Madeleine L'Engle, *A Wind in the Door*

Am I alive and a reality, or am I but a dream?

—Edgar Rice Burroughs, *The Return of Tarzan*

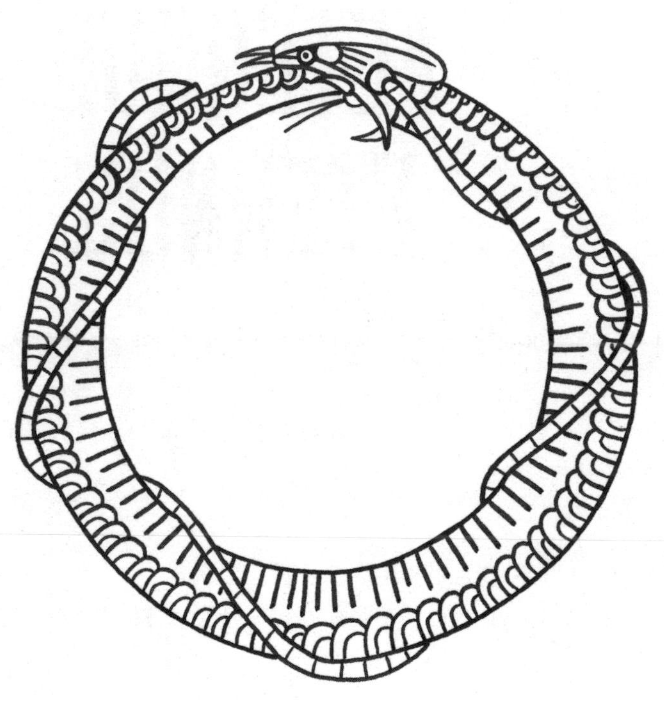

Chapter 28

THE WORLD THAT WAS

In a matter of minutes, Myra lived a whole other life.

It was Elianna Wade's life.

o o o

She saw the world that was.

Before it had been unmade.

And it was beautiful.

She walked on the Surface.

She beheld the endless sky, bluer than the purest cornflower blue.

She chased lightning bugs through the fields at night, the soft tendrils of wheat caressing her skin.

She looked upon the stars, and she understood what they were.

She drank from the rivers, and they were not salty. Her thirst was quenched, as it had never been before.

She watched as the rivers fed into tributaries and lakes and, eventually, emptied into the sea. And this sea was exposed and unstill and restless with waves.

And when she saw the sun and felt its heat, she fell to her knees and wept tears of joy. And her flesh was warmed, as it had never before.

This world was teeming with life through and through.

It was a world of plenty.

And she absorbed all of it.

She beheld vivid greens, saturated reds, dignified purples, dazzling oranges, glittering yellows, and oh, the blues.

She had been living in a gray world, she realized then.

And when she had seen all of that, she saw everything that man had built.

Cities upon cities upon cities.

Asphalt paths that blanketed the unquiet earth.

Skyscrapers, gray and hulking and seemingly as tall as the sky.

Computers that grew more intricate and more intelligent with each iteration.

Locomotion machines, too numerous to comprehend.

But comprehend them, she did.

And somehow it all became a part of her, this remembrance of a world that had long since passed into oblivion. She was one with this world, and this world was one with her.

Chapter 29
A BLESSED GIFT

The images began to resolve themselves into a scene.

Though Myra did not know how exactly, she understood that this memory—above all others—was something that Elianna Wade wanted her to witness.

And then she was inside of it, and it was all around her.

The world from Before Doom pulled into stark focus.

o o o

She stands in a circular room.

The walls are rounded—even the door is curved.

Her father sits behind an imposing desk.

Her father, the president.

These details come to her all at once.

She catches a glimpse of her young face in the gilded mirror on the wall—and she is Elianna Wade. Her lips move of their own accord and speak words that are not her own. She is merely an observer, she understands then. This is the past, and that's why she can't control her actions. The past cannot change; it can only be recorded and replayed.

"Papa, you wanted to see me?"

Another man steps into view. He's garbed in a crimson robe with a golden seal—a serpent swallowing its tail, entwined around the words Aeternus Eternus.

"Elianna, I would like you to meet Professor Divinus," her father says. His eyes shift to the man. "Professor, this is Elianna, my firstborn."

"Elianna, what a lovely name," the professor says and smiles warmly. "Mind if we sit for a spell? My joints just aren't what they used to be."

They sit in the stiff-backed chairs positioned in front of her father's desk. Now they are close enough that she can examine the professor's weary face, long white beard, and eyes as blue as the bluest sky. They probe her face.

"Elianna, do you know about the Doom?"

"Of course, everybody does," she says, taken aback by this turn in the conversation. She's lived with this threat her whole life—every kid her age has.

"And what do you know about it?"

She glances at her father, but he doesn't intervene. He sits silently, observing. "Well, just that it's a weapon more powerful than any other weapon on Earth."

"Yes, the Doomsday Machine. That's the official name given to it by our military. I think it's important to remember the truth about these things, don't you agree?"

She nods, for it is all she can think to do.

"As it happens, we were the first nation to possess it, but many have now followed in our footsteps." A troubled look passes over his face, making him appear a decade older.

Though that matters not—all that matters are the consequences, should it ever be activated. Do you know what they are?"

"It'll destroy the world."

"You are only partially correct this time," he says, not unkindly. "It'll render the surface of our planet uninhabitable for a thousand years, at a minimum."

She looks down. "It's too horrible to even consider . . ."

"But consider it we must," he says. "That is—if we wish to survive."

Her eyes widen in fear. "You think the Doom . . . might actually happen?"

"I don't just think it, I know it," he replies. "I've done the calculations, taking into account man's genetic predisposition to violence, human error, chaos theory, among other variables, and the probability is not as insignificant as you might wish."

"If you're right, then there's no hope."

He smiles in a way that exudes kindness. "There is always hope, my dear. Don't ever forget that."

"But . . . how?" she says, reeling from it all.

"The same way that we got ourselves into this mess—by using our wits." He strokes his beard. "I've created something called the Continuum Project. It's top secret, of course, but your father has assured me that you're most trustworthy."

She risks a glance in her father's direction, where he sits behind his desk, still observing their interaction. She sits up straighter and squares her shoulders, as if sensing the burden about to be placed there. "My father . . . is correct about me."

"Yes, well, I thought so," the professor says with a glint in his eyes. "The Continuum Project's purpose is to preserve life on Earth and the knowledge of human civilization should the Doom come to pass. With the help of my sworn brothers and sisters, I've constructed an underground vault that we call the First Continuum."

"The First Continuum—what is it?"

"A vessel."

"What does it hold?"

"Everything—the sum total of life."

"But how is that possible?"

"Well, for over two decades, we've been cataloging and archiving human knowledge in a supercomputer. At the same time, the biology professors have been collecting and freezing seedlings and embryos of all known species in incubators, so that they may be resuscitated hundreds of years in the future with the push of a button."

She struggles to comprehend this knowledge, to adjust her worldview to allow for it. "If that is the First Continuum, then there are more of these Continuums?"

He looks pleased by her reasoning. "Twelve more, to be exact. Only they aren't repositories like the first—they're colonies built into my college's existing research facilities, which we've retrofitted to support human life. Five are deep underground; three are in outer space, including the Mars colony; and four are in the trenches at the bottom of the ocean. This is because we don't know which environment will prove the most conducive to long-term survival."

"Thirteen in all," she says. "How many people can you save?"

The troubled look—which she can now positively identify as guilt—passes over his face again. "Space is limited, and we have the entire world to consider. Though we've been most diligent in our choosing, we can't possibly save everybody. However, that brings me to the reason we're sitting here right now, having this conversation."

He leans forward and steeples his fingertips under his chin. "Elianna, your family has been chosen—your father, mother, sister, and you."

She feels a sharp pang, as if somebody has stabbed her. "But not my grandmother?"

He frowns, and his sadness is genuine. "She's an elderly woman who has already lived out most of her days . . . and even if we were to choose her, then I'm quite sure she'd prefer to surrender her spot to somebody younger, don't you agree?"

Elianna thinks of her grandmother—her wiry hair, her sharp eyes, and her charitable smile—and she knows that the professor is right about her.

"Nana is very giving," she says, though her voice wavers.

The professor smiles grimly. "I'm not going to lie, the choosing has been the hardest part of this entire operation—a necessary evil, as I think of it."

He reaches inside his robe and produces a golden armlet. It shimmers and glows, casting off the light. She can see her reflection in its luminous surface.

"What's that?" she asks, captivated by the armlet.

"The Beacon."

"Like a homing beacon?"

"That's right, it's a homing beacon, but also so much more. One will be given to each of the colonies. Its central purpose is to lead those who survive the period of exile back to the First Continuum after the proper amount of time has elapsed. I consider it my greatest invention. It's made using very complex science. You do not just wear the Beacon—it actually bonds with your physical body."

She looks at the professor in confusion. "But then why do you need me? Surely my father can wear the Beacon. He's the leader of the free world, after all."

The professor exchanges an amused smile with the president. "Ah, I'm sure that he would wear it if he could," the professor says.

"So why can't he?"

"Only the least among us may possess the Beacon," he says cryptically. He leans forward and strokes his beard. "It was an unforeseen complication, but the Beacon can only bond with a person whose body isn't fully mature yet. When I approached your father with my quandary, he suggested that you might be an appropriate choice."

Her nerves flare up, and she feels unworthy. "You want me to wear it?"

The men exchange a worried glance, and that is when she knows that there is more to this task than it appears on the surface. She steels herself, before asking: "So then, what's the catch?"

The professor regards her solemnly. "Once the Beacon bonds with a Carrier, it can only be removed after they die. If you volunteer for this duty, then you will wear the Beacon for the rest of your life. Trying to remove the device prematurely . . . well, it would be too damaging. None of our test subjects survived such a trauma."

She grips the arms of the chair to steady herself. She does not want to appear afraid, not in front of the professor. "And the bonding process? Is that dangerous, too?"

"Not for someone like yourself. Disorientating, maybe. You might experience some nausea. It'll be an adjustment, to be sure, but it's entirely safe, I promise."

"But what if I grow older before the Doom happens?"

He smiles warmly, the corners of his eyes crinkling up. "Well, then, my dear, we shall all rejoice. Every day that we live freely on this fair earth without the Doom happening is a blessed gift. And, in that case, the burden will pass to your sister."

"Sari," she whispers. "And if she grows older?"

"Then we shall rejoice again and identify a new Carrier."

"But why approach me now?"

"We've installed early warning systems, but they're imperfect at best. Should the Doom come to pass, I fear that there will be precious little time to evacuate. And, well, we don't want to force this on anyone—we want the Carriers to have a choice."

The professor levels his gaze on her. "Elianna Wade, will you become a Carrier?"

Her eyes dart to the golden armlet clutched in the professor's gnarled hand. For a moment, she is captivated by its radiance—and by everything that the professor has just told her. She has always assumed, like almost everybody else, that the Doom would kill every living creature on Earth and wipe out all that mankind has endeavored to build. To learn that they have hope—any hope at all—is a blessed gift indeed.

Tears well in her eyes, but they are not tears of sorrow or fear.

They are tears of tremendous joy.

"Eli, we need your answer," her father says. "Will you carry the Beacon?"

o o o

It was then that the edges of the memory began to fray and fade into a blur of memories.

They overtook Myra and flooded through her, each moving faster than the one that came before. They were snapshots taken through the eyes of Elianna Wade and preserved by the Beacon all these hundreds of years later, like mosquitoes trapped in amber. She witnessed them through Elianna's eyes as if they were one person.

o o o

Elianna evacuates the White House with her family and boards a helicopter. Sari breaks down in a fit of tears as they forsake their grandmother to the Doom.

They arrive at the docks and board a submersible marked with the number 13.

It is then that she knows their destination—The Thirteenth Continuum.

A red-cloaked professor kneels before her and presents the Beacon.

She grasps it, and under her touch, the golden metal morphs and splits apart. She knows that there is no turning back now—the enduring bond is thus forged.

The submarine shudders to life with a great rumble.

They dive and dive and dive into the depths of the sea, while many miles above them, the Doom wreaks havoc on the exposed surface of the Earth.

And then, the world that was—the world of Elianna Wade and her beautiful memories—ceases to exist altogether, and a new world is born underneath the sea.

Chapter 30
RECREATION

When Myra finally awoke with the Beacon bonded to her flesh—to the essence of her entire being—she was a different creature altogether.

Not *Myra Jackson* exactly, but not *Elianna Wade* either.

Sort of like a *Myra-Elianna* composite.

The knowledge of this other life had invaded every cell in her body and filled her up in a way that she had never been filled before, and it had recreated her in its image.

And now, without any shred of reluctance or uncertainty, she knew exactly what it was that she must do.

Chapter 31
MALFUNCTION

Captain Aero Wright

"Captain Wright I heard there was a computer malfunction?"

Supreme General Brillstein leveled this question on Aero as they stood on the bridge with Earth projected on the monitors.

Aero wasn't dressed in his everyday uniform but in a spacesuit. Though lightweight, the silvery material was more durable than it appeared. His Falchion was strapped to his waist. Before the Supreme General had summoned him to the bridge, he'd been readying his unit for deployment. His eyes flicked to the monitors. The storms had finally abated. To take advantage of this lull, they would deploy immediately.

The fact that two of his soldiers had died and another had lost his Falchion wouldn't hinder his unit's ability to perform their duty. They took no time off to mourn their dead or hold funerals. By this time, the Euthanasia Clinic had already delivered Starling and Tristan's bodies to the incinerator, where, in one final burst of productivity, their remains were used to help fuel the ship.

Aero pictured the combustion—the searing blaze that would consume their flesh and bones. Now his soldiers were likely nothing more than smoke and ash.

"Yes, sir!" Aero said with a crisp salute. "We encountered a problem with the simulator." He couldn't bring himself to say *malfunction* when he suspected it was something far more insidious. "I didn't program any environmental interference, but we experienced an earthquake. And the safety controls were . . . switched off."

His eyes darted to Major Vinick, who sat behind his console, monitoring the ship's position. The other Majors—Doyle, Oranck, Kieran, Cole, and Mauro—were diligently manning their stations, but they all seemed to be listening to his conversation.

"I read the report, Captain. You were wounded?" Supreme General Brillstein said. He nodded to Aero's bandaged shoulder. "Not too badly, I hope?"

Aero smiled sheepishly. "Nothing that won't heal. I'm almost good as new."

Despite his adamant and, in retrospect, foolhardy protests, Wren had forced him to go to Medical after all. They had worked on his injured shoulder and applied a special bandage that sped up the body's natural restorative processes. "The bandage is only a precaution to facilitate the healing. Medical's cleared me for deployment."

Brillstein appeared relieved, which surprised Aero. He studied the Supreme General's face but arrived at no definitive conclusion. *Emotions are slippery like that*, Aero thought. *They can appear one minute, only to vanish the next without a trace.*

"Very good, Captain," Brillstein said. "But you lost two soldiers?"

Aero couldn't help it—he looked down. "Yes, two *good* soldiers. Starling and Tristan." He forced himself to meet Brillstein's gaze. "And one of my privates lost his Falchion. It melted down."

There were murmurs on the bridge. Losing one's Falchion was considered a fate worse than death. As was the protocol,

Zakkay was being held by Medical for observation to make sure that he didn't try to harm himself—or anyone else.

"But three privates have already been transferred from another combat unit," Aero said, trying to keep his voice devoid of emotion. "And two transports are being readied for my unit. We should have enough provisions to last two weeks—"

But Aero didn't a chance to finish.

Suddenly, Major Vinick unsheathed his Falchion and leapt at the Supreme General with a surprising amount of agility. In midair, he expertly shifted his weapon into a dagger and buried it deep in Brillstein's back. It was perfectly placed—the blade stabbed right through his heart, the golden tip protruding from his chest.

The wound hissed and spat as sparks flew from the dagger. Brillstein clutched at his Falchion's hilt, trying to unsheathe it, but he was too late. His body began to convulse as the electric charge ran through it. Blood spilled down his chin. The Beacon also appeared to be in its death throes—the green light flickered and began to fade.

"No!" Aero screamed as his father's body slumped to the ground in a bloody heap. His reflexes took over, and he acted like a creature of pure instinct. He whipped out his Falchion, morphed it into a broadsword, and hurtled himself at Vinick.

But Vinick reacted just as quickly. He pressed his foot into Brillstein's back to free the dagger from his ribcage and then shifted his Falchion into a broadsword and raised it just in time to meet Aero's blade. Their swords clanged together with ferocity, emitting a shower of golden sparks. They both leaned into the attack, their faces illuminated by the flaming blades.

Vinick glared at him malevolently. "Are you upset about your father?" he said. He redoubled his efforts and forced Aero back several steps. "He didn't care about you, silly boy."

"Shut up!" Aero seethed and held his ground. "You murderous traitor!"

Why aren't the Majors wrestling Vinick to the ground? he thought frantically.

They stood around the bridge, watching the fight. Some had unsheathed their Falchions and clutched them loosely in their default forms, but they made no move to intervene. They'd known that Vinick was planning this treason, Aero realized furiously. And they were supporting him, at least passively. So they would not interfere.

Vinick forced him back another foot, pushing him into the wall. "*Only the strongest shall lead us*," he quoted their teaching. "Well . . . your father was . . . sadly . . . unfit for leadership. I am the strongest soldier. I always was!"

"That why you were second at the Agoge?" Aero said.

This infuriated Vinick—he broke the connection and swung again. His Falchion tore through the air with blinding speed. Aero could only deflect the blow; he didn't have enough time to recover and launch an attack. He was a skilled soldier, but Vinick was older and also exceptionally skilled. Plus, Aero was still healing from his wound. His injured shoulder started to throb. If he wasn't careful, he could tear it open again.

Aero gritted his teeth and switched his Falchion to his right hand. He flexed his fist and strengthened his grip on the hilt. Vinick paused to recalibrate his attack.

"Ambidextrous?" he said. "I read your file from the Agoge."

"Then you know that I was first in my class, like my father," Aero said and took a cautious step toward Vinick, feeling him out. Vinick swiped at him, but Aero sidestepped the blow. "And that I'm undefeated in Falchion-to-Falchion combat."

Vinick's lips curled back. "Being first will not save you, boy!" He gestured to Brillstein's body. "Just like it didn't save your father."

"Then I'll just have to win, won't I?"

"This isn't the Agoge or a simulation," Vinick said as he swung his blade.

Aero ducked out of the way. "Oh, but it's not so very

different, is it? In my last simulated battle, somebody changed the safety controls to kill."

Vinick flinched and that was when Aero knew—Vinick was responsible for the deaths of his soldiers. Anger surged through Aero, overwhelming his rationality.

"So it was you! You killed my soldiers!"

"The earthquake killed them," Vinick said, circling Aero and thrusting when he spotted an opening. "I just made sure they didn't have any protection."

"You're a murderer!" Aero screamed.

"I prefer to think of myself as a good soldier. If the Supreme General had ordered you to kill for him, would you have done it, Captain?" Uncertainty clouded Aero's face. Vinick saw it and plowed forward. "We all kill when it benefits our side. Well, it's just a matter of perspective, isn't it? Whether you're the victor or the vanquished."

Doubt surged through Aero, but he forced it back down. His moral compass was strong, he reminded himself. It had been calibrated over the course of his training and studies. He wouldn't let Vinick skew his thinking, the way he had the other Majors.

"You're a murderer—you'll never convince me otherwise."

With that, Aero launched his attack, blocking Vinick's blows and then advancing, retreating when it proved beneficial, and pressing his attack when his instincts told him the moment was right. Vinick was swinging his Falchion with less control now, Aero noticed, advancing less and defending more. *Just a little bit longer*, he thought.

Digging into reserves of energy that he didn't even know he possessed, Aero backed Vinick into a corner and trapped him between two computer consoles. He kicked a chair at Vinick, forcing him to dodge it. Vinick stumbled and went down, recovering just in time to meet Aero's swift blow.

But it was too little too late.

Fear flashed across Vinick's face. He was losing now, and he knew it. It only took a few more strikes for Aero to finish the fight. He knocked the Falchion from Vinick's hand and kicked it away. It skittered across the floor and came to rest a few feet from them. A few more swings brought Vinick to his knees. One final blow and Vinick fell flat on his back.

Aero towered over him with his Falchion raised for a kill stroke, one that he had delivered many times before in the simulator. But this time was different—a wave of doubt flooded through him. Despite all of his experience in Falchion-to-Falchion combat, he'd never actually killed anyone, not in real life. And he'd certainly never struck down an unarmed opponent.

The other Majors were watching, but still they didn't intervene. They also hadn't bothered to help his father, Aero noticed angrily. They hadn't called Medical—or the Euthanasia Clinic.

"What are you waiting for, boy?" Vinick hissed. Spittle flew from his lips. His face and uniform were splattered with the Supreme General's blood. "Finish me!"

Aero's muscles tensed as he gripped his Falchion. It would be so easy to strike him down in the passion of the moment.

So very easy . . . and so very wrong.

He lowered his blade. "Then I'd be no better than you," Aero said.

"You're a fool, just like your father."

"I thought I told you to shut up!" Aero said as he swung his Falchion. But the blow wasn't intended to kill Vinick. Instead, it knocked him unconscious.

Aero didn't waste another second on the traitor. He morphed his Falchion back to its default form and sheathed it and then sprinted over to his father's body. The puncture in his chest was leaking blood at an alarming rate.

Aero tore the sleeve off his spacesuit and used it to apply pressure to the wound. His eyes darted to the Beacon. It still throbbed with greenish light. It was faint—a shadow of what it had been—but unmistakable.

Was it possible he was still alive?

"Call Medical, you cowards!" Aero screamed at the Majors. This jolted them into action. Major Doyle moved to a console and hit the emergency button.

"Medical to the bridge!" Major Doyle said. "Two soldiers down!"

Aero cradled the Supreme General's head in his arms. Suddenly, his eyes fluttered open. He tried to smile, but it morphed into a grimace.

"*Aero* . . . is that you?" he rasped, coughing up blood.

The use of his first name stunned Aero, but dying men sometimes experienced delusions. The Supreme General had lost a lot of blood. He probably wasn't in his right mind. "Please, try to be still, sir," Aero said. "You're . . . badly wounded."

"*A good commander . . . knows when the battle is lost*," he quoted their teaching. "This is a . . . mortal wound, I am finished . . . my son."

Aero froze—*did he just call me his son?*

"There isn't . . . much time left," Brillstein rasped. His eyes were glassy, and coughing fits interrupted his speech. "You must . . . listen to me . . . carefully."

"Yes . . . father," Aero said. The word felt strange and unnatural on his tongue, but it also filled him up in a way that he had never been filled up before.

"Take the Beacon after I die. Don't let Vinick change our course . . . go to Earth . . . go alone if you must. There are others . . . you will see . . . you must find them—"

A coughing spasm interrupted him.

The light of the Beacon had begun to fade.

"No, you're going to make it, sir!" Aero blinked away tears. He hadn't even realized he was crying. "Medical is on the way! They'll fix you up good as new! And we'll journey to the First Continuum together. Please, hang in there."

"Just promise me, damn it!"

"I promise," Aero said. More tears welled in his eyes. They fell from his cheeks, mingling with his father's blood. "I swear it on my life as a soldier."

A smile played across his father's lips, as the Beacon throbbed with a vivid flash of green light. He placed his hand on his son's cheek.

"You are my son . . . there's no doubt about it," he said weakly. "I wish I could have known you as a child . . . that it wasn't forbidden."

His hand slipped from Aero's cheek and fell to the ground.

The Beacon emitted once last flash of light and then went dark.

"No," Aero sobbed, shaking his father's limp body.

Dimly, he was aware of movement and rustling around him. The swish of uniforms as the Majors surrounded him, trying to pull him away from his father's corpse, and then Medical arriving on the bridge with a gurney.

Somebody else with them, too.

Was it Wren? Or was he imagining things now?

His emotions threatened to overwhelm him, and he was powerless to stop the deluge. He shook his head to clear it—only one thing mattered now:

The Beacon.

He had made a promise—he had sworn it on his life as a soldier—and he would not fail his father now. He crawled to his body and seized his wrist. There, still latched around his pale flesh, was the Beacon. Aero had never seen it up close like this. He had no idea how the device functioned, let alone how to unfasten it. Its exterior was smooth and unbroken. He ran his hand over it anyway, searching for a hidden joint or switch.

And that was when it happened.

The Beacon came alive, as if sensing Aero's suitability as a Carrier. It split apart, the metal liquidly shifting, and fell open in his outstretched palm. Though solid, it was lighter than he'd expected. Aero did not hesitate—time was of the essence now. Almost like some outside force had seized control of him, he latched the Beacon around his right wrist. It glowed with a blinding flash of green light as it sealed itself around his flesh.

Vaguely, Aero heard the Majors shouting at each other in panicked voices. "He has claimed the Beacon . . . now they are bonded for life . . . only death can part them."

The pain that Aero felt as the Beacon sunk into him, though reminiscent of when he'd bonded with his Falchion at the Agoge, was infinitely stronger. His flesh burned, and he felt searing pain traveling up his arm, spreading through every molecule in his body until it reached his brain.

And that was when another assault began altogether.

Aero struggled to remain conscious as all of the Supreme Generals' collected memories forced their way into his neural synapses.

But he was failing.

The world around him was dimming.

He drew on all of the skills that he'd learned at the Agoge, the same ones that had allowed him to master his Falchion. The world drew into sharper focus for a moment.

And that was when he saw the shadow.

It stretched over his prone body, which lay right next to his father's. Major Vinick towered over him with his Falchion clutched in his hand. Blood seeped from a deep laceration in his forehead, where Aero had struck him.

"Foolish boy! What have you done?"

Aero tried to move his lips, but he found that he could not speak. He ordered his hand to seize his Falchion, but it remained limp by his side. It did not even twitch.

The horror of his situation dawned on him.

I am paralyzed. Helpless. Unable to defend myself.

"You've claimed the Beacon for yourself," Vinick said as he raised his Falchion, still in the shape of a broadsword. "And so now you must die."

Chapter 32
TWO NAMES

The Synod

"Now that didn't take long, did it?"

The priest allowed the disdain to filter into his voice as it reverberated through the locked chamber. He liked to let them know when they had displeased him. He pushed aside the crate filled with dusty objects. Several more were stacked behind him.

The man in black, though physically large, cowered in his presence. "Padre, you were right . . . as always!" he stammered, nervously bobbing his head.

"But you wasted my time." His lips curled back like they always did when he was cross. "We should have deployed this tactic at the first sign of resistance."

"Well, the prisoner proved more defiant than we anticipated, but after we arrested his daughters and roughed them up a bit, he found his voice. He won't shut up now."

"What did he cough up?"

"Two names."

"Are you sure he's telling the truth?"

"More than sure." The man in black held up two thick

files with the names scrawled across the bindings. "Both were already under surveillance."

"For what?"

"Being suspected heathens."

"Arrest them."

"But my men have been working around the clock—"

"Now."

"Yes, of course!"

This man was afraid of him, terrified even. A cruel smile stretched across his thin lips. He loved having this effect on people. "And see that you don't waste my time with ineffective tactics again."

"We didn't waste time—"

"Silence!"

He rose to his full height. Though he was not larger than this man—*this Factum*—he stood on an elevated platform, and this made him appear taller than he actually was. He made sure the man was properly chastised before he continued.

"If they prove defiant—as you put it—don't hesitate to arrest their children," he pronounced with a flick of his wrist. "Don't wait two days this time."

"As you command, it shall be done!"

"As *the Oracle* commands!"

The man swirled his hand over his chest. "Of course—the Oracle!"

"Amen."

As the man fled from the chamber, he found himself comforted by the thought of the two names. The investigation was already going better than he'd hoped. Soon—very soon now—he would have more sacrifices for the Holy Sea. And maybe even information that would lead to the Beacon. His eyes flicked to the crates and narrowed. So far it had eluded him, but that could change now. This pleased him greatly.

He loved doing his holy work.

Chapter 33
'TIL DEATH DO US PART

Myra Jackson

Myra regained consciousness to Tinker shaking her. He was silent—deadly silent, as if he had lost the ability to speak—but terror shone brightly in his eyes.

Her head felt as though somebody had shaken it up. Her temples throbbed, her lips were dry and cracked, and she felt terribly disoriented. It took her a moment to realize that she was still in the bedroom that she shared with her brother, in her family's assigned compartment, in the Thirteenth Continuum—and that the year was 1000 Post Doom. She had traveled through space and time, and she had experienced things that she'd never imagined existed, not even in her wildest dreams.

"You're alive . . . " Tinker gasped.

Once the worst of the disorientation passed, Myra struggled to sit up. As her vision cleared, she realized that it seemed like there was another person in the room, in addition to her and Tinker—Elianna Wade. It felt as though she were sitting next to them on the bunk or hovering in the periphery just out of sight, though Elianna had been dead for nearly a millennium. There were no such things as ghosts, Myra reminded herself.

But doubt flooded through her anyway.

"How long . . . was I unconscious?" she rasped through parched lips.

"Only a little over five minutes," Tinker said.

She looked at him in shock but detected no lie in his eyes. "But how is that possible?"

Her journey had felt much longer—like years, or maybe even decades—not mere minutes. She jerked her gaze to her wrist, where the Beacon had welded itself to her flesh. It pulsed in a steady rhythm with emerald light. Tinker reached out and laid his palm on it. She felt warmth traveling from his hand into the Beacon, and then into her, like it was hotwired to her body. "It feels . . . like a part of me now," she whispered.

Tinker was equally captivated by it. He examined her wrist closely, then retrieved his computer and typed in a few observations. He stopped typing abruptly. "It appears to carry an electrical charge, though I don't know how exactly. Maybe it's drawing on your body's energy to power it?" He typed a few more things, and then reached for her wrist and found her pulse. He counted it out, his eyes widening.

"It's pulsing with the same rhythm as your heart," he said, confirming what Myra already sensed. "Well, I guess it really is like a part of you now."

"'Till death do us part," she joked before growing more serious. "Tink, I can feel her . . . Elianna Wade . . . "

She trailed off, aware of how crazy that sounded. She didn't know how to properly explain it.

"What do you mean?" Tinker said, looking up from his computer.

She had his full attention now. She considered how best to translate it into words. "Her memories . . . her essence . . . her feelings . . . her thoughts . . . her everything."

Tinker's eyes widened even more. "But that's impossible."

"I know, but that doesn't mean it isn't true."

Tinker thought hard for a minute. "I guess the Founders must have discovered a way to preserve a person," he said, gesturing to his computer. "To download and record Elianna's thoughts and memories, like a computer downloads a piece of data."

Myra felt Elianna pushing on her.

Tell him what you must do.

Elianna's words echoed through her head, clear and undeniable. Myra froze—how was this possible? Elianna could talk to her?

The world threatened to dissolve again, but Myra concentrated hard and somehow forced Elianna back down. She didn't want to fall unconscious again.

"Well, it's hard to explain," she said. "But when I was unconscious, I saw the world from Before Doom through Elianna's eyes and absorbed everything she knew."

As best as she could, Myra recounted what she had experienced. *The World That Was*. The *sky* and the *stars* and the *sun* and the *oceans* and the *cities* and the *roads* and the *machines* and the *people*, carefree and plentiful and doomed.

She told him about evacuating the White House, boarding the submersible, and the weapon that had obliterated the Surface. She finished by telling him about the professor—*Professor Divinus*, Elianna communicated to her—and the Beacon and the Continuum Project.

When she had done that, she told him what Elianna most wanted: "Tinker, I know what we're supposed to do now! I have to lead us back to the First Continuum, so we can recolonize the Surface. This is what the Founders intended. A thousand years have come and gone, and now the time has arrived for us to return to our rightful home."

Tinker blinked and said nothing for a long while, and Myra worried that she had burdened him with too much.

Finally, he let out a long whistle. "That is some story."

"So you believe me then?"

"Do I have a choice?"

She shook her head. "None of us do."

He fixed her with a determined look. "I believe you, and I'm coming with you."

"Oh, Tink, I want you to come . . . more than anything.

You have to believe me! But it will be difficult and dangerous, and I don't even know how I will manage it."

"I don't care," he insisted. "I'm coming."

Myra wanted to protest, but it was no use trying to convince him otherwise. Her brother was many things, but above all, he was stubborn.

"Fine, you're coming. Happy?"

He nodded, but then his eyes flicked to the door.

"It's time, isn't it?" Myra said.

She'd been dreading coming clean to her father, but now that she'd found the Beacon, there was no avoiding it. But before Tinker could respond, a noise shot through the compartment.

Bang! Bang! Bang!

Somebody was pounding on the front door.

Fear surged through her. It was still the middle of the night. Only one type of visitor came calling at this hour—the Patrollers. She leapt from her bunk, ignoring the dizzy feeling that still muddled her brain, and padded to the door.

Tinker started to follow, but she stopped him. "Wait here!" she said. "And keep the door locked."

She peered into the dark living space. Her father was already up and heading for the door. He wore his nightclothes and clutched a flashlight, which cast a dim beam of light. He looked exhausted, like he'd just woken from a deep slumber.

"Papa, who is it?" Myra whispered, but he didn't hear her.

He padded up to the compartment door, but before he could scan his wrist, it beeped and retracted into the wall. The Patrollers barged through the opening, their pipes raised over their heads. Her father was shocked by the sudden intrusion.

"Hey, you can't just break into my compartment—"

"Silence, heathen!" snarled Jasper. Another Patroller stormed in right behind him. Myra recognized him immediately. It was Patroller Bates. Two pledges flanked them—Baron and Horace. Baron spotted her and grinned viciously.

Her father looked furious. "Stop, I demand to know why you're here!"

They didn't answer, at least not verbally. Jasper pounced on her father and started beating him with his pipe. Her father cried out, but that didn't stay the blows. Without thinking—acting on pure adrenaline—Myra hurled herself at the Patroller. She clawed at Jasper's face with her nails. This made him stop beating her father but only so that he could beat her instead. His pipe connected with her abdomen, knocking the wind from her chest in an explosion of pain. She collapsed into the sofa, gasping for breath.

"Leave her alone, you bully!" her father yelled.

He charged at Jasper and punched him in the face, his fist connecting with Jasper's jaw and knocking him down. Then he ran to Myra's side, and his eyes landed on her wrist—and the golden cuff that was fastened there. They widened in shock. "But how did you find it?"

Myra didn't get a chance to answer.

Jasper, who had recovered from the blow, whacked her father in the head with his pipe. But it did serve as a warning—Myra yanked her sleeve down to hide the Beacon, grateful the Patrollers hadn't noticed it.

She glanced up to see Tinker watching from the bedroom door. "Tink, get out of here!" she yelled at him.

When he didn't obey, she ran over and shoved him back into their room, shutting the door. He pounded on it angrily, but she ignored him. Better that he be angry—even terribly so—than risk him getting hurt.

She watched the horrific scene unfold in front of her. Jasper beat her father until he was crumpled on the ground in a bloody heap. Baron bound his wrists behind his back with thick rope, though it was unnecessary. Her father was immobilized and clearly not going anywhere. Jasper inspected the knot and shot Baron a satisfied grin.

"Nice job, pledge! Now get the prisoner on his feet."

"But what about the girl?" Baron said to his assigned apprentice. "She's a heathen, I swear it. We ought to arrest her too, save ourselves another trip."

"Pledge, our orders are only to arrest the father," Jasper

said. "Don't ever question your superiors, you got that? Or you won't last long with the 'Trollers."

Baron looked furious, but he didn't protest. "Yes, sir."

"Now get the prisoner up, so he can hear why we're here."

Baron yanked her father to his feet with more force than was necessary. He groaned and struggled to remain standing. Blood seeped from a nasty gash on his forehead. He'd lost a few teeth and maybe broken a rib or two.

"Myra, don't even think about it!" he yelled. "Just keep Tinker safe."

She wanted to disobey him, but she knew it was futile. "Yes, Papa," she said through angry tears.

She felt her heart rending apart, but she stayed planted in front of the bedroom door to protect Tinker. Besides, there was nothing she could do. She had no way to defeat four Patrollers and free her father. She'd never felt more helpless in her life. Tears clouded her vision, but she blinked them back, refusing to let the Patrollers see her cry.

Bates pulled out a roll of parchment and cleared his throat. "Jonah Jackson, by order of the Synod, I hereby place you under arrest. For plotting to find the *blasphemous object* and return to *the place that shall not be named*." He looked up and frowned darkly. "May the Holy Sea have mercy on your soul."

Chapter 34
ONLY THE STRONGEST SHALL LEAD US

Captain Aero Wright

Major Vinick was standing over Aero to deliver the kill stroke when what looked like an angel leapt on top of him and saved his life. She was silvery and lithe and unafraid.

"Stay your blow, Major!" she yelled.

And that was when Aero realized through the haze of semiconsciousness that she was not an apparition after all—but a flesh and blood woman.

It was Wren.

Vinick hesitated, less because he was afraid of having another corpse on his hands and more from sheer surprise. He glared at her with his Falchion still raised to strike.

"Out of the way, Lieutenant! Unless you want to die, too."

Wren glared back at Vinick. "You can't just strike down two unarmed soldiers in cold blood!" She turned to the other Majors. "How can you stand by and let one of your own commit coldblooded murder like this? It goes against all of our teachings!"

Vinick narrowed his eyes. "Captain Wright stabbed the Supreme General in the back," he said in a clear and unwavering voice. "I'm merely doling out punishment."

Aero was still in the grip of the Beacon and utterly paralyzed. Wren glanced at him, wishing that he'd wake up and defend himself.

"Come on, talk to me!" she hissed in his ear, but he didn't respond. Didn't even blink. She knew Vinick was lying—Aero would never attack the Supreme General, especially since Brillstein was his father—but she didn't have any proof.

The Majors began to look uncomfortable. A few whispered to each other, but they didn't intervene. They feared Vinick, and they feared being on the losing side.

"Now stand aside, Lieutenant," Vinick said. "That's an order." When Wren didn't budge, he began to look furious. "In case you've forgotten, I outrank you significantly."

But Wren was thinking frantically. "Even if Captain Wright killed the Supreme General, you can't just kill him—not until he gets a fair trial." She gestured to the Medical team waiting by the elevator in stunned silence. They hadn't attended to Brillstein yet, though he looked beyond their salvation. "There are witnesses, and they'll know you haven't administered justice."

Wren turned to the other Majors. "We are a people of discipline, not savages. Or have you forgotten?"

Major Vinick raised his Falchion again, but he hesitated. "A trial before the Majors?" Vinick said with a sneer. "Fine, let's get it over with right now."

He turned to the other five Majors.

"As we witnessed, Captain Wright attacked the Supreme General and stabbed him in the back with his Falchion in the shape of a dagger, resulting in the Supreme General's untimely demise. The punishment for such an offense is death by beheading."

The lies poured forth from Vinick's lips naturally. The Majors whispered among themselves. Wren glanced down at Aero. He appeared mostly unharmed, aside from the blood seeping from his shoulder, yet he remained unresponsive. She couldn't begin to understand the reason. "Why don't you speak up and defend yourself?" she whispered.

But there was no response—Aero didn't even blink.

"Well, it's time to render our verdict," Vinick said. "I vote . . . guilty."

He turned to face Major Doyle. "Major, what say you?"

The officer looked down, but he uttered his verdict nonetheless.

"Guilty."

Majors Oranck, Mauro, Cole, and Kieran pronounced the same word in unison.

"Guilty."

Their voices echoed through the bridge. Wren couldn't believe her ears. This wasn't a fair trial, and the Majors knew it. Vinick grinned triumphantly.

"The Majors have spoken! Now stand aside, Lieutenant."

But Wren had one last card up her sleeve. Though she'd always hated her studies at the Agoge, she was grateful for them now. She turned to the other Majors.

"As you've just ruled, Captain Wright bested the Supreme General in combat. They both had their Falchions, didn't they? And Captain Wright has claimed the Beacon for himself. *Only the strongest shall lead us*. I don't need to remind you of this—it's our most sacred teaching. By defeating the Supreme General and claiming the Beacon, he's proven himself to be the strongest soldier and should be the next Supreme General."

Vinick frowned darkly. "He's not the strongest—I'm the strongest! And I'll prove it right now. Once I kill him, I'll be the next Supreme General."

He raised his Falchion to strike Aero and take his life, but Wren narrowed her eyes and didn't budge, not even one millimeter. She lay draped over Aero's prone body to protect him from Vinick. She deployed her final maneuver.

"Striking down an immobilized opponent won't demonstrate that you're the strongest soldier. According to our teachings, you must prove it—through a duel."

"I don't have to prove anything," Vinick said, but his voice wavered.

The other Majors whispered among themselves and appeared conflicted. Though Vinick didn't swing his blade yet, he also didn't surrender and sheathe his Falchion, which was still morphed into a broadsword. Wren bit her lip nervously.

Finally, Major Doyle spoke up. "Major Vinick, you know the Majors support your bid to be our next Supreme General. However, it seems that Lieutenant Jordan is right about our teachings. Captain Wright triumphed over the Supreme General in combat and claimed the Beacon, so he's next in line to command us—unless you beat him in a duel. If you strike him down now while he's injured and unarmed, then the soldiers will question your leadership."

Doyle's eyes flicked to the Medical team. Though only a few witnesses, rumors and gossip had a way of spreading through the ship. Aero still lay paralyzed on the floor, his mind hijacked by the Beacon and its complex bonding process.

Vinick didn't look pleased by this pronouncement. "What are the parameters of this duel?" he asked.

It had been hundreds of years since such a circumstance had occurred, and few remembered the arcane rules anymore. Doyle conferred with the other Majors.

"Falchion-to-Falchion combat in the simulator, and the Majors will select the venue. Neither you nor Captain Wright will be privy to the venue in advance. Oh, and the safety controls must be set to kill. It will be a duel to the death with only one victor."

"And when shall this event take place?" Vinick asked.

Doyle shrugged. "There's no specific rule, at least not that I know." Wren was forced to agree, and she nodded. "But I'm of the opinion that the sooner we settle this vacuum of leadership, the better. It'll help prevent unrest and dissent in the ranks."

Vinick caught his drift and shot him a smile. "Yes, of course I'm of like mind, Major Doyle." His eyes flicked to Aero's wounded shoulder. "The sooner the better."

"Tomorrow then?" Doyle suggested.

"But Captain Wright is wounded!" Wren said.

"There's no rule on that," Doyle said. "It's best if we settle this now."

"But you must see reason!" she begged. "Two days! And then I'll drop my objection. If Major Vinick defeats a wounded opponent, then the soldiers will always question his leadership. Isn't it better if Captain Wright is ready to face him? It would secure Major Vinick's claim to be the Supreme General and shore up his support."

"Major Vinick, what say you?" Doyle asked.

"Fine—two days," Vinick said. "But no more. And we should confine the Captain to his barracks to make sure he doesn't try anything in the meantime."

"Of course. We'll post guards," Doyle said. "So it's decided then?"

Nobody had any further objections, not even Wren. She signaled to the Medical team, who descended on Aero and began bandaging his shoulder.

Though still paralyzed and shifting in and out of consciousness, Aero was dimly aware of the fate that had been decided for him. Before he faded away completely, giving into the power of the Beacon, he saw Vinick standing over him like a dark shadow.

"Then it's decided," he said. "In two days we shall duel to the death."

That was the last thing Aero heard before he drifted away.

Chapter 35

THE DREAM THAT WAS NOT A DREAM

When Aero awakes, he is dreadfully cold.

His eyes flutter open and all he sees is white everywhere. He tries to move but can't—something is trapping him. He looks down and that's when he sees the reason for his paralysis. He's buried in ice up to his shoulders, and then he knows with certainty.

This is his Kryptcia.

He's back on Pulsar B1257+12, back on that icy rock of a planet, back in that moment where he fell asleep and the snow almost buried him completely.

Almost ended him forever.

He can't feel his extremities, but his shoulder throbs. Blood seeps into the ice, staining it crimson. He struggles to free himself from the arctic shroud, but it's no use. He tries to grab his Falchion, but it's buried in the ice beside him. He can't reach it.

Despair descends on him then, hard and fast and deadly. When you lose hope, you surrender to death. *This is one of their teachings. He tilts his face upward. Sleet pours down from the leaden sky, burying him still further. It won't be much longer now, he knows. Soon it will cover his mouth and he'll suffocate, if he doesn't freeze first.*

He squints against the sleet, though it cakes onto his eyelashes and threatens to weld them shut, and spots a lone figure in the distance.

Grayish. Obscured by the precipitation. A dark stain on the world.

Probably a soldier planted here to kill me, *he decides.*

He watches helplessly, for that is all he can do.

Gradually, the figure looms larger and more distinct, even through the veil of sleet. His breath catches in his throat when he realizes it's a woman—and a young one at that. She looks like she's only recently left girlhood behind. As she nears, he glimpses more details. The flimsy sandals strapped to her feet that leave her pale skin exposed to the cold. But she doesn't appear to notice that she isn't properly attired for this world.

This girl is no soldier, *he realizes with a start.*

Her eyes burn brightly, and they are fixed on him. A piece of crimson ribbon secures her curly hair, but it looks wild and unkempt, like it yearns to be set free from its restraints. He decides then that he must be dying to be visited by such a creature, for this girl cannot possibly be human—she's so unlike any human that he's ever known.

She is carrying something. A metal box of some kind, he realizes, when she sets it down next to his ice-bound body. She kneels beside him. Her face is freckled and quite beautiful in its otherness. Tendrils of smoke curl out of her full lips. She is slight—he guesses at least a foot shorter than him—and precise in her movements.

Girl, who are you? *he thinks.* Why are you here?

Her eyes snap to his face as if she can hear his thoughts. I fix the broken things.

Her lips don't move, and she doesn't utter these words aloud. This is her thought, but somehow he can hear it. His eyes probe her face, searching for some answer. But how is this possible?

She shakes her head, and a few curls tumble free from the ribbon. Her hair is long and unruly, so different from how the women in his world keep their hair shorn. I don't know any more than you do.

She sticks her finger into the discolored ice by his shoulder and tastes it. Her nose scrunches up at the briny, rusty taste. Concern flashes in her eyes. You're bleeding—quite a lot.

She reaches into her box, searching through the tools, when a flash of gold catches his eyes—she's wearing a Beacon. It's the twin to his own, buried under the ice but still bonded to his wrist. Suddenly, he remembers his father's last words:

There are others . . . you will see . . . you must find them . . .

Was this what he meant?

She produces a knife from the box, and he flinches away.

Don't fear me, *she thinks. Her eyes dart to his wound.* You have many enemies, but I'm not one of them. Now hold still, I'm going to cut you free.

The girl sets to work on the ice, sawing at the hard crust that's formed around his body. Suddenly, she gasps and draws her hand away. Blood pools on the tip of her finger.

Now you've hurt yourself, too.

It's only a scratch. *Her face hardens against the pain, and she starts sawing again.*

Behind her, in the middle distance, he catches a glimpse of something through the sleet. A dark, amorphous shadow. He can feel its intent somehow, and he knows that it is sinister. She follows his gaze and frowns at the shadow.

The Dark Thing, it was following me, though I don't know what it is.

It's coming closer.

She sets her lips. Then we must hurry, I don't like the feeling it gives me.

She works faster to free him. Once she uncovers his shoulders and chest, he's able to rip his right arm free. His fingers are bloodless and numb. He flexes his hand several times to restore the circulation. His eyes dart to his Falchion, buried blade-first in the ice, and he's gripped by a powerful yearning for it.

Stand back, *he thinks, and she obeys without question.*

He reaches for the hilt and grasps it firmly. With a mighty tug, he unsheathes the blade from the ice. The weapon flashes and sparks, melting the frost. Water drips from the blade. The girl watches as he morphs the weapon from its default form into a shorter blade, and then uses it to slice himself free, assisted by the electric charge. He glances behind her apprehensively—the Dark Thing is larger now and more distinct. He can feel its menacing presence growing stronger.

Feeding off them, even.

With great effort, he rises from his icy grave.

The girl staggers back.

He stands at his full height now and towers over her. He was right—he is over a foot taller than this girl, this strange creature from another world.

The Beacon welded to his wrist, now fully exposed, captivates her. It pulses with emerald light. She tilts her face up. Her eyes are wide and bright; her breath puffs out in smoky coils; melting ice dribbles down her flushed cheeks. He thinks then that she is the most beautiful creature that he's ever laid eyes on. She gasps at this thought.

Nobody's ever called me that before.

Called you what?

Beautiful.

He goes to her then, and she goes to him. Without hesitation—or even conscious thought—they're in each other's arms. He buries his face in her curls and inhales, letting her scent fill him up. He feels her stiffen and then relax against him. Every place where their bodies connect reminds him of the Falchions—it tingles and sparks and flames.

The Beacons on their wrists catch fire with blazing emerald light.

She gasps and pulls away.

Her lips part; they invite him in.

He's helpless to resist her, nor would he want to try. He presses his mouth to hers, drinking her in. This kiss overshadows any sensation that he's ever felt before. It's so pleasurable that it aches. The light from the Beacons blazes up their arms and burns through their torsos, engulfing them in an emerald inferno. The light binds them together. His mouth moves against her lips—his tongue probing her mouth hungrily. She reciprocates eagerly and then kisses the melting sleet from his eyelashes and cheeks.

She has more experience kissing than him, he understands, but he finds that he doesn't mind. If anything, it makes the encounter more thrilling. This is a girl who isn't afraid to love with her whole heart—who doesn't fear her emotions.

They morph together—him into her, and her into him.

He can feel her thoughts. Her dreams. Her entire essence.

He no longer knows where she ends and he begins.

The rush of thoughts and feelings build and pulsate and grow and finally climax in an electrifying shudder of sensation. The release is incredible, beyond his wildest dreams. She cries out and clings to him, burying her fingernails into the flesh of his back. They stare into each other's eyes, the awe and revelation apparent in their shared gaze.

Myra Jackson, *he thinks.*

And then she thinks back: Aero Wright.

And when they eventually part—when the emerald light dies down and they're two distinct entities again—he wishes they could have remained morphed together forever. The Dark Thing still hovers in the distance, but it's been driven back by the power of their embrace. He tries to cling to her, but she is already fading.

Myra, don't leave me!

She frowns sadly, and it pains him to see such agony assail her lovely face. This is only a dream—it can't last forever. Eventually we must awake, eventually it must end.

Then I'll gladly sleep forever.

Don't wish such a thing! The time will come for us to claim what is rightfully ours, but for now we must be patient—there are Dark Things looming.

Her eyes dart to the black shadow cast against the white snow.

But when can I see you again?

He tries to embrace her, but she is merely a wisp of smoke that passes through his outstretched fingertips. She is growing fainter by the second, fading into white against the whiter backdrop of this arctic world. Even her thoughts are fainter.

Maybe tomorrow . . . maybe never . . . though I hope that's not the case . . . I don't know how to control it yet. *Her words are filled with the deep sorrow of having loved and lost before.* I'll try to come back . . . I swear it. Until then . . . farewell.

And then she is gone, as if she were nothing more than a figment of his imagination. The white world around him begins to dissipate and dwindle.

Until it is gone, too.

And he is alone in the darkness once more.

Chapter 36
BONDED

Myra Jackson

Myra woke from the strangest dream.

She opened her eyes to the darkness of her bedroom, and the images came back to her all at once. A man was stranded on a strange world covered by ice. They were both wearing Beacons, and he could read her thoughts. She cut him free from the ice, and then he kissed her. A shudder tore through her body at the memory, though it was one of pleasure, not fear. She reached up and touched her lips—they still felt tingly.

The more she thought about this dream, the stranger she realized it was. It didn't dissipate under the scrutiny of wakefulness. The details of it—the textures and contours—remained sharp and unblemished in her mind. That kiss felt as real as any Kaleb had planted on her lips when they were courting. More real even, she thought.

His name was Aero, she remembered. She pulled the blanket over her head and clicked on the flashlight to study the Beacon. He was wearing its twin.

And that was when she saw it:

The blood splatters on her pillow.

Crimson on white.

Stark and unmistakable.

Still wet, not even dry yet.

She jerked her gaze to her hand—there was a cut on her finger. Upon closer inspection, she saw that the wound was clean. It looked like it had been made by a knife, just like in her dream. She had sliced it open when she was trying to free him from the ice.

That was no dream, she realized with sudden clarity. He was real—as real as anything in this world—she was sure of it. The Beacons must have connected them somehow. That would explain the mind reading and the way they had . . . morphed together. She blushed at this reminder of their coupling, as the sensations surged through her again. She felt tingling on her lips and on other parts of her deeper down. A soft moan escaped from her throat.

Embarrassed, she glanced at Tinker's bunk, but he was still fast asleep, curled around the needlepoint pillow that their mother had made. Myra wondered if it had nudged out his computer as his most prized possession.

Unobserved, she sank down in her bunk and let the vibrations course through her. How she felt for Aero was different than anything she'd ever felt before. The emotions were scorching and fervent and—above all else—wholly consuming. She'd never harbored such strong feelings for Kaleb.

Affection, certainly and maybe even love.

But nothing like . . . this, she thought as her body gave off another shudder. Aero had entered her—her body, her mind, and her soul—and become one with her, and now they could never be parted. They were connected by the Beacons. They'd be connected for the rest of their lives. She glanced down at the golden cuff shackled to her wrist.

He must be from one of the other colonies, she realized.

But there was another being in the dreamscape, she remembered. *The Dark Thing*, she called it. The shadowy, amorphous presence made her feel afraid, but she had no idea what it was exactly. Confusion swept through her like a violent wave, pitching and churning and tossing her about. There was only one thing she understood for sure:

Now she knew about the Dark Thing—and now it knew about her.

o o o

Myra padded into the living space with her flashlight. Though the automatic lights wouldn't come on for another hour, she'd given up on sleeping.

The battle was lost—maybe it always had been.

She shifted the flashlight's beam, assessing the damage from last night. The sofa rested on its back from when Jasper had knocked her into it. She didn't bother to right it. Blood splatters stained the concrete floor. *My father's blood,* she thought, as her stomach churned sickly. But she didn't bother to clean that up, either. She just didn't have the heart to try to make it look as if nothing had happened.

She sat down at the kitchen table. Her sleeve pulled back, revealing the Beacon. It cast off greenish light, which pulsed in steady rhythm with her heart. She clicked off the flashlight and sat there, bathed in its throbbing glow. Her head hurt, and she had a touch of nausea, though that could have been from grappling with Jasper.

But she was already growing used to the Beacon. She was even becoming accustomed to hosting Elianna Wade and her memories. Elianna always seemed to be lingering at the back of her mind now, like she'd taken up permanent residence there, only occasionally shifting to the forefront when she demanded to be heard.

"Lot of good finding you did," Myra muttered to the Beacon.

She'd thought the Beacon would solve their problems, but, if anything, their situation had only worsened. She was at a complete loss for how to proceed. Even Elianna remained silent on what to do. Myra put her head down and let out a choked sob.

"Holy Sea, we're doomed," she said aloud to no one in particular.

There was no response—only the continued pulsing of the Beacon.

Myra sat at the kitchen table in a state of near-total paralysis of both mind and body until the automatic lights flashed on and Tinker padded into the living space. He rubbed his tired eyes and frowned at the mess.

"I had hoped it was only a bad dream."

"Me too," she said. She stood up from the table and started rummaging through the larder, pulling out a bag of rice and a bottle of almond milk. "Breakfast?"

He shook his head. "I'm not hungry."

"Me neither, but we have to eat something. It's what Papa would want."

Tinker frowned. "He won't know."

"Even so, I will. So sit." She pointed to the table. "I'll make the porridge."

He obeyed but didn't appear comforted by this sham reenactment of their morning routine. He watched as she staggered around the kitchen, trying desperately to make something . . . anything . . . seem normal. It didn't work, not really.

"Think he'll ever come home again?" Tinker asked.

This stopped Myra in her tracks. Her heart lurched in her chest, and she nearly overturned the scalding porridge. There was a lilt to his question, which meant he hadn't given up yet, but there was also a strong undercurrent of doubt. It almost shattered the brave façade that Myra had put on for his sake. Otherwise, she might have been a comatose, weeping shell of a person, still hiding out in her bunk.

She wanted to tell Tinker that of course he would. She wanted to shelter him from the more likely possibility that their father would soon be taking a swim in the Holy Sea. But she knew that Tinker was too smart for such empty assurances. Besides, hiding the truth wouldn't do him any good in the long run. Their world was dimming—it was already gasping for its final breaths. Death now lurked around every corner, and without their father's help to build the submarine, they had precious little chance of making it to the Surface and saving their colony, if they'd ever had any at all.

"I hope so," she said instead.

And it was true. She did hope.

What she served them did not resemble porridge so much as wet concrete. Her cooking skills had never approached those of her father or Tinker. She forced down a bite anyway, reminding herself to be grateful. She knew from experience that her father wouldn't be getting anything to eat today—maybe not even a cup of water.

They ate in silence, and Myra tried not to look up from her bowl. The kitchen table felt like it had grown considerably larger overnight. There were now two empty chairs, not just one. *They may never be filled again*, she thought and set her spoon down. Any desire to finish her porridge had fled from her.

Suddenly, the doorbell chimed.

It startled Myra. Her arm shot out, knocking her bowl off the table. It hit the floor and shattered, sending gruel and shards of pottery flying around the compartment.

"Are the 'Trollers back?" Tinker asked.

"Well, they don't usually ring. They prefer to barge in unannounced, so it's probably somebody else. But go in the bedroom . . . and lock the door just in case."

He looked relieved to be excused from finishing the dreadful porridge. He retreated to the back of the compartment and headed for the bedroom. "And don't unlock it until I say so," she added before he shut the door.

Once Tinker was hidden, Myra padded up to the door and flashed her wrist under the scanner. The door beeped and dilated into the wall, revealing Kaleb. He clutched a cloth bundle in his arms. Rickard and Paige stood behind him. A few passing Factum slowed down to stare at Myra and then whispered among themselves.

They know what happened, she realized. The news must have spread through the colony. Wordlessly, she let her friends inside. It wasn't safe to talk in the corridors, which were packed with Factum heading to work or school. Kaleb handed her the bundle. “It’s from Maude,” he said. “She had to hurry to the Souk, but she’ll stop by later.”

Myra accepted it. There was a note attached: “Stay strong! Love, Maude.” She still had no appetite, but if anything was going to stay down, it was sweetfish.

Her friends followed her inside. Myra called to Tinker, alerting him that it was safe to come out. Rickard and Kaleb righted the sofa and then straightened up the room, while Paige scrubbed the bloodstains from the floor. Myra tried to help out, but Paige waved her off, saying she’d grown used to cleaning up bodily fluids at the Infirmary. Though Myra still felt gutted by what had transpired, she was grateful for her friends.

Once the compartment was clean—or at least, as clean as it was ever likely to get—they gathered in the living space. Myra, Paige, and Kaleb settled on the sofa; Rickard and Tinker sat cross-legged on the floor. An awkward few seconds passed.

“So . . . does everybody know what happened?” Myra said eventually.

Kaleb nodded. “The gossip is spreading through the corridors and the Souk. It’s the only thing the Factum and Hockers are talking about.” He exchanged an uneasy glance with Rickard and Paige. “And, well, the ’Trollers didn’t just arrest your father last night. They pulled Stan Decker out of his compartment, too.”

Rickard glanced around nervously. “And there’s more. Two days ago, they arrested the Bishop twins. I heard the news from one of their neighbors.”

“Stella and Ginger,” Tinker said softly.

“But they’re just kids!” Myra said. “Only a year older than Tinker.”

“That didn’t stop them from arresting you,” Kaleb said.

Rickard looked down in shame. “Sorry I didn’t warn you about the arrests, but the ’Trollers kept me in the dark—they know I’m friends with you.”

“Lynch, it’s not your fault,” Myra said and patted his arm.

"If they arrested Bishop and Decker, that means they aren't guessing that my father is a heathen . . . they have evidence. Somebody must have betrayed him."

"Right, I've been thinking about that," Kaleb said. "Trying to put the pieces together. We know Bishop was digging around Records, looking for the Beacon. He took those pictures of the Wade family, remember? Well, maybe somebody informed on him. Factum are often willing to betray other Factum to curry favor with the 'Trollers."

"That makes sense," Myra said. "So what happened next?"

Rickard scratched his head. "Then the 'Trollers grabbed Bishop from his compartment and threw him into the Pen. We saw him get arrested . . . remember?"

Paige screwed up her face. "But then why'd they arrest his daughters?"

"Because he wasn't talking," Myra said, the horror dawning on her. "They knew if they arrested his kids . . . maybe even tortured them . . . then he'd tell them anything."

Paige looked like she might be sick. Even Kaleb looked pale.

"Well, the timing makes sense," he said weakly. "The 'Trollers arrested his daughters two days ago, and I'll bet it didn't take long for him to break. Then they arrested Decker and your father last night, after Bishop supplied them with their names."

Myra's eyes roved over their faces. "You realize what this means? They're not just arresting heathens now, but their children, too. Who's next? Other family members? Neighbors? Friends? Where do you draw the line? Nobody is safe, not anymore."

Myra felt the pull of Elianna and the Beacon. *Tell them*, Elianna urged, as the Beacon pulsed insistently. In the rush to talk about the arrests, she'd almost forgotten about it.

"Uh, well, there's something else I need to tell you . . . " Myra trailed off. For reasons she didn't entirely understand, she felt strangely protective of the Beacon. She wanted to keep it secret but forced herself to finish anyway. "I found . . . the Beacon."

"What?" Kaleb exclaimed. "But when? I mean, how?"

Rickard also looked stunned. "You actually found the bloody thing?"

"Why didn't you tell us right away?" Paige demanded.

"I guess I was distracted . . ." Myra said.

"Of course," Kaleb said quickly. "But how'd you find it?"

"Remember the statue with the message from Sari?" Myra said. "Well, the Beacon was hidden in the base, just like the riddle said. *Buried under a city of old*. Tinker figured out that Paris is actually a city from Before Doom. The statue is called a snow globe. And that white stuff that floats around when you shake it up? That's snow. On the Surface, ice crystals fall down from the sky, or at least they used to Before Doom."

"But how do you know all that?" Paige asked.

"Because . . . I'm wearing it."

Guiltily, Myra pulled back her sleeve. And there it was, welded to the tender flesh of her right wrist, radiant and undeniable.

Then, as quickly and as best as she could, Myra recounted everything that had happened. The First and Second Warnings came and went, and still she kept talking, though she left out the part about Aero and the Dark Thing and the strange dream. Of all the unexplained things that had happened to her in the last twenty-four hours, she understood the dream the least. Her friends listened with rapt attention.

When she finished telling them as much as she could—and there was precious little time left before the Final Warning—she told them the most important part.

"My purpose is to journey back to the Surface and find the First Continuum. The Beacon will guide me and show the way. Only without my father's help . . . what hope do I have of reaching it?" Her voice caught in her throat. "He drew up the plans for the submarine. He's the only one who can build it. I wouldn't even know where to begin."

Her words hung in the air, full of despair. Tears spilled down her cheeks. Though Kaleb reached out to comfort her, none of her friends could provide an answer. It was just as she thought—her situation was completely hopeless. She allowed that knowledge to wash through her as she leaned into Kaleb. The fight drained out of her completely.

Tinker was the only one who didn't appear upset. "I've already thought about our options," he rasped. "And we only have one choice if we want to reach the Surface."

"And what's that?" Myra said, wiping away tears. They kept falling anyway.

"We have to free Papa," he said in a firm voice.

Myra shook her head. "It's not that simple! The Pen is impenetrable."

"Not for you," he insisted. "You have your secret ways."

"Tink, even if I could get inside using the pipes, he's still locked up in a steel cage! I can't get him out, not even if I could bring heavy-duty tools with me. Sawing through the bars would be impossible, not to mention make a bloody racket."

"But there has to be a way." To him, this was just a problem, and he was hell-bent on solving it. "Can you get into the area where they keep the prisoners?"

"Uh, right, I think so. There were vents in the ceiling," Myra said, dredging up the memory of her imprisonment. "The cells were built after the Founders, that's why they're not set into the walls. I guess they didn't think they'd need to lock people up."

"Then you just have to get his cell open."

"Tink, I wish it were that easy! They're locked with deadbolts. I wouldn't even know how to go about picking them. Seriously, there's no way to get his cell open—"

"Unless you had the key," Rickard interjected.

All eyes snapped to him.

"I could get the key for you. My father keeps a spare set in his office. I could take them at work, and then you could break your father out tonight. And I can put them back first thing tomorrow. I'll bet my dad won't even notice they're missing."

"But what if he does?" Myra said. "It's too dangerous."

"Doesn't really matter," Rickard said. "If we don't do this, then your father and Decker and Bishop and his daughters will go to the Holy Sea. And everyone else—including us—will only outlive them by a few months or so."

"Lynch, are you sure about this?" Myra said. "I release you from helping me. This . . . well, it goes way beyond anything I had imagined, to say the least."

Her eyes darted over their faces—Rickard, Kaleb, Paige, and Tinker. But none of them retracted their help, especially not her stubborn little brother.

"Fine, we break my father out of the Pen tonight," Myra agreed. "But what do we do after we get him out? The 'Trollers are bound to notice he's gone missing and search for him. Our compartment obviously isn't safe, nor is the Engineering Room."

"We hide him," Paige suggested, "in the secret room."

Kaleb nodded. "That just might work! We can bring him rations and keep him hidden. And he can work there in secret to build the submarine."

"The Final Warning is about to flash," Myra said. "Are we decided then? Lynch will take the keys today, and then we can meet in the secret room after the automatic lights go out. It will be dangerous—deadly even—if we fail. I won't think any less of you if you decide to pull out now." But nobody did; they were steadfast in their oaths to her.

"This is our only hope," Kaleb said. "We're dying anyway."

His words were the last spoken among them that morning, for his statement was so true—and so irrefutable—that there was simply nothing left to say.

They exited the compartment and headed off in various directions to begin their days. Kaleb would report to the Synod's chambers in Sector 6. Myra hoped he could stomach serving them after what had transpired last night. Paige was headed to the Infirmary, Rickard to the Patrollers' headquarters in Sector 3, and Tinker to the Academy. None of them could afford to skip their duties, not with so much at stake. They all had to do their best to act cheerful and oblivious and pretend that *everything we need is under the sea.*

As Myra hurried through the corridors to the Engineering Room, which would feel so much emptier without her father, she thought about what Kaleb had said:

We're dying anyway.

She felt Elianna nudge her from inside her skull. *You know it's true,* she communicated. *But fear not—worlds end all the time, and then new ones spring up from their ashes, and the cycle begins again. This is your purpose—you can do it.*

"But how do you know?" Myra whispered under her breath, and she felt slightly crazy for talking to herself. She hadn't completely grown used to this other entity's intrusion into her thoughts and feelings—to the reality of the Beacon's bond to her.

Because I'm you, just as you're me now, Elianna answered.

Then you know that I'm afraid. Myra thought back this time instead of whispering aloud. It worked, for Elianna seemed to understand her perfectly.

It's not fear that determines our fate, but how we choose to react to it, Elianna communicated to her. *That's the meaning of courage.*

Chapter 37
A RARE VISITOR

The Synod

He sniffed the air and grimaced.

It was pungent with the stench of blood, sweat, and other human filth. He rarely ventured down here, preferring to leave such work to his underlings, but they'd already made too many mistakes, including the man in black leading him down the passageway. *If he wanted something done right,* he thought, *he had to do it himself.*

The man in black carried a thick ring of keys that clanked with each footfall as they strode down the row of dark cells. Each housed a prisoner in varying states of putrefaction. As they passed, they shrieked and hurled themselves at the bars of their cages. Many uttered curses that denigrated his most sacred beliefs, only reinforcing why they were imprisoned here. The ones with some wits left in their skulls pleaded with him.

"Padre, save us! The Oracle have mercy!"

Of course, he ignored them—their fates had already been determined. Only the Holy Sea could save them now. He glimpsed the cell that contained the girls, their broken bodies huddled together. The man in black shone his flashlight at them, and for a split second, their pupils refracted the beam, crimson as four coals stoked in a dying fire. He could feel hatred wafting off their tiny bodies like a wave of heat from a furnace.

Uncharacteristically, this caused him to shudder. But he shook it off, comforting himself with the thought that the Holy Sea would soon claim them and the heathen who was their father. It would crush their bones and suck the air from their lungs and bathe them in frigid saltwater, and, most importantly, it would cleanse them of sin.

At the end of the row, they reached their destination. The man in black shone his flashlight inside the steel cage, where a sorry-looking creature was crumpled in a bloody heap on the floor. *Jonah Jackson*, he thought with disdain. This man—his entire family, in fact—had been a thorn in his side for too long, but that would end today. So far, the heathen had refused to talk or divulge anything. He would change his mind soon.

"Head Patroller Lynch, your pipe!" he ordered. His lips curled back from his teeth in anticipation. Though he'd taken a vow of celibacy, this provided him with a thrill.

"Yes, Padre!"

The man in black complied without hesitation. The priest gripped the pipe and rolled back the finely woven fabric of his robe. He preferred not to bloody it, or soil it too much. Then he raised his arm and went to work with the pipe.

It wasn't long before the prisoner's wretched cries filled the sector, echoing through the darkness and silencing the other inmates. He paused to catch his breath and stepped back to survey his handiwork.

The prisoner was writhing on the floor of his cell. That was just how he liked them. There was only one more thing he had to do to break him.

"Well, well, I should've known you were a heathen." He allowed the revulsion to cloud his voice. "Just like that wife of yours. She was a pretty thing, wasn't she? But more trouble than she was worth, I'd imagine. Now, remind me. What was her name?"

"Tessa," the prisoner gasped.

He pursed his lips in mock sympathy. "Pity how she died . . . so very young. A terrible misfortune indeed. In childbirth . . . wasn't that what the Head Doctor told you?"

"Wh-what do you mean?" the prisoner sputtered.

The preist reared up to his full height and sneered down at the prisoner. "She was a sinner—snooping around Records, sticking her nose where it didn't belong, looking for a blasphemous object, causing problems for the Synod."

The prisoner lunged at the priest suddenly, which seemed a feat beyond his ability, given the broken state of his body. "You monster! What'd you do to her?"

The preist sidestepped him easily and whacked him in the head. The prisoner moaned piteously and collapsed but continued to glower at the priest.

"Only what she deserved! Back then, the other Chancellors weren't as sympathetic to my need for more sacrifices. They objected to putting a pregnant woman out to sea. They claimed the unborn child was an innocent that had to be spared. So I waited until the heathen went to the Infirmary and delivered the bastard, and then I had Head Patroller Lynch do it for me and make it look like an accident."

The sound that the prisoner made then didn't sound human. It was a low wail that gradually built to a high-pitched shriek. He flailed around with the force of it.

The priest saw his opening; he relished the prospect. "Now let's, talk about that daughter of yours," he said in a cheerful voice. "She slipped through my fingers once, thanks to Chancellor Sebold and his appeals for mercy. He swayed the other members, but that won't happen again. So either you start talking right now, or that will be her fate." He pointed to the twin girls in their cell, their tiny bodies bruised and broken. "You're a smart man, so what's it going to be?"

The priest savored how the prisoner glared at him with such deep hatred that it almost felt like a physical force. "May the Holy Sea have mercy on your black soul!" the prisoner spat through bloody lips and broken teeth.

The priest let out a bored sigh. What was it with these heathens? They thought themselves so noble in their rebellion, but make no mistake—they were sinners all.

He turned to the man in black. "Head Patroller Lynch, go arrest the girl—and the boy, too. Bring them both here." He turned to face the prisoner. "Then maybe he'll change his mind about talking."

For a split second, the man in black appeared troubled, but it quickly passed. "Yes, Padre! As you command, so it will be done."

"Amen!" said the priest. "You do the Oracle's good work."

Chapter 38
THE WAITING

Captain Aero Wright

Aero's eyes popped open to see a hazy figure.

"Myra!" he gasped and sat up quickly—too quickly, it turned out, for the dizziness overtook him and forced him to lie back down. He let out a frustrated groan. "Damn it all to hell!" he muttered. He hated being an invalid almost as much as he hated Major Vinick, though such emotions were strictly forbidden.

"Who's Myra?" the figure asked. And she sounded a little bit . . . perturbed.

He recognized her voice first, and then his vision slowly resolved itself. Of course, it was Wren. Her arms were crossed, and she was doing her best to look ticked off, but relief was the predominant emotion.

Aero glanced at his surroundings. He was in his private room in the barracks, a perk of being an officer. His soldiers slept together in another large room. The door was closed, but two sentries were stationed just outside of it, per Major Vinick's orders. Usually, he could come and go as he pleased, but now he was a prisoner in his own room.

"Well, if I were allowed to express my emotions, then I might be jealous," Wren added with a wink. "So tell me . . . who's this *Myra*?"

Just a strange girl from another world, Aero thought, grateful that Wren couldn't read his mind like Myra. He wasn't ready to tell her about the girl yet.

"Nobody," he rasped. He must have lost his voice screaming over his father's death. His lips were dry, and he was terribly thirsty. "Just a strange dream."

"You've been having a lot of those lately."

She perched on the edge of his bed and laid a hand on his forehead. "You're still burning up, but not as bad as yesterday." She poured a glass of water from the pitcher next to the bed and handed it to him. "Drink," she said—it wasn't a request.

This annoyed him, but he was too weak and thirsty to protest. He chugged the glass and handed it back to her. "More?" he said. He was still terribly thirsty.

Wren set the glass down on the bedside table but didn't refill it. "Let that settle first, and then we'll see how you feel. I'd rather not clean up your puke today."

He frowned. "You used to do what I said."

"That was before . . ." she trailed off.

"Before I donned this cursed thing?" he said, raising his right arm, where the Beacon was latched around his wrist. To his surprise, she shook her head.

"Before Vinick almost killed you."

"Oh, right . . . that before." So much had happened that it was hard to keep it straight, especially with the Beacon clouding his thoughts. "So how long was I out?"

"You've been in and out of consciousness for about twenty-four hours, though I'm not sure if it's from the Beacon, the shock of losing your father, or the blood loss."

He looked down at his shoulder. It was heavily bandaged and still throbbed from the wound. He must have torn it open in the fight with Vinick. "All of the above, I think."

"A fair assessment, Captain," she said. "Glad to see you've

developed a sense of humor at long last. Starry hell, you used to be so serious."

"A lot has changed," he agreed. "But I'm still pretty damned morose." She smiled, genuinely, and then busied herself with changing his bandages.

"So, what'd I miss while I was out?" he asked.

"A lot . . . and, well . . . you're not going to like it," she said. "Major Vinick has sworn that if he defeats you in the duel and becomes the next Supreme General, then he'll abandon Earth and continue on Stern's Quest to find a new home."

"Vinick is a fool! Earth is our true home."

The Beacon pulsed in support.

"You believe that, and I believe that—but we're in the minority," Wren whispered, her eyes darting to the door. "The Majors are backing Vinick and many of the soldiers, but you still have some supporters. Most of our unit is on your side."

"Most . . . but not all?" he said. The betrayal stung.

She didn't dispute that point, for she never lied to him. "Xing, Etoile, and Hoshiko wanted to visit you," she said instead. "But I thought it'd be too much for you right now. You need to rest and get your strength up—those are Medical's orders."

"I hate resting," he said. "I feel so damned useless." He struggled to sit up, but she placed her hand on his chest and forced him back down.

"Right now, rest is the best medicine, and I won't have you wearing yourself out on my watch." Her bossiness annoyed him—he was used to giving her orders, not the other way around. But he knew she was right, and so he complied and lay still.

"And the duel?" he asked.

"It's tomorrow at 0900 hours."

They both shifted their gaze to his wound, which was visible now that the gauze had been stripped away. The angry, red gash had begun to close up, but it wouldn't be fully healed by tomorrow, no matter how many miracles Medical and Wren tried to work on it. He would just have to fight around it.

Wren studied his face and frowned. "You're allowed to be

pissed off about it, you know," she said. "I'm pissed off. It's not right—the whole damned system is rigged! They call that charade on the bridge a fair trial? It's a travesty of justice! It goes against all of our teachings."

"Anger won't help me tomorrow," Aero said. This had been drilled into his head endlessly at the Agoge—that mental clarity was preferable to emotion in a soldier.

"So sure about that?" she asked, her eyes flashing.

"What do you mean?"

"Only that . . . maybe emotions aren't as bad as they make them out to be. Maybe they want us to be emotionless because we're easier to control that way."

Her words rang out loud and clear. Aero worried that the sentries heard her—or, worse, that the room was bugged and Vinick was monitoring their conversation. He didn't want anything bad to happen to Wren, but one look at her face told him that she didn't care—that she'd gladly die for the values in which she so passionately believed.

"Point taken . . . and I am angry," he said. "In fact—I'm already past angry and well on my way to furious. I'm just better at hiding it. We all have emotions, Wren. You're not the only one. You're just not as good at hiding it as the rest of us."

This made her smile, and a little color crept into her cheeks. "Thanks. I appreciate it, but right now it's my job to make you feel better, not the other way around."

Her eyes were trained on him in a way that made him feel uncomfortable. He had the sense again that she felt something for him . . . something forbidden.

A few days ago, this would have terrified but also thrilled him. Although they'd both been betrothed to others since their births, he'd always secretly wished that Wren was his betrothed, that when his summons came ordering him to the Magistrate for his Connubial Service, her name would be printed next to his name, even though he knew that was impossible. Betrothed never trained together at the Agoge, and they also never served together after they graduated. This was to prevent emotional attachment.

But now, something inside of him had changed. Something had shifted, and he wasn't sure if it could ever shift back. *Myra Jackson*, he thought, remembering the girl from another world and the strange dream and the way that they'd merged together into one single entity, bound together by the Beacons. Emotions—especially something as dangerous as love—were strictly prohibited, but his heart pounded anyway.

He felt completely torn between Wren, who'd been his best friend and constant companion, and Myra, whom he'd only just met and in a dream no less, but to whom he felt an undeniable connection. A tide of confusion swelled up and enveloped him in its icy waters. Even if Wren felt something for him, he resolved not to lead her on.

He broke their eye contact and cleared his throat. "That everything?"

She shifted her gaze to the golden cuff fastened to his wrist. "So . . . what's it like?"

He could hear the curiosity in her voice. He thought for a minute, searching for a way to explain something that felt so inexplicable. "Like a thousand voices in my head, all trying to talk to me at once. Every Supreme General who's ever worn it . . . they're all preserved by it somehow."

"That sounds overwhelming."

He nodded. "But it's comforting, too. My father's in here somewhere. I can sense him . . . though I haven't figured out how to focus on individual voices yet."

Now he understood the burden that his father had borne and how the Beacon had changed him irrevocably. It explained why he'd ended Stern's Quest and reversed course for Earth. Aero felt the urge to return to the First Continuum, just as his father had, like a yearning that couldn't be denied. It was painful and urgent and always with him now.

"You'll get better at controlling it, just like the Falchions," Wren said. "Remember how we learned to clear our minds and focus them? Well, I paid a visit to your favorite Forger yesterday. He said that you have a special talent; that's how he put it. He also said the Beacon would have rendered most people comatose for days, but that you've bonded with it well. He believes that you'll soon learn how to master it."

He thought of Myra and wondered if she also had a special talent—if that explained the nature of their bond and why they'd connected so strongly. "How does the Forger know all that?"

"He came by yesterday when you were unconscious and inspected it. He said your father also struggled with the burden of the Beacon, that they'd had many training sessions together to teach him how to control the voices."

"Wait, my father spoke to the Forger?"

"You both had a preference for him. Is that so hard to believe?"

Aero was forced to acknowledge that it wasn't. His world had been upended in the last twenty-four hours by a great many things, but learning that his father had cared about him was perhaps the most shocking of all, and it was certainly the hardest to wrap his head around. Although Aero had dreamed of the moment when his father would acknowledge him as his son, he'd never believed that it would actually happen. And he'd certainly never imagined that a second later, his father's heart would stop beating.

"Did the Forger tell you anything else . . . about my father?"

Wren shook her head. "He promised to return tonight to retrieve your Falchion and charge it so it's fresh for the duel tomorrow. You can ask him about it then."

Aero felt fatigue stretching its weary tendrils into him. His eyelids were growing heavy. *If I can't even stay awake, then how am I going to defeat Vinick in a duel?*

Wren finished applying the fresh bandage to his shoulder. "There . . . all done," she declared, but before she could pull away, Aero placed his hand on top of hers.

"Wren, I don't know how to thank you. Without your help, well . . . I'd already be dead at Vinick's hand."

"You can start by promising me something."

"And what's that?"

"That you'll make that traitor suffer," she hissed. The fire was back in her eyes now, burning brightly. "For Starling and Tristan . . . and your father."

"I swear it on my life as a soldier; I'll make him pay!" He grinned, and the Beacon flashed. "Now, can I have another glass of water?" he added hopefully.

She smirked. "See, sense of humor. It's very charming."

"I'm not sure I'm so charming. You didn't actually get my water."

"That's because you neglected to say please."

"Damn it, you're enjoying this caretaker stuff a little too much," he grumbled. "I won't be an invalid forever. You will have to obey my orders again soon."

"Yes, sir," she said crisply. "But until then, you're at my mercy."

"Fine . . . please," he said with a roll of his eyes.

This time she acquiesced. He savored the water as it trickled down his throat. It was the best thing he'd ever tasted, and it quenched his thirst at long last.

o o o

The Forger came that night, just as Aero was waking from another dream.

He had been back on the icy planet that was the venue for his Krypteia, back under the shroud of ice, back with the amorphous, sinister shadow. But Myra didn't return. He remembered her words. *Maybe tomorrow . . . maybe never . . . though I hope that's not the case*. He'd waited for her anyway as the sleet poured down, piling up around his body until it covered his neck, and then his mouth, and then his nostrils. As he gasped his last breaths, the shadow descended on him and devoured him whole.

He woke up screaming and shivering uncontrollably, though his body was bathed in sweat, like it had been burning up. The two sentries posted at his door burst into his room, their Falchions at the ready, but the old Forger shooed them away.

"Privates Yang and Rodriguez, I'll handle this," he said, fixing them with a disapproving stare. "That means you may leave us now."

They hesitated, but most soldiers feared the Forgers since they presided over their most precious possessions, and so they left and shut the door behind them. Suddenly, a second figure stepped from behind the Forger. He was also dressed in a crimson robe. It was the boy formerly known as Xander who'd been in Aero's class at the Agoge.

The old Forger laid a hand on the hilt of Aero's Falchion, which was tucked under the covers with him. Aero wasn't taking any chances. Though the Majors had confined him to his room, they hadn't stripped him of his weapon.

"Will you relinquish your blade?" the old Forger said.

"Only to you," Aero said. There were few people that he trusted anymore, but this Forger was one of them. "If anything happens to it, then I'm a dead man."

"My brother will deliver it to the Foundry and oversee the charging process," he said, referring to Xander. "You can trust him. So, will you allow him to take it?"

The young Forger approached Aero's bedside and knelt to accept the blade. Aero surrendered his Falchion. "Brother, please don't let it out of your sight."

"I wouldn't think of it! You are the Chosen."

"The chosen what?" asked Aero.

The young Forger glanced nervously at his mentor, realizing he'd just spoken out of turn, but the old man didn't chastise his young charge. Instead, he smiled warmly.

"*The Chosen one who carries the Beacon and lights the way*," he quoted. "It's one of our most sacred teachings in the Foundry, little known to those who study at the Agoge. Our teachings overlap in many places, but they diverge notably in others."

He shifted his attention to the young Forger. "Brother, you may go now. Return as soon as it is done."

"Yes, brother," the young Forger said with a bow before he left, his robe swishing behind him in a swirl of crimson. Aero was left alone with the old man.

"May I see the Beacon?" he asked.

Aero held his arm aloft so that he could inspect it. The Forger's sharp, gray eyes roved over its golden surface. "Looks like a strong bond . . . how's it treating you?"

"Well, for starters, it's disorienting," Aero admitted. "And completely overwhelming . . . but also comforting at the same time. I love it . . . and feel strangely protective of it. For example, I had to force myself to let you examine it."

He halted, feeling like he'd made a fool of himself, but the Forger looked pensive. His withered fingers roved over the device, fingering the Ouroboros seal.

"The Beacon was forged using ancient science, made by the First Ones in the time Before Doom. The protectiveness that you feel is actually a security measure built into the device so that the Carrier wouldn't cast it aside or try to destroy it. The Beacon's purpose is threefold—to preserve the knowledge of prior Carriers, to guide you back to the First Continuum, and to connect you to the other Carriers, if there are any left."

This part caught Aero's attention. "Right. I think maybe . . . I might have met another Carrier . . ." He trailed off uncertainly.

The Forger raised his bushy eyebrows. "Are you certain?"

"Well . . . no," Aero was forced to admit. "It was in a dream."

"Very interesting! Well, it's been a long time since we've been in proximity to other potential Carriers. We've been journeying too far away from Earth, but with the rendezvous time having arrived, other survivors might be coalescing on Earth's surface. According to our records, back when the space colonies were in the same galaxy, the Carriers could communicate with one another unassisted."

"They could read each other's minds," Aero said. "That's how it was with the girl. She was wearing a Beacon . . . I'm sure of it." He blushed as he remembered their coupling and hoped the Forger didn't notice. "She had long hair and was dressed in crude clothing . . . she wasn't a soldier . . . or from our colony . . . and she helped me."

The Forger thought for a moment. "It's possible that she's a Carrier from another colony. And if so, that's big news indeed! For a long time, I've feared that we were the only ones left. Where was she—underground? Underwater? On the surface already?"

He shook his head. "I should've asked her that, but the dream just kind of happened, and I wasn't really able to control it. And there was another thing in the dreamscape . . . *The Dark Thing*, she called it. It wasn't friendly, not like the girl."

The old man appeared troubled. "The Dark Thing? Was it human?"

"I don't know. It was formless and shadowy . . . and it's possible that it's just something I dreamed up . . . the girl too. My thoughts have been jumbled lately."

The Forger nodded. "For now, I suggest you keep this to yourself. Major Vinick has vowed to destroy the Beacon after he kills you. He mistrusts it and wants to continue on Stern's Quest, so he's ordered the Foundry to oversee its unmaking."

Anger—an emotion that Aero had never seen from a Forger—flashed across the old man's face.

"You're unhappy with the Major's decision?"

"Oh my . . . that is a rather euphemistic way of putting it," the Forger said with a chuckle. "Destroying a thing such as the Beacon . . . well, it goes against all of our teachings, to say the least. We're the Creators and the Descendants of the First Ones and the Preservers of Science and Knowledge and Human Life. We're not destroyers."

Aero considered everything that he knew about the Forgers. "Is the Beacon made with the same science as the Falchions?"

"That's a very astute observation! The Order of the Foundry developed the Falchions for the Interstellar Army of the Second Continuum, at the behest of the first Supreme General. His name was Milton Wright, most likely your ancestor. They did make the Falchions using the same science as the Beacons, but with some improvements. The Falchion bonds with you, but it can be set aside without resulting in death."

"I'd say that's an improvement," Aero said wryly, glancing down at the armlet shackled to his wrist. "This isn't exactly the softest thing to sleep with."

"Glad you approve!" the Forger said. "Anyway, the Falchions are weapons, make no mistake, but they were forged in the service of a greater calling. Do you know what the original purpose of our army was?"

"Peacekeepers," Aero said. "Wright believed that with man's propensity toward violence, a peacekeeping force might be necessary to protect us from ourselves."

"That's correct—our soldiers are meant to keep the peace, not to be aggressors. *First do no harm.* Only some have forgotten that teaching in their quest for power."

"Vinick," Aero said darkly. "If I lose, will the Order obey his command and destroy the Beacon?"

The old man looked aggrieved. "We haven't delivered our answer yet—and it's our hope that we won't have to." His eyes locked onto Aero's face. "That you'll triumph over Vinick tomorrow, and then this shall all be put to rest. It's our belief that you're the rightful Supreme General."

"And if I don't win?" Aero asked, his voice thick.

The thought of the Beacon's destruction horrified him, both because of its bond to him and because of the ramifications of forsaking their home planet. In one swift and destructive act, Vinick could undo everything that the First Ones had created.

"There's hope, as long as your heart still beats," the Forger said. The Beacon pulsed in perfect rhythm to Aero's heartbeat. "I'm sending my young brother with you tomorrow in case you need help with your Falchion. He is most trustworthy. If anything happens, you should turn to him for help. Remember, the Forgers are on your side."

The way he emphasized this statement made Aero aware that there was more to it than met the eye. Did the Forger suspect that Vinick might cheat? Or that something could go wrong? But before he could ask, the door opened to reveal the young Forger. He had returned with the

Falchion. The golden blade, in its default form, surged with the fresh charge.

He approached the bedside and presented the weapon to Aero with a bow. "Captain Wright, your Falchion," he said in a solemn voice.

Aero accepted the blade and said his thanks to the Forgers. The old man left with the boy, promising that his charge would be at Aero's door first thing in the morning to accompany him to the duel, whose venue still remained a mystery to all but the Majors.

Aero wondered what they were plotting. Feeling a surge of anger, he shifted his Falchion into a broadsword and slashed at the air, imagining that it was Vinick's heart he was tearing open instead. His shoulder ached less, he noticed with relief, and his strength was returning. Even better, the cacophony of the Supreme Generals' voices had begun to fade. They sounded less like an angry mob now and more like a soft chorus.

He wondered if the conversation with the Forger had set his mind at ease, thus allowing him to better control the Beacon. And who knew, maybe the knowledge of the Supreme Generals would prove an asset tomorrow—or it could be his undoing.

Either way, he'd find out at 0900 hours.

Chapter 39
THE PENITENTIARY

Myra Jackson

Myra came to a halt over a vent and peered into the darkness below.

Faintly, she could hear the rustling of bodies. She inhaled, and the stench hit her full force—it was the smell of the dying. And that was when she knew her trajectory had been accurate. She was right above her old cell. The Pen was pitch black, so no Patrollers were lurking about right now. They always carried flashlights.

Her heart pounding, she unhooked the grate and lowered herself through it, coming to rest on the top of the steel bars. They easily bore her weight. She climbed down and landed on the floor in a crouch. The keys in her pocket gave off a soft clink.

She froze and listened, but aside from the rustling, the sector remained eerily quiet. It was only a precaution anyway. The last thing most prisoners wanted was to summon the Patrollers and their pipes. She reached down and fingered the bulky key ring in her pocket. Rickard had swiped it from his father's office and delivered it to her in the secret room.

Though her friends had offered to accompany her, they'd have only slowed her down. She could move through the pipes faster alone. Also, more people might draw unwanted attention. And worst case—if she were caught—then they'd be spared, at least.

It was paltry comfort now that she was actually inside the Pen. Her heart thudding, she crept down the row of cells. The only light came from the greenish pulsing of the Beacon, peeking out from the sleeve of her dress. It was faint, but it made it possible to see in the perpetual night. She whispered into each cell she passed.

"Jonah . . . "

She prayed her father would be strong enough to answer. One prisoner pressed himself against the bars. "Please . . . bloody get me out! Don't leave me here to rot!"

"I'll come back, I promise . . . if I have time," she whispered. She felt torn, but she couldn't start releasing random prisoners. Though desperation clouded his eyes, the prisoner seemed to understand and let her pass without causing a disturbance.

She neared the end of the row.

"Jonah . . . "

The figure huddled in the back of the cell shifted and suddenly separated into two smaller figures. "Look, it's Tinker's sister," one of them croaked out.

"Myra," rasped the other one.

"Stella and Ginger?" Myra said.

Myra held up her wrist and saw that the Bishop twins were in a dreadful state—bloodied, bruised, and obviously famished. Fury surged through her at the Patrollers, but she wasn't surprised. They hadn't treated her any better when she was locked up.

"By the Oracle, I'm breaking you out," she hissed through the bars. She flipped through the key ring, trying several different keys until one fit. With some effort, the stubborn lock turned with a squeal, and the heavy door swung open on its hinges. The girls hobbled out of the cell. "My father's cell . . . can you show me where it is?" she asked.

They both nodded but exchanged a troubled look.

"Follow us, this way," Ginger said.

They pointed her to the last cell and then signaled that they would wait for her. Myra crept up to the bars and pressed her face to them. "Papa . . . are you in there?"

She held her breath—but there was no response.

Then she heard a weak voice. "Myra . . . but how's it possible?"

"Papa! I've come to save you."

Myra fumbled through the keys until she found the right one and then hurried into his cell. He was slumped in the back corner, and as the light from the Beacon caught his face, she gasped. It was a patchwork of welts, gashes, and bruises. His nose had been broken, more than once from the looks of it, and a few teeth had been knocked out. But he was still alive and breathing, and that was all she cared about for the moment.

She rushed to his side, and that was when her heart sank. His wrists and ankles were shackled to the steel bars by heavy chains. One glance at the lock told her no key on her ring could possibly fit it. They were all too large.

"You're chained up, and I don't have the key!" she cried in frustration. Angry tears brimmed in her eyes. He cracked open his swollen eyelids.

"By the Oracle . . . how'd you get in here?"

"Through the pipes and ducts," she whispered. "I use them to get around, that's why I've never been caught out in the corridors after the Final Warning. It was Tinker's idea to use them to get into the Pen and rescue you."

"A foolish mission! You shouldn't have risked your life for me! What if you get caught?" He strained against the shackles, but they held fast. A wry smile graced his swollen lips. "They're steel, topnotch craftsmanship, virtually indestructible."

A horrible realization dawned on her. "You made them, didn't you?"

He nodded, the irony not lost on him. "Last year, Padre Flavius ordered me to make them for special prisoners. Holy Sea . . . I never imagined he'd use them on me."

"Bishop and Decker?"

His eyes flashed in surprise. "They're chained up, too. Padre Flavius isn't taking any chances with us. But Myra . . . how do you know about them?"

She looked down. "I overheard you meeting with them. I hid in the vent above your office. That's how I learned about the Animus Machine breaking down and your plan to return to the Surface. That's also how I found out about the Beacon."

Guiltily, she reached down and slid back her sleeve and held up her wrist. His eyes shifted from the golden armlet and its pulsing green light back to her face.

"Why didn't you tell me?"

"I was scared you'd be angry . . . and, well, I didn't think I'd actually find the bloody thing! I was going to tell you, but then the 'Trollers arrested you."

"That's right, I saw it on your wrist before Jasper grabbed me, but Padre Flavius beat me so much, I started to think that I'd probably imagined the whole thing."

She looked up at him. "Papa, you were right! About everything."

In a low voice, and as quickly as she could, she told him everything that she'd learned since donning the Beacon. She told him about finding the Beacon, Elianna Wade, and her purpose to return to the First Continuum.

"Papa, I need your help to build the submarine," she said. "But obviously that's impossible now. The blueprints are so complicated . . . and require so many parts. I can't possibly build it without you."

A smile twisted her father's swollen lips. "You don't have to build it."

"What do you mean? It's the only way to reach the Surface."

"Myra . . . I've already built it."

"But when? Where? I mean . . . how?"

"You're not the only one with secrets," he said with a twinkle in his eyes. "I've been working on it for months, ever since I discovered the Animus Machine was failing and I couldn't fix it. I recruited Decker to help since he runs the Spare Parts Room. The submersibles were destroyed in the Great Purging, but many of the parts were salvaged for other uses. That's why I've been working around the clock lately. I hated leaving you and Tinker alone so much, but it was the only way."

"Holy Sea, I had no idea," Myra said in a stunned voice. She remembered seeing the many deliveries from Decker in the Spare Parts Room arriving for her father, but she didn't think much of them at the time. "But how'd you hide something that large?"

"You know the area in Sector 8 that's sectioned off?"

Myra visualized a map of the colony and zeroed in on Sector 8, where the Docks were housed. "Of course, it's structurally unsound. Nobody's allowed in there."

He smiled, though it pained him. "Oh, it's perfectly sound alright, though I declared the area hazardous and forbade anyone from entering it due to safety concerns. Then, it was just a matter of pushing it to the bottom of the list of repairs, which wasn't hard since I'm in charge of the assignments. The submarine is hidden there by the portals that open to the sea."

She threw her arms around him and hugged him fiercely. "Oh, Papa, you're a genius!"

He wanted to hug her back, but he couldn't. His arms were shackled. His eyes probed her face. "Myra, have you studied the plans? Do you know how to operate it?"

She nodded quickly—she had a photographic memory for blueprints. "Yup, I've already memorized them," she admitted. "You designed it brilliantly."

"Then you're the only one who knows how to pilot it, aside from me." He glanced miserably at his manacled wrists. "It's designed to rise swiftly, which should minimize the exposure to the water pressure, which will be your biggest enemy."

"Eight tons per square inch," she whispered. She'd learned all about it for her Apprentice Exam. The colony's structure had to withstand it—and so would the sub.

"The structure should bear it, but I haven't had a chance to test it yet. Holy Sea, I only finished building it three days ago." What he didn't state explicitly, though it was clear from his voice, was that it could fail. Myra swallowed hard at that thought.

"Myra, it'll hold, I promise you," he said, "or I'm not the Head Engineer."

"Of course it'll hold," she said, forcing a brave smile.

"With Maude's help, I've stocked the hull with supplies—food preserves, water filters, flasks, tarps, coats, boots, tools. Many Hockers donated to our cause."

"The Hockers helped you?" she said in surprise. "You mean you actually told them about the submarine and your plans? But wasn't that dangerous?"

He shook his head. "They don't know the exact nature of our mission, nor do they know who's involved. Maude just told them we were defying the Synod—a cause they readily support. The Hockers are more united than it appears on the surface, and they've been discriminated against for too long. Most of the sacrifices come from their ranks. If the Synod isn't careful, they could have a bloody revolution on their hands."

"A revolution," Myra said warily.

Their eyes met, the ramifications of that clear to both of them. "Now listen carefully," he said. "I don't know what you'll find when you reach the Surface. I've tried to include everything you'll need, but you've got to be prepared for anything."

"You act as though I'm leaving without you!"

"Myra, that's exactly what you must do." He strained against the shackles. They dug into his wrists. "Look, I've never wanted this burden for you, but I fear that it's chosen you anyway. There's nobody else I trust to see this journey through." His eyes locked onto her face and held her gaze. There was more urgency in them now.

"Myra, it's up to you now. Take your brother with you and whatever companions you trust. There's room for four, or maybe five including Tinker."

"I'm not leaving you, and you can't make me!" Myra cried, the tears spilling freely from her eyes now. "I'll come back tomorrow night and find a way to free you. I'll bring tools next time . . . and friends to help. You're coming with me."

"No, I forbid it! Listen to me. Padre Flavius ordered the Patrollers to arrest you and Tinker not two hours ago. By some miracle, they haven't come for you yet."

"Right, we've been hiding in the secret room."

"Clever girl! You always have been."

"Like father, like daughter."

"Like mother, like daughter is more like it." His voice caught in his throat. "Myra . . . there's something else you need to know . . . and it's about your mother."

"What about her?" She was caught completely off guard. They almost never talked about her mother.

Pain flashed across her father's face and contorted it. "Padre Flavius had her killed."

Her mouth dropped open in shock. "I thought she died giving birth to Tinker."

"That's because Padre Flavius made it look like an accident. He confessed while he was beating me. He thought the knowledge would break me."

"But why'd he do it?" she asked, too stunned to cry.

His eyes darted to her wrist and the golden armlet. "Because she was looking for the Beacon," he said. "She was pledged to Records and secretly dug through her family history until she came across a journal entry from her ancestor, President Elijah Wade, where he wrote about the Beacon. Well, she became convinced that we were supposed to leave the colony and return to the Surface."

"Her name used to be Wade, didn't it?"

"Exactly, before she married me—Tessa Wade."

"Is that how you found out about the Beacon?"

He nodded. "But shortly after she told me everything, she died giving birth to Tinker . . ." His voice caught in his throat. "Or so I thought. Padre Flavius must have found out that she knew about the Beacon and decided to get rid of her."

Myra took this all in, forcing her emotional response back down—it would have to wait for later. "But why didn't you keep looking for the Beacon after she died?"

"After she passed away, I couldn't bear to think about

any of it, so I just tucked my head down and worked around the clock, anything to take my mind off missing her. I forgot all about the Beacon until I discovered the Animus Machine was failing."

"And then you remembered?" Myra said.

"Right, I recruited Bishop to help search through Records. Padre Flavius put his wife out to sea, too, so he was sympathetic to our cause. Only, aside from finding some old photographs of the Wade family, we hadn't made any progress."

"But I overheard your meeting and took up the search."

"Yes, and you succeeded where so many have failed!" He fixed her with a proud smile. "Myra, your mother would have wanted you to find it. She'd be so proud that you're a Carrier, just like Elianna Wade. And she'd want you to go to the Surface."

"Papa, I won't leave without you! They'll kill you."

"But you must!" he insisted. A devious smile crept onto his lips. "Besides, Padre Flavius won't kill me—he needs me too much. I'm the only person who knows how to run half the machines that keep this bloody place going. And until I train a replacement—and Royston assures me he's a very slow learner—he'll have to keep me alive."

"That's no guarantee, and you know it," Myra said.

Her father's strength was fading, but he forced himself to continue. "Padre Flavius can beat me all he wants, that doesn't scare me. I'm just afraid of what he'll do to you and Tinker. But if you leave with your brother, then at least I'll know you're safe from him. For all his power, even he can't follow you into the Holy Sea."

She wanted to argue with her father—or just refuse to go—but she knew better than that. The tone of his voice told her as much. Her father was as stubborn as Tinker, and his logic was sound. She felt her heart rending in two.

"Yes, Papa," she said reluctantly.

"Myra, you must leave tonight! The 'Trollers will be looking for you and Tinker. Use your secret ways to get around if you can—"

Beep!

Suddenly, the sector door activated—somebody was coming.

Myra's eyes jerked to her father's face, and she could tell that they were both thinking the same thing: *This could be the last time we ever see each other.*

She hugged her father fiercely. "Papa, I won't fail you!"

"Myra, I love you," he said. "Don't ever doubt that! I'm sorry if I've ever acted distant or detached. You just remind me so much of Tessa, and it was excruciating to see her ghost walking around the compartment every day."

"Papa, I love you, too," she murmured into his shoulder.

"Now you must go!" he whispered and pulled away from her.

She let go of him, tears streaming down her cheeks. "I'll come back for you, I swear it!"

Any second now, the sector door would dilate. She backed out of the cell, locked the door, and forced herself to look away. As she retreated down the dark passage, she said a silent prayer to whatever deity might be listening: *Please let my father endure until I can return to save him—to save everyone. For if I don't, then they're all doomed.*

The Beacon pulsed fervently, urging her onward. She sensed Elianna's support flooding through her, and also her concern, and Myra felt comforted. She wasn't alone—in fact, she realized, she'd never be alone again, not so long as she lived.

The Bishop twins were waiting by their father's cell. They were saying their final good-byes. Myra marveled at their similarities—Padre Flavius had killed their mother and imprisoned their father, too. She wanted to give the twins more time, but they didn't have that luxury now. "Hurry, we have to go!" she whispered. "Somebody's coming."

She grabbed their hands—tiny like Tinker's—and led them back to the cell beneath the vent. "Can you climb?" she asked, worried they were too injured.

"Yes," they said in unison.

Myra helped them up and then started climbing behind them. With another beep, the sector door dilated, and Myra glimpsed two flashlight beams—

And a swirl of crimson.

The light careened wildly around the Pen, but then it fell on her and froze.

"It's that Jackson girl!" snarled a voice so distinctive that every man, woman, and child would have recognized it. It belonged to Padre Flavius. The beam of his flashlight landed on the Beacon, which exploded with golden light. "And she has the Beacon!"He turned to the Patroller next to him—Bates. "Catch her or if you fail, it'll be the last thing you do!" Flavius thundered.

Myra scrambled the rest of the way up the cell. She heard pounding feet drawing closer. The Bishop twins slithered through the grate and reached down for her. Myra started to climb through the narrow opening when something grabbed her foot.

It was a hand, and it belonged to Bates.

He yanked hard, and she almost lost her grip and plummeted down. "Get back here, heathen!" he growled.

She tried to kick him off, but he held on. She could hear more pounding feet approaching. *Reinforcements*, she thought grimly. More flashlight beams lit the sector. She glimpsed Baron and Jasper. She strained to reach the edge of the vent, but it was too far away. Bates gave another hard tug, and she started to lose her grip, when she felt tiny hands latch around her wrists. The Bishop twins had her.

With their combined strength pulling on her, Myra kicked at Bates. This time, her foot connected solidly with his jaw. She heard a sickening crack and felt something implode beneath her foot. He cried out in pain and released her. She didn't wait for him to recover. She slid through the grate and hooked it shut behind her. Then, she jammed the key ring into the latch to prevent anybody from trying to follow them.

As quickly as she could travel with two injured companions, Myra led them through the pipes, pointing the way through the darkness. She kept her flashlight off—only the pulsing of the Beacon lit their way. Her heart hammered in her chest, and the Beacon pulsed faster and brighter. The Bishop twins quickly tired, but she urged them forward. They could rest when they reached the secret room, where they'd be safe.

Once Myra had put enough distance between them and the Pen, she allowed them to slow their pace. The Patrollers couldn't follow them this deep into the bowels of the colony. But now they knew about her secret ways. This trick wouldn't fool them again. Her father was right—she and Tinker had to leave immediately. They didn't have a choice. The Patrollers were already searching for them. Even Kaleb, Paige, and Rickard might not be safe anymore, even if their only crime was being her friend.

Her mind was made up—there was no going back now. Padre Flavius had killed her mother and imprisoned her father. Soon he'd do the same to her and Tinker, and would probably sacrifice them to the Holy Sea. Their world under the sea was doomed—it was already dying. She would take her father's submarine and escape to the Surface.

The only question was who would be coming with her.

PART V
THE SURFACE

"Why have not we an immortal soul?" asked the little mermaid mournfully; "I would give gladly all the hundreds of years that I have to live, to be a human being only for one day, and to have the hope of knowing the happiness of that glorious world above the stars."

—Hans Christian Anderson, *The Little Mermaid*

He was enchanted by the mystery of coming ashore naked on an unfamiliar island. He resolved to let the adventure run its full course, resolved to see just how far a man might go, emerging naked from salt water. It was a rebirth for him . . .

—Kurt Vonnegut, *Cat's Cradle*

Chapter 40

A DUEL TO THE DEATH

Captain Aero Wright

Aero approached the door to the simulation chamber, as he had many times before to face hundreds of opponents over the course of his sixteen years.

The young Forger, whom he still thought of as Xander, trailed behind him. His robe rustled with every movement. As the old Forger had promised, his young charge had been waiting at Aero's door at 0800 hours when Major Doyle had come to escort him to the duel. Wren had accompanied them, too. She emerged from the supply closet with the helmet that he always used. She inspected it to make sure that it was functioning properly and hadn't been tampered with, and then relinquished it to Aero. He shrugged it on.

"Lieutenant, will you fasten it?"

"Yes, sir." She went to work on the straps. She was close to him, standing on her tiptoes, with her left ear right by his lips.

"So, you're back to following my orders?" he whispered. He noticed her blushing.

"Well, I informed you yesterday that my disobedience was temporary," she whispered back. She hit the power button, and he felt the helmet booting up. A green light appeared in the visor. Her hand came to rest on his uninjured shoulder.

"Captain, I'm here to support you," she said and stepped back. Their eyes met, and he nodded once.

The sound of footfalls reached their ears. They both turned to look as Major Vinick strode into the corridor, accompanied by Majors Oranck and Doyle. He wore a lightweight uniform, the preferred garb for simulator combat. An angry welt stood out on his brow where Aero had struck him. It looked like it would leave a nasty scar.

But then another soldier stepped into the corridor, trailing behind the officers and carrying Vinick's helmet. Aero's eyes tracked over her face and then backtracked swiftly. Her shock of coppery hair and freckled face were unmistakable—it was his mother.

"Lieutenant, proceed," Vinick said and gestured for her to approach, and she started fastening his helmet. She glanced quickly in her son's direction, but her face remained stoic. There wasn't even a hint of recognition buried in her features.

Watching her help Vinick sickened Aero. His heart lurched in his chest, and his thoughts started to swim, drowning in the Supreme Generals' voices. And, for the briefest of moments, his felt his father's presence surface from the sea of chatter.

Lydia Wright, his father thought. *Oh, Lydia, what are you doing?* But then the voice receded, drowned out by the cacophony.

Another soldier stepped into the corridor and approached Vinick. She had brown hair—cropped short, of course—dimples in her cheeks, and looked young. Aero had never laid eyes on her before. "Who's that soldier with Vinick?" he whispered to Wren.

Her eyes snapped up. "The young one? No idea," she said, scrutinizing the girl's face. "She looks about our age but didn't train with us at the Agoge."

"Danika Rothman," the Forger said in a low voice. Every soldier visited the Foundry, so the Forgers knew all their names. "She was our year at the Agoge. She's skilled with her Falchion and serves in a combat unit."

Vinick jerked his eyes to Aero and caught him staring at her. A cruel sneer stretched across his lips. "What's wrong, Captain? Haven't met your betrothed yet?"

Aero felt the blood rushing and roaring in his ears.

Danika Rothman.

The young female soldier with Vinick was his betrothed. His eyes roved over the stranger's face, taking in her milky skin, her placid brown eyes, her full lips, the soft swell of her bosom, and the curve of her hips. She was lovely, there was no doubt about it. He should have felt lucky to be betrothed to such a girl, and many soldiers would have envied him the honor, but all he felt was a dreaded swirl of emotions. He paled suddenly, as the dizziness and nausea returned with a vengeance.

"If that's your betrothed, then who's that other soldier?" Wren asked.

"My mother," Aero said furiously.

She paled now, too. "But why are they here?"

"No doubt Vinick has been enjoying perusing my confidential files. He must be trying to throw me off and stir up my emotions."

"Then he's a monster and a coward!" Wren snapped. "He fears you, that's why he's resorting to dirty tricks. He doesn't want to face you at full strength. You already bested him once on the bridge, and he knows that you could do it again."

"But that was before I was wearing the Beacon," he said weakly, as the torrent of voices assailed his neural synapses. "Vinick knows that I have to control my emotions in order to control the Beacon and wield my Falchion at the same time . . ."

He trailed off as the voices swelled, overwhelming him. He felt consciousness slipping away from him, consumed by the chorus. He swayed on his feet and grasped onto Wren for support. Vinick noticed and exchanged a smile with Major Doyle.

Wren shot a troubled look at the young Forger. "Quick, we have to help him," she whispered.

The Forger nodded and turned to Aero. "Captain, it's not so different from controlling your Falchion," he said in a soothing voice. "Just remember the breathing exercises you practiced at the Agoge—take deep breaths and still your mind."

Aero did as the Forger instructed, slowing his breathing and working to clear his mind of irrational impulses and emotions. Gradually, the voices grew quieter—as quiet as they were likely to get—which was manageable, like the soft whirring of an engine.

"Five minute warning!" Major Doyle announced. "The Majors will be watching from the control room. Major Vinick, Captain Wright, any last questions?"

"Thank you, Major Doyle," Vinick said with a salute. Then he turned to Aero. "Enjoy your breathing exercises, boy! They're some of the last breaths you'll ever take."

Aero set his jaw but didn't respond—he didn't want to give Vinick the satisfaction. But then his mother stepped up to Vinick and saluted him.

"Major, I hope that you triumph in the duel," she said.

"Thank you, Lieutenant Wright," Vinick said. "Your loyalty today won't go unrewarded. There can be only one outcome—I am the strongest soldier."

"*Only the strongest shall lead us*," she quoted with another salute.

It was the ultimate betrayal. Aero felt the calm that he'd worked to achieve slipping away, like water through a sieve. Sudden panic seized him, and the voices swelled and engulfed him completely. He felt helpless to stop them. He staggered and doubled over, fighting to keep from losing consciousness. Wren tried to help him.

Vinick checked his helmet and, finding it secure, proceeded into the simulation chamber. The door emitted a soft hiss and contracted behind him. As usual, they'd each be in their own chambers and meet face-to-face only in the simulated venue.

Dimly—as if very far away from him—Aero heard the hiss of the door and knew what had happened, but he didn't glance in Vinick's direction. Nor did he allow his gaze to wander to his mother or his betrothed. Instead, he kept it fixed firmly on Wren.

Major Doyle's ghostly voice, also sounding very far away, resonated through the corridor. "Captain Wright, it's time!" he barked. "If you don't proceed into your simulator, then you'll forfeit the duel—and be sentenced to death by beheading."

But consciousness was leaving Aero. The world was dimming. He was barely holding on. Only one thing kept him there, kept him from leaving this time and place, swept away by the Beacon.

It was Wren—she held his gaze and never wavered.

"Captain Wright, this is your final warning," said Doyle.

"You can do this," Wren insisted to Aero. "Just remember what the Forger told you; it's just like your Falchion. Quiet your mind and control your emotions."

Doyle unsheathed his Falchion and shifted it into a battle-ax. "I'll only say it one more time—step into your chamber or risk forfeiture and execution," he ordered.

"Stay with me!" Wren whispered fiercely. "Don't listen to Doyle!"

Whether it was the words that she spoke or simply her presence that finally snapped him out of it, Aero didn't know, nor did it matter. All that mattered was that the dissonant voices lost their hold on him, fading away to nothing.

"Thank you," he whispered to Wren.

Then he turned to Doyle. "Yes sir, Major," he said with a calm salute. Doyle appeared surprised at his sudden recovery but quickly hid it.

Aero unsheathed his Falchion so that the Forger could inspect it one last time. The weapon was still in its default form of a curved blade. He didn't know the venue yet, so he'd wait to morph it. The sword surged and flashed with the fresh charge.

"Sir, your Falchion is fully charged," the Forger said with a bow.

Then, without hesitation, and under Major Doyle's careful watch, Aero strode into his simulation chamber and found the grooves on the floor where he was supposed to stand. Then he squared his shoulders and bent his knees a few times to loosen them up, his blade at the ready. The door hissed shut behind him, sealing him inside the chamber.

"Two minute warning!" he heard Doyle say through his earpiece.

Breathe, Aero commanded his body as the voices swelled in his head and threatened to overtake him again. *Just breathe.* If he didn't focus his mind—if he didn't push back against the voices—then this duel would be very short.

"Thirty seconds!" said Doyle. "Remember, the safety controls are set to kill. This is a duel to the death—only one victor shall emerge from the chambers alive."

The lights in the chamber flickered and went dark. The blackness was all encompassing. Aero was swimming in it, flailing around in it, beginning to drown in it. The voices morphed and grew into a discordant chorus. The Beacon pulsed brighter and faster, mimicking his quickening heart rate. Aero tried desperately to slow it.

Breathe. Breathe. Breathe. Breathe.

He repeated this mantra over and over again, fighting back against the cacophony reverberating in his skull. Against all odds, his lungs obeyed him, and oxygen flooded into his bloodstream. The panic began to recede, and his mind slowly cleared.

And in the silence that emerged, a singular voice rang out clear as day.

You will avenge me, said his father. *Just remember that I love you. I have always loved you. You've trained your whole life for this moment—and you will triumph.*

The voice fell silent, and Aero's mind went quieter than it ever had before. It felt as if his father was protecting him—as if he'd wrangled the other voices into submission. The Beacon pulsed at Aero forcefully, and he felt his Falchion surge back in response.

"0900 hours!" Doyle said. "Soldiers engage!"

The lights surged on, flooding his neural synapses. Aero tensed his muscles, gripping his Falchion tighter, and then stepped into the venue to face Vinick.

Only one of them would emerge alive.

Chapter 41
DELIVERANCE OR OBLIVION

Myra Jackson

The thin beam of the flashlight lit Myra's route through the pipes.

It was still night—or at least the artificial thing they called night, which was created by the dimming of the automatic lights. This night already felt endless, and morning was still several hours off, she thought wearily.

There were many things that made leaving difficult, abandoning her father foremost among them. It went against every instinct in her body. She wanted to disobey his order to leave, but the Beacon—and Elianna—overrode the impulse. They reminded her of her purpose, that this was what her mother would have wanted, and that returning to the Surface was her best chance to save her father and everybody else in the colony.

Myra gave in, but that didn't make it any easier. The image of her father's bruised and bloodied face flashed through her mind, filling her with sorrow. That was the last time that she'd seen him, before she fled with the Bishop twins.

Myra couldn't see behind her—the pipe was too narrow—but she could hear the sounds of her companions as they crawled in tandem behind her. Tinker, Kaleb, Paige, and Rickard. If all went according to plan, then this would be their final journey through the pipes. *We're leaving tonight,* she thought, *and we may never come back.*

When Myra had returned to the secret room, she'd tried to talk her friends out of coming, arguing that they didn't have to leave since the Patrollers weren't after them. They were only coming to arrest her and Tinker. They could stay behind in relative safety. But they'd all refused—and, in truth, Myra was grateful. She needed their help, not only to navigate to the Surface, but also to find the First Continuum, for not even Elianna could tell her exactly what to expect once they reached the Surface.

So many variables and possibilities, Elianna had communicated to her. *No prediction, not even from a brilliant scientist like Professor Divinus, is certain.*

This filled Myra with confusion. *But what do you think it'll look like?* she thought back.

There was a weighty pause. *A wasteland as far as the eye can see.*

The image of blackened earth stretching into the horizon flashed through Myra's head as emotions that belonged to Elianna swept through her, grief foremost among them—grief for the world lost to the Doom. Myra forced it back and asked, *How do you know the First Continuum will still be there?*

I don't, Elianna had thought. *I can only hope.*

Myra had briefly considered bringing the Bishop twins, but they didn't have room in the submarine. It could only hold five people, including Tinker. Also, the girls were injured and needed immediate medical attention. They were in no shape for a long journey, especially one that promised to be perilous.

But Stella and Ginger were fugitives. The Patrollers would be looking for them everywhere. She'd racked her brain for somebody that could help, and eventually she'd settled on the one person that she trusted above all others—*Maude.*

Myra had given the old woman a terrible fright when she'd popped out of a vent in her compartment's living space.

Maude had come running out of the bedroom in a nightgown, wielding a flashlight and a glass bottle for protection. Once she'd ascertained that the intruder meant her no harm, she'd broken into a toothless grin. "Myra Jackson, aren't you full of surprises?"

That was when Stella and Ginger had peeked their heads out of the vent and given Maude another surprise.

"And you've brought two friends!" Maude exclaimed. "Now don't be afraid, sweethearts, I won't hurt you." When she glimpsed the extent of their injuries, she added, "The 'Trollers and the Red Cloaks have already had that honor." News of their arrest had spread through the colony, and Maude was always the first to hear about anything.

Myra hugged Maude. "Can you keep them safe?"

"Of course! You're not the only one with secrets."

She led them back to the spare bedroom that served as her distillery and showed them a secret panel hidden in the wall. "Well, I used to hide firewater back here, before the 'Trollers started to patronize my establishment. I'm guessing it's just large enough for two little girls, and I've got plenty of supplies—plus all the candy they can eat."

Stella and Ginger looked less afraid then. Maude slipped them some sweetfish from her pocket. They gobbled them up and looked up at her with hopeful eyes.

"Oh my, you must be famished!" Maude fussed and retrieved more sweetfish from the kitchen for them. "What were the 'Trollers feeding you down there?"

"From experience, next to nothing," Myra said.

Just then, Stella wobbled on her feet, and her sister had to support her. "Now, where are my manners?" Maude exclaimed and ushered the twins over to the sofa in a flurry of movement. "Just rest, you hear me? You've been through quite an ordeal."

Once the twins were off their feet, Maude pulled Myra aside. "They're injured," she said in a low voice. "Quite badly, from the looks of it. Scrapes, a few broken ribs, I suspect, and that's the least of it," she said, tapping one finger to her forehead.

"Paige went to her mother for help," Myra said. "Head Doctor Vanderjagt should be here soon to examine them. She'll bring medicine and bandages."

"You trust her?" Maude asked, narrowing her eyes. Most Hockers had a natural distrust of Factum—and vice versa. Paige's mother also held a position of power, which probably made Maude even more suspicious.

Myra nodded. "I trust Paige, and her mother is appalled by what Padre Flavius has been doing. She dedicated her life to helping people, this goes against all her beliefs."

"All our beliefs," Maude snorted. Her eyes lingered on Myra, whom she'd known since she was just a little girl. "You've got something else to tell me, don't you?"

When Myra hesitated, Maude set her hands on her hips. "There's more to this story than you're letting on, so don't even bother trying to lie to me, sweetheart."

"Right. I'm going . . . away . . . far away," Myra admitted. "Tinker, Paige, Rickard, and Kaleb are coming with me. And we're leaving tonight, but I hope that we'll return . . ."

She trailed off and decided that she'd already said too much. She didn't want to put Maude in any more danger than she already had.

Maude didn't look nearly as shocked as Myra had expected. "This is about your father's special project, isn't it?"

Myra nodded slowly. Maude didn't try to pry more information out of her, but she did look saddened. She enveloped Myra in her ample arms and squeezed tight. Myra blinked back tears and glanced at Stella and Ginger, who were fast asleep on the sofa.

"You'll take care of them?"

"As if they were my own," Maude said, her voice catching. "I lost Quentin and Bertha to the Pox. They were about the same age as those girls."

"Thank you," Myra said. "I knew you would." She wanted to linger in the seeming safety of Maude's compartment, but time was running out. They needed to escape under the cover of darkness.

Maude saw the expression on Myra's face. "The Oracle be with you!" Maude bid her and pressed a satchel of sweetfish into her palm. "For the journey ahead; I know it's not much."

"It's plenty! You've already done more than enough," Myra assured her. She tucked the satchel into her pocket, backed away, and unhooked the grate. She glanced behind her one last time. "Good-bye—" she started, but Maude cut her off like always.

"It's not good-bye—it's see you later."

"See you later," Myra revised her statement.

And she hoped it was true.

o o o

It had only been thirty minutes since Myra had left Maude's compartment, but it already felt like a lifetime ago. A single tear crept down her cheek, sluggish and alone.

After crawling through the pipes for a little under half an hour, Myra and her companions reached Sector 8, which housed the Docks that opened to the sea. One by one, they climbed out and stole across the sector to the far side. Their flashlights lit the way. Engineering had sectioned off the back area with thick tarps and posted signs:

DANGER:
Structurally Unsound & In Danger of Collapse!

NO TRESPASSING:
By Order of Engineering

Myra smiled to herself at her father's clever ruse. Feeling a rush of nervous excitement, she drew back the tarps that concealed the area and beheld the submarine for the first time. She couldn't believe her eyes. It had come alive from blueprints that she'd committed to heart. Her eyes roved over every inch of the vessel, taking in each detail.

The submarine itself was a feat of engineering, shaped like a narrow cylinder with pointed ends. A bulbous window encapsulated the cockpit. Stabilizer fins and rudders jutted out of the stern at the back of the ship. Lining the hull were panels that concealed the ballast tanks, which took on water or released it to control the buoyancy, or how fast the submarine would rise or sink. It was suspended off the ground by a motorized crane fitted with wheels so that it could be loaded into one of the portals.

Though made from mismatched parts, the exterior had been expertly insulated and welded together. Tinker ran his hand over the smooth surface.

"It's . . . incredible," he whispered. He glanced at Myra, and a look passed between them. She could tell they were both thinking of their father.

Myra wanted to linger over the design more, but time was wasting. She climbed the metal rungs to the hatch on top of the submarine, turned the wheel, and swung it open. Then she disappeared through the hatch and aimed her flashlight at the interior deck. The cramped space would hold all five of them, she thought, but just barely.

In the stern, she glimpsed supplies that her father had promised would be there—backpacks, blankets, coats, boots, food, and water. She began divvying up the coats and boots. "The water is freezing at this depth," she explained, though Tinker already knew. "So as soon as we plunge into the sea, the submarine will grow very, very cold."

As she handed Kaleb a coat, he leaned in closer. "Then I get to sit next to you," he whispered, his breath kissing her earlobe. "So we can keep each other nice and warm."

Myra rolled her eyes. He was a hopeless flirt. *Even our dire circumstances haven't altered that part of his personality*, she noted wryly.

"That honor goes to Tinker," she said. "He's my copilot."

Tinker flashed a grin.

They pulled on the thick coats and traded their flimsy sandals for the boots, which her father must have pilfered from the Engineering Room. Rickard was still dressed in his black Patrollers uniform and had two pipes strapped to his waist.

He handed one to Kaleb, who accepted it warily. "Hey . . . just in case," Rickard said.

"Let's hope that *case* never happens," Kaleb replied grimly. "Since I've had no fight training." But he tucked the pipe into his waistband anyway.

Once they'd changed, Myra examined the crane. "It's mechanized, but we'll need to steer it over to the portal. Looks like number 3 is the closest. Kaleb and Rickard, why don't you get it open? Paige can help me operate the crane, and Tinker will guide us."

Myra approached the control panel at the back of the crane. After scanning it, she hit the power button. The crane roared to life, causing the submarine to shudder and undulate from where it was suspended above them by a thick cable.

Paige squinted at the control panel like it was an impossible math problem. "How'd you know to hit that button? They all look exactly the same to me."

Myra shrugged. "Engine Rat instinct—it's the same way you can diagnose what's wrong with a patient when I wouldn't have a clue."

Myra placed her right hand on the joystick, feeling her pulse quicken. "Sure hope this bloody thing works," she muttered as she nudged it forward.

For a stomach-churning second, the crane didn't move. But then, with a mighty jolt, a gear shifted into place, and it lurched forward, dragging Myra along with it.

With Tinker guiding them, Myra used the joystick to pilot the crane toward Portal 3. When they drew closer, Rickard triggered the button that opened the thick door. It beeped and dilated into the walls, revealing the cavernous interior. The Founders had designed the portals to hold much larger vessels than her father's humble design.

Indeed, they did, Elianna communicated to her.

Images of a great fleet of submersibles flashed through Myra's head—hulking ships filled with frightened refugees. Men, women, and children streamed out of their hulls, clutching their precious few belongings, and glimpsed their new home under the sea for the first time. Myra had been impressed by her father's design, but it paled in comparison to those of the Founders. She felt a surge of anger that the Synod had destroyed this once mighty fleet, dooming her people to the isolation of the deep.

Now all that remained was this singular vessel, cobbled together from mismatched parts that her father had salvaged. It would soon hold all of their lives—and the fate of their entire world—in its cramped hull. Myra just prayed that it would withstand the powerful and temperamental sea, which wanted nothing more than to crush them into oblivion. *It'll hold*, Elianna reassured her. *It has to hold.*

I hope you're right, Myra thought back.

Flicking the joystick from side to side to make corrections in their trajectory, Myra piloted the crane into the portal. She breathed a sigh of relief. The submarine was now in place—she just needed to release it from the crane. She located the right button and depressed it. The crane whirred to life and automatically lowered the submarine to the ground. It landed with a great thud that rocked the entire sector.

Her friends broke into jubilant cheers. She even caught Kaleb, who had no natural affinity for anything mechanical, running his fingers over the smooth exterior.

Though Myra was anxious to get going, there was more to do first. She thumbed the crane's joystick, guiding it out of the portal and back to the sectioned-off area. Paige drew the tarps back and made sure the warning signs were visible, while Myra kicked dust over the tracks that the crane had made on the floor.

As they walked back to the portal, Myra noticed tears brimming in her friend's eyes. She didn't need to ask why Paige was crying, for it was obvious. They were leaving everything familiar behind. She threaded her arm through Paige's and squeezed.

Suddenly, the sector door beeped.

They both froze—*somebody was coming!*

A split second later, the door dilated, revealing dark figures clutching flashlights. The beams of light careened wildly around the sector. Paige and Myra tried to duck behind the tarps, but the light landed on their faces and blinded them. Through the blazing whiteness, Myra could make out only one thing—the shadows grasped pipes.

The Patrollers had found them.

"Heathens, freeze!" yelled a voice that could only belong to Jasper. The shadows around him resolved into sharper focus. Myra glimpsed Bates, and standing behind him were the new pledges, Baron and Horace. Their pipes were unsheathed.

"By order of the Synod, you're all under arrest!" yelled another voice, this one deeper and more authoritative. It was Head Patroller Lynch. His flashlight beam landed on his son, standing next to Kaleb and Tinker. The beam jerked to the right, hitting the submarine.

"The Holy Sea save us!" Baron yelled. "What's that in the portal?"

"It's a sacrilege of the highest degree!" another voice boomed through the sector. The flashlight beams grazed over his crimson robes. "I'm glad I decided to join you on your search, so I could witness this abomination with my own eyes."

It was Padre Flavius.

His face was twisted up with deadly fury. "Patrollers, your orders have just changed—kill them all."

Chapter 42
DIRTY TRICKS

Captain Aero Wright

The venue was humid, oppressively so.

Aero was already sweating before he'd even taken one step. The air was scorching and steamy. As his eyes adjusted to the sunlight, he saw green everywhere. The venue was overgrown with vegetation, sprouting up in the primordial heat. He scanned the immediate area—ferns, underbrush, mossy trees with vines strung around their branches like ropey necklaces and roots arching out of the sodden earth.

They are all hazards, he thought. Every piece of vegetation here posed an obstacle.

This was a *jungle*, Aero remembered from his Planetary Biology class. They were in a simulation of Earth from Before Doom. He listened for signs of animal life, for that could prove an even bigger hazard, but the jungle remained eerily quiet. There were no sounds of insects buzzing, birds chirping, frogs bleating, or predators prowling.

That was the first—and perhaps only—piece of good news so far.

And lastly, all in a matter of seconds, Aero realized that Major Vinick was nowhere to be seen. He blinked, hoping it was merely a glitch in the simulator and Vinick would materialize before him at any second, but there was still no sign of him. This unsettled Aero—usually an opponent appeared right away and engaged him.

He gripped his Falchion tighter but didn't morph it yet. *Damn it, where's that coward hiding?* he thought as he scanned the area. All he saw was *green* and *green* and more *green*. There was no sign of his opponent anywhere in the venue.

Aero felt a surge from the Beacon and heard his father's voice.

Why did the Majors choose this venue?

"I don't know," Aero said uncertainly, his voice drowning in the muggy air. Frustration coursed through him. Usually, he could break down battle strategy instantly.

How does this venue adversely affect you?

That deep voice again, which should have been comforting but only aggravated him. Why was his father asking him questions? Why didn't he just tell him the answer?

"Well . . . it's a jungle," Aero said, his eyes scanning the thick foliage. "And it seems to be filled only with plant life—underbrush, ferns, trees, and vines."

He trailed off on that last word and tilted his gaze up, and that's when he glimpsed a flash of silver and gold in the trees. Then he had his answer.

"They know that my shoulder is injured!" he whispered. "And I can fight just as well with my right hand, but I need both arms to climb."

The speed with which Vinick had disappeared into the treetops meant the Majors had tipped him off. *More dirty tricks*, Aero thought angrily. He felt the Beacon pulse, indicating that his father agreed with him. His voice echoed through his head again.

Now you know—so what are you going to do?

"Right. I need to exploit Vinick's weaknesses and even

the playing field. I need to make him climb down somehow . . . and engage me on the ground."

What's his biggest weakness?

Insecurity, Aero thought right away.

He felt that his father agreed, and then his presence receded into the back of Aero's mind. The Beacon fell silent again, though it continued to pulse.

"Major Vinick!" Aero yelled. "Stop hiding like a coward!"

At first there was only silence, but then Vinick spoke. "Come up and get me, boy! Then we'll see how strong you are."

It came from the left. Aero jerked his head in that direction, but then he heard a twig snap to his right. He turned that way and slowly circled, on full alert.

"You're a damned coward!" Aero taunted his opponent. "Always have been! That's why you're hiding. That's why you brought my mother and my betrothed to the duel. You're afraid to face me in an even fight, right? You know I'm the strongest!"

"Liar!" Vinick screamed. "You're weak, and I'll prove it!"

Aero continued circling. His left boot sunk into the earth and stuck there. *Quicksand*, he realized at the last second and jerked it back. He'd have to be careful where he stepped. Rivulets of sweat poured down his brow, stinging his eyes.

"If you don't engage me, then the soldiers will know you're a coward! They'll never respect your leadership, and eventually they'll overthrow you!"

For a second, nothing happened. And then in a blur of motion, a silvery figure swooped down from the sky. Vinick swung from the treetops on a vine, his Falchion raised in the shape of a menaulion—a heavy spear with a thick shaft. Aero ducked out of the way and tucked into a tight roll. His injured shoulder collided with a root in a burst of pain. The spear stabbed into the ground right next to his head, penetrating through the mud with a sickening *thunk*. It had missed, but just barely—it clipped his hair.

Vinick yanked the spear from the ground and stabbed again, but this time Aero was ready. He shifted his Falchion into a shield and raised it. The spear ricocheted off in a shower of golden sparks. Aero didn't wait for Vinick to land another blow. He leapt to his feet and retreated, careful to avoid the roots and the deadly quicksand.

They circled each other, but the playing field was more even now. Aero's taunts had worked—Vinick had left the treetops to face him on the ground.

"Earth is a dead world, boy!" Vinick hissed, gesturing to the simulated venue around them. "It'll never look this way again! We should plunder it for resources and then continue on Stern's Quest to find a new home. That's our purpose!"

Aero inhaled and smelled the scent of life all around him—pungent, bitter, gritty, and so very alive. He felt the Beacon pulse, reminding him that it could be so again.

"You're wrong! Our purpose is to return to the First Continuum."

"And you're a fool, just like your father!" Vinick said as he stabbed at Aero with his spear. The blade swished past Aero's temples as he bobbed away. Vinick retracted his arm and stabbed again in rapid succession. His lips pulled back into a sneer.

"How was it seeing your mother today? She's a wonderful soldier—obedient, good with a Falchion, and, most importantly, she chose the right victor."

"Damn it, you had no right to read my file!" Aero said furiously.

He felt long-buried emotions flooding his brain, and with them came a torrent of voices from the Beacon. The dissonant chatter distracted him, and he tripped over a thick root and almost fell, just as the spear shot out at him again. He barely got his shield up in time—it felt impossibly heavy now. The golden metal started to ripple and shudder, the first sign that it might melt down.

Aero started to panic, struggling with the voices.

"And Lieutenant Rothman?" Vinick said. "What'd you think

of her? A lovely thing, isn't she? Pity you'll die before you get to bed her—"

"Shut up!" Aero managed weakly.

He had to go on the offense before his emotions and the voices overwhelmed him completely. He gripped his shield tighter and prepared to morph it, right as Vinick's voice cut through the air, almost making Aero lose control of his Falchion.

"Oh, what form will you choose?" Vinick jeered.

Aero averted his weapon melting down, but just barely. His heart was pounding, and the Beacon pulsed faster and brighter.

Vinick saw this and smiled viciously. "A broadsword like always?" he taunted his opponent, sensing the weakness. "I enjoyed perusing your file! You're so predictable. It's quite disappointing, really. Well, two can play at that game," Vinick said and shifted his Falchion into a broadsword.

He swiped at Aero with the heavy blade, and Aero sidestepped the blow. *Breathe*, Aero told himself. *Just breathe, damn it! And don't listen to Vinick!*

"You always begin on the defensive with a shield," Vinick went on in a bored voice. "And once you've worn out your opponent, you switch to a broadsword, using the strength that you've conserved and the more powerful weapon to win."

Vinick stabbed at Aero, but he dodged the blow and kept his focus on his breathing. He had to control the Beacon and the voices or his Falchion would melt down and Vinick would kill him. But the breathing exercises weren't working this time—the voices in his head weren't quieting down. And his father, whose help he desperately needed right now, was nowhere to be heard, probably lost amidst the cacophony.

Right when Aero thought all hope was lost—when his shield was rippling and convulsing—a vision of Myra popped into his head in her strange clothing on that icy world. Suddenly, a golden aura enveloped her body, blowing away the voices.

Everything drew into stark focus. If Aero didn't win this duel—if he didn't journey to Earth—then he'd never get to meet this strange and wondrous girl from another world. Vinick stabbed at him, but Aero had regained his mental focus. The power of the Beacon surged through him, syncing up with his Falchion's charge.

"Oh, I'm not so predictable as that!" Aero said and chose his form. At his command, the golden shield liquidly shifted and transformed into a katana. "This was Private Tristan's preferred weapon form."

Aero brought his newly formed sword up to meet Vinick's blow. Their Falchions clashed together with a jarring clang. Sparks flew from the point of impact.

"A very sentimental choice, boy!" Vinick scoffed.

"Maybe, but also highly effective," Aero said and swung again.

The longer, lightweight blade moved easily, cutting through the muggy air. Their Falchions collided, but Aero could wield his lighter blade faster. He forced Vinick back, who was struggling under the weight of the heavier broadsword. Vinick's heel caught on a root and he tripped but caught himself just in time. Sweat dripped down his brow, darkening his uniform. He tried to retreat further, but his back hit a tree trunk.

"You're trapped!" Aero said and raised his blade to swing.

"Not quite!" Vinick said. He morphed his Falchion back to its default form, quickly sheathed it, and climbed up the tree, using the vines to pull himself up.

Aero's sword collided with the trunk, giving off a shower of sparks. He briefly considered going after Vinick but stopped himself. Though he was fighting right-handed, his left shoulder was throbbing. The wound hadn't fully healed yet. If he tore it open again, then it could cost him his life. Better to wait and lure Vinick down again.

His father's voice rippled through his head. *Let your opponent make the choices—and also the mistakes.*

Aero heard rustling in the treetops and prayed that it was Vinick. He didn't want to contend with other life-forms. There were already enough obstacles in this venue. He crouched down and crept in the direction of the noises. This respite was giving his opponent the chance to catch his breath from wielding the heavy broadsword. It was costing him the advantage. But still he waited, the katana gripped in his sweaty fist.

His father was right—he had to wait for Vinick to make mistakes. He kept his eyes glued above him. The air felt moist and heavy. It clogged his lungs.

If you cannot climb, his father communicated, *then what can you control?*

Aero thought for a moment.

"My position on the ground," he replied, as a strategy began to take shape in his mind. His father and the other Supreme Generals understood it and approved of his plan. The pulsing of the Beacon synced up with the surging of his Falchion.

Abruptly, the rustling and snapping of branches ceased. Not even a breeze disturbed the muggy air that hung around Aero like a thick cloak. His uniform was drenched with sweat. He carefully selected a patch of ground that would benefit him and planted his feet. Then he waited for the attack to rain down from above.

He didn't have to wait long.

Just as before, in a flash of silver and gold, Vinick swooped down on a vine with his Falchion morphed into a deadly menaulion.

This time Aero didn't duck.

He waited for as long as he could, and then he sidestepped out of the way and swung at the vine, slicing it cleanly. One minute Vinick was hurtling through the air, and the next he was plummeting. He landed right where Aero had intended. The soft ground cushioned his fall.

"Nice try, boy!" Vinick said with a sneer. "But I'm unharmed!" He raised his spear to strike and tried to take a step forward, but to his surprise, he couldn't lift his foot. It was stuck in the soft quicksand that had cushioned his fall.

The surprise quickly dissolved into horror and then downright panic. Vinick thrashed around in the quicksand, trying to free himself, but he only sunk deeper the more he struggled. He dropped his Falchion. It fell into the thick mud and sank with a burble. Fear, pure and unadulterated, inhabited his features, freezing them in place.

"Having a little trouble, Major?" Aero asked with mock pity.

"You wouldn't dare strike down an immobilized opponent!" Vinick shrieked, as he continued to struggle against the quicksand. Aero clutched his blade and advanced.

"Mercy!" Vinick screamed. "*Mercy!*"

Aero reached the edge of the quicksand and narrowed his eyes. "*No mercy in the face of weakness*," he quoted and lifted his blade to deliver the kill stroke.

"He's going to finish me!" Vinick yelled. "What are you waiting for?"

His eyes darted around in a fear, looking up at the sky. *Men on the cusp of death often panic*, Aero thought as he knelt before his opponent—the man who had killed two of his soldiers and his father, who had schemed to kill him, who foolishly planned to turn their ship away from Earth, their only hope for a permanent home.

"But I'm unarmed!" Vinick cried. "You can't strike me down!"

"Sadly, you're correct," Aero said, lowering his blade. "It goes against all of our teachings. But I don't have to finish you—the quicksand will do it for me."

"No!" Vinick screamed as he sank up to his neck. Now his arms were trapped at his sides. He cried out as the quicksand covered his mouth and nose, cutting off his piteous screams. Only his eyes could be seen now, darting around in a wild panic. And then the quicksand enveloped him completely with one final burble.

Sudden blackness enveloped them.

Caught off guard, Aero stumbled, flailing around in the darkness. He ripped off his helmet and found that he was standing in his simulation chamber.

But he wasn't alone.

The chamber door gaped open.

The Majors stormed through it, their Falchions morphed into various deadly weapons. He saw his mother and his betrothed among them. All at once, Aero realized what had happened—the Majors had interrupted the simulation to prevent Major Vinick from perishing in the quicksand and Aero from winning the duel.

This was the ultimate betrayal.

And then the soldiers advanced on him with their weapons drawn. Aero could see it in their eyes, his mother's most of all.

They meant to kill him and make it look like he'd died in the duel.

Chapter 43
KILL THEM ALL

Myra Jackson

Padre Flavius's furious voice boomed through the sector as he screamed for the Patrollers to attack. The dark figures immediately diverged, with two of them heading straight for Myra and Paige and the other three toward Portal 3. Acting purely on instinct, Myra grabbed Paige's hand and yanked her toward the tarps. She couldn't worry about the others right now. She just prayed Kaleb and Rickard could protect Tinker.

"Where did the heathens go?" Baron yelled.

"That way!" Jasper said. "Hurry up, pledge—don't let them get away!"

Their flashlights grazed over Myra and Paige as they sprinted across the sector. Myra felt the heady rush of adrenaline. She glanced back at Portal 3. The three shadows were closing in on Kaleb and Rickard. It took her a moment to locate Tinker—he'd climbed into the submarine. She spied his face in the cockpit. He must have flicked the power switch because it roared to life with a deep rumble that rattled the floor.

Myra and Paige ducked under the tarp. The cable dangled listlessly from the crane in front of them. She thrust the hooked end at Paige. "I'll hit the release button," Myra whispered. "Stretch it across the path and hook it around that pipe over there."

As Paige took off, Myra sprinted over to the crane and hit some buttons. Baron and Jasper's flashlights lit up the tarp, creating shifting patterns of light and shadow. Further away, she could hear sounds of struggle and the clanking of pipes. *Rickard and Kaleb must be fighting back against the Patrollers*, she realized. But they were outnumbered three to two. They wouldn't be able to hold them off for long.

She heard Baron's voice from behind the tarp. "*Structurally unsound*? That doesn't sound good."

"Don't be a coward, pledge!" Jasper snarled. "Probably just some Engine Rat trick. They went back there, didn't they? So it can't be that structurally unsound."

Jasper swept the tarp aside, and they both dashed under it. Their flashlight beams quickly found Myra and Paige and blinded them. "Look, there they are!" Baron said.

"Get the heathens!" Jasper yelled.

Myra couldn't make out their facial expressions, but she guessed they were both sneering. She abandoned the crane and grabbed Paige, dragging her toward the back of the area, but it was a dead end. They were trapped against the sector's thick wall. Myra quickly scanned it, but there weren't any vents that she could crawl through.

Jasper and Baron sprinted after them. "You're trapped!" Baron said when he saw them. "Heathens can't escape from those who serve the Oracle—"

Suddenly, both Patrollers pitched forward and face-planted into the concrete floor. Their flashlights also hit the floor and went out. The area fell into darkness, but Myra could hear Baron and Jasper's anguished cries. She guessed that their noses were broken—and maybe other things, too. Their flashlights had been aimed at Myra and Paige, so they'd never seen the cable that was stretched across their path.

"Hurry, we have to help the others!" Myra hissed to Paige.

Myra snatched a hefty wrench from a toolbox wedged against the wall. She handed a hammer to Paige. Then they slipped under the tarp, trying not to make a sound.

They neared Portal 3. The main area of the sector was still bathed in darkness, but the submarine's exterior lights illuminated the portal. Tinker must have turned them on when he powered up the sub. Bates was trying to pry the hatch open, but he didn't seem to be having any luck. *Tinker must have locked it*, Myra thought proudly.

Meanwhile, Kaleb was fighting Horace, their pipes clanking together, but he looked like he was losing. He had a nasty gash on his temple where Horace must have struck him. They weren't the only ones engaged in fierce battle. Rickard and his father were dueling with their pipes. They both wielded them with terrific force.

Myra looked around, but she didn't see Padre Flavius anywhere. That troubled her, but she didn't have time to dwell on it. Right now, she had to make a choice—and it was clear which one of her friends needed more help right now.

"Horace is going to bludgeon Kaleb to death if we don't do something!" she whispered to Paige. Tightening her grip on the wrench, Myra crept up behind the Patroller and swung at the back of his head. The wrench connected solidly. Horace never saw her coming—he went down like a sack of potatoes.

Kaleb looked shocked and then relieved when he saw Myra.

"Hey, we have to help Rickard—" Myra started, but then a dark figure swung at her with a pipe. She hit the floor hard and bit down on her tongue. She tasted blood and her head spun sickeningly. She tried to stand up but couldn't.

Bates raised his pipe to strike her again when Kaleb tackled him. They rolled around on the ground. Myra scrambled over to Horace's unconscious body. His pipe was still gripped in his closed fist. She pried his fingers from the metal and seized it for herself. Then she swung at Bates's head, but he was a more skilled fighter.

He knocked Kaleb aside and raised his pipe to meet hers. The impact sent a shock up her arm, rattling her shoulder in its socket and making it go numb. Bates leered down at her. "Heathen, you may have snuck up on Horace, but you won't beat me!"

She tried to lift the pipe but couldn't move her arm. The experienced Patroller grinned and raised his pipe to strike, when suddenly he froze mid-stroke.

Why didn't he hit her? Myra wondered.

But then his eyes rolled back in his head and he pitched forward, revealing Paige standing behind him with the hammer clutched in a two-handed grip. Blood gushed from the back of his skull. "Holy Sea . . . I can't believe I just did that." Paige dropped the hammer and started hyperventilating. "I think I'm going to be sick. Is he . . . dead?"

"Just unconscious, I think," Myra said.

The sound of clanging drew their attention.

"Rickard," Paige said in alarm. They helped Kaleb to his feet and then sprinted into the main sector. Rickard was engaged in a fierce battle with his father. Their pipes were dented and chipped, but they kept swinging at each other with tremendous force.

"Head Patroller Lynch," Myra yelled. "What're you doing? He's your son."

"He's no son of mine!" Lynch spat. "Not anymore!" He swung at Rickard again, this time landing a blow on his ribs. Rickard staggered and went down on his knees. His father towered over him and raised his pipe raised to strike a terminal blow.

"Father, please!" Rickard cried. "Padre Flavius is the heathen."

"No, you're the heathen," Lynch said, but his voice wavered.

"But we are dying!" Rickard said. "The Animus Machine is breaking down, and the Synod won't do anything. Don't you know what that means? We're all going to suffocate to death in less than a year. That's why we have to go to the Surface."

"Blasphemy!" Lynch shrieked. "You've been corrupted by that girl!"

"You're the one that's been corrupted by the Red Cloaks!" Rickard shot back. "And if you don't let us go, then everybody in the colony will die. Padre Flavius is the real heathen. He's the one who's sacrificing his own people, even children now."

"Lies, they're all lies!" his father said, but doubt flashed across his face.

Rickard threw down his pipe and looked up at his father with pity. "Dad, I won't fight you anymore. Now you have to believe me—I've got no motive to lie! What kind of person orders a father to kill his own son? Isn't that the definition of a heathen?"

Lynch raised the pipe as if to strike, but tears brimmed in his eyes. His arms started to tremble. Finally, he cast down his pipe with a great sob. "The Oracle forgive me. I can't strike down my own son."

"Oh, father," Rickard said and hugged him. They look so much alike,—Myra found herself thinking. "So . . . you believe me, then?" Rickard said.

"I've been having doubts for some time," Lynch admitted. "Especially after Padre Flavius ordered me to arrest the Bishop twins . . . and torture them." His voice faltered, the shame evident on his face. "By the Oracle, they're only young children."

"Then you understand why we've got to leave?" Rickard said.

A grim look passed over his father's face. "Well, if what you said is true . . . if the Animus Machine really is failing . . . then we're all doomed."

"Unless we return to the Surface," Rickard said softly.

His father swirled his hand over his chest but then came to his senses. "Holy Sea, if you mean to go through with this errand, then we've got to hurry! Padre Flavius went to summon more Patrollers—he'll be back soon."

That snapped them into action. He helped Rickard, who was limping, over to the portal. They rejoined Myra, Kaleb, and Paige. "Rickard, are you hurt?" Paige asked.

"Not mortally, thank the Oracle," Rickard said, casting a sideways grin at his father, who looked sheepish. "Well, I'm no Head Doctor, but I think I'll survive."

Paige turned to Myra. "I should bandage his wounds."

Myra shook her head. "There's no time—Padre Flavius is coming."

Paige still looked worried, but she didn't object.

They hurried over to the submarine. Rickard and his father dragged Bates and Horace's bodies out of the portal. They were both still unconscious. Then Myra signaled to Tinker that it was safe to unlock the hatch. He disappeared from the cockpit window. A second later the hatch swung open, revealing her little brother's grinning face.

"Hey, what took you so long?"

Myra rolled her eyes. "Did you power it up?"

"All systems are go," he replied. "I was just waiting for the pilot and her crew."

Myra grinned and started to climb the ladder. "Nice work, Tink."

Beep!

Suddenly, the sector door activated.

Myra jerked her head around right as Padre Flavius stormed through it with a group of Patrollers. Myra spotted the other six members of the Synod, including Kaleb's father, and the entire order of priests. She counted more than twenty Patrollers, not to mention the Plenus behind them.

"Get them, they're about to escape into the Holy Sea!" Flavius shrieked. "They'll poison it with their sins and bring another Doom upon us! You must stop them!"

The Head Patroller turned to his son. "Rickard, you must go! I'll hold them off as long as I can and shut the door to the portal! The Oracle knows, I've had enough practice with the sacrifices."

Rickard hesitated, but Myra leapt into action. They didn't have much time. She scrambled through the hatch and took her place in the pilot's chair. Her eyes grazed over the levers and instrument panels. Through the cockpit window, she could see the Patrollers streaming toward them like a black tide. Tinker squeezed in next to her, his computer at the ready. He'd already jacked it into a port. Kaleb and Paige slid into the seats behind them and buckled their safety harnesses, tightening them to fit their waists.

Myra glanced over at the Head Patroller. He stood behind the control panel, hitting buttons and trying to close the portal, but it didn't appear to be responding. Padre Flavius and the Patrollers had almost reached the submarine now.

"Rickard, they're almost here!" Myra yelled. She looked back to see him straddling the hatch. His eyes were locked on his father. "Hurry up!"

"I have to help my father!" Rickard said.

"But they'll kill you!" Myra gasped. "Don't be foolish."

"They'll kill us all if I don't help him!" Rickard said. "He can't fight off twenty men and seal the portal at the same time! Myra, just promise me this—you'll go to the Surface and find the First Continuum, and then you'll come back to save us."

Myra opened her mouth to protest, but Rickard was already gone.

Tears pooled in her eyes and slipped down her cheeks. Through the cockpit window, she watched Rickard scoop up the two pipes that had been dropped by Bates and Horace. Wielding both at the same time, Rickard fell on the Patrollers. He knocked two down, and then swiveled around to engage a third, but there were just too many. They kept coming at him, one after the other. He couldn't keep this up for much longer.

However, it did buy his father some time. The Head Patroller worked feverishly at the control panel. He must have hit the right combination of buttons at last because the portal started to contract with a slurping sound.

Before it closed completely, Myra saw Rickard fall to the ground as the Patrollers spilled over him. His face was bloodied and bruised, and his strong body looked broken beyond repair.

And then the portal shut, cutting off her view and sealing them inside. Jasper got caught on the wrong side of the door and trapped inside with the submarine. He pounded on the thick door, but it didn't budge. Myra watched his panicked face, and the grief over leaving Rickard washed over her. She couldn't believe he wasn't coming with them.

"Quick, shut the hatch!" Tinker yelled. "Or the water will crush us, too!"

This snapped Myra out of it. Though she wanted to succumb to her grief, she had to keep it together. She remembered Rickard's last words to her. *Myra, just promise me this . . .* She hadn't been able to respond in time, but her answer was *yes*.

She would go to the Surface.

She would find the First Continuum.

And then she would return to save them.

Or she would die trying.

Myra jabbed the button that operated the hatch. She heard it lock into place and then felt a shift in the air as the cabin pressurized and the heating system kicked on. She started sweating from the hot air, heavy coat, and the closeness of the bodies around her.

And then the portal gaped open, allowing the saltwater to flood inside. Jasper got swept up in the deluge. Under the extreme pressure, his body imploded in a swirl of blood and tissue. The submarine rocked and shuddered as the water hit it—and though it could have been Myra's imagination—felt like it shrunk a few inches, too.

But mercifully, it held.

Myra hit a button and felt the ballast tanks filling with water to control their depth and give them stability. The exterior lights illuminated the landscape outside the colony. The rocky terrain—which she'd only glimpsed through tiny windows—came alive before her eyes. A few strange creatures, gelatinous and transparent, darted out of the reach of the submarine's lights. The blackness of the deep extended into infinity before them.

Myra's pulse quickened, as did the flashing of the Beacon. Sweat streamed down her brow, but the temperature was already dropping precipitously thanks to the frigid water. They'd be thankful for the extra layers and the heat in a matter of minutes.

She felt the Beacon surge. It seemed to have grown stronger now. Elianna's voice rang out in her head—truer and clearer than ever before.

The time has come for us to return to our rightful home.

Buoyed by that thought, Myra set her hand on the joystick and urged it forward. The submarine responded effortlessly to her command. It swam through the portal door like a creature begat by the deep and plunged into the darkness of the sea, carrying them beyond the strict confines of the Thirteenth Continuum for the first time in their lives.

For all they knew, they might never see it again.

Chapter 44
INTERFERENCE

Captain Aero Wright

"Didn't think we'd actually let you win, did you?" Major Doyle sneered.

Aero flung off his helmet, his eyes darting around the simulation chamber. The other Majors—all except Vinick—stood behind Doyle in the doorway with his mother and betrothed. Their Falchions were unsheathed and morphed into various weapons.

"Major, this is the ultimate betrayal!" Aero yelled. "Interfering in a duel goes against all of our teachings! Everything we stand for as soldiers."

"Oh my, you're naïve, Captain," Doyle said. "It'll be the end of you." He turned to Aero's mother and his betrothed. "Soldiers, kill him!" he ordered.

"Yes, sir!" they said in unison.

Without hesitation—for they were obedient soldiers—the women advanced on their son and betrothed, respectively. His mother's Falchion was morphed into a nandao, a curved sword with a knuckle guard. She gripped it two-handed. Meanwhile, Rothman clutched an ahlspiess (or awl pike), a thrusting spear with a razor-sharp point.

Rothman jabbed her pike at Aero, which he dodged. *She's testing me*, he thought, *seeing how quickly I react to her thrust*. With a mighty yell, his mother swung at him two-handed. He ducked, spinning away. His back hit the wall; he was trapped.

"Mother, I won't fight you!" he said and morphed his Falchion from a katana into a shield. "Or you, Lieutenant Rothman. You're my betrothed."

"Not for much longer, I pray!" Rothman said and jabbed at him again.

He blocked the strike with his shield, as his mother swung at him. "Mother, you don't have to obey Major Doyle."

"Stop calling me that!" she cried and swung again, barely missing. "You're a foolish boy. You're too sentimental and needy, an emotional hazard if I've ever seen one. When I abandoned you at the Agoge, I was delighted to be rid of you."

Aero gasped as if he'd just been struck.

Rothman took advantage of his emotional lapse and jabbed him in his wounded shoulder. Blood blossomed where she struck him, but he barely felt it, barely felt anything physical at all. His mind was reeling from his mother's words—his Falchion was failing him. The shield rippled and softened liquidly, beginning to lose its form.

His mother saw the effect her words had on him—more damaging than any material weapon—and grinned in satisfaction. The voices from the Beacon swelled to a cacophony. Aero felt like his head was going to explode. Madness gripped him and hurled him like a gale force wind. He wanted nothing more than to fling down his Falchion and devote his strength to casting off the Beacon, even if it would kill him.

He sank to his knees, his shield heaving and undulating in his weakened grip. Black spots danced before his vision. His mother approached with her sword raised.

"Major Doyle, with your permission?" she said.

"Finish him, Lieutenant," Doyle said, "and you shall be named Captain."

"Thank you, sir!"

"Mother, I won't fight you," Aero stammered. He slid his arm from his shield, shedding it like a frostbitten limb that needed to be amputated. In its present state, it was useless anyway. He bowed his head in surrender and waited for the blow that would take it off with one clean slice.

His mother peered down at him, as she had when he was a small child hanging on her every word. Except something was different this time. With her coppery hair, cruel gaze, and deadly sword, she looked nothing like the mother whom he'd once loved and idolized with every fiber of his being, the woman that he'd wished would return to love him again. That mother was gone, if she'd ever existed at all.

"Then so be it," Aero said. His last thought was of Myra Jackson. *I'm so sorry we'll never meet in person*, he thought. The Beacon pulsed forcefully.

He kept his head bowed and waited for his mother to swing her sword, when another voice penetrated into the simulation chamber.

"Soldiers, attack!"

A stream of silver and gold rushed into the simulation chamber and engaged the Majors. Through his confusion, Aero looked up to see Wren leading half the soldiers from his unit. He spotted Xing, Etoile, and Hoshiko.

Wren wielded her Falchion in the shape of a talwer, the curved sword that she favored. She whipped it through the air like the hefty blade weighed nothing at all. Her beauty was a powerful thing to behold as she spun and pivoted and twirled and clashed like she was performing some sacred dance, not fighting for her life.

She fought her way through the thick of the battle. She easily dispensed with Major Oranck, knocking him aside, and then unarmed Major Kieran with a few well-placed strokes. Kieran's sword flew from his hand and hit the floor, melting down and pooling into a puddle of gold. Kieran cried out in agony and sank to his knees.

Wren covered the final four strides across the chamber

to Aero. "Lieutenant Wright, stand down!" she yelled at his mother, who stood over him with her sword raised.

His mother turned just in time to meet Wren's blow. Their swords collided, sparks erupting and fizzling out in the air. In fact, the whole chamber sparked and clanged and burned with the furious light of a Falchion battle. It would have been beautiful, if not for the carnage. Private Etoile had taken a blow to her sternum, blood trickling from the wound, while Major Kieran lay in a fetal position, undone by the loss of his Falchion.

Rothman joined Aero's mother in battling Wren. She jabbed her spear while his mother swung her blade. Though Wren was a better soldier, she was fighting two opponents. They forced her back several paces.

My son, you must rise! Aero heard his father communicate over the din of the battle and the other Supreme Generals' voices. *Lieutenant Jordan needs your help.*

Aero felt his strength returning to him. He reached for the discarded shield, amazed that it had retained its shape. He swept his arm through the straps and felt the bond flood through him. *Broadsword*, he thought. The weapon shifted effortlessly into his preferred form, and the Beacon pulsed. He understood that his father was with him, and this gave him courage. He stepped right next to Wren, clutching his blade.

"Need a little help, Lieutenant?" Aero said.

"Nice to have you back, Captain!" she said with that feisty spirit he'd grown to love in her. Sweat dripped down her brow, and she was winded, but otherwise appeared no worse for the wear. She swiped aside a jab of Rothman's spear and then parried a blow from his mother's sword. "What're you waiting for—permission?" she gasped.

Fighting side by side, Aero and Wren quickly disposed of their opponents. With his height and superior strength, Aero battled his mother into submission. A few quick thrusts and a flick of his wrist and her Falchion went flying from her hand.

"Mercy!" she said as she fell to her knees. "My son, grant me mercy!"

He studied her face. She'd invoked their biological bond, but he could see that it was just a clever manipulation. She didn't care for him as a son. "Mercy is more than you deserve," he said with disdain. She cowered in fear, but then he lowered his sword. "But as you wish."

She bowed down at his feet. "Thank you, sir! You're the strongest soldier, I was mistaken."

Aero turned his back before she could finish. It was over—he had nothing left to say to this woman who had birthed him, raised him for the first five years of his life, and then discarded him like refuse bound for the incinerator.

He turned just in time to see Wren knock Rothman's spear from her grip. His betrothed dropped to her knees and cried, "I surrender!"

His eyes met Wren's, and they both grinned. This was how it had always been between them, from the first time they'd fought side by side at the Agoge. They both lived for the heat of battle.

"Major Doyle called for reinforcements," Wren said. "And the soldiers will obey the Majors. We've no evidence of their treachery. Sir, we can't stay here!"

Aero knew she was right. They were only a few soldiers. They couldn't withstand the force of an army, which numbered in the thousands. "Then where do we go?" he asked, but then saw the look in her eyes. "You've already got a plan, don't you?"

She nodded. "Our mission. We go to Earth."

The Beacon flashed, and his father urged him onward.

"Earth it is, then!" he agreed. "Let's get the hell out of here."

They fought their way through the Majors that were still standing, locked in frenzied battle with his soldiers. Aero saw Xing fighting Major Doyle, and with pride he noticed that his soldier was holding his own against the more experienced officer. He reached the door with Wren right on his heels, but something held him back.

"Lieutenant, we can't abandon our soldiers!" he said.

Sadness cut across her face. "Sir, they're *good* soldiers. You taught them well. The plan has already been decided, and I gave each of them a choice."

"But I can't let them die for me!" Aero said, straddling the doorway.

"They've trained their whole lives for this. *A soldier aspires to a clean death at the hands of a worthy opponent.* If not this fate, then what would you wish for them?"

This was one of their teachings, and it was undoubtedly true. He knew because he hoped for the same thing. But still he hesitated, his hand twitching on his Falchion.

"Sir, your time hasn't come yet," Wren said. "The old Forger told me as much. Your destiny lies elsewhere—on Earth. Captain, we must get away! I've readied an escape pod, but we've got to hurry. Reinforcements will be here soon."

The Lieutenant is right, his father communicated. *You know your true purpose.*

This snapped Aero out of it.

He followed Wren, their boots pounding through the corridors. They tried the quickest route but heard a unit approaching from that direction, so they reversed course and dashed into an elevator. It whisked them down to the ship's lowest level, where the escape pods were docked. The elevator doors dilated with a soft hiss.

Wren craned her neck out. "It's clear!" she reported.

They dashed out of the elevator and sprinted down the corridor. As they rounded the bend, the sound of footsteps and shouts could be heard right behind them.

"Another unit is chasing us!" Aero yelled.

"This way!" Wren said as she ducked down a different corridor.

They emerged in a vast bay filled with transports. Some were being loaded with supplies. A few soldiers from an engineering unit were milling about. Wren pulled Aero behind a pallet of oxygen tanks. "Look, the transports are too heavily guarded, but the escape pods are defenseless. I've already loaded one with supplies. It's this way."

Crouching low behind the pallets, they scuttled to the far side of the Docking Bay, where several escape pods were housed. Wren was right—this was the only way. She led him to a panel in the wall marked Pod Bay 7, when suddenly a figure stepped in front of them and blocked their path. He wore a flimsy medical gown and his dark skin had a sickly pallor. A needle protruded from his inner elbow, the IV line trailing behind him. In his shaky hands, he clutched a blaster. The deadly weapon was aimed right at them.

Aero recognized him right away—it was Zakkay. Ever since his Falchion had melted down during their ill-fated Mars simulation, the Medical Clinic had been holding him for psychiatric observation. Wren exchanged a worried look with Aero.

"Captain, watch out!" Zakkay yelled.

"Drop your weapon!" Wren shouted. "That's an order, Private!"

The blaster wobbled in his grip. He looked like he was struggling very hard to hold it aloft. Aero shot Wren a warning look and then raised his hands in surrender.

"Zakkay, you don't have to do this," he said in an even voice. "Just turn around and go back to Medical. Nobody has to know you found us."

"Captain, with all due respect, duck now!" he yelled.

And that was when Aero heard the footsteps right behind him. He didn't turn to look—instead his hand shot out and dragged Wren to the floor with him.

"Die, you bastards!" Zakkay screamed and fired the blaster in rapid succession.

The shots zipped right over their heads. Aero heard a series of thuds as two bodies hit the ground behind them. He risked a glance back, his eyes falling on Majors Oranck and Mauro. The fronts of their uniforms were still smoking.

Aero rose to his feet and turned to Zakkay. "I misjudged you, Private!" he said with a salute. "My apologies."

Zakkay looked down. "No, sir, you were right about me. I'm an emotional hazard. Medical confirmed the diagnosis, that's why my Falchion melted down."

"Private, with all due respect—medical is mistaken," Aero said. Zakkay stared at him in disbelief. "You're a good soldier, Private."

"You mean that, sir?"

Aero took a step toward him and laid a hand on his shoulder. "Today, you've served me well. Your emotions are what made you rise from your sickbed and perform this heroic act. Don't ever forget that. You have my gratitude."

Just then, there was rustling in the shadows. Out stepped the Forger formerly known as Xander in a swirl of crimson. A pack was slung over his shoulders.

"Brother, what're you doing here?" Aero asked in surprise.

"I'm to accompany you on your journey to Earth," he said. "Yesterday, the Order of the Foundry convened and arrived at this decision as a unified brotherhood."

"Brother, I appreciate the offer, but I can't allow it."

The Forger lifted his hand to silence him. "Captain, I won't be swayed, so don't waste your words. My Order knows more about the nature of your quest than any soldier on this ship. Our teachings have foretold of your ascendancy for nearly a millennium. We've always been sworn to serve the Carrier of the Beacon. Besides, you'll need my help to tend to your Falchion's charge."

"But how is that possible without the Foundry?"

The Forger gestured to the hefty pack slung across his shoulders. "With permission from the Order, my older brother has been laboring to produce a portable charging station in preparation for this mission. And he finally succeeded."

"I really hate to break up this gathering," Wren interjected. "But reinforcements will be here soon. If we're going to do this, then we'd better get moving."

"Good luck, sir," Zakkay said with a salute.

Aero returned the gesture. "Now get back to Medical before they notice you've gone missing."

Zakkay obeyed the command. He tossed the blaster into a refuse bin, which would whisk it to the incinerator and destroy all evidence of how it was used. As he retreated down the corridor, Wren hit the button that activated the door to Pod Bay 7. The panel in the wall dilated, revealing an escape pod. She climbed inside and took her place in the cockpit. The Forger slid into the passenger seat and fastened his harness.

Aero took one last look back at the place that had been his home for the last sixteen years. Instead of fighting his emotions, he allowed them to surge through him. The mix of sentimentality, combined with a strong sense of yearning, flooded through him. He might never set foot on this ship again.

Your true home lies on Earth, he heard his father say in his head. The other Supreme Generals echoed this sentiment in a harmonious choir of voices.

Suddenly, Myra's face flashed before Aero's eyes—a fleeting glimpse of a diminutive girl strapped into a chair and piloting a strange vessel through a dark and murky world. He tasted her fear and her sorrow and her expectation on his tongue. Some terrible loss had befallen her, he could tell, someone she loved had been hurt. Had possibly even died. *A friend*, he realized after more thought.

Myra felt closer to him now than ever before. In the heat of the moment, he almost called out her name, but then the vision was gone, sucked away from his consciousness like space junk caught in the pull of a black hole.

"Captain, waiting for company?" Wren yelled.

This snapped Aero out of it. "Well, I wouldn't want to make our escape too easy, now would I?" he said, pushing back against the pulsing of the Beacon.

She arched her eyebrow and shot back, "Not sure this qualifies as easy."

Aero grinned and then ducked into the pod, taking his place behind the controls. He'd participated in countless evacuation drills and was familiar with the pod's operation. He saw that Wren had already powered it up. The alarms were probably sounding, alerting the Majors of their impending escape. They had to hurry.

He hit a button, and the cabin door sealed itself shut behind them. He felt the engines ratcheting up as the pod bay door yawned open in front of them. Through the cockpit window, he glimpsed the impossibly black vacuum of outer space, broken up by its constellation of stars—and, overshadowing all of it—Earth.

The grayish orb pulled at him, and he felt the pulsing of the Beacon. The planet was calling to him, urging him onward. He was helpless to resist it. He set his hands—steady as a rock—on the controls and hit a few more buttons. The thrusters fired up.

"Commencing launch!" said a soothing female voice. "In *three* seconds, *two* seconds, *one* second . . . "

The escape pod shot out of the bay like a rocket, a shower of sparks trailing behind it. For a moment, it was only the pod against the void of outer space, but then a halo of blasts rained down on it from the mothership. Explosions rocked the hull. A blast connected with the starboard engine, striking a damaging blow. Aero pitched forward, his harness the only thing keeping him from smashing into the cockpit window.

An alarm blared, and red lights flashed.

"Captain, we've lost the starboard thrusters!" Wren yelled. Behind her, the Forger had turned white. He was chanting in a low voice, "*Aeternus . . . eternus . . .*"

The trail of sparks was now a trail of smoke and debris.

"Switching to manual!" Aero shouted, seizing control of the crippled ship.

As the pod shot through the emptiness of space, streaking like a fallen star through the heavens, the intercom blared to life. Aero's hand jerked to disconnect it, but words slipped through the static. The voice belonged to Vinick.

"Captain Aero Wright . . . you are hereby . . . banished for life!"

Chapter 45
THE MIDNIGHT ZONE

Myra Jackson

Navigating through the trench was no easy feat.

There were so many ways to die in the deep. Myra ticked through a few in her head. For starters, there was implosion. Though she trusted her father's abilities as an engineer, he hadn't had a chance to test the seaworthiness of the vessel. Any weak spot in the design or tiny flaw in the construction and—with a sickening crunch—the submarine would collapse and instantly crush them.

If that wasn't bad enough, they could also freeze to death. Even with the thick coat and the heating system running full blast, her teeth were chattering and her breath puffed out in smoky tendrils. The temperature in the deep hovered around zero degrees Celsius. If they got stuck in the trench somehow—or, worse, lost power altogether—then they would die of hypothermia long before they ran out of oxygen.

And that brought her to fire. They were carrying a significant supply of pure oxygen, which would last them about sixty hours, according to her instruments. Her eyes flicked to the small extinguisher stowed onboard. It would be paltry defense if a glitch in the electrical circuits gave rise to a spark that set the oxygen tanks ablaze.

Adding to these risks were the swiftness of the ocean currents, which batted them around like a child's plaything; the sharp rock formations that jutted from the seabed and threatened to puncture the hull; and the hydrothermal vents, fissures in the crust that spewed out superheated water at unexpected intervals that would melt their ship.

Myra didn't elect to share these concerns with her companions. It would only upset them more, and they were still heartbroken over leaving Rickard behind. The last image that Myra had glimpsed of him—his broken body crumpling to the ground as a black tide of Patrollers swept over him—kept replaying in her mind. She hoped that he'd survived the assault but had no way to know. She tried not to consider the alternative.

"Thermal vent!" Tinker called out. He tapped away on his computer, monitoring their progress and immediate surroundings. "Port side!" he added.

Myra adjusted their trajectory, veering right. Off the port side, illuminated by the exterior lights, she glimpsed the rock formation spewing out superhot water. Strange life-forms were crawling on the vent. *They must live off the heat*, she thought in awe.

"Tink, what's our speed?" she asked.

"Thirty knots," he replied. "Max speed."

Though her eyes remained fixed on the rocky seabed, suddenly she was in another place altogether. A vision flashed before her eyes—it was Aero. She could sense that his thoughts were trained on her, and the intensity of his yearning almost bowled her over. She had to grip the controls harder to keep from crying out his name.

The vision resolved itself, more details coming to her now. He was also piloting a ship of some sort, though the strange environment through which he navigated was even more desolate than the trench. His emotions stretched into her—a murky cloud of fear and heartbreak and sadness. Something terrible had just happened to him, she realized.

A dreadful word zapped her—*banishment*.

For a moment, she felt as if they were coupled again, their bodies and their Beacons merged together into one being. *He's an exile from his world now, too*, she understood. But then—just as quickly as the vision had come over her—it receded. This was the first time she'd experienced such a connection in her waking state.

He's closer now, she realized. *We're both bound for the Surface.*

Kaleb's voice jerked her back to the present.

"How long until we reach . . . the Surface?" he said, not used to speaking those words out loud.

His eyes were fixed on the map displayed on the monitor, but Myra didn't consult the instruments. She shut her eyes and sought out the Beacon's will.

"Only a few hours once we begin the ascent," she said as the response flooded through her. "According to the Beacon, we're almost to the right coordinates."

She checked their pressure and nodded in satisfaction. They shouldn't have trouble adjusting to the Surface since the colony and the sub were both pressurized.

A few minutes later, the Beacon flashed, alerting Myra it was time. "De-ballasting!" she called out and hit a few buttons. Water rushed out of the ballast tanks to assist with their ascent. Myra manipulated the joystick, angling the nose upward. The rudders swiveled down and directed the submarine to rise through the ocean. To her great relief, her father's design held true. They began to rise through the crushing water.

As they ascended through the layers of the ocean—out of the Abyss and into the Midnight Zone, which began four thousand meters below the Surface, according to her instruments—Myra gripped the controls and fought to keep the ship steady against the currents that threatened to sweep them off course. Soon—very soon now—they would cross into the Twilight Zone and be less than one thousand meters from the Surface.

She glanced back and saw that Paige had dozed off with her head resting on Kaleb's shoulder. Their eyes met, and Kaleb shrugged sheepishly. "Well, I thought one of us should get some rest."

His head wound had clotted and was starting to scab over. If anything, this blemish only rendered him more handsome. It had roughed up his soft edges, imbuing his face with character. *He's no longer the spoiled son of Plenus*, Myra thought. Despite the cold, her cheeks started to feel hot, but then Paige stirred and mumbled.

"Almost there yet?"

Myra turned away from Kaleb and cleared her throat. "We're almost to the Twilight Zone, that's only one thousand meters from the Surface. Once we reach that depth, it won't be long before we cross into the Sunlight Zone."

"Oh, sunlight," Paige murmured sleepily. "I've always wondered what it would be like. Is it brighter and hotter than the automatic lights?"

That it is—Elianna communicated to Myra—*and so much more.*

Myra repeated this to Paige, who seemed to delight in the knowledge. Suddenly, Tinker's voice grabbed her attention. His eyes were glued to his computer, and the urgency was palpable in his voice. "Look, there's something else out there."

"What do you mean—something else?" Myra said and jerked her eyes back to the monitor. Outside the cockpit window, the water was still pitch black.

The exterior lights only illuminated a small halo of a few feet around their ship. For all intents and purposes, they were blind. Tinker clacked on his computer and then paled.

"I don't know . . . but it's large. Twice as big as our ship."

Myra felt panic rising in her but tried to quell it and focus on piloting the submarine. "Tink, anything else you can tell me?"

"Yup—it's coming right toward us. And it's moving fast."

"How fast?" Paige gasped.

"Faster than us," Tinker reported. "By the Oracle, it's gaining on us. Visual contact in *three* seconds . . . *two* seconds . . . *one* second."

A dark shape bulleted past the exterior lights, blotting them out completely, and slammed into the hull. If not for their safety harnesses, they would have flown out of their seats and hit the ceiling. The straps cut painfully into Myra's shoulders, but she stayed put. A red warning light lit up the console, followed by an urgent beep.

"Holy Sea, what was that?" Myra yelled. She struggled to right the submarine, which had pitched over from the impact. She prayed it wasn't too damaged.

"A kraken!" Kaleb said. "I saw tentacles—big ones!"

Tinker's eyes widened. "But you said that they weren't real!"

"I guess I was wrong," Myra muttered. Though the Hockers loved to tell tales about giant tentacled monsters called krakens, nobody had ever laid eyes on one.

Until now.

The dark shape rammed into them again, this time with more force. It seemed to be growing bolder now that it had them in its sights. Through the cockpit, Myra glimpsed its bulbous body, enormous eyes, and powerful tentacles grasping hungrily at their ship.

More warnings lights went off, beeping urgently for her attention. Their vessel had sustained significant damage in the attack—it couldn't take much more of this.

"Tink, I'm losing control!" Myra yelled.

Outside the window, the water began to lighten. They were almost to the Surface now. Myra fired the thrusters, angling them upward. They sped away from the kraken, but it gave chase. They'd surprised it with the burst of speed, but it was gaining on them.

Soon it would catch them.

They had only one choice.

Myra bore down on the controls. Traveling at maximum velocity, they sped through the Sunlight Zone and blasted out of the ocean like a projectile, piercing the turbulent water and lifting off into the air. Sunlight—blinding and glorious—enveloped them. She hit the engines full throttle, aiming for the rocky landmass visible in the distance. Their ship cut through the water, skirting over the frothy waves.

"Look . . . the Surface!" Tinker said excitedly. He pointed through the cockpit window. "It's really here. Mom's stories . . . they were true!"

Suddenly, a tentacle shot out of the water and latched around their rudder.

"No!" Myra screamed when she saw it.

The aim was dead on—the kraken had them in its grip. It yanked them back into the sea and dove quickly. It was dragging them back into the deep. Even the thrusters couldn't power the ship upward again. Angry warning lights lit up the console. The tentacle had cracked the hull, and saltwater was pouring into the cabin and rising quickly. It was already up to Myra's shins. Not only would the submarine not survive another dive, but also based on the amount of water flooding the cabin, they'd soon drown.

Through the cockpit window, Myra glimpsed the kraken's hungry mouth with rows of razor-sharp teeth. They snapped open and shut in anticipation of its meal.

She jammed the controls forward, but it made no difference. They were still descending rapidly.

"Squeeze as much power out of the batteries as you can!" she yelled to Tinker, whose fingers began to fly over his computer in rapid succession. She tasted saltwater on her lips and felt it stinging her eyes. The deluge was now up to her knees.

"Discharging the batteries!" Tinker shouted over the beeping of the warnings and the roaring of the seawater. The noise was deafening.

"Diverting all of the power to the rear thrusters!" Myra said.

The lights faltered and flickered. As they plunged deeper, the submarine began to creak and moan, and more water flooded into the hull. Soon it would implode from the pressure. Suddenly, a green light flashed on the console—a lone beacon of hope drowning in a sea of red lights. The rear thrusters were at their fullest charge.

Myra didn't hesitate—she fired them right away.

A blast shot out, meant to propel the submarine through the water, but it hit the kraken's body with tremendous force. The creature roared and released them, and then shot out a dark cloud of ink and vanished into it. Myra didn't wait around to see if it was coming back—she thrust the joystick forward, and they swam upward again.

A few minutes later, they shot out of the ocean, and this time they came to rest up there. Choppy waves slapped into the submarine, batting it around. Seawater was still flooding into the cabin—it wouldn't remain buoyant for much longer.

"The sub is compromised!" Myra yelled and sprang into action. She sloshed to the stern, where the emergency life raft was stowed. "We've got to evacuate now!"

o o o

The escape pod sputtered and flickered through space.

The blast from the mothership had damaged it, but somehow they'd survived the attack. None of their vital systems had been compromised. However, Aero didn't know the extent of the damage to the insulation designed to protect them during re-entry, and without donning a spacesuit and inspecting the exterior, he couldn't evaluate their risk. Since this was an escape pod and not a proper transport, they lacked the equipment to perform such a maneuver. It was a moot point and therefore not worth dwelling on.

Aero pushed it from his mind and instead focused on piloting the ship. Soon Earth loomed larger before them, blotting out everything else. The tiny escape pod aimed for the thick atmosphere and plunged into it. While Aero couldn't control their exact landing point, especially with the damage they'd sustained, he just hoped that he could land them on the same continent as the First Continuum.

Flames erupted around the pod and tore at them from all sides. Friction from the atmosphere slowed their descent and created intense heat. Any weakness in the insulation could mean their fiery demise. Emergency lights started flashing on, a new one every few seconds. Wren surveyed them from her seat in the copilot's chair.

"Captain, can the escape pod survive the descent?" she asked in a shaky voice. It was shaky from fear perhaps, but also because the pod was now vibrating with frightening intensity.

Behind them, the Forger bowed his head and chanted softly.

". . . *Aeternus . . . eternus . . .*"

"We have to," Aero replied grimly.

The shaking intensified, and more warning lights flashed on. The world outside comprised only flames—orange and red and white hot—that licked mercilessly at the ship.

"Did the blast compromise the insulation?" Wren shouted over the noise.

"No way to know for sure!" Aero yelled back. He gripped the controls tighter and tried to hold them steady. "My ship, Lieutenant!"

Wren flipped a switch, giving him full control of the escape pod. "It's your ship, Captain."

Their fate was now in his hands—and his hands only.

Using everything that he'd learned, Aero manipulated the controls and did what he could to ease their entry. The heat only increased the more they penetrated into the atmosphere. According to his instruments, the temperature outside their ship was a toasty 1600 degrees Celsius. He prayed that the insulation would protect them.

As he watched the flames tearing at them from all sides, Aero felt grateful that at least Earth still had an intact atmosphere. Some had feared that the Doom would destroy even that, but the scans that the Majors had run indicated that they'd be able to breathe the air unassisted. It was paltry comfort at the moment.

The escape pod shot out of the heavens, an alien intruder into an alien world. The surface came into stark focus below them—rocky, dusty, and utterly destitute of any life. It wasn't ruddy like Mars, but grayish and drab, as colorless as it was lifeless.

This is our true home?

That was the last thought that flashed through Aero's mind before the parachutes deployed. A cluster of silver air bags erupted around them and engulfed the pod. The parachutes did their job—but it was a graceless and inelegant way to decelerate. The escape pod jerked back with such astounding force that Aero's neck snapped back and smacked the headrest. Though his head throbbed from the impact, he felt relieved.

The worst part is over, he thought.

They drifted down slowly, the shrouding of airbags obstructing their view. Aero couldn't see the surface rising up to greet them but knew they'd meet it soon.

A few minutes later, they finally touched down. The airbags connected first and then flung them back into the air. They crashed down again, only to bounce back up and tumble down again. The world somersaulted in an endless blur around them. Aero caught sight of Wren's pale face and hoped that they could both keep down their last meals. He hated to think of what might occur otherwise.

Behind him, he heard the Forger's chanting. He repeated the same phrase over and over again: ". . . *Aeternus eternus* . . . *Aeternus eternus* . . . *Aeternus eternus* . . ."

The escape pod touched down one last time, cartwheeled over the surface and smashed into a rock formation. The hatch ripped open from the impact, debris and rocks spewing into the hull, followed by a puff of grayish dust.

The last thing that Aero remembered was the scent of ash and the taste of powdery grit on his tongue before he lost consciousness altogether.

Chapter 46
MAROONED

Myra Jackson

The slapping of cold water woke Myra from her stupor.

Groggily, she pulled herself to an upright position. Her body was draped across the side of a rubbery raft that was partially deflated. A life vest was strapped across her chest. Where was she? She squinted against the dimming sunlight out across the desolate, rocky shoreline. Further down, she could make out some shapes—they looked like her companions, and they were inert. Terror gripped her heart then and squeezed.

It all came rushing back in a torrent:

Their escape from the Thirteenth Continuum in the submarine. Leaving Rickard behind, as the Patrollers beat him mercilessly. Their journey from the trench—rising, rising, rising. The kraken that had almost destroyed them. Seawater flooding the cabin. But after that, nothing.

Myra lurched to her feet unsteadily, wincing from the pain. Her lips were cracked, and she was terribly thirsty. Her skin looked bright pink and burned to the touch. *From the sunlight*, she realized with shock. As fast as she could, she hobbled down the beach to the other figures. As she neared, they drew into sharper focus. Kaleb lay flat on his back with Tinker and Paige tucked under each arm. *He saved them,* she realized.

Suddenly, Paige cracked her eyes open and rolled onto her side, while Tinker sat up and rubbed his head. They were both alive, but Kaleb wasn't moving. His skin looked grayish and lifeless, just like the rocky shore.

Myra knelt down and shook him. "By the Oracle, wake up!"

Vaguely, she realized Paige was helping her. "Hurry, roll him over!" she instructed. "Maybe he swallowed water, it could be blocking his airway."

With some effort, they got Kaleb onto his side. Paige pushed on his chest, and just as she'd predicted, saltwater poured from his mouth. But he still wasn't breathing.

Paige turned to Myra. "We have to give him CPR!"

"Just tell me what to do!" Myra gasped, tears blurring her vision.

While Paige gave him chest compressions, Myra waited for her signal and then pressed her lips to Kaleb's mouth, which was blue and icy. Whenever their lips had touched in the past, he'd always kissed her back eagerly. His lack of response terrified her, and she swore to herself that if he lived—that if by some miracle he survived this—then she'd never forsake him again.

With that promise, she exhaled breath into his lungs. But still Kaleb remained unresponsive—he wasn't breathing, and his heart was still. They continued like this for a few more minutes with no response. Kaleb didn't so much as twitch. His lungs only moved when Myra moved them for him; his heart only pumped when Paige pumped it for him. She drew back and wiped tears from her eyes.

"Myra, it's over—he's dead."

"No . . . I won't believe it!" Myra cried and exhaled into his mouth again. "We have to keep trying. I already lost Rickard. I can't bear to lose him, too."

Dimly, she felt Tinker's hands on her shoulder. He was trying to ease her away from Kaleb, but she resisted. She couldn't believe she'd been so afraid of everything—his father finding out, her own feelings, him abandoning her again. All those excuses seemed so trivial now—so utterly ridiculous. Tears coursed down her cheeks.

She bent over his face—oh so beautiful even in its morbid repose—and remembered all the times that he'd held her in his arms and caressed her; how he'd stopped courting her only to protect her from his father and the Synod, a sacrifice that was excruciating for him; how he'd helped her find the Beacon and then braved this journey to the Surface, leaving behind his comfortable life as the son of Plenus.

"Kaleb . . . I love you," she whispered in his ear. Cradling his head in her arms, she craned her neck down and kissed him, exhaling oxygen into his lungs. She kept kissing him long after she had run out of air and dark stars danced in front of her eyes. The world around her dimmed, and still she kissed him, as she'd never kissed him before. Soon she'd probably join him in unconsciousness, she realized, yet didn't care.

As she began to slip away, she felt something.

A slight warming of his pale flesh. A twitching of his blue lips. A shudder in his chest. A spasm behind his eyelids. A gust of air emptied from his lungs. And then, all at once, he came back to life in her arms.

One minute he was seemingly dead—and the next he was gasping and sputtering. Myra rolled him over and rubbed his back. More seawater came up, spewing out of his mouth.

Once the worst of it had passed, he lay back in her arms and smiled weakly. "Holy Sea, I should die more often," he rasped. "If you'll kiss me like that."

"Don't ever do that again!" she said in relief. "I mean it."

Paige regarded Kaleb as if he were a ghost. "I . . . can't believe it," she stammered. "His heart was stopped for . . . well . . . a long time. I've heard stories in the Infirmary about people drowning in cold water and coming back to life . . . but I always thought they were made up."

Tinker thought for a moment.

"The world is full of mysteries," he said softly.

After what they'd just been through, nobody could argue with that.

o o o

Farther down the beach, they located the remains of their vessel.

The submarine—or, rather, what was left of it—had washed up on the blackened shore. Myra took one look and knew it would never embark on another voyage. The sun was sinking lower on the horizon, and soon night—*true night*—would fall.

In the last vestiges of daylight, Myra, Tinker, and Paige salvaged what supplies they could, pulling them out of the wreckage and strewing them along the beach to dry. But it was far less than they'd set out with. Many provisions had been ruined by the saltwater's incursion or simply lost to the insatiable appetite of the sea.

Paige had ordered Kaleb to rest, so he sat with his back pressed up against the twisted, volcanic rocks. His eyes never left the sky, and Myra suspected that he was still adjusting to this new world without boundaries. They all were. They'd lived their whole lives in the tight confines of their colony, never once glimpsing anything as spectacular as the sun hoisted aloft in the expanse of the sky. A few lazy clouds drifted by.

As the sun sank even lower, it transformed the clouds into a kaleidoscopic light show. They all stopped to watch. Brilliant pink and purple hues danced in the sky, fading, fading, always fading, until they were gone and night was falling.

This world is full of mysteries, Myra thought.

That night, they feasted on a meager dinner of fish jerky, which had been wrapped tightly and survived the deluge. The water-filtering canisters worked perfectly, converting the saltwater into freshwater. They drank thirstily, replenishing that which the sun had stolen during the day. With the first aid kit, Paige tended to their scrapes and cuts and applied cooling salve to their sunburns.

Myra reached into her pocket and found the last satchel of sweetfish that she'd been saving. Miraculously, it had survived the evacuation. She shared the candy with her friends. The sweetfish were delicious, and this small reminder of home cheered them up. They'd need to ration their food, but Myra didn't have the heart to lay down the law on their first night. *Let them rest and recuperate,* she thought. *We'll sort it out tomorrow.*

When the sun had dipped below the horizon and stars lit up the sky like a million tiny pinpricks, they huddled around a heater to sleep. It was her father's design, Myra could tell, and she felt as if he were right there with them, warming them on this dark night, at least in spirit. He'd planned this journey, and Myra could sense his care and attention in every aspect of it, and this comforted her a little.

She glanced at Kaleb, who dozed beside her with his head resting on her shoulder. She didn't push him away, like in the past. She was just grateful that he'd survived. Her confusion about her feelings hadn't resolved—not even slightly—but she was determined to honor her promise to him. Meanwhile, Tinker was curled up with a trail of drool dribbling down his chin, and Paige rested with her head on a backpack and her arm draped over Tinker's tiny shoulders. They were all fast asleep, except for Myra.

Despite her best efforts to doze off, she remained wide awake. In the last two days, her life had changed irrevocably. The Patrollers had captured Rickard—he might even be dead, she thought with a shudder. Maude was hiding the Bishop twins, but could she keep them safe from the Synod and the Patrollers? Even worse, her father was still locked up in the Pen, shackled and deprived of food and water. She hoped that Padre Flavius wouldn't take out his wrath over their escape on her father's frail body.

She hoped—but it was flimsy reassurance at best.

And still the Animus Machine was failing.

The Thirteenth Continuum was dying.

Myra glanced at the unsalvageable remains of the

submarine. How would they rescue their people without it? Surely, they would find help at the First Continuum. She tried to comfort herself with this thought and sought to override her doubts. It worked, but only partially.

They still had to reach the First Continuum.

The enormity of her quest hit her full force then, and she felt wholly inadequate. Elianna tried to reassure her, but this too felt flimsy. There was only one other who shared her burden. She allowed her eyes to close and her mind to drift away. She sought him out through space and time. Then—and only then—did sleep claim her.

o o o

Her dream that night was stronger than any that had come before it.

The edges and contours were sharp and clear. A ruined vehicle—one that flew through the air, she realized with astonishment—smoldered like an empty husk on the volcanic earth. Yet there was no risk of fire, for there was no organic material that it could set ablaze. And there he was, sleeping in the shadow of his smoking ship.

A girl not much older than Myra slept with her back pressed up to him. She cradled a golden blade in her arms. She was guarding him. Her blond hair was cut short, like a boy's, and her cheekbones were sharp and contoured. She was lovely, this girl—perhaps incomparably so. But Myra could tell that he didn't think of her in this way. Another person slept a few feet away, also their age from the looks of him, though Myra couldn't be sure. He wore a long crimson robe that reminded her of the robes that Padre Flavius and the priests wore. His arms were wrapped around a strange backpack.

Myra cast an anxious glance behind her. She could just make out the Dark Thing looming in the middle distance, its vile intentions fixed on her, as if it were trying to penetrate her thoughts, but she closed her eyes and pushed it away. She was growing better at controlling the Beacon, and the Dark Thing seemed remote and diffuse.

But still it worried her—its malevolent presence here in this placid dreamscape. What exactly was it? And, more importantly—what did it want? But the more she focused on it, the blurrier and more shadowy it became. So she dragged her gaze away and focused on the reason she'd come here. She crept over and knelt before him. His slender torso was chiseled with muscles, forged by years of hard training. They bulged under his silvery uniform. He held his golden weapon, hugging it tightly to his chest.

His face was so peaceful in its repose that she didn't want to disturb him, but the desire to talk to him was more powerful. She nudged his arm and whispered in his ear.

"Aero Wright . . . you've come for me."

"Myra," he gasped as his eyes popped open.

She heard him, but she also felt him. The Beacon on his wrist throbbed in rhythm with the one shackled to hers. She understood that she was experiencing the world through his senses, that they were inexorably linked in this way. She didn't just see and hear him, but she could also feel him—his thoughts, his feelings, his essence.

"Where are you?" he asked, squinting into the distance. "I see the ocean."

Another revelation—and so just as she was visiting him in this landscape of smoke and ash, so he was visiting her in the vista by the sea.

"Some distant shoreline," she said with a weary sigh. "We traveled many miles from the bottom of the sea . . . but our vessel didn't survive the journey."

"Nor mine, I'm afraid."

His eyes darted to the smoking ruin behind them. But then he raised his arm—the one bonded to the Beacon—and pointed to a twinkling star, brighter than the others.

"Look . . . I came from up there."

Her breath caught in her throat. It was so impossible to believe such a thing, but reinforced by the throbbing connection of their Beacons, she knew it was true.

His gaze shifted from the brilliant star back to her face and stayed there. The fire from the crash had kissed his face, she saw. It was a black mask. Blood seeped through the bandage on his shoulder, crimson on white. But neither injury distracted him from her.

"We're closer together now than ever before, aren't we?" His voice was gravelly, yet gentle—that of one who could listen but also who could command.

"But still so far away," she said despairingly. She cast her eyes down in shame. "I'm afraid that I'm not cut out for this journey. I'm losing my faith."

He smiled grimly. "Me too."

"Then what can we do?" she asked, her eyes searching his face.

He thought for a moment before arriving at his answer. "The only thing that humans have been able to do for more than a thousand years—endure and hope."

Myra rested her head on his shoulder and listened to the insistent beating of his heart. She stayed there, comforted by the illusion of his proximity to her. Right then, Aero felt the most amazing sensation—it was as if the shattered pieces of his heart hewed together and mended themselves. The reformed organ pulsed and flexed with renewed vigor. His cheeks flushed with the increased blood flow.

He looked up at Myra in awe. "You've fixed me! I've been broken for so very long."

And that was when they kissed—their bodies interlocked and melded together, urged on by the Beacons bound to their flesh. He wrapped his strong arms around her and pressed his hips against her, making her shudder. Though Myra felt guilty—and Aero sensed that she did, since he understood her thoughts—it paled in comparison to the desire to merge with this stranger from a distant star. She was helpless in his grasp.

Kaleb, she felt him thinking, *you love him, don't you?*

But it's nothing like what I feel for you.

Myra, don't feel shame for your affections, he communicated to her. *The only shame you should feel is in not loving enough. There may come a time when you have to make a choice, but that time is not now.*

And she surged into him as never before, feeling that their connection was unbreakable. Their coupling lasted for as long as there was night. And when they eventually parted, she began to fade away. The sun was rising and rousing her from sleep. Any minute, brilliant light would explode over the horizon.

"What should I do now?" Myra asked, though her voice was growing fainter. Uncertainty gripped her then. He took her face in his palms—calloused and strong.

"Follow the Beacon—go to the First Continuum."

"But what about you?"

She felt him focus on her and project toward her. She could tell that what he wanted—no, what he needed—to communicate to her was of vital importance. She waited, her heart thumping in her chest. Finally, he released the thought, which traveled to her instantly, though untold miles of lifeless surface physically separated them.

"Myra, I will find you!" he swore. "No matter what happens, I will find you."

The thought zapped her like an electric charge, and she knew that he meant it—that he was not one who swore oaths lightly. And she also knew that it was true.

He would find her.

○ ○ ○

When Myra awoke on that rocky shore to daylight—*true daylight*—with her friends clustered around her, still caught in the throes of sleep, the dream didn't fade or dissipate. It stayed with her, like something corporeal and true.

Even when the sun rose higher in the sky, shocking her with its brilliance, even when her companions rose and doled out that morning's rations (it wasn't nearly enough, but would have to suffice), even when they packed up their encampment and shouldered their heavy packs, filled with as many supplies as they'd been able to salvage, the dream stayed with her, as real as anything that she could hold or touch in her palms.

The Beacon throbbed with her heartbeat, reminding her of Aero's oath. He would find her—or he would die trying.

As Myra led her companions over the volcanic earth, guided by the Beacon, the sunlight poured down, brighter and hotter and more magnificent that anything they'd ever experienced before. She drank it in like a woman dying of thirst who'd never tasted anything more delectable and satisfying. Before this moment, she'd only been existing, she realized. Now she was living—*really* living for the first time in her life.

We're not creatures begat of the deep, as the Church proclaimed, she thought. *We're creatures of the sun and the sky and the land and the freshwater.*

Tinker paused and hoisted his hand to his brow, squinting against the sunlight. "Where are you leading us?" he asked in his way—softly, but firmly.

"To the First Continuum, of course," Myra replied. She stopped to muss his hair, while Kaleb and Paige soldiered forward over the blackened terrain. The ocean, frothy with waves, churned and beat up against the shore behind them. It stretched into infinity. She could still taste saltiness in the air, but soon they'd be leaving that behind, too.

"But how will we find it?" Tinker asked.

"The Beacon will guide us."

"How far is it?"

"Far," she said.

"How long will it take?"

Her pupils dilated as she probed the Beacon for some answer. "Weeks—if not months."

"Will we make it?"

She thought for a moment. "Well, we have to," she said at last, for it was the best answer she could give. Tinker considered this for a second and studied her face.

"There are others, aren't there?"

A smile played at her lips then, mysterious and musing. "Yes—they will find us."

He nodded as if he believed her.

"Now come along," she chided him. "The daylight is wasting." This was the first time that she—or any inhabitant born of the deep—had ever uttered such a thing.

And so Myra and her companions began their journey into this great land that their ancestors had forsaken a thousand years ago. For the first time in their lives, they were no longer constrained by ceilings or walls or narrow passages. The shadows that they cast were deeper and truer than ever before. And still the sun rose and rose and rose, until it was a burning beacon suspended aloft at the pinnacle of a cornflower-blue sky.

It lit their way.

Epilogue

THE DOOR IN THE WALL

Seeker

The Door in the Wall opened, and the Light came in.

If she could have uttered anything other than an unintelligible scream, it would have been this:

It burns! It burns! It burns! It burns! It burns! It burns! It burns!

Seeker clawed at her eyeballs, wanting to pluck them out of her skull with her nails. It only made the pain worse. Blood, thick and wet, dripped down her face. She tasted it on her lips, coppery and still warm. With her eyes shut tight, she scuttled back into the Moving Room, which terrified her, too, but it was better than the Light.

The nasty, burning, evil, stinking Light.

The Strong Ones had warned her. They'd told her that her curiosity would get her into trouble. That was why they'd named her Seeker. They sang out in the Darkness to taunt her, their voices reverberating through the subterranean caverns.

Seeker, Seeker,
Can't get any weaker!
She creeps and she sneaks,

Sticks her nose where it reeks,
And soon we shall eat her!

In between flashes of white-hot pain, Seeker wondered if she was blind now. The thought came from the rational part of her, the part that wasn't currently directing her body to thrash around and claw her eyeballs out. She could get around without her sight well enough, that much she knew. Her other senses were strong—they'd been sharpened by the Darkness. She could hear and smell and feel in the blackness. But without her eyes, the Strong Ones would prey on her and feast upon her flesh. She wouldn't last long.

But that was to be expected—none of the Weaklings did.

Though her eyes were open, she could see nothing but white—a thick, milky fire of pain that flamed before her vision—but she could hear. There was a slurping noise first, as the Door in the Wall began to contract. Next there was a feeling of air being sucked inside the Moving Room, followed by a dull thud that rattled the walls.

Then—and only then—did the Light stop.

The nasty, burning, evil, stinking Light.

The Darkness was back, the Darkness that was her home.

Seeker drank it in, worshipped it, knelt in prayer to it, let it fill her up until she drowned in it. She vowed to the Darkness that she'd never leave it again.

But curiosity was a funny thing.

It fled from her at the first sign of trouble. But it always crept back into the dark corners of her mind. Needled at her. Told her to do things that she shouldn't do.

It would be back, she knew.

And then she'd be back at the Door in the Wall.

If the Strong Ones didn't kill her first.

. . . to be continued in

November 2016

from

WITH GRATITUDE

To my fabulous agent Deborah Schneider, for signing me based on a completely different book and not flinching when handed a sprawling sci-fi trilogy, her colleagues Victoria Marini, Cathy Gleason, and Josie Freedman, and everyone at Gelfman Schneider/ICM. Also, to Stephanie Thwaites and Sophie Harris and everyone at Curtis Brown for taking my book to the UK and the wider world.

To Elizabeth Guber Stephen and Alicia Lipinski at Gables Media, for believing in my book and connecting me with my publisher. Without your help, this series might not be seeing the light of day. Also, to Sarah Ganzman at Fake Dare Productions, whose tireless faith kept me going in my darkest moments.

To my editors, Stephanie Beard and Jon O'Neal, my publisher Todd Bottorff, and everyone at Turner Publishing, for taking a chance on this trilogy and pushing it out into the world with verve, vision, and velocity. You all rock! I can't wait to hold the book with its dazzling cover in my hands.

To my earliest readers, Scott Andrew Selby and Jennifer Pooley, whose comments made this book exponentially better. Also, to Leanne Crowley and Nicole Pajer, for always being my biggest *freaking* cheerleaders, and to all the members of my book club. You're my girls! Can't wait to read my book with you.

To the Sirenland Writers Conference, where I workshopped a sizable chunk of this manuscript in one of the most gorgeous locales imaginable (hint: it takes the edge off . . . so does Prosecco). Special thanks to Meg Wolitzer, for your wisdom, humor, and yes, notes! And to everyone in our workshop, especially Edna Ball Axelrod.

To my Mom, for taking me to the library and nourishing my insatiable appetite for books. To my Dad, for paying me ten bucks to read *The Hobbit*, mostly out of fear that I'd never read anything besides Nancy Drew. To my brothers, Jackson and Jared, for always keeping my life interesting, even to this day.

Finally, to my husband—my rock, my toughest critic, my support system, my life. Thanks for introducing me to Kurt Vonnegut, *Star Trek: The Next Generation,* and jointly raising our dog Commander Ryker. I love you always.

ABOUT THE AUTHOR

JENNIFER BRODY lives and writes in Los Angeles. After graduating from Harvard University, she began her career in feature film development. Highlights include working at New Line Cinema on many projects, including *The Lord of the Rings* trilogy, *The Golden Compass*, and *Love In The Time of Cholera*. She's a member of the Science Fiction and Fantasy Writers of America. She also founded and runs BookPod, a social media platform for authors. This is her first book.

You can find her online at:

@JenniferBrody

www.jenniferbrody.com

www.facebook.com/jenniferbrodywriter